PRAISE FOR
THE NOVELS OF
CATHERINE PALMER:

Falcon Moon:

"A captivating story penned with unusual warmth and compassion . . . a wonderful read!"

—Lori Copeland

"An excellent realistic historical romance . . . You will be transported into a world of bushwhackers, ex-slaves, and primitive conditions."

—*Rendezvous*

Outlaw Heart:

"Ms. Palmer has created a fast-paced Western and sensuous love story in a lawless land."

—*Romantic Times*

"A journey to love filled with warmth and tenderness."

—*Rendezvous*

Sometimes Forever

CATHERINE PALMER

JOVE BOOKS, NEW YORK

SOMETIMES FOREVER

A Jove Book / published by arrangement with
the author

PRINTING HISTORY
Jove edition / August 1996

All rights reserved.
Copyright © 1996 by Catherine Palmer.
This book may not be reproduced in whole
or in part, by mimeograph or any other means,
without permission. For information address:
The Berkley Publishing Group, 200 Madison Avenue,
New York, New York 10016.

The Putnam Berkley World Wide Web site address is
http://www.berkley.com

ISBN: 0-515-11922-9

A JOVE BOOK®
Jove Books are published by The Berkley Publishing Group,
200 Madison Avenue, New York, New York 10016.
JOVE and the "J" design are trademarks
belonging to Jove Publications, Inc.

PRINTED IN THE UNITED STATES OF AMERICA

10 9 8 7 6 5 4 3 2 1

For Timothy Charles Palmer

Special thanks to Judith Stern Palais for believing in my vision for this book, to Steven Fluker for teaching me about weapons of the early nineteenth century, and to Sharon Buchanan-McClure for her valuable membership in the M.S.G.

Sometimes Forever

O*ne*

LIKE THE FINEST SILK THREADS TWISTED AND CROSSED to form a net of gossamer lace, Anne Webster's plan had to be executed perfectly or it would unravel into a thousand fragments. The seed cake must be steaming, the ripe quinces baked to perfection, the tea piping hot. The Limoges cup and saucer must gleam in shades of blue and gold on the black lacquer tray. Every facet of the silver teapot must reflect the fire crackling on the grate. Nothing must be out of order, for this afternoon Alexander Chouteau, son of the Duke of Marston, was taking tea in his bedroom alone.

A shaky breath clouded the creamer Anne took down from the Welsh cupboard at the back of the large, dimly lit kitchen. Lifting the hem of her apron, she buffed the silver vessel. She must not tremble when she poured Lord Alexander's milk. Her voice must not quaver when she offered him the sugar. Above all, she must remember to shut the bedroom door behind her when she went in. If anyone heard her speaking to him . . . if anyone knew what she had planned . . .

"Anne, do stop your dawdling." Mrs. Smythe slid a dish

of baked fruit down the slick boards of the scrubbed pine worktable. The glass clinked as it hit the tea tray. "Sugar those quinces, and be quick about it. I won't have Mr. Errand screeching at me because the tea was late and His Grace complained at it being too cool. The duchess can't bear frigid toast, and you certainly know how their son demands punctuality."

"Of course, Mrs. Smythe." Anne glanced at the pink-cheeked cook and wondered what the portly woman would do if she knew about the roll of delicate Honiton lace tucked into the bodice of her housemaid's dress.

Mrs. Smythe must never know. If she found out, Anne would be forced to sell her work to the laceman who came out in his chaise every month from London. The long, narrow panel of lace had taken her three months to design, its pattern two months to prick onto parchment, and its silk threads another ten months to weave with her pillow and bobbins.

In France, where it was illegal to own lace, such a panel would be worth a king's ransom. Even in London, the laceman could sell her work for a small fortune, though he would pay her only a fraction of its value. Thus she had designed the pattern for the Chouteau family alone, praying that her plan would succeed. Into this bit of lace she had woven her future.

Quickly Anne took the nippers and broke several lumps from the hard sugar cone. She slipped one lump into her pocket as a treat for Hercules, the duke's mastiff, then sprinkled a spoonful of sugar crystals across the peeled quinces. Dear heaven, she hoped they satisfied Lord Alexander's exacting tastes.

As she carried the dish across the kitchen, the chill of the black-and-white-tiled floor crept through her thin slippers and around her ankles. Her toes ached. She had been on her feet since before dawn, and she would work at Slocombe House until the last dinner plate was cleared and washed that evening. In between, she must pray that the duke's son would have the temper to listen to an impertinent, headstrong housemaid, that he would have the patience to inspect her length of Honiton, and that he would have the wit to realize the value of the lace.

As she set the dish of quinces on the tea tray, Anne squeezed her eyes shut. Oh, God, this was her only hope. If Lord Alexander paid her even half the market value of the Honiton, she would have enough money to quit her position at Slocombe House and return to Nottingham. She could hire a barrister to secure her father's release from prison and save her sisters from the factories.

Satan's workshops, her father called the drafty, machine-filled buildings with their deafening clatter and sooty windows. The factories, he had preached in more than one sermon, led women to sicken and children to die early deaths. As the eldest child of the Webster family, Anne knew that what her father said was true, and she had supported his association with the Luddites even though their activities had landed him in prison.

Now the family's only hope lay in her hands. Could a length of lace, more air than thread, save them? Anne swallowed at the gritty lump in her throat. It had to.

"Head in the clouds as usual," the cook huffed as she bustled past with a plate full of steaming cinnamon and currant scones. "Have you remembered to put tea in the pot, Anne?"

"Yes, Mrs. Smythe."

"She probably put in coffee." Sally Pimm, the first kitchenmaid, eyed Anne as she sifted salt into a copper pot of soup on the stove. In the scullery a cluster of maids giggled at the notion while they scoured stewpans, utensils, and colanders.

"Won't Lord Alexander be surprised," Sally continued, "if he sips up a mouthful of coffee when he's expecting his afternoon Darjeeling?"

"No more than when his oxtail soup tastes as if it's been made with water from the English Channel," Anne returned.

Mrs. Smythe's wooden spoon cracked across Sally's knuckles, and she let out a shriek. "Have mercy!"

"Then stop your chatter and pay heed to the supper, girl! Shall we all be tossed out on our ears thanks to your heavy hand with the salt? Have this as a reminder!"

Ignoring Sally's screeches as the cook added three whacks for good measure, Anne laid a starched cloth over the tray and set the tea things on it. She knew the kitchenmaid was envious of her position. Under normal circumstances, Anne would have come into Slocombe House as a scullery maid. After several years, she might have worked her way up to the positions of second kitchenmaid, first kitchenmaid, and then, possibly, cook.

Circumstances were not normal. Anne had journeyed to the south of England after the Luddite riots in Nottingham. She brought references from the Right Honorable Lady de Winter, the baroness who had preferred her father to the rectory of a small parish. Despite Lady de Winter's recommendation of the clergyman's daughter, the housekeeper at Slocombe had intended to put Anne into the kitchen, until Mr. Errand intervened.

"Look at the girl, Mrs. Davies," the butler had intoned, one bushy white eyebrow arching as he inspected the newcomer. "With that face she will be wasted in the kitchen. She has kept all her teeth, her eyes are clear, and though she's no beauty, she has a certain grace to her carriage. The letter from the baroness indicates she may have a measure of wit, as well. Put her in the house, and you will please His Grace, for you know how the duke despises the fishermen's daughters we normally get."

Anne had been given a place in the house, though the discriminating Duke of Marston had not laid eyes on her in the eighteen months she had labored at Slocombe. She had seen the duchess only three times. But on Saturday afternoons, when the footman took his leave, she did have the great honor of serving tea to Lord Alexander.

"Now what?" Mrs. Smythe mopped her forehead. "More charity at the door? Sally, see to them."

"I beg your pardon, mum, but I'm in the midst of beating eggs." The kitchenmaid shot a glance at Anne. "Perhaps Anne will do it, if she's not too proud."

"I should be happy to feed the poor if I had the time," Anne said, surveying the hungry men, women, and children who had gathered around the door that led outside the kitchen. She could so easily be one of them, and yet she had worked hard to improve her lot. Now she must press forward with her plan.

Touching the lump that was the roll of lace hidden in her bodice, she lifted her chin. "I'm afraid Lord Alexander is most particular—"

"Do it now, Anne, and quickly," the cook cut in. "We can't have them loitering about and gawking at us. The leavings are in a basket by the back door."

"But the tea. The duke's son—"

"Ooh, she is in a hurry to be off," Sally Pimm observed. "Have you an assignation with Lord Alexander today, Miss Webster?"

Anne's cheeks went hot. "He's awaiting his tea."

The cook gave a snort. "There's time to tend the charity first. His Grace's tea has just gone up to the library, where he is meeting with the vicar. The duchess is in the drawing room with two ladies from the church, and I'm sending theirs now. Lord Alexander's scones won't be ready for five minutes." She pointed her spoon at the door. "See to them, or I shall have to tell Mrs. Davies of your impudence."

Anne grabbed a ladle. "Yes, Mrs. Smythe."

As she hurried past Sally Pimm, the kitchenmaid smirked. "Don't dirty your apron now, Annie. They say

Lord Alexander likes his girls pretty, unsullied, and clean. You must try to please him on at least one count.''

"Lord Alexander admires respectful manners and silence,'' Anne retorted. "These are, you can be certain, the reasons his attendant at tea today is I and not some other.''

In the scullery, she stacked clean bowls and spoons. She must ignore Sally and hurry. Trying to steady her fingers, she set up a tray and carried it back into the kitchen.

The poor of Tiverton watched her, eyes shining with hope in their dirt-darkened faces. How could she think only of her own plans when such people were starving around her? Yet how could she let her father go on languishing in prison? And what of her sisters?

"Thank ye kindly, miss.'' An elderly man tipped his battered hat as she handed him a bowl of leavings.

"God bless the duke.'' A man with no teeth gave her a smile. "And God bless the duchess.''

Hurrying down the row of outstretched hands, Anne ladled each person a bowlful of the mixture of bread, soup, and meat scraps. Quickly now, quickly. In all the months she had served Lord Alexander, this would be his first Saturday to take tea alone. Her only chance to speak with him! If the tea was late, he would be in a foul mood and would send her away at once.

"Thanks.'' A little girl looked up, her tiny face pinched and white as she wrapped one arm around her full bowl. "Be ye an angel from heaven, then?''

"Oh, I'm only a housemaid.'' Unable to resist the child's sweet expression, Anne dug from her pocket the lump of sugar she had saved for Hercules and tucked it into the little one's hand. "There you are. A gift from the duke himself.''

The girl turned the lump one way and another. "What is it?''

Anne could hardly imagine she had never seen sugar. "Put it in your mouth.''

The child eyed the gift for a moment, then gingerly

placed the small lump on her tongue. "Mmm," she whispered. Her eyes drifted shut. Long lashes fanned her cheeks. A smile spread across her lips.

The door blew open in the March wind as yet another of Tiverton's needy slipped into the kitchen. Anne took little notice. She knelt before the ragged girl and took her sparrow-thin hands.

"For this moment, you are a duchess," she said softly. "In your mouth is the taste of Christmas plum pudding, black currant ice cream, treacle, and Turkish delight. You are dressed in a gown of fine green silk caught up with rosettes of pink ribbon. At your ankles sweeps a ruffle of the most exquisite Point d'Angleterre lace. Your hair is braided, looped, and curled. Your skin is scented with fragrant heliotrope."

"Now that's a good 'un," a man said with a laugh. "She smells more like coal dust, I should think."

"Hush!" A woman gave him a sharp elbow. "Don't spoil it."

Anne watched the little girl drift in the vision she had created. "White gloves slide up your fingers and over your arms, all the way to your elbows. You have in your possession a lace fan figured with little Chinamen trotting across a footbridge. On your feet you wear thin slippers of emerald green kidskin. Pale mint ribbons wind around your ankles. You dance like the wind; your voice sings as high and clear as a bird's; you can draw and stitch and play the pianoforte better than anyone in the realm. In short, my little one, you are the most enchanting duchess in all of England. That is the taste in your mouth. It is dreams."

"Coo!" The little girl's eyes popped open, and everyone chuckled as she threw her grimy arms around Anne's neck. "I almost thought it was true!"

"And well it should be." The man who had just tramped in from the street swept off his dusty hat and gave the child an elegant bow. "The Marquess of Blackthorne, my lady duchess.'' Then he turned to Anne and repeated the bow. "I am at your service, madam.''

Though heavily bearded and scruffy, he possessed a pair of gray eyes that sparkled with fun. What could she do but curtsy in return? "Queen Anne, of course.''

"Your Majesty, the pleasure is all mine.'' Before she could react, he took her hand and lifted her bare fingers to his lips. Warm in spite of the chill outside air, his mouth brushed across her skin, lighting a tingle that skittered up her arm. His mustache surprised her in its softness, and she jerked her hand away.

"I beg your pardon!''

"Lavender,'' he pronounced, straightening. "A clean scent, slightly astringent, with all the promise of spring. Very appropriate.''

"I was putting up . . . putting up the linens this afternoon.'' She shoved her hand beneath her apron. "Tucking lavender among the sheets.''

Disconcerted more by her reaction than by the stranger himself, Anne filled a bowl with leavings and handed it to him. Never mind. She must put him aside. He was the last of the charity, and she hadn't yet heard Lord Alexander's bell. There was still hope. She started down the row again, this time collecting spoons and bowls.

"If yer going to play at peerage, ye won't want to be Blackthorne,'' the toothless man said to the tall newcomer. "He's reported to be dead.''

"Dead? Good heavens, how did it happen?''

"Met with an accident while traveling in America. Scalped by them red savages.''

"Better him than Lord Alexander,'' a woman uttered in a low voice. "The marquess was nothing but a rogue, he was. Roved about the country, spent money like water through a sieve, sired bastards everywhere he stopped but couldn't be bothered to marry here at home and give the good duke an heir.''

"Good riddance to the blackguard," Anne affirmed. Then she added, "God rest his soul."

"Abominable, was he?" the stranger asked. "Well, the devil take him."

"I should never wish to set the forces of darkness upon anyone." She set a handful of spoons on her tray. "But an heir apparent has his duties. The Marquess of Blackthorne rightly should have seen to his father's duchy. He was said to wager large sums at cards, and he engaged in more than one duel. He was even known to attend glove matches."

"Bare-knuckle boxing," the toothless man confirmed. "If yer bound to play at royalty, man, be the duke. He's well loved by everyone."

"Ah, the Duke of Marston." The tall man turned to the housemaid. "Your Majesty, Queen Anne, be so good as to acquaint me with the health of the master of Slocombe House."

Stacking the bowls on her tray, Anne tried to suppress her growing irritation with the dusty intruder. She didn't have time for games. "His Grace is well. He's taking tea in the library."

"And the duchess?"

"With friends in the drawing room." As she approached the man, she realized he was still lounging by the door, his bowl untouched. "You must eat, sir. I'm to serve Lord Alexander his tea at once."

"Is that a royal command, Your Highness?"

Unamused, Anne stared into the man's deep-set gray eyes. In his brown tweed coat with its tarnished brass buttons, though clearly no better off than his companions, he had a demeanor that spoke of some wit. His features were all of angles and planes, and his nose slashed down the middle of his face like an arrow, straight and determined, nostrils flared slightly to either side. Beneath that uncompromising nose, his mouth tilted upward at one corner. Perhaps he was entertained.

"If you will not eat," she told him, "give me your bowl."

"My dear queen, I have not finished my inquiry. How fare the duke's daughters, the Ladies Claire, Lucy, Elizabeth, Charlotte, and Rebecca?"

"I could lose my position at the House," she shot back, her voice low. "Will you eat or not?"

He took a mouthful of mush and grimaced as he chewed. "The ladies?"

"They're fine, of course, all of them married and gone away."

"Even Lady Rebecca?" He raked a hand through his hair. Coal black, it was a rumple of uncombed curls. "She's young to be wed. What of Alexander, the duke's son?"

"He's to marry in six months' time."

"Good Lord, who's the lucky lady? Not Miss Mary Clark, I hope. She may be a beauty, but she's only the daughter of a baronet. He can do much better."

Anne stared. How did such a beggar know the names and ranks of Society? With his heavy beard, unruly hair, and dark eyebrows, there was a certain air of wildness about the man. His large hands in their tattered knit gloves appeared so strong as to make him dangerous.

He dipped his spoon into the leavings. "This supper actually gets better as it goes along. Alexander's not still bedding Mrs. Kinnard, the actress, is he?"

"Lord Alexander's fiancée is Gabrielle Duchesne, the daughter of the Comte de la Roche."

"Damn! Hasn't he better sense than to choose a Frenchwoman? With Napoleon restless and France in a muddle, there's no guarantee what her fortune will be."

Anne pressed the tray into her stomach as Lord Alexander's bell began to jangle on the far wall. Absorbed in his own musings, the stranger tapped his spoon against the rim of the bowl. She had to go. But this last remnant of Tiverton's needy was clearly odd, perhaps even lunatic, and she didn't want to irk him. The others began to file out the door as he straightened, focused on her eyes, and gave her a brief nod.

"Is Smythe in?" he asked.

Surprised at his common use of the formidable cook's name, Anne glanced behind her. "She's seeing to the seed cake and—"

"What of Errand? Is he still butler at Slocombe?"

"Excuse me, may I have your bowl?" She tried to grab it away, but he walked past her into the center of the kitchen. "Sir! You must go out the back way! Please, sir!"

"Mrs. Smythe," he called. The cook lifted her head from sniffing the seed cake and swung around. "Mrs. Smythe, have you any gingerbread nuts for my tea today?"

"Awwk!" At the first sight of the man, she dropped the plate of seed cake and threw up her hands. "It's . . . it's . . . it's—"

"Lord Nicholas Ruel Edward Chouteau, Marquess of Blackthorne." He winked at her as he gave his thick beard a tug. "Not quite as hairless as the red savages might have wished me. In fact, I'm a little on the bristly side, I'm afraid."

"Lord Blackthorne!" Mrs. Smythe shrieked, her tongue loose at last. "Great ghosts, you're dead!"

"On the contrary. I'm quite alive and eager for a cup of your finest Darjeeling. And do send for a barber, will you? I'll speak to Errand on my way up. Perhaps he should prepare my father with the news that his son has arisen from the grave."

"The marquess is in my kitchen!" As Lord Alexander's bell jangled, the cook stepped over the shattered dish of seed cake and shouted at her kitchenmaids as if they might have some explanation for what had just occurred. "He walked into the kitchen from the back! Where's his carriage? Where are his footmen? Where's the valet? Oh, how could we have known it was Lord Blackthorne? He came in with the charity!''

"Calm yourself, Mrs. Smythe. You know, I always believed the only place to learn the truth about life at Slocombe House was in the kitchen. Besides, I must have my gingerbread nuts.''

"Gingerbread," the cook repeated. "Gingerbread nuts. It *is* you! Oh, my lord! Oh, criminey! Mary and Lissy, run to the larder for ginger and treacle! Sally, find Mr. Errand at once. Anne, see to Lord Alexander's tea, for heaven's sake. Gingerbread. We must have gingerbread nuts.''

Sucking air back into her lungs, Anne slid the tray of used bowls and spoons onto a kitchen table and picked up her skirts. She edged around the room to avoid the tall man in its center, swept up the tea things, and made for the curtained doorway that led into the hall. Her legs felt as though they'd been jellied.

That ragged, dusty specimen of charity was the marquess? But the marquess was dead, scalped, and buried in America. And she'd only just wished him good riddance. She'd called him a blackguard. Straight to his face!

"Your Majesty," he called out. "Good Queen Anne!"

She paused, every jellied limb suddenly rigid. She couldn't bring herself to look at him. "Yes, my lord?''

"Would Your Royal Highness be so kind as to extend Alex cordial greetings from his brother?''

"Yes, my lord," she whispered. "Of course, my lord.''

The Marquess of Blackthorne was chuckling behind her as she brushed past the green baize curtain and fled into the hall.

Anne remembered to shut the bedroom door. It was the only part of her plan that was not lost. How dare she show Lord Alexander a length of Honiton lace when she had been ordered to tell the man that his brother, the marquess and heir to the duchy, had suddenly returned from the dead?

If she failed to carry out her duty, she would be dismissed.

"Set the tea on the table there," the duke's younger son told her as she approached the fireplace. He barely glanced up from the tray of cosmetics he was perusing.

Known to enjoy the company of dandies, Lord Alexander cut a fine figure as he took his carriage about Tiverton. Of course, in London he was said to shine even more brightly, a veritable star among Society's eligible bachelors. With his tall, slim, well-proportioned figure, thick golden hair, and brilliant blue eyes, he was known to have broken many a young lady's delicate heart.

"Sugar, my lord?" Anne asked softly. She had managed to pour his tea without spilling any into the saucer, but she hardly trusted herself with the tiny silver tongs.

"Please." He lifted his head and scrutinized the dish of quinces. "Do pass my compliments to Mrs. Smythe. The fruit appears quite agreeable."

"Yes, my lord." She got the first lump of sugar into his tea without incident. The second landed with a loud splash. "Milk?" she asked quickly.

"Dare I? I fear it may end in my lap."

"I beg your pardon, sir." Anne glanced up at him. "I shall take the greatest care."

His bright blue eyes greeted hers with a light sparkle. "Pour away, then."

He studied her as she lifted the creamer and tipped it over his cup. She held her breath. *Please, dear Lord, don't let me spill it. Give me strength. Give me courage.*

"Well done, miss."

"Thank you, my lord." She let out her breath.

"Have you served me in the past?"

"On Saturdays."

"Ah, yes. Perhaps I do recall you." He scrutinized her so intently that she felt a heat creep into her cheeks. "Surely, then, you are familiar with your duties and with the proper decorum required of a housemaid. Are you aware, my dear miss, that you have shut the bedroom door?''

"Yes, my lord."

"Ahh, I see." He settled back in his chair and stretched out his legs. Deeply set beneath his pale brow, his blue eyes took on a glitter that sent a knot into the pit of Anne's stomach. He didn't understand at all, and his shameless advances with the female household staff were common knowledge. She gripped her hands at her waist until the blood drained from her fingers.

If she were to save her father, she must do it now. She must bring out the lace. But if she were to keep her position at Slocombe House, she must tell him about his brother's arrival.

"Pray, what am I to make of this tightly shut door, miss?" Lord Alexander cut into her dilemma. "Have you a certain purpose in mind?"

Anne watched dark spots dance across her eyes. Her blood had puddled in her knees. "Indeed, I do have a purpose, my lord."

"A purpose beyond splashing sugar into my tea and milk into my lap? This is intriguing. Perhaps you wish to comment on my selection of rouges." He held out the cosmetics tray. "Is this pink a little strong for my complexion? Should I use the salmon?"

Anne stared at the little pots of paint. The lump that had been in her throat all afternoon wedged tight. "I know nothing of rouges, my lord."

Ignoring his tea, he set the tray aside and stood up. Anne's mouth turned to glue. He tugged at the hem of his striped waistcoat and loosened the spotted silk cravat at his neck as he took two steps toward her. She lowered her focus, concentrating on the way his narrow-cut trousers came together under the high instep of his leather pumps.

"What is it you know, my dear?" he asked. "Something more than serving tea in the afternoon?"

She dug her nails into her palm. "Yes, my lord."

"How engaging." He reached out and touched the side of her face. "Your cheeks are aflame, yet you tell me you know nothing of rouges. Let me see your eyes now. Ah, they're blue. Quite nice."

"My lord," she managed, "I do not wish to speak of my eyes."

"But you did wish for a tête-à-tête with me, did you not?" He tugged the white cotton mobcap from her head, and her hair spilled to her waist. "Oh, dear, it's brown. I cannot deny I have never been partial to brown hair, but your eyes are certainly enchanting. And your figure is—"

"My lord, it's about lace." Anne shrugged away from the long, thin fingers that had reached to explore her bodice. "I've come to speak with you about lace. Honiton, to be exact."

"Lace?" He looked up, confusion written across his brow.

"I was taught lace design by Mr. Samuel Beacon in Nottingham, and he says I'm the finest pattern pricker he has ever seen and certainly one of the cleverest artists. My execution of lace is said to be most exquisite." She gulped down a breath, determined to get it all out before he could say another word or touch her again. "Thinking only of your future happiness with the Lady Gabrielle Duchesne, the daughter of the Comte de la Roche, I contrived to fashion a design with her wedding gown in mind. I have created a length of the most delicate lace, my lord, using silk threads and more than a thousand bobbins."

Stepping back from him, she dipped her fingers into her bodice and lifted out the roll of lace. "As you can see," she hurried on, unwinding the length, "I have carefully created the Chouteau family's lozenge. I centered it here, believing my lady Gabrielle may wish to use the lace on her veil or perhaps at her bodice. Bearing your esteemed heritage in mind, I designed a row of English roses along the edge, while ribbons twined with morning glories loop around the lozenge.''

When he said nothing, she gathered her courage, lifted her chin, and continued. ''Ferns, of course, have been interwoven throughout the pattern to create a lush sense of the beauty of England. As I designed this border, I envisioned a garden of the sort that only my lady's future home here at Slocombe House could boast, a profusion of blossoms, vines, and birds. I have given the lace a certain fragility, you see, thinking of the misty air in the south and wishing the fabric to whisper against your bride's skin in a most delicate fashion.''

Forcing herself to meet his eyes, she laid the lace in his hands. ''I come boldly before you, my lord, only because of my great reverence for your excellent taste in fashion, knowing that you would wish the very best for your wife. Had I sold this to the laceman, the crest would be useless to any other purchaser, and so I . . . I would beg you to . . . to consider a fair price—''

''Alex!'' The deep voice rang through the cavernous room like a gong. ''Alex, old man, how are you?''

Lord Alexander glanced up from the lace, focused on the man who had just burst into his room, and faded to a deathly shade of white. ''Ruel?'' Anne's lace drifted to the floor. ''Can it be?''

She watched in horror as her months of work, her only hope for her father's freedom, came to rest at the edge of the carpet beside the fire. Lord Alexander took a step forward, and the sharp heel of his pump impaled the lace.

''Ruel!'' he cried, hurrying across the room with the length of lace trailing behind him. ''You're alive! Oh, God, we thought you were gone. We had heard appalling rumors that you were dead. Father has been beside himself, sending out parties of inquiry, mailing letters left and right. But you're all right! Thank heaven!''

The two men embraced, the one a dark pirate and the

other a golden youth. Anne looked down at her tattered handiwork, remembering her father in prison and the damnable lace machines that had put him there. Then she covered her hand where, in the kitchen below, a dusty beggar's lips had heated her skin. She decided she agreed with his earlier sentiment.

The devil could take the Marquess of Blackthorne.

$\mathcal{T}_{wo}$

"ALEX, YOU'RE LOOKING CAPITAL." RUEL CLAPPED HIS brother on the back. "What are you now? Twenty, at least."

"Three-and-twenty, Ruel, and you look like hell. Your skin is as brown as a seaman's. And your hair! Good Lord, where have you been these last months? When did you get to Slocombe?"

"Not an hour ago. May I join you for tea? I assume there's plenty."

Ruel glanced at the housemaid. She had backed up against the fireplace, her face as white as chalk and her cheeks a pair of pink roses. This must be the young lady who had served him leavings with the charity in the kitchen, yet she looked different now. Her hair, a rich brown cape around her shoulders, glistened in the red firelight. Her mobcap lay on the floor. Ruel appraised the situation. Alex was still up to his lecherous pranks. Had the maid been a willing partner?

"I shall see to the pouring," he said, aware that the woman would wish to escape and restore her appearance.

"I'll fetch Mr. Errand." Her voice was low. "He will dispatch a footman to serve you, my lord."

"Nonsense." Alex settled into his chair and waved a hand at her. "Pour the tea. My first cup is cold already, and I haven't the patience to wait for a footman when you'll do just as well. Seat yourself, Ruel, and tell me what you've been about. The last intelligence we had of you was from our cousin, Auguste Chouteau. He wrote that you were staying with him in St. Louis in the Missouri Territory.''

''The last I heard of me, I'd been scalped by Indians.'' Ruel looked at the maid again. She was carefully ignoring him. Unable to rescue her cap, which had fallen beneath the tea table, she had tucked her hair behind her ears and bent to pour a second cup of Darjeeling. ''Fortunately I've kept the hair on top of my head, and I've just had a barber whack off what lingered on my chin.''

The maid's attention darted from the teapot to his face. Their eyes met, and the flush spread from her cheeks down her neck. Caught, she shifted her concentration to her tasks again, as though nothing had passed between them.

How did he appear to a woman, Ruel wondered. Though a common house servant was no judge of aristocratic manliness, it comforted him to see the blush of color that made her fair skin glow. Perhaps he hadn't lost all his looks during the three months of hell he had spent at sea.

''Before you go out in Society, you'll want to do better than a shave,'' Alexander informed him. ''The Regent has developed a bit of a tousled mop, but he manages to make it appear rather dashing. You, on the other hand, look a veritable rake. So where have you been, Ruel? No doubt pirating, smuggling, or something else equally illegal.''

''Your opinion of my talents has grown since I've been away, Alex. I'm flattered.'' He accepted the warm cup Anne handed him and held it to his lips. Tea. Closing his eyes, he took a deep drink. The steaming liquid seeped into his body and unknotted his muscles. He let out a long breath.

''In spite of my appearance,'' he told his brother, ''I've been the perfect gentleman. I left St. Louis half a year ago. I've been traveling homeward since that time. Down the

Mississippi River to New Orleans. Around Florida. Across the Atlantic.''

"It took you six months to get here?''

"The ship was becalmed at sea for five weeks.'' He opened his eyes. "We were in danger of starvation. I shall be grateful when sails are put away in favor of steam.''

Alex laughed. "Steam! Ruel, you're dreaming again. No one in his right mind would undertake a sea crossing with nothing better than steam power. Ridiculous!''

Ruel waved a hand in dismissal. "Never mind. I'll leave that enterprise to the shipyards.''

"I should hope so!''

"We've other missions to discuss, Alex.'' He leaned forward, elbows on his knees. He had missed his brother in the years away. Though the younger man's propensity to waylay housemaids and his fondness for dandy fashions had never pleased Ruel, he counted on Alex for companionship and counsel. From their boyish exploits sneaking about in the smuggler's tunnels along the coast to their united conquest of London's most enchanting female company, they had been the closest comrades in adventure.

"I've made plans to absolve the duchy from debt,'' he confided. "With hard work and determination, we can do it.''

Alex lifted one golden eyebrow. "Not with steamships, I hope.''

"Textiles.''

"Oh, God.'' Alex leaned back and covered his eyes. "We haven't the sheep of the Lake District, the factories of the Midlands, or the roads of London, yet we're going to build a fortune on fabric.''

Ruel couldn't suppress a grin. "Your dramatics could be staged in London, Alex. Look at you, rouge on your cheeks and a red silk cravat at your throat. Your trousers are so tight it will be a wonder you can ever father children.

You've even managed to impale a bit of lace on your heel.''

Reaching across the tea table, he tugged the strip of lace free from his brother's pump. ''You do still fancy women, don't you?''

Alex chuckled. ''I'm to be married in six months. Gabrielle Duchesne is quite the most buxom Frenchwoman I've ever met, and I'm looking forward with great anticipation to liberating her bounty from its torturous imprisonment.''

Ruel wound the lace scrap around his finger. ''What is her fortune?''

''Fifty thousand pounds, but I'm far more interested in her bosom. Especially now that I know we shall save the duchy with your textile enterprises. Do apprise me as to how it is to happen.''

''A trade triangle. We shall send raw linen and flax from England to St. Louis. The opportunities there are unfathomable. We shall use our own port, of course, and I hope to acquire ships eventually.''

''Steamships, no doubt.''

''We shall export our fabric from St. Louis to the United States and France. In France, we shall add to it machine lace from the factory I intend to build in Douai, and voilà! We shall revitalize French fashion and fill our coffers.''

Alex guffawed. ''Bless my soul, I've missed you, Ruel. I haven't had this grand an entertainment since you left. More tea, please, miss.''

''Laugh all you like, Alex, but with only your wife's fifty thousand pounds, you won't be purchasing rouge and silk cravats for too many more years.'' Ruel stuffed Anne's panel of lace into the pocket of his waistcoat and held out his cup. ''I left Devon three years ago for one reason. The duchy was running aground in debt. You knew it. Father knew it. Now I'm back, and I've brought a workable plan. I shall expect your cooperation.''

He watched the housemaid pour his teacup full. Too full. The tea edged up to the brim, over the top, and down the sides into his saucer. "Enough!" he said, grabbing her hand and forcing the pot upright.

"I beg your pardon, sir." She dabbed at his saucer with the hem of her apron. "I shall fetch Mr. Errand at once."

"Stay! If you send for Errand, he'll alert the duke to my presence in my brother's chamber. I must have this moment for private discussion." He glanced up at the woman. Instead of cowering beneath his wrath as she properly should, she was glaring at him. He frowned back.

"Ruel, permit me to understand you," Alex said, setting down his cup. "The duchy grows almost no flax, yet we're somehow to send a grand shipment of it to the Missouri Territory. Are we not at war with the United States, brother?"

"You've been sequestered in the country too long. A peace was signed last December." Ruel took mental note that his brother had not gained any greater interest in world matters than he'd had as a boy. "I have calculated the initial cost of our investment in raw materials, Alex. The duchy can afford it."

"We have no factory in St. Louis, yet we're somehow to make fabric from this quantity of flax."

"Exactly. Auguste Chouteau is sixty-nine years old and a man of vision. He believes St. Louis will one day become a hub of commerce. He has committed himself to the expansion of the city and her industries. Even as we speak, our cousin is beginning construction of a mill."

"American fabric? French lace? Are you mad?" Alexander jumped to his feet, reached out, and pulled the length of lace out of his brother's pocket. "Assume we manage to purchase this quantity of linen," he said, wagging the lace as if it were a lady's handkerchief at the opera. "Assume we manage to ship it all the way to St. Louis. Assume we manage to build a mill there and weave the raw stuff into fabric. Even assume we ship our product all the way to France. That country is in chaos, man!''

"Perfect for our purposes. Did you know Napoleon has just returned to Paris?''

"You must be joking. He's in exile on Elba.''

"Not any longer. He's free, and by my best guess, all the sovereigns of Europe will unite forces against France. It can mean nothing less than war.''

"Wonderful! We're to establish our revolution of French fashion in the midst of an international war. Have you taken leave of your senses, Ruel?''

"Perhaps, but a man cannot depend on logic alone in these times. Without vision, without dreams, the world will overtake us. We must be ready to run with the best of the thinkers, Alex.'' He stood. "We must not be quick to ridicule the advancements of our age. Factories are springing up everywhere you look. Steam is taking the place of water power. The middle class has its hands on the source of money—manufacturing. Money is power. Power in the hands of the middle class spells doom to the aristocracy. And that aristocracy, my dear Alexander, is us.''

The younger man stared at his brother. "You're raving.''

"I'm the sanest man in this society of rouged dandies. If we mean to save our fortune, we must think. Think!'' He punched the air with a forefinger. "What does little Tiverton have to offer the world? Agriculture? Mining? Timber?''

"Fishing.''

"Fishing? Good Lord, we can barely supply our own villages.''

"Then what can you be thinking?''

Ruel jerked Anne's scrap of lace from his brother's hand. "Textiles! We are the source of Honiton lace. John Heathcoat has brought his lace machines from Nottingham to Tiverton in order to escape the damned Luddites and their determination to smash and burn him out of business. We shall take one of Heathcoat's lace machines to France, and there we shall ùnite their product with our cheaply made fabric to supply every languishing Frenchwoman in the empire.''

"How shall we export lace machines to France when you know it is perfectly illegal to do so? Lace itself has been banned since the Revolution."

Ruel dropped his voice and leaned close to his brother's ear. "With France in wartime chaos, we shall smuggle our machinery."

"Smuggle it!" Alexander threw up his hands in disbelief.

"Quiet! If we're found out, the plan is dashed. We must arrange a meeting with Heathcoat at once. Do you know him? I understand he's brilliant. I mean to learn all I can about—''

At that moment the chamber door flew open. Ruel clamped his mouth shut as Laurent Chouteau, the Duke of Marston, entered. He was followed close behind by Mr. Errand, the butler, his personal valet, and two footmen.

"Ruel!" The duke's blue eyes shone in his face. At eighty-seven, he was frail and white-haired, but his bearing was undeniably regal. "So, the intelligence I have had of you is true. You've returned!"

"Father!" A flood of feeling ran through Ruel as he strode across the floor toward the old gentleman. Like the little boy who had always adored his father, he threw his arms around the smaller man and hugged him warmly. "You should not have walked this distance, Father. I fully intended to come to you before dinner."

"I could no more await you than a child in anticipation of Christmas. We've had vicious rumors of your death, my boy. But here you are, safe, sound, and hale." He held his son at arm's length and looked him up and down. "Good heavens, what plagues your hair? And have you no better clothes?''

Ruel grinned. "I've just returned from sea, Father. I only managed to shave off my beard a few minutes ago, or you wouldn't have recognized me at all. My wardrobe and hair will have to wait. But how are you? You're looking well."

"Tolerable, tolerable." The duke gestured to a short, round-headed man at the rear of the party. "Do you know our vicar? I was taking tea with him when news of you arrived."

Introductions were made, and before Anne could escape she had been ordered to attend to tea for the Duke of Marston, his sons the Marquess of Blackthorne and Lord Alexander, and the vicar of Tiverton. She nodded quickly, swept up the tea tray with its cold silver pot, and ran out of the room.

"Annie!" Vera Peterson caught her best friend in the corridor as Anne was rushing back up to Lord Alexander's room. "Annie, what's possessed you? You're pale as a ghost, your hair is wild, and you're running with a tray full of Slocombe's very best silver plate!"

Anne stopped, plunked the tea things on a hall table, and grabbed Vera by both arms. "He has my lace!"

"Who?"

"Blackthorne, that's who, and I mean to have it back."

"The marquess? He's home?"

"He took my lace after Lord Alexander stomped a hole through it, and he put it in his pocket. They grabbed it back and forth from each other, waved it about, and abused it in the most abominable fashion. All the while, the marquess went on and on, blathering about lace machines, damning Luddites, and never knowing he was holding the finest length of Honiton he shall ever have the good fortune to lay eyes on."

"Anne!"

"I'm going to take it back from him."

"You can't! He's the marquess."

"He's a blackguard!"

"Oh, Anne!"

"I shall rework the lace the best I can and sell it to the laceman. I mean to pay my way back to Nottingham and hope I never set foot in Devon again."

"What about your father?"

Anne sobered as she picked up the tea tray. "I don't know. Oh, I can't think." Her voice was almost a whisper. She walked toward the door. "But without my lace, I'm lost."

"You can't go in there!" Vera caught her arm. "Annie, the duke's inside."

"I'm to serve them all tea."

"But you're not even wearing your mobcap!"

"How can I? Lord Alexander pulled it off my head and threw it to the floor. They're demons, those brothers, the both of them."

"You'll dip your hair into the tea!" Vera tried to stop her friend as Anne pushed open the bedroom door. "Oh, Annie!"

Careful not to spill a drop, Anne walked across the carpeted floor toward the party gathered around the fire. The duke's valet and the butler stood aside to allow her to place the tray on the central table. One footman began to pour the tea while the other handed around the cakes, toast, and biscuits. Anne picked up the plate nearest her and turned to the marquess.

"Mrs. Smythe sends you gingerbread nuts, Lord Blackthorne," she said, holding the dish before him. "At your request."

He took one of the small baked cakes and met her eyes. His voice was nearly inaudible. "My compliments, Your Majesty."

"You have my lace panel," she whispered through clenched teeth. "I want it back."

"Ruel, do be so good as to join the vicar and your family

at the table,'' the duke commanded. ''We must hear of your adventures.''

''Lace?'' He mouthed the word.

''In your pocket. I made it. Give it to me.''

''Ruel, what can you tell us of my nephew, Auguste Chouteau?'' The duke tapped his cane on the floor. ''Did his mother, Madame Marie Therese, welcome you? I understand she is quite prominent in Society in St. Louis, though you must give us to understand her relationship with this gentleman, Pierre Laclede, of whom I have heard so many remarkable things.''

Frowning at Anne, the marquess stepped around her and sat down in a chair by the fire. ''I'm sorry to tell you your sister-in-law passed from this earth last year, Father.'' He accepted a cup of tea from the footman and turned his attention to the company. ''Madame Chouteau was indeed highly esteemed, and with Pierre Laclede she was the mother of four children after Auguste. While in her presence, I found her to be a most charming and cordial hostess.''

''She married this Laclede, then?'' the vicar of Tiverton asked.

The marquess gave a small smile. ''Difficult, given her presence in a Catholic territory and the small matter that her husband, my father's brother, René Chouteau, did not die until 1776, well after she had given Monsieur Laclede his four children.''

''Harrumph.'' The duke cleared his throat and took a sip of tea.

''Indeed,'' the vicar put in, ''I have heard it said that Americans are more than a little coarse and unrefined. Rough about the edges, so to speak. Did you discover it to be so, Lord Blackthorne?''

Immoral, Anne thought as she studied the group of men gathered around their tea. A married woman giving birth to four children by a man who was not her husband! But how much better was England?

Many Sunday mornings she had heard her father denounce immorality from his pulpit. At the family dinner table, he told stories of King George III, who was still alive at his home in Windsor Castle, though he had gone utterly mad. His son, the Regent, had ruled England in his father's place for five years now, and Anne's own father could not name a more dissolute, contemptible, and immoral man in the entire realm.

She watched the marquess take another gingerbread nut. No better than their Regent were these high-born Chouteaus with their penchant for chasing housemaids about and bedding ladies of Society without benefit of marriage. They were indecent, the whole lot of them. America, for all its wild savagery, could hardly be worse.

"What of your plans now, Lord Blackthorne?" the vicar asked during a pause in the duke's inquiry about his son's travels. "Will you settle at Slocombe House until the Season?"

Ruel thoughtfully stirred his tea. "Perhaps." He lifted his gaze and fixed it on his father. "Or I may travel again. I am thinking of a tour of pleasure in France."

"France!" The duke rapped his cane on the floor. "Nonsense! We shall be at war with France again in six months' time. You must stay here and take your place, my boy. I am not long for this world, and Marston will be wanting a duke."

"Now I must respond with a hearty 'nonsense,' my lord. I expect to be taking tea with you well into your hundredth year."

The duke laughed, and Anne could see by the glow in his eyes that he deeply loved his son. The marquess reached out and laid his hand over his father's. Unwilling to witness the mutual tenderness between two men she was determined to despise, she lifted her focus to the fireplace and began counting the statuettes on Lord Alexander's mantelpiece. Blackthorne had her lace, and she didn't care if he and his father lived to be two hundred, she wanted it back.

"You cannot deprive Society of your presence for another Season," the duke was saying. "Alexander simply cannot bear the press of admiring ladies alone, can you, my boy?"

"I'll warrant my brother's charms have been missed," Lord Alexander conceded.

"I fully expect you to get yourself to London and select a young lady to marry, Ruel," the duke continued, his voice taking on an imperious tone. "Alexander has engaged the lovely daughter of the Comte de la Roche, have you heard?"

"I've given him my congratulations."

"You are the heir apparent," the vicar reminded him. "You must think of the duchy."

"I am thinking of the duchy."

"Then you've found a woman?" The duke sat forward.

"No!" Ruel gave a laugh and leaned back against his chair. "Father, marriage is the last thing on my mind."

"Surely not! You are a healthy young man with duties clearly spelled out. You will go to town this Season and select a wife. I shall leave the duchy in good hands, and I fully intend to see your heir before I die."

"Be reasonable, Father. I've been away from England three years, and my own brother tells me I'm browner than a sailor. What lady would have me?"

"Any lady with good sense!"

"I have not the slightest inclination to dress myself up as a dandy and parade from one ball to another all Season. Before I left England, it was common intelligence that the Marquess of Blackthorne had the manners and bearing of a rogue. I was considered arrogant, thoughtless, insolent, headstrong, and rude."

"Ruel! You are shocking!"

"Shocking was not the least attribute of my reputation, Father. Ask any lady in London and you will hear the same. I am disagreeable and ill-tempered. I am willful and boorish."

"Nonsense!"

"I'm afraid it is quite true, Father," Lord Alexander put in. "Blackthorne performs with greater success at cards than he will ever do with the ladies. Swoon at his beauty they will, but marry him they will not."

"I can't believe it," the vicar of Tiverton said firmly. "Lord Blackthorne is to be a duke. Why, anyone would be—"

"My manners have only grown more coarse," Ruel interrupted, "with the influence of Americans. I believe even the servants at Slocombe House have labeled me a blackguard."

He lifted his focus to Anne, amusement written in the tilt of his handsome mouth. She glared at him from her position by the fire. He knew he had toyed with her in the kitchen, he knew he had her lace in his pocket, and he knew he was teasing her even now. She would not be sorry if the marquess found a wife as headstrong and insolent as he.

"You are not a blackguard!" the duke cried. "You are my son and my declared heir! Any woman with half the sense of a toad would marry you!"

"Any woman?" Ruel leapt to his feet and took two strides from the tea table to the hearth. "Any woman, Father? Shall we put your assertions to the test?"

He dropped to one knee at Anne's feet and grabbed her hand. She gasped, but before she could jerk her fingers away he placed a firm kiss on them once again. Flourishing one hand in a grand gesture, he looked straight into her eyes.

"My dear Miss . . . what's your surname?"

"Ruel, don't be absurd!" The duke cut in, chuckling. "Come, come now, my boy."

"Your surname, madam?" Ruel repeated.

"Webster," Anne managed.

"My dear Miss Anne Webster, in the course of our acquaintance I confess I have fallen most violently in love with you. From the moment I took note of your magnificent eyes, I have been bewitched. Never before have I witnessed in any woman such tantalizing almond-shaped eyes. Their upward tilt is charming, and their color . . . the shade of the evening sky just past sunset . . . the whisper of dark indigo . . ."

"Her eyes are blue," Lord Alexander spoke up. "I've had a look at them myself. Blue eyes."

"My dear Miss Webster, your hair falls about your shoulders like a sheet of molten bronze, a river of the finest liqueur, a cascade—"

"Brown hair," Lord Alexander pronounced. "Brown, brown, brown. Brown as a mouse's rump."

Ruel's eyes softened as he studied Anne. "Chocolate, I think. Hot chocolate laced with cinnamon."

"You have quite terrorized the young lady, Lord Blackthorne," the vicar said. "I should think you've gone far enough."

"On the contrary." Ruel leaned his arm on his knee and scrutinized Anne. "By heaven, she's a beauty. She actually is truly fascinating."

He turned to the assembled company. A chorus of "Nonsense" and "Absurd" followed his proclamation. Ruel ignored the comments and gazed at Anne a moment longer. Mortified, she could do nothing but stare back.

"Miss Webster," he said in a low voice, "your cheeks blush with the damask pink of new roses. Your skin is as soft as the down of a petal. Your lips are like ripe peaches in the heat of summer."

"Peaches!" Lord Alexander exclaimed. "Oh, very good, Ruel. You'll win her heart with that one."

"Your brow speaks of high intelligence and your speech of good breeding." His eyes narrowed. "I think, perhaps, you can even read books. Can that be true, Miss Webster?"

Anne longed to pull her hand away, but the marquess was looking at her with such intensity. His fingers on her wrist were warm and firm. His eyes had melted to rain-cloud gray, and his lips curved with the hint of pleasure. He was making sport of her, of course. She was nothing but a housemaid, the object of everyone's derision.

"The Bible," she said, lifting her chin. "I read it nightly."

"The Bible? Then you are a moral and virtuous woman, two strong qualities to add to your engaging beauty." He looked at her a moment longer, then caught himself. "Well, to get on with it. My dear Miss Webster, you cannot be indifferent to the fact that I have come to admire you devotedly. At the hour of our parting this afternoon, I felt that I could not go on. Indeed, I cannot release you now without telling you my heart and asking you if I may not have your affection in return. Will you not take me, Ruel Chouteau, Marquess of Blackthorne, Earl of Glascock, Viscount Billings, and so forth, and allow me to be your husband and protector through life?"

Anne stared at the man who held her hand. The vicar cleared his throat, but Ruel never took his eyes off her. She knew she could play the blushing housemaid. She could run from the room in horror and leave them laughing in her wake. Or she could play the affronted parson's daughter and hand Blackthorne a moralizing sermon on the evils of dissimulation. Or she could be herself.

"You have professed your admiration of me, Lord Blackthorne, and I thank you," she said clearly. "Although you intended to ridicule and mock me for the amusement of your company, I believe your esteem is merited. I am, indeed, educated and virtuous. The shape of my eyes and the color of my hair are the endowment of my parents, but my skill as a designer of bobbin lace has been honed through my own diligence. Few in Nottingham and none in Tiverton surpass my ability to envision and design lace borders, fans, shawls, caps, and collars. Few can equal the skill with which I am able to prick my designs onto parchment. Some may have similar deftness in the twisting and winding of silk from a thousand bobbins across such a parchment pattern pinned to a pillow, but I am surely one of the most accomplished.''

''Good heavens!'' the vicar exclaimed in a hushed voice. ''Young lady, your impudence is not to be tolerated.''

''Let her continue,'' Lord Alexander countered. ''This is diverting.''

''Miss Webster?'' Ruel signaled her to go on.

Anne glanced at the duke. He rolled his eyes and waved her on. She stared at each of the Chouteaus one by one. Vain, self-important, heedless pagans. Perhaps she was only a servant in their house. All the same, her dismissal was imminent, and she wanted her lace.

''I descend from a proud line of Britons,'' she stated, turning her focus on the marquess. ''My family are not nobles, but the surname Webster speaks to our profession. We are weavers. We create fabrics, fashion them, stitch them, and mold them to the pleasure of the aristocracy. Without us, Lord Blackthorne, you would appear in Society no better dressed than the legendary pompous emperor whose new clothes were made of invisible thread.''

''My goodness!'' Ruel swung around and gave his brother an incredulous look. ''Did you ever think of that, Alex? Without this charming young lady and her family, we should all be as naked as eels.''

''Bestow a title on them!'' Lord Alexander declared. ''Reward their grand contribution to our cause. Make the Webster family barons or knights!''

"You have requested a difficult thing of me, Lord Black-thorne," Anne said to her mocker. "I am a woman who places high value on honesty, charity, and prudence. You have asked for my affection. You do not have it."

"No?" Turning to his father, he held up his hands. "I do not have her affection. What did I tell you?"

Anne squared her shoulders. "Now I would ask something of you, Lord Blackthorne. I require the return of my lace panel."

He tugged the lace out of his waistcoat pocket and draped the fragile masterpiece across his knee. Anne stared down at the craftsmanship that represented more than a year of her labor. Though torn where Lord Alexander's heel had spiked it, the narrow panel was still clean. She could pick out the tattered edges and rework them. Perhaps she could even cut away the central medallion that formed the Chouteau lozenge. She might place a bouquet of roses in its stead and sell it to the laceman for a price, small though it would be.

Lord Blackthorne lifted the border and held it to the firelight. For a terrible instant, she thought him so cruel as to toss it into the flames. She held her breath as he turned the lace first one way and then another.

"You designed this, Miss Webster?" he asked.

"Yes, my lord."

The gossamer silk caught the sparkle of the blaze and glowed with an inner radiance. "By heaven, I'm deuced. This lace is a work of art. Here is our lozenge, Father, depicted in a most accurate and delicate fashion. These roses are . . . well, they're magnificent."

"Thank you, my lord." She bent slowly toward the lace as she spoke. "I spent more than a twelvemonth in the border's design, and I should very much like—"

"I'm afraid I shall have to keep it," he interrupted her, stuffing the lace into his pocket before she could grab it.

"When I have your answer, Miss Webster, the lace will be yours again."

"She told you she could not like you," Lord Alexander said with impatience. "What more can you ask of the wench?"

"Until I know whether or not she intends to accept my hand in marriage, I fear my father will pursue me relentlessly on that account. I must have Miss Webster's formal rejection, and then His Grace will understand there is not a woman in the land who would willingly yoke herself to me."

"Now, then, Lord Blackthorne," the vicar intoned, "do leave this poor serving girl in peace. You have tormented her beyond reason already."

"Indeed." The duke gave his son a scowl before turning his attention to Anne. "Miss Webster, go and find Mrs. Davies at once. Tell our housekeeper to prepare the chambers of the marquess. They are to be dusted and aired with no little care. Then you may inform Mrs. Smythe to ready an elegant dinner on my son's behalf. Stop at nothing. We shall have the finest from our larder."

"Yes, Your Grace." Tearing her eyes from the marquess's waistcoat pocket, Anne gave the duke a curtsy.

"Prepare the fatted calf," Lord Alexander declared with a grand sweep of his hand. "The prodigal son has returned."

"Let us make merry and rejoice," the vicar quoted from Scripture, "for this brother of yours was dead and has begun to live, and was lost and has been found."

"Amen!" the duke pronounced, as if he were God Himself.

The other men in the company chuckled, relaxed, and went at their tea once again. As Ruel watched the dismissed housemaid slip away, three things occurred to him at once.

First, it occurred to him that in Christ's parable of the prodigal son, the younger brother had in no wise welcomed home his wandering sibling. He had been, in fact, jealous, angry, and resentful. Was Alex as pleased as he seemed at Ruel's return? The turn of events meant Alex had lost the opportunity to be declared heir apparent. All the same, the younger man wore his usual cheerful demeanor, and Ruel could not believe his brother had meant anything of substance by his allusion to the parable.

Second, it occurred to him that Miss Anne Webster did possess the most intriguing pair of indigo eyes and the most luxurious mane of chestnut hair he had ever seen. She spoke with fire and wit, and had shown not the slightest fear in declaring her utter dislike of him. Moreover, she was undoubtedly as talented in the creation of lace as she had asserted.

Finally, it occurred to Lord Blackthorne that he still held that panel of ethereal lace in his possession and that Miss Anne Webster had not given him her answer.

$\mathcal{T}hree$

"WHATEVER CAN YOU DO?" VERA WHISPERED. "YOU can't steal it back."

Anne studied the shadows creeping across the moonlit ceiling above the narrow iron bed she shared with her best friend. The row of five beds in the small room on the top floor of Slocombe House mirrored rows in fifteen other rooms filled with sleeping housemaids, kitchenmaids, scullery maids, ladies' maids, parlormaids, and maids-of-all-work.

Dimly lit and musty, the rooms were little used and contained nothing more homelike than beds, trunks, hooks for dresses and aprons, washbasins, and chamber pots. Their thin, yellowed walls and bare wood floors contrasted sharply with the opulent lower stories of Slocombe House, outfitted with luxurious carpets, velvet draperies, gilt wallpapers, and roaring fires. The poorly ventilated servants' quarters stayed hot all summer and frigid all winter.

In her tenure at Slocombe House, Anne had discovered she was never alone. At mealtimes, the kitchen staff dined all together in the kitchen, the household staff in the servants' hall, and the upper servants in the steward's room. She bathed, dressed, read her Bible, and worked her lace in the company of no fewer than ten young women at a time. Even on her rare afternoon off, she was ordered by Mrs. Davies to attend church or to stroll in the park with

the other maids of the House. Since she had come to Slocombe, Anne had shared this bed with Vera, a tiny housemaid whose small face, limp hair, and pale skin belied her
great inner fortitude and practicality.

The tall clock in the corridor outside their room chimed
the hour of three in the morning. In two more hours the
bell would ring, young ladies would fly out of bed, scrub
their faces, pull on dresses, aprons, and mobcaps, and
scurry to their posts. Anne and Vera would be among them,
though neither had slept for a moment.

"You're not actually thinking of stealing the lace from
the marquess, are you?" Vera asked, the note of hope in
her voice heavily tinged with dread. "I know your father
was a Luddite and upheld their creeds. What were they?"

"Determination. Free liberty."

"Yes, but look what their determination for freedom got
them, Anne. Look what they got for all their sledgeham-
mers and muskets." She paused, then shook her head.
"You have to know your place in this world. If you're a
stockinger making seven shillings a week, you'd better stay
a stockinger, no matter how many machines the hosiers
bring in. That's your place. Your father may have preached
that all people are the same in God's eyes, but I'm sorry
to tell you he was wrong. There's royalty, nobility, merchants, and laborers. You can't go from one to the other,
Anne. You're a housemaid, and your job is to serve the
duke's family and to keep your mouth shut. You can't go
independently selling lace to Lord Alexander or stealing it
from the marquess. You could be put in prison like your
father . . . or worse."

Anne rubbed her eyes and focused on the ceiling again.
Peeling paint where rainwater had seeped through the slate
roof formed fantastic curls that made her think of a dra-
gon's misty breath. She could almost see the lace she could
design of that undulating, magical pattern of swirls and
shadows. Of course, no one would purchase a piece of lace

so imaginative. The aristocracy wanted their standard roses and bows, perhaps a fern or two, and if they were unusually daring, a cherub or an urn.

"Here's my advice," Vera said, offering her seventh new stratagem that night. Anne had counted. "You should forget you ever made that lace panel. It was a foolhardy notion in the first place, thinking you could sell it to Lord Alexander. You're too much the dreamer, Anne. You have no practical sense."

Anne wondered, as she often did, how lace would look dyed in all the colors of the rainbow. At the moment, blonde lace was becoming all the fashion, lavishly trimming dresses, caps, pelisses, and aprons. Only a woman with especially dry hands could make blonde lace. In the summer it must be worked in the out-of-doors, and in winter it could be worked only in special rooms built over cow houses, where the animals' breath warmed the air. The smell in those rooms, as Anne well knew, was pungent, but any form of flame heat would cause soot damage to the lace's fine threads.

"This is what you should do, Anne," Vera said. It was her eighth attempt at dispensing advice. "You should start another piece of lace, this one more marketable, strewn with roses and lilies and such. In one or two years' time, if you save your wages from your work at the House and add to them what you earn from your next lace, you should be able to go back to Nottingham and eventually pay a barrister to defend your father."

One or two years. Anne thought of her father living night and day in the darkness of his small prison cell. How different from the snug parsonage with its little library, writing desk, and warm rugs. He had suffered from ill health for many years, and Anne feared he could not live much longer in the confines of a prison.

It was not his physical strength that would suffer so much as his spirit. Mr. Webster considered his books sus-

tenance, his pen and inkstand friends, and his pulpit the
very breath of life. His communion with God through
prayer and Bible reading were foremost in his priority—
followed by his determination to serve mankind. He viewed
the Luddites and their war against machinery as a cause as
noble as the great Crusades, and he was willing to give his
life on their behalf. Without Anne to secure his release, he
surely would.

"Here's what you should do," Vera whispered. Sugges-
tion number nine. "You should go down to Tiverton with
me for church tomorrow and take your afternoon off to visit
that new factory Mr. Heathcoat has built. You could ask
for an interview with Mr. Heathcoat himself and show him
what you can do with lace. He might put you to work as a
designer of embroidery patterns for the machine lace he's
manufacturing."

Anne turned her head and scowled at Vera's moonlit
profile. "Machine lace!" she hissed.

"Oh, it can't be all that bad. It's nothing but a lot of
boring net without the handwork anyway. You mustn't feel
so threatened." In contrast to Anne's straight nose, Vera's
tilted upward at the end, giving her a pert look, even though
Vera, at her happiest, was anything but pert.

"You must be reasonable and prudent, Anne," she continued. "You can continue as a housemaid here at Slocombe like the rest of us, or you can think of something
else rational to do. It's not as though there are many
choices."

Anne stroked her fingertips across the hem of the worn
sheet. "I could always be a duchess."

"There you go again. You won't be logical."

"Who's talking?" Sally Pimm lifted her head from the
next bed and glared at Anne. "Is that you, Webster?"

"Go back to sleep, Pimm."

"How can anyone sleep with the two of you chattering
away?"

"Vera is advising me what to do with my future."

"Tell her to jump in a stew pot and put the lid on it," the first kitchenmaid groused. "It must be nearly morning."

Anne tugged the sheet up to her neck. She knew she should try to sleep, but every time she shut her eyes, she saw the Marquess of Blackthorne winding her lace around his finger and then stuffing it into his pocket. He had known its value at once. He had also recognized the significance of the lozenge, and he understood that the lace had no value to anyone but the Chouteau family. He wanted it for himself, the blackguard!

Clenching her fists, Anne fought the rising tide of helpless anger. He had trapped her! Stealing the lace from him would send her to prison. Begging would be useless. Working another lace border in hopes of freeing her father would take far too long. And she could never betray him by using her skills in the manufacture of machine lace.

"What about taking a husband?" Vera whispered. "The gamekeeper has asked to marry you twice already. I understand he's more than a little angry at your rejection. In spite of his jealous manner, he's not so bad, is he? You'd have your own cottage, and you could send all your wages to your family in Nottingham."

Anne tilted her head to one side and eyed her friend. "And be subjected to the gamekeeper's brutishness and vanity night and day? Now it's you who won't be reasonable."

"Then look for a soldier to wed. Everyone is saying England may go to war with France due to that little emperor escaping from his island exile. As near as we are to France, Tiverton should be full of regiments. Soldiers earn solid pay, I'll wager."

Anne lifted herself up on one elbow and gave her friend a kiss on the cheek. "You must try to rest, Vera. You know how Mrs. Davies likes us to be fresh."

"But what will you do?" Vera looked at Anne with luminous eyes. "Oh, you won't do anything foolish, will you?"

Anne let out a deep breath. "Of course not," she said. "Do try to get some sleep now."

As Vera's breathing began to slow, Anne studied the curls of ceiling paint. Again she thought of the marquess, a man of shadows and darkness. She remembered perfectly the way his fingers had raked through the thick rumple of black curls on his head, the way his cold gray eyes had assessed her, the way his mouth had curved upward in a cynical smile.

She remembered, too, how his hand had felt as it held hers—warm, firm, strong. She recalled the timbre of his voice as he had pronounced her a beauty, had called her eyes indigo and her hair a sheet of bronze, had asked to be her protector.

Protector? There was only one way a man like Blackthorne could protect a woman like Anne Webster.

"You will forget about that lace, won't you, Annie?" Vera murmured, half asleep. "You will heed my advice?"

Anne watched the sky lighten outside the small window of her bedroom. The tiny square patch faded from black to cobalt and finally to a familiar shade of silver gray, the gray of a man's eyes shining in firelight.

When the Marquess of Blackthorne arrived at church in his chaise and four the following morning, not a female in the room failed to take note. The kitchenmaids whispered at how villainously shiny and black his hair appeared in contrast to the blond locks of his younger brother. The housemaids murmured their observations on the massive firmness of his chin, the wondrous breadth of his shoulders, the disdainful expression of his mouth, and the immense height to which he rose as he strode down the aisle toward the family pew.

The merchants' wives and daughters commented among

themselves on the fine cut of the marquess's blue coat, its M-notched lapels, shiny brass buttons, flapped pockets, and French cuffs. The mayor's daughter and her friends regarded with admiration his double-breasted waistcoat of striped valencia, his cream-colored trousers, and his fine leather boots.

The landowners' daughters and their mothers took note that the future Duke of Marston had returned to England with his skin abominably tanned and his attention no more fixed upon them than it ever was. They observed, however, that in spite of his rakish manners and malevolent air, he had returned all the same and was as eligible as ever.

Anne Webster, seated on the second row from the back, saw only one thing. The Marquess of Blackthorne had tied around his high, stiff collar a cravat of the finest and most elegant silk Honiton lace.

Almost deaf with fury, she heard little of the vicar's lengthy sermon. Instead she watched Blackthorne as he whispered some comment to his brother, chuckled at a tidbit of humor the vicar put forth, and ran his finger around the inside of his collar. Unable to quell it, she had the unChristian wish that her lace would come to life and strangle the man.

After the service, the Chouteau family exited the church first, followed by the inhabitants of their duchy. The duke and duchess departed for Slocombe House in their carriage, and Lord Alexander joined some town friends for a ride on horseback. When Anne emerged into the springtime sunshine, the marquess stood at the bottom of the steps deep in conversation with the vicar.

Vera grabbed her arm. "Don't say a word!"

"He's wearing it. Do you see?"

"You can't be sure it's yours."

"It's mine."

"Oh, let him have it. It bears his crest anyway."

By the time Anne reached the marquess, it was all she

could do to hold her tongue. She crossed her arms, lowered her head to hide her face inside her bonnet, and took a deep breath. She was almost past him when he touched her elbow.

"Your Majesty," he said in a low voice tinged with mock servitude. "How well you look this morning."

"Thank you, my lord," Anne managed through gritted teeth.

Vera let out a muffled gasp as the man turned away from the vicar and joined them in their walk across the drive toward the road. He slowed his long stride to match theirs and tipped his hat at acquaintances they passed, as though strolling with housemaids were a perfectly acceptable pastime for a marquess. Anne knew Vera would bolt given half the chance, so she caught her friend's puffed sleeve in her fist and hung on.

"Your gown is fetching, Your Highness," he continued. "Such a shade of sapphire reminds me of a Missouri morning, a color that brings a glow to your lovely eyes."

Anne stared at the road, hardly daring to let herself speak. He was teasing her again, of course, and she had no idea why he found such revolting behavior so amusing. Poor Vera was wilting with shock, her pale skin ashen and her fingers visibly trembling.

"I regret to see," he went on, "that you chose to cover your stunning hair with a mobcap and straw bonnet. The lavender and crocuses with which you adorned your hat, however, are an exquisite touch. Your Majesty, you could not look more lovely."

She lifted her chin and fixed him with a glare. "And you could not look more like yourself."

The marquess threw back his head and laughed loudly. "Ah, I'm pleased to find your tongue has lost none of its acidity. Did you note my choice of cravat this morning? I selected a fine length of Queen Anne's lace."

"How very witty," she returned. "Yet the lace does not belong to you."

"Do you brand me a thief, Miss Webster?"

Vera let out a low moan. It was all Anne could do to keep her friend upright. They had left the enclosure of the church and were walking in the lane that led to the main road. Had they turned west, they soon would have entered Tiverton, but they set their direction toward Slocombe House to be in time to serve the noon meal. In a moment, they would walk onto the road and begin the two-mile journey to the House. As the marquess had left his chaise and four at the church, Anne knew his interview could not go on much longer. If only she could keep her wits.

"I merely speak the truth," she told him. "The lace is mine, and a true gentleman would return it to its owner."

"Unfortunately I have never been considered a true gentleman," the marquess retorted. "I believe you yourself referred to me as a blackguard."

"A reputation you only etch more clearly in mind with your unseemly behavior."

"My reputation is among the least of my concerns, Miss Webster."

"Mine, on the other hand, concerns me greatly, and if you do not return to your chaise at once, Lord Blackthorne, you will endanger it irreparably. I hope you do not believe that your brother's pursuit of me yesterday in his chamber was in any way encouraged. I have no interest in becoming a momentary fancy for either of the two sons of the Duke of Marston."

Vera's groan could have been heard by anyone passing. To Anne's dismay, she realized the road was deserted, all the household staff having hurried ahead. The marquess was showing no signs of returning to the churchyard for his transportation.

"Momentary?" he said. "My dear Miss Webster, you may recall that my proposition to you yesterday was in no way to expire at day's end. If truth be told, you intrigue me more than a little. Where did you come by such pleasant manners?''

"If my manners are seen as pleasant, my lord, you are mistaking me. I have no pleasant feelings toward you whatever.''

Again he chuckled and shook his head. Ruel had not met anyone he could converse with so easily in years. Certainly never a woman. Who was Anne Webster, and how had she come to be working as a housemaid at Slocombe?

This morning's observation of her confirmed everything he had remembered as he lay alone in his bed the night before. He had turned their conversations over in his mind, first one way, then another. There could be no mistaking the fact that she spoke with the words of an educated woman. Her manners were acceptable if not noble, and her wit was delightfully sharp. She didn't care for him in the least and had not the slightest fear of his rank. In short, she was so refreshing a creature, he had made up his mind to confront her again immediately following the church service.

"I concede your evident displeasure with me, Miss Webster,'' he told her. "I am deeply wounded, of course.''

She shot him a disparaging glance, and he was happy to find that her eyes were as blue as he had remembered them. A pink flush colored her high cheekbones, but her skin was fair, clear, and creamy. Though she was scowling at him, he took note that her lips were full and slightly damp. The image of kissing them took him by surprise, but he reminded himself that the prim Miss Webster would be no willing conquest.

"Your father is a schoolmaster,'' he guessed. "You hail from Tiverton, and your house is filled with books which you delight to read.''

"My father's occupations are none of your concern, Lord

Blackthorne. We are not under your jurisdiction. Our family dwells in Nottingham.''

"You're a long way from home. What brings you to Devon, then? Surely you could find employment in Nottingham.''

Anne swallowed. She could never tell this man about her father's imprisonment with the Luddites. As a parson, Mr. Webster had been expected to preach, tend the ill, take tea with the baroness, Lady de Winter, and nothing more.

That he had joined the secret group of men who met in Sherwood Forest and had followed the orders of their leader, who called himself General Ludd, had brought utter disgrace to the Webster family. That he had broken into factories and smashed machinery had besmirched his own name forever. He had lost his position with the parish, of course, though the countess allowed his family to go on living in the parsonage until she could find someone to replace him.

Captured and thrown into prison, Mr. Webster had expected the usual sentence for stocking frame breaking—transportation to Australia. Exile from England for fourteen years would have been bad enough, but during the time he was awaiting trial, the House of Lords passed a bill making such violence a capital offense. Without a skilled barrister to plead his case, he would be hanged.

No, Anne could not have found employment in Nottingham. Without the countess's recommendation of her to Slocombe House, she would have joined her mother and sisters in destitution. As it was, her wages barely kept them alive.

"My presence in Devon can be of no concern to a man such as yourself," she told the marquess. "I am employed to serve your family in the House along with a hundred other young women no different from myself."

"I beg to point out, Miss Webster, that yesterday you stated in no uncertain terms your very great difference from the hundred other young women in Slocombe House. You claimed to be a better lace designer and pattern pricker than anyone in Tiverton.''

"Oh, Annie," Vera moaned. "You didn't."

By now there was no hope that he would abandon them and return to his chaise. The hilly, wooded property belonging to the Duke of Marston had closed them in on either side, a glorious display of budding trees dressed in pale green. Along the hedges at either side of the road sprung bright white daffadowndillies and purple crocuses. The scent of newly turned earth mingled with the perfume of spring buds. Birds, busy with nest building, chirped and sang and fought over fat worms they pulled from the soft dirt at the side of the road. Anne would have given anything to be able to drink in the morning and dream out a lace pattern to reflect its glory.

Instead she was shackled by *him*. She glanced at the marquess from beneath the brim of her straw bonnet. Oh, he was handsome, of course. No woman could deny that. His high-crowned black felt hat with its curled-up brim added imposing height to his already tall physique. The cut of his clothing, the width of his shoulders, the length of his legs— everything about him was the picture of the manly aristocrat. Only the brownness of his skin gave his face the cast of a pirate. But the twinkle in his gray eyes and the amused angle of his lip showed him for the scoundrel he was.

"As you have surely discovered," Anne said, "by observing my lace panel which you wear around your neck, I am a skilled designer."

"Indeed, Miss Webster, you are. In fact, it is this quality about you that intrigues me more than any other. Not only are you lovely, articulate, and mannered, but also you possess a skill most remarkable." His brown fingers touched the crest on the lace. "May I inquire where you learned such technique? Surely no common lace school could teach a young woman how to create a lozenge such as this."

"My technique came from the lace school at Nottingham," she said. "What talent I possess is God-given."

"God? Ah, yes, I do recall that you are religious. Nightly Bible readings and—"

The unmistakable, familiar crack of flint striking steel silenced him. An instantaneous report echoed from the hillside. Before Ruel could call out "Ambush," a projectile raked across his left arm at a downward angle. His flesh split wide. The round continued on undeflected. It tore into Anne's thigh, taking with it a piece of her gown, and came out the other side. It ripped a hole near the hem of Vera's dress before plowing into the dirt at her feet.

Vera screamed. Anne crumpled to the road.

"Down!" Ruel jerked Vera's arm. She shrieked in hysteria, rolled into a ball, and covered her head with her arms. "The hedge," he grunted. "Get to it."

He drew his coat pistol from an inside pocket as he swept Anne up in his arms and ran with her toward the shelter of the hedge. A puff of smoke, smelling of black powder, drifted across the open road. Still screaming, Vera unwound herself and scrambled for cover.

"Silence," he commanded her. Holding the loaded pistol with one hand, he jerked it from half to full cock and shouted up the hillside. "Show yourself, villain!"

Through the black spots that danced in her eyes, Anne could distinguish a circle of bright blood forming on the marquess's shoulder. She reached out to him, but no words reached her tongue. Overcome with nausea that swept over her in a rising tide of pain, she shut her eyes.

Oblivious to his wound, Ruel peered through the dense hedge.

"Damnation. He's gone." He turned to the women and noted Anne's blood-soaked dress. At the sight of her ashen face, a wave of fear curled through his stomach. A crimson stain covered the torn hole in her gown, spreading quickly and dripping onto the ground. Dear God, she could die.

"What about you?" he demanded of Vera. "Are you

hurt?'' When he took her shoulder and shook her, the paralyzed girl let out a little squeak. ''Are you injured?''

''No!'' she sobbed. ''I'm all right.''

''Then help me.'' He shrugged out of his coat, vaguely aware that his shoulder throbbed as though a bee had stung it, and tossed the garment to Vera. ''Make a pillow of this. We must stop the blood.''

He reached for his cravat, realized he had only the bit of flimsy lace, and swore. He grabbed Anne's dress and ripped the hem away with his hands. ''Miss Webster, do not flinch. And don't look as if you're swooning either. I know you're not the sort.''

Anne's eyes fluttered open. She could see the marquess bending over her, could feel him touching her leg. Mortified, she tried to push the demon away but found she couldn't lift her hands. He slid what was left of her skirt up her legs, took her thigh in his hands, and blotted the blood.

''Torn clean through,'' he muttered. ''At least the ball is out. We shall require an apothecary.''

Anne stared at the man whose head hovered somewhere above her body. His tall hat had fallen off. A streak of blood marred his clean-shaven jaw. His black hair fell in a tumble of curls over his brow as he wiped and wrapped her thigh. The tendons in his neck bunched, and the small muscle at the side of his jaw flickered in his anger.

''Who could have done this?'' he growled to himself. ''A highwayman would have come out onto the road after my money. Surely Barkham would have challenged me to a duel if he still held a grudge. It's been three damned years since the incident with his wife. . . . Wimberly can't still be nursing his anger about that money I won. . . . Of course, there's Droughtmoor. He might still—''

''It was the gamekeeper,'' Vera croaked. ''I saw his brown coat.''

''William Green? What have I done to him?''

"Not you. It's her he's sworn to kill." Vera took Anne's hand and squeezed it. "He wants to marry her. He's asked twice, but she won't have him. I couldn't tell her what was rumored, but everyone knows it."

"Absurd. To kill a woman because she won't marry? Ridiculous."

"She spurned him. A man of his stature—"

"A gamekeeper? He's a peasant! He doesn't deserve a woman like this."

"She's only Annie Webster, my lord. She's only a housemaid."

Ruel looked down at the woman whose shadowed eyelids had drifted shut. Her face, so animated before, was motionless, her breathing shallow. Only a housemaid?

"Stay here with her," he ordered the smaller woman, whose large green eyes brimmed with tears. "I'm going for my chaise. It's at the church, and I'll send it here at once for both of you. Then I'll go into the town and find the apothecary. We should return to Slocombe within the hour."

When he started to get up, Vera caught his arm. "No, my lord, please don't go. You . . . you're wounded yourself. Your arm . . ."

He glanced at the tattered flesh of his shoulder and frowned. "Hellfire. This is a deuce of a circumstance."

"Please guard your tongue, my lord," Vera whispered. "She's a minister's daughter."

Studying the injured woman for a moment, he decided he had no choice. "I'll go for the chaise. If we lose her—"

"I'll go! The gamekeeper has no reason to shoot at me. I'll send the chaise and fetch the apothecary." Vera leapt to her feet, clapped one hand over her straw bonnet, and darted away.

"Miss!" He called after her, but she was already flying around a bend in the road, her tattered, blood-spattered skirts dancing at her ankles.

Four

HE SUPPOSED IT HAD SOMETHING TO DO WITH THE WAY she had woven a royal tale of imagination for the little beggar girl in the kitchen. Or perhaps it was the manner in which she had boldly demanded the return of her lace panel. Maybe it was nothing more than the range of emotions that had flickered across her face during his farcical marriage proposal—indignation, amusement, anger, shy pleasure.

Ruel lifted Anne's shoulders and placed her head on his thigh. Whatever the reason that drew him to this woman, she intrigued him. He stared in dismay at her blanched face. The thick hedge cast blue shadows beneath her cheekbones and over her neck. Though a tiny pulsebeat flickered in her throat and her breath came regularly, she had lost too much blood. Even now, it soaked through the binding on her thigh and seeped onto her bare leg. He rubbed his fingers together, aware that they, too, were stained with her bright blood.

A strange sensation crept over Ruel as he looked at the woman. He had always viewed his own existence with the cynicism of the rakehell that he was. He had been born late in his mother's life, to everyone's immense surprise. And though the duke clearly loved his elder son, Ruel's mother found him abhorrent. "That dark, vile little thing," she called him as she chose either to abuse or to ignore him.

Yet the duchess doted on her second son, "that golden gift from God," Alexander.

Ruel had learned not to care. All women, he had decided while still quite young, were useless except as entertainment. Claire, sixteen years his senior and the eldest of the five flaxen-haired Chouteau sisters, had done her best to encourage tenderness in him by playing with the little boy, teaching him songs, bringing him toys from London. But Claire had married the Viscount Eagon the year after Ruel was born, so he saw her rarely. His other sisters could hardly be bothered with him.

Ruel touched the tip of his knuckle to Anne Webster's cheek. He had always thought of women rather the way a huntsman views his prey. They were to be admired, pursued, conquered. As many as possible, as often as possible.

A man could be respected for a variety of things—his intellect, his wit, his shooting skill, even his wealth and position in Society. Women focused their whole existence on balls, fashions, and romantic intrigues. They spent their time on such fripperies as playing the pianoforte, stitching fire screens, beading purses. No, Ruel had nothing but a passing carnal interest in the female gender.

He had little use for religion, either, thinking it a grand collection of gibberish intended to give the weak-minded hope. He agreed with his friend George Gordon, Lord Byron, on the subject. The poet had commented to him one day, "We are miserable enough in this life, without the absurdity of speculating upon another."

Women. Religion. Shooting. Balls. Fashion. Grand dinners. The royal court. All of them a great waste of time. Ruel had found his education boring, most of his peers simpering, and his prospects for the future deadly dull. Travel, adventure, and gambling—whether at cards or in speculative exploits—were the only things that interested him.

He cared little for life, his own or that of others. He had

shot two men in duels, several more during a misadventure in America, another at the gaming table. He disregarded his own existence and had almost lost his life more than once. In fact, he realized as he looked down at the young lady who lay in his lap, he could hardly count the number of men who would be happy to see him dead.

Why did the thought of losing this woman send an aching emptiness through his chest? She was only Annie Webster . . . only a housemaid . . .

He tried to straighten the mobcap that had slipped askew during the shooting. A ribbon of her hair had fallen out and lay across her shoulder. He picked it up and draped it over the back of his hand. As light as silk, it gleamed with golden highlights in the late-morning sunshine. Chocolate laced with cinnamon, he had called the color. No wonder Miss Webster disdained him.

The mobcap refused to go right, so Ruel pulled it off and let her hair spill across his thigh. He traced one finger over each of her eyebrows, marveling at the way they echoed the upward-tilted shape of her almond eyes. She was a housemaid, a minister's daughter, a lace worker. She ought not to have those lips. So full, though pale now, they all but begged to be kissed.

Had any man ever kissed Miss Anne Webster? He thought not. The tone in her voice warned men away. The tilt to her chin instructed them to keep hands off. Even the design of her simple cotton gown spoke of her maidenhood. Where most women, maids and ladies alike, took to extremes the fashion of necklines cut as low as possible, waists cut as high as possible, and breasts molded as tightly as possible, Anne wore a modest bodice covered by a discreet cotton shawl. She was as untouched and new as that crocus growing beside the hedge.

Swallowing at the hard lump that had somehow lodged in his throat, Ruel stared down at her leg. Slender, firm, and white, it was a sharp contrast to the deeply tanned skin of his own hands. He had seen women's legs, lots of them. They had been displayed for him wantonly. Anne Webster's leg was not meant for his eyes. He tugged at her skirt, but it was too torn and bloodied to cover her.

"Oh, God." He shut his eyes, searching for answers. In the blackness he saw nothing. Emptiness. Void.

When he lifted his head again, he saw that she was staring at him. Her eyes were a deep shade of blue, the lashes long and black around them. She took a breath, and her face contorted in pain.

"My leg hurts."

"Don't move it."

She bit back tears. "Where's Vera?"

"Gone for the chaise and the apothecary."

"Never mind that." She spoke in a murmur. "I'm prepared to die."

"You're not going to die."

"I think I shall."

"No." He leaned over her and took her face in both his hands. "No, Anne Webster, you will not. You will get into the chaise and go to Slocombe. You will recover and make lace panels and read your Bible and stand up to the nobility just as you always have. Yes?"

She looked into his gray eyes. At first she had thought the man speaking to her was the Marquess of Blackthorne, but now she saw she had been wrong. The marquess had eyes of cold, hard iron. This man's eyes were soft, tender, filled with compassion.

"Who are you?" she whispered.

"Ruel."

"I think you should know . . . Ruel . . . were I to paint your eyes, I should make them the color of a dove's wings."

He clenched his jaw, fighting the lump in his throat. "Thank you, madam."

"I could make your eyes in lace, I think. I'm good with

patterns . . . and your hair is curly . . . like the paint on my ceiling. . . . You look very like the marquess, but much more gentle. I must tell you, Ruel . . . I think the marquess was wounded. I saw blood on his shoulder . . . like that on yours.''

"I shall look after the marquess."

"Oh, you are good." Her eyes drifted shut. She tried to remember why her leg hurt so terribly, but a cloud had drifted across her mind, a gray cloud that made her think of Ruel's eyes.

"Ruel," she said. She opened her eyes as far as she could. His were damp and red-rimmed, so she shut them again. "Ruel, the marquess asked to be my protector."

"Yes, he did." His voice was ragged.

"I prefer you."

"Thank you, Anne. Thank you very much."

The apothecary predicted she would die during the night. She had lost a great quantity of blood. If not that night, she would surely perish within the week. The lead ball had driven bits of dress fabric into her wounded leg, he informed Mrs. Davies, the housekeeper. Gangrene was certain to set in. He gave the housekeeper a small bottle of laudanum to dose Anne for the pain, instructed that the vicar be called in the hour of the young lady's death, and hurried up to the rooms of the Marquess of Blackthorne.

There, the apothecary blotted, cleaned, and stitched the grave wound in the marquess's shoulder. He then bled him, gave his valet a variety of powders along with a quantity of laudanum, and prescribed bed rest until the injury healed—a month at the least. The marquess was not to use his shoulder in any way during that time, but was to be fed, bathed, dressed, and pampered.

Beatrice Chouteau, the Duchess of Marston, swooned the moment she was told of the dreadful event, and the apothecary rushed from the marquess to her bedside. She recovered quickly enough but was confined to her rooms with a headache.

She concurred with the intelligence that the gamekeeper was to blame for the shooting incident. It was against Slocombe House rules for female servants to have male followers, she reminded her lady's maids, and such appalling violence was exactly the reason. Romantic liaisons between members of the lower classes always led to trouble.

While the apothecary was tending his elder son and wife, the duke stormed up and down the corridors of Slocombe House, rapping his cane on the floor and issuing commands. Footmen flew at his beck and call. He ordered the roadway from Tiverton to Slocombe searched. He ordered all possible witnesses to the dire event to be summoned. He ordered the family's physician to be driven out from London. He ordered William Green brought to him at once. The gamekeeper, to no one's surprise, was not to be found. The duke dispatched a party of footmen to find and arrest the villain.

On hearing the report of the shooting, Lord Alexander immediately departed the home of his friends in Tiverton and rode to his brother's chambers. He stayed at Ruel's side through the apothecary's visit and afterward during the long hours of the night.

Weak from loss of blood and dizzied by laudanum, Ruel found it difficult to recall exactly what had happened on the road to Slocombe House. He knew his shoulder hurt like the devil. He recalled the uproar when his chaise arrived at the House with him and . . . and who? Two women. He couldn't place their names. Who were they? There was something about one of them, and he just couldn't . . .

"The shot must have come from the south," Alexander was saying when Ruel finally recognized his brother's voice. "A hill rises just beyond the hedge where you were shot. It's well-wooded property, and the shooter must have been standing at the top of the knoll in order to have taken such accurate aim. He almost had you through the heart, you know.''

Ruel knew. He clenched his jaw against the pain as he straightened his shoulders on the mound of pillows beneath them. Sunlight filtered through tiny slits between the heavy velvet draperies, but the room was almost as dim as night. The scent of burning wax mingled with the vile smell of the powders at his bedside. His mouth tasted of cotton.

"Draw apart the damned curtains, Alex," he muttered, grabbing the nearest bottle from the bedside table. It was rum. He grimaced and took a swig. "For God's sake, open the windows and let some air in here. Where's my valet? Where's Foley?"

His brother laid a hand on Ruel's brow. "Be still. The apothecary left strict instructions for your rest. Have some more laudanum, why don't you? It'll calm your nerves.''

Ruel scowled at the small container. "Dash it, Alex, I don't want laudanum. It puts me in a foul humor, and I can't think. There's something . . . someone . . .''

"You're to take two hundred and fifty drops, enough to keep any man in bliss. I confess I've had a little myself just to calm my nerves. Come now.''

His hand started toward Ruel's mouth. "No, I said!" Knocking the vial to the floor, Ruel let out a growl. "My head feels like a bloody pumpkin! And my shoulder . . . Where's my valet? . . . Damn, I can't even think of his name. I should have eaten breakfast long ago. I have things to do today. I've got to find out . . . to see . . .''

"If you won't lie down and rest, I shall end up the next Duke of Marston, and by all accounts, that will be a devil of a situation. Father has been ranting all night, storming about the place in fits of apoplexy.''

"Why?"

"No one can find the gamekeeper, of course."

"Gamekeeper . . ." Ruel gripped his sheets in his fists as

pieces of the puzzle began to fall into place. If only his head would stop throbbing.

Alexander leaned back in his chair and propped a foot on the bed. Despite Alexander's obvious worry, Ruel noticed that the young man had managed to find the time to have his valet lace him into a corset in order that his outrageous blue knee-length coat would button over his pinched-in waist. Voluminous cossack trousers tied at the ankles with yellow bows were draped about his legs. Ruel considered tossing out a barb against dandy fashion, but he couldn't make his befuddled brain or his thick tongue function.

"Personally, I hold it was a highwayman who shot you," Alexander said, rearranging the red flowered-silk cravat at his neck. "He must have used a rifle for the ball to have gone so far and with such accuracy. He might have had a blunderbuss, but I understand there was only one ball. Can you recall?"

When Ruel didn't answer, he went on. "I'll wager the highwayman knew you'd be leaving church Sunday morning, saw that you were afoot, and determined to have your money."

"I wasn't robbed."

"Perhaps the highwayman didn't expect you to be armed. It was rather rash of you, I think. Do you always carry a coat pistol, Ruel?"

"Since America."

"I should continue the practice if I were you. I've had it on good authority that more than one gentleman is displeased at your return to England. Have you considered that the assassin might not have been the gamekeeper or a highwayman at all? It might have been Barkham. When you were caught with his wife—"

"Fiancée."

"Whatever. At any rate, I don't think he's forgiven you. Wimberly, too, has every reason to come after you. You ruined him, you know. He hasn't been the same since you took his money—"

"Won it."

"Fairly? He doesn't think so, and it would be like him to travel from London with a rifle that could shoot right through a man's arm and a woman's—"

"Where is she?" Ruel interrupted, remembering suddenly. He tore back the sheets and surged out of bed. "The woman . . . where is she?"

Alexander leapt to his feet and grabbed the bellpull. "Ruel, do calm yourself. Foley! Come at once."

Ruel's valet ran across the carpeted floor, closely followed by two footmen. "My lord, my lord!" the valet cried. He turned to one of the footmen. "Fetch Mr. Errand."

"Stop!" Ruel commanded. He caught the bedpost for support as the three servants stiffened into obedience. Turning to his brother, he grabbed the ridiculous floral cravat and pulled Alexander close.

"Where . . . is . . . she?" he repeated slowly, anger burning each word into the silence of the room.

"Who?" Alexander asked. "Please, Ruel, you're making no sense at all. Foley, the laudanum!"

"The two women who were with me—where are they now? One of them was wounded."

"I don't know where they are. Really, Ruel—"

Pushing past him, Ruel staggered toward the door. The damned room spun like a child's top. He could hear the mad scramble behind him, the shouted commands. Idiots.

Where was she? He lurched out into the corridor and leaned on a marble bust to catch his breath. *She's only Annie Webster . . . only a housemaid.* The servants' quarters, of course. Upstairs.

"Lord Blackthorne." It was Mr. Errand, the butler. He approached from the rear, gave Ruel a formal bow, and cleared his throat. His bushy eyebrows floated on his face like a pair of matched clouds. "My lord, please do be reasonable. It is imperative that you follow the apothecary's orders and return to your bed."

"To hell with the apothecary. Where are the stairs?"

"Your father, His Grace the Duke of Marston is below, down the staircase at the end of the second corridor beyond—"

Not *that* staircase. Ruel swung away from the wall. The bust he had been leaning on tottered, fell to the floor, shattered. Marble fragments bounced across the carpet. He'd never been in the servants' halls, but their staircases meandered up and down, giving access to every floor. He had played in them as a boy. Now, if he could only remember . . .

"Lord Blackthorne!" Mr. Errand picked his way past the scattered marble shards and tottered down the corridor after him. "Your wound is most grave, my lord. Please do consider your father, I beg of you. The duke is beside himself with worry. Quite, quite frantic."

Ruel turned a corner. The walls swayed. He caught a rope to steady himself, then realized it was a bellpull and knew he'd probably summoned Mrs. Smythe and half the kitchen staff. Cursing laudanum, he worked his way down the corridor. A green baize curtain hanging at the end of the hall promised a door. A door promised a staircase.

"Ruel! What on earth are you doing?"

It was Alexander. As he reached the curtain, Ruel glanced behind him. His younger brother was running down the corridor, ankles swaying to and fro as he attempted to balance on his high-heeled shoes. His voluminous cossacks billowed around his legs, the bows at his ankles fluttering like yellow moths.

"Ruel, be reasonable!" Alex's roughed cheeks puffed with the effort of the chase. "The apothecary has ordered you to bed. You must be prudent."

"Prudent?" Ruel muttered as he pushed back the baize

and slipped through the door. This household was filled with a grand lot of damnable circus clowns.

The staircase, narrow and dimly lit, proved almost impossible to navigate. As Ruel staggered up it, the stairs dipped. He clung to the crumbling wall. The woman . . . had to find her . . . had promised to protect her.

They poured up the stairwell after him—his brother, the butler, his valet, the footmen. Like the pied piper, he worked his way up past the fourth floor, then the fifth, barely ahead of the rats. He threw open the door at the top of the House and careened out into the narrow corridor.

"Anne!" he bellowed. "Anne Webster!"

Like blank-faced sentinels, an endless row of shut doors lined the hallway. He flung them open one by one. Identical rows of empty beds filled the dank rooms. Was this where they slept . . . housemaids . . . kitchenmaids . . . footmen? He shook his head, as if he could dislodge the irreconcilable image of this rodent warren above the splendor of Slocombe House.

"Anne Webster!" he called again.

A door at the far end of the corridor fell open. The vicar of Tiverton, round-headed, ashen-faced, and perspiring heavily, emerged. He leaned against the door frame, mopped his face with a white handkerchief, and gaped at the oncoming parade.

"Lord Blackthorne," he uttered. "But you . . . she . . ."

"Is she in there?" Ruel didn't wait for the answer. He pushed past the clergyman and through the doorway. "Miss Webster?"

A loud gasp greeted him. "The marquess!" Vera leaped up from a low stool beside a narrow bed.

Ruel stopped. Anne Webster lay propped on a brown pillow, her face as still as death. A thin gray wool blanket covered her fragile body. Her hands, white and limp, were crossed at her breast.

"Dear God." Ruel covered his eyes. This hellhole had

been her home. This rusted iron bed her last resting place. *She's only Annie Webster . . . only a housemaid.* Of course. That was true. But she was Anne with the indigo eyes and the sharp tongue and the keen mind.

"God in heaven," he muttered, turning away.

"Ruel?"

At the soft sound, he lifted his head. She was looking at him, her blue eyes as dark and liquid as ink.

"Anne?"

"Oh, it is you . . . Ruel. I remember you sat with me after I was shot." She smiled, glad she hadn't imagined those gentle dove-gray eyes. She had imagined so many things in the dark hours of her pain. "You protected me under the hedge."

"Yes, I—"

"Lord Blackthorne!" The butler burst into the room. Lord Alexander rushed to his brother. Footmen swarmed.

"Ruel, you must go back to your chambers," his brother insisted. "This roving about like a madman will never do. The servants' quarters! Good heavens, think what will be said of you."

Anne stared in confusion as Mr. Errand, whom she had seen only once in her life and knew was next to God and the duke in importance at Slocombe House, fluttered about her bedroom. Footmen made vain attempts to usher everyone out into the corridor. The vicar slipped back inside and stood trembling against the far wall. Who was the man she thought had protected her? They called him Ruel, but . . .

"My Lord Blackthorne, Lord Alexander." The vicar gulped down a bubble of air as he executed a deep bow in the room. "Gentlemen, I beg of you—"

"Ruel?" Anne's brow narrowed as she looked her savior up and down. *Nicholas Ruel Edward Chouteau, Marquess of Blackthorne, Earl of Glascock, Viscount . . .*

"The marquess!" She looked at Vera for confirmation. "Oh, but I thought . . ." Her friend had wilted in one corner. So, it was true. The handsome, gentle, wonderful Ruel was the marquess. That lace thief, that cocky villain, that blackguard . . .

"Miss Webster, are you suffering much?" he was asking as he approached her bed. "Your leg?"

She lifted her chin, anger overriding her pain as she saw the man for who he really was. "I'm well enough. I had sent the vicar to hold a private conference with you, but I see you've chosen to bring all your rabble here."

Ruel glanced at the clergyman in confusion. The man was as pale and damp as the handkerchief he dabbed across his forehead. "I beg leave to speak with you, my lord," the vicar mumbled. "It is a matter . . . a matter of some consequence."

"Do let's go down at once," Alexander concurred. "The odor up here is appalling. This woman is clearly delirious, ordering the vicar about and addressing us as rabble."

Ruel held his brother back with an outstretched hand. "Miss Webster, on the road you informed me you were prepared to die."

"I am," she said firmly. "My soul rests in the hands of God."

He studied her for a moment and recognized that the peace underlying the pain in her blue eyes meant she had spoken the truth. He couldn't understand it. The woman had nothing—no wealth, no position, no future. Yet she possessed such calm confidence. Such grace.

"In contrast to you," he told her, "I have no faith in the existence of souls or of God, and I'm not at all content to let you die."

He turned to the butler. "Errand, send to London for our physician. He shall come at once and have a look at Miss Webster's leg."

"My lord, His Grace the duke has already requested him to attend you."

"It's this woman, not I, who needs his attention."

"Blackthorne!" Lord Alexander glowered at his brother. "You cannot mean this. Your wits have been dimmed by laudanum. I insist you return to your chambers immediately."

"Don't be ridiculous, Alex. This is a scratch. An annoyance."

"But . . . but she's a housemaid."

"On the contrary." As he spoke, Ruel realized that somewhere in the fog of the past night, his brain had discovered a perfect solution to the problem that had plagued his financial blueprint for the duchy. "Perhaps you will recall that our dear Miss Webster is the finest lace designer in Nottingham, the best pattern pricker in Tiverton, and one of the most skilled lace workers in England."

Anne flushed with heat. "Have you come to ridicule me again, Lord Blackthorne?"

"I have never ridiculed you yet." He squatted on Vera's little stool, his long legs folding up almost to his chin and his great knees spread wide. He propped his arms on them and gave her the cocky grin she knew all too well. "In fact, Miss Webster, I have been altogether most serious on every occasion of our acquaintance."

Anne gritted her teeth. Her leg hurt much worse this morning, and she was quite certain infection had set in. Death was sure to come, Vera had confessed sometime in the night, but it would bring peace from the fever already beginning to rage through her body.

Misery had flooded through Anne at the realization that she would die without ever helping her father, without ever marrying or bearing children, without designing another scrap of lace, without starting her lace school. She had done nothing of much use to anyone, and her conscience tormented her.

Early that morning as her fever rose, she had arrived at the one solution that might save her family. She had sent for the vicar and given him her requests, but his horrified reaction had only made her more despondent. Why now had God chosen to allow the marquess to persecute her? Wasn't she suffering enough?

"About William Green," Lord Blackthorne said. "I have the unwelcome intelligence that he may have been our assailant, Miss Webster."

"I didn't see anyone in the forest."

"Nor did I, yet I understand he may have had motive. You rejected his proffered hand in marriage, did you not? I wonder at that. Tell me, is our gamekeeper as great a blackguard as I?"

Anne glanced at Vera. She had covered her face with her hands and seemed to be in ardent prayer.

"Mr. Green is not a man with whom I wish to link my life, though that hardly matters under the circumstances," Anne told the marquess. "The gamekeeper is unkind, vain, and rude, but I don't think him capable of murder."

"Why not? Surely your extraordinary beauty and keen wit merit such passion."

"My lord Blackthorne," the vicar cut in, anguish lifting his voice an octave. "I beg of you to guard your tongue."

"I shall not. Miss Webster is a promising young lady. Since our fortuitous meeting in the kitchen, I have been considering her situation here at Slocombe House and her obvious skill with lace. Once she is recovered from her injuries, I mean to make good use of her."

"She means to make use of you," the vicar muttered.

"I beg your pardon?" Ruel turned on the stool.

The vicar twisted his hands together. His round head glowed with perspiration. "Lord Blackthorne, I have been requested to tell you . . . to tell you that Miss Anne Webster . . . she accepts your offer of marriage."

"Does she now?" Ruel slowly faced Anne again. "Well, I'm deuced."

$\mathcal{F}ive$

SILENCE DROPPED LIKE A THICK WOOL FLEECE OVER THE room. Anne looked at the marquess. Ruel stared at her. Vera dabbed her eyes in the corner. Alexander shifted from one foot to the other and glared at the vicar. The footmen held their breath.

"Perhaps I misunderstood you, sir." Addressing the clergyman, Ruel stood slowly. "Please repeat yourself."

"She . . . she accepts." The vicar blotted his round chin with the handkerchief. "I tried to tell her . . . tried to warn her . . . but I do think she's dying after all, which would remove the problem immediately . . . on the other hand, everyone who heard your declaration that afternoon knew it was made in jest."

"I have witnesses," Anne said softly. "The Duke of Marston, the vicar of Tiverton, and Lord Alexander all heard your offer, Lord Blackthorne. You proposed marriage to me. I accept."

"You said you couldn't like him," Lord Alexander burst out. "I heard you tell him you felt no affection for him in the least."

"Surely a nobleman such as yourself, my lord, knows affection is not necessary to marriage."

"I'll be damned, Ruel. Say something to the wench!"

The marquess returned his attention to Anne. His gaze traced the narrow outline of her body as she lay in the bed.

Her blue eyes never left his face. Again he was struck by her unwavering fortitude.

"Out," he commanded, waving a hand at the assembly. "Everyone, out. I shall speak with her alone."

"Oh, don't hurt Annie!" Vera rose from the corner, her cheeks damp. "She's dying, the apothecary said so, and you mustn't torment her, I beg you!"

"Out!" Ruel pointed at the door.

"Yes, my lord."

When the door shut behind the maid and everyone who had preceded her into the corridor, Ruel turned to Anne and crossed his arms over his chest. "You accept, do you?"

"I do."

"Are you dying?"

"Yes."

"Then why do you want to marry me, and why on earth should I marry you?"

Anne summoned her strength. "Because you know you won't have a wife to burden you more than a day or two. Because you can extend your mourning a year or longer and stave off your father's demands that you wed in Society. Because as my husband, you'll see to the safety of my family in Nottingham. Because I have information about you that would be most useful in the hands of an enemy."

The corners of his mouth tipped up. "My goodness, Miss Webster, you astound me."

"No more than you astound me."

"Let me see if I grasp your logic." He settled onto the bed next to the one where she lay, stretched out his legs, and propped a pillow under his shoulder. "I'm to marry you because you'll soon die, and I can play the merry widower. My father cannot expect me to wed for more than a year after your passing, and that should keep me quite happy and allow me to fulfill my own goals."

"Yes."

"You wish to marry me because your family is in some sort of financial straits in Nottingham, and you believe that as the son of a duke I could do nothing less than to rescue them."

"I would expect that of you, yes."

He stared at the peeling paint on the ceiling and recalled her confession that his hair reminded her of the curling shadows. For a moment, he could not think beyond it. She had lain just here, looking up at this ceiling, thinking of him.

A strange sensation slid through his stomach. He turned his head on the pillow and studied her. Eyes shut, she breathed in a shallow, pained manner. Would she die? Did he care?

How odd that his own mother had fallen so ill at news of the shooting that she had been unable to visit her son. Yet Anne Webster, mortally wounded herself, had managed to concoct a grand plan to save her family. From her deathbed this little woman with the courage of a lion had intimidated the vicar and everyone else into believing she meant exactly what she said. Amazing.

"About this information that would be so useful to my enemies," he said. "Could you expound?"

She lifted her head and swallowed against a wave of pain. "Lace machines," she said in a ragged whisper. "Smuggling them into France. I heard your plan."

"Good Lord. You were there, weren't you? Serving tea in Alexander's bedroom."

She couldn't hold back the little smile that tugged at her mouth. "You must learn to be more discreet, my lord."

He studied her for a moment. How could a pair of blue eyes be so entrancing? She was a servant, that's all. And near death. Yet the intelligence and determination that sparkled in her eyes made him feel he was speaking to an equal.

"And what will you do with your ill-gotten information about my plan to smuggle lace machines into France, Miss

Webster?'' he asked. ''How do you propose to use it against me?''

''Blackmail is a harsh word.''

''Extortion, then?''

She let out a deep breath and shut her eyes. She desperately needed more laudanum, yet with the drug swimming inside her head she wouldn't be able to speak clearly. ''I prefer to think of it as encouragement.''

He chuckled. ''Exactly how will you encourage me?''

''I shall inform my family's patroness, the Baroness de Winter.''

Ruel sucked in a breath. The de Winter family held Nottingham's lace industry in the palms of their hands. They were rich and well connected with English royalty. The baroness—a small, withered old lady who scented herself heavily with rose water—was a close friend and confidante to Queen Charlotte, wife of the mad King George and mother of the Regent.

Worse, perhaps, the baroness abhorred the Revolution that had brought an end to the French monarchy. She knew every aristocrat in Paris, she had been personally responsible for smuggling vast quantities of lace into that country, and she would stop at nothing to keep England foremost in the manufacture of lace.

''Trump!'' Ruel said, sitting up and leaning across the space that divided their beds. ''Miss Webster, you have played your hand like an expert.''

She tried to concentrate, but she could make little sense of his words. ''I know nothing about cards,'' she murmured.

''Ah, yes, the innocent minister's daughter. She reads her Bible every night, wears her collars buttoned to the throat, and wouldn't dream of playing cards. Can she be the same Anne Webster who would hazard her position in order to sell lace to the son of a duke, who would boldly announce that her family's trade of weaving was equal to the calling of the nobility, who would dare to force a marquess into marriage—''

"You asked me!" she hissed, struggling up onto one elbow. "I had nothing to do with it."

Ruel slid from his bed onto hers, leaned over her, and placed one hand on either side of her head. Her eyes widened. She could feel his knee at her hip, the weight of the man sinking her into the mattress.

"You had everything to do with it," he said.

Anne stared into his face. His mouth hovered no more than three inches above hers. His gaze flicked from her eyes to her lips and back again. In spite of the pain in her leg, she felt a strange flush creep through her chest, spread out to the tips of her breasts, and send her heart into an erratic beat.

It occurred to her that he might kiss her . . . that she wanted him to . . . or didn't . . . that it hardly mattered what happened between them. Her soul was God's, her body was swiftly betraying her into the hands of death, and this man . . . this very odd, very handsome man . . . who smelled of rum and soap . . . was so close . . .

"You made a beggar child believe she was a duchess," he whispered, his eyes softening. "You wove a lace that captured the essence of my homeland in springtime. You faced down my father, my brother, and the vicar of Tiverton. You very sweetly blackmailed me. And, yes, Miss Anne Webster, yes, indeed, you had everything to do with it."

Before she could work up the courage to speak, he turned his head and shouted at the shut door, "Alexander! Get the damned vicar in here. I'm getting married."

Anne clutched the sheets to her neck as the bedroom door burst open. People poured in like a swarm of angry bees, chattering, shouting, shoving. Anne wanted to turn her head, but the marquess held her gaze. Still pinning her to the bed, he leaned close to her ear.

"You win this round," he whispered, and a shiver poured down her spine. "But we've only begun our game, Miss Webster. You see, I have a use for you as well."

She pressed the heel of her palm against her chest to try to steady her heart. "There's no time for games," she returned. "I'm dying."

He straightened up away from her and gave a little grin. "I'm afraid not."

Lord Alexander reached his brother just as Ruel turned. "Take care of the arrangements between the vicar and our father, will you, Alex? This afternoon should be soon enough. Have the young lady carried down into the House. See that she's washed, fed, and dressed in something suitable."

"Ruel, you can't be serious."

"Of course I am." He spread his hands to indicate a path to the door. "You'll excuse me now, ladies and gentlemen. There's someone in Tiverton I must see."

Without a backward glance at the woman to whom he had just become betrothed, the Marquess of Blackthorne walked out of the room.

"No!" The Duke of Marston turned from the fire in his wife's drawing room and stared at his youngest child. "Alexander, you cannot mean this."

"Father, the vicar has gone to prepare the ceremony, the young lady has been carried down to the east wing, and your son is nowhere to be found should anyone wish to contradict his purpose."

"This is just like something he would do!" The duchess threw up her hands. "I tell you, Ruel should have been ordered to stay in America where people are less civilized. He's not reasonable. He's not prudent. He simply cannot be trusted with the duchy."

"I'm afraid his sanity cannot be verified," Alexander confided to his father. "Your Grace, I can attest to the fact that my brother's health—both physical and mental—is not strong. He was under the influence of laudanum when he confirmed the marriage proposal.''

''What? He's gone off to Tiverton in a cloud of laudanum?''

''Well, he was capable of some function—''

''Where is this brazen young lady? I shall speak to her myself.'' The duke stalked across the floor, his cane striking the tiles. ''Errand, send someone to Tiverton after my son. I shall interview him before this nonsense continues a moment longer.''

''Yes, Your Grace.''

''Now take me to the girl.'' He ignored the duchess, who had summoned her younger son to her side for a whispered conference.

The butler escorted the duke out into the corridor and down the staircase. ''Your Grace, the young woman is wounded and is expected to perish within the week. It is reported that her injury is most grave and that infection is setting in. Putrefaction is assured, and not even removal of the limb can insure her survival.''

''Good heavens.'' The duke turned to the head of his household staff. ''You're quite certain of this?''

''Absolutely. Restraining your son's rash impulse for a few days should solve the problem. I should not concern myself overmuch with this unfortunate situation, Your Grace.''

''It's not unlike something Blackthorne would do. And yet . . . you tell me she's a housemaid?''

''Yes, sir. She has been at Slocombe less than two years.''

''A fisherman's daughter, no doubt.''

''A minister's daughter from Nottingham. She arrived at Slocombe with a most flattering recommendation from the Baroness de Winter. Of course, we could do no less than employ her. I confess it was I who recommended her to the household staff rather than to the kitchens.''

"A beauty, is she?''

"Not at all.'' The butler pushed open a heavily carved door. "You may recall her attending your party at tea the afternoon Lord Blackthorne arrived from his travels.''

"I gave the wench no heed. She was little different from any other of the household's female staff—merely a vague, trivial creature. I can't think how Blackthorne noticed her in the first place.''

"Indeed, Your Grace. Miss Webster is quite plain, with no redeeming quality to have aroused interest in such a man as your esteemed son.''

"The woman possesses a sumptuous figure, perhaps? Large breasts, a narrow waist, full hips? I am well aware Blackthorne had been at sea a long time.''

"She is very thin.''

"Eyes?''

"Nondescript.''

"Then the attraction cannot be due to her appearance.''

Mr. Errand drew back a curtain. "May I suggest, Your Grace, that the situation has more to do with him than with her? Perhaps Lord Blackthorne believes that in wedding this dying woman, he will excuse himself from the obligation of marriage during the mourning period.''

"Nonsense, Errand. My son may be headstrong, but he would never go to such an extreme.''

The duke studied the huge bed at the far end of the long room he had just entered. The bed's canopy of blue and gold velvet rose almost to the ceiling. At the side of the bed, in a chair of carved walnut, sat a small figure with a wisp of blond hair and a face so thin as to be almost gaunt.

"That's her, is it?'' he murmured to the butler. "That pale thing?''

"That is the woman Miss Webster selected to attend her. I believe your son's affianced lies in the bed.''

His cane tapping softly on the thick, rose-patterned carpet, the duke approached and scrutinized the mound of white pillows, the rumple of heavy blankets, the tangle of silk sheets. "There's no one here," he said. "Has she died already?"

"Begging your pardon, Your Grace," Vera managed after executing the clumsiest curtsy of her life. "Anne . . . Miss Webster, that is . . . well, she's dressing for her . . . for her wedding."

The duke lifted his focus to the dressing room just as Anne hobbled between the curtains. One hand on a maid and the other on the door frame, she forced herself erect when she saw her visitor.

"Miss Anne Webster," Errand intoned, "His Grace, Laurent Chouteau, Duke of Marston."

Anne wobbled through a curtsy, thankful she had refused laudanum. In spite of her excruciating pain, she had been determined to remain clearheaded through the coming hours. Now, facing the duke, she was doubly glad.

"Your Grace," she said softly. "I beg your pardon for my disruption of your day."

"My day? My life, don't you mean?" He waved a hand at her. "Sit down, sit down, girl! For heaven's sake, don't perish right in front of me. Errand, what did you mean telling me she was plain? Look at her!"

The butler inspected Anne up and down. "Perhaps I was mistaken, Your Grace."

Disconcerted, she touched her hair. One of the maids had curled and pinned it, but she didn't have any idea how she looked. The dress Vera had found for her in an unused wardrobe of the suite was positively appalling. The neckline of the blue silk gown swept in a huge curve all the way down her bosom. Though she wasn't buxom, it was all Anne could do to keep herself tucked in.

Soft puffed sleeves came only halfway to her elbows, exposing her gloveless arms. The gathered skirt fell from just beneath her breasts to her ankles, a whisper of sapphire blue that might have been lovely had it not been so indecently transparent. In a certain angle of light, a person might be able to see straight through the dress, and Anne had the terrible feeling she was standing in just such an angle.

"I believe I recollected her wrong," the butler added. "Upstairs she was decidedly more peaked."

"May I be seated?" Anne asked. The duke nodded as she limped to a brocade settee and lowered herself onto it. She decided she could manage the duke better than his son at this moment. Every time she thought of the marquess, she remembered him hovering over her as she lay in her little bed, his mouth so close and his breath so warm and sweet with the scent of rum.

"Do you plan to perish quickly, Miss Webster?" the duke asked, seating himself across from her. "Everyone has assured us you will, and yet I find you're looking quite rosy."

Anne tried to swallow the hurt his words caused her. "The apothecary from Tiverton predicted infection, Your Grace. Though I do not wish to die, I understand little can be done."

"My deepest regrets, of course. Now, Miss Webster, it is my understanding that you are the cause of my son's grievous wound."

"It is possible, my lord. Vera . . . over there . . . believes the gamekeeper fired on us."

"You may have led to the injury of the marquess," the duke said, leaning forward and pointing at her with his cane, "yet you presume to hold him to his marriage proposal amusement?"

"I did not find the proposal amusing."

The duke stared at her as though he had not expected such a prompt response. "Yes, well, neither did I. It was clearly a jest, however, Miss Webster, and you were not to take my son's words to heart."

"My heart holds no place for your son. I merely considered his proposal and decided to accept." She lifted her chin. "You yourself stated that any woman would have him."

"I beg your pardon," the duke spluttered. "I said no such thing."

Anne glanced at the butler. "Witnesses will confirm the statement, Your Grace."

"You are a shameful young lady!"

"I bear no shame for my actions. On the contrary, I consider my behavior exemplary under the circumstances. Your son derided, mocked, and ridiculed me before such esteemed persons as yourself and the vicar. He then appropriated a very dear possession of mine, which he refused to return until I gave him my answer. He further tormented me by walking at my side after church and exposing me to the scrutiny and gossip of all my acquaintance."

"Well!" the duke exclaimed.

"Although the ball that was fired upon us may have been meant for me, Your Grace," Anne continued, unable to hold her tongue, "it just as easily may have been intended for your son. I have the unwelcome intelligence that the marquess has made many enemies, some of whom would think little of his demise."

"Upon my word!"

"At the hand of the Marquess of Blackthorne I have been ridiculed, robbed, exposed, and mortally wounded." Anne fought back the sudden tears that sprang to her eyes. "I am a godly and moral woman, Your Grace. I was made a proposal of marriage, I accepted that proposal, and I intend to see myself wed. Your son has shown no inclination to withdraw his offer, and to my way of thinking, the matter is settled."

"Good heavens!" The duke stared at the butler. "Mr. Errand, she is eloquent!"

"Agreed, my lord."

"Young lady, what do you mean to gain by this marriage? Surely your motive to wed the Marquess of Blackthorne lies deeper than the redemption of your wounded pride."

"My motive is monetary."

"Aha, I thought so! You may claim to be godly and moral, but greed flows through your veins."

Anne's eyes narrowed. "I am far less greedy, Your Grace, than any more socially suitable mate. You cannot deny that the family of another woman would demand titles, property, retirement of debt, and all manner of other material advantage of you."

"You do not believe my son capable of a marriage founded on love?"

"I doubt Lord Blackthorne would know the meaning of true mutual affection. I am even more certain that no woman could ever find reason to love him."

"That bad, is he?" The duke dipped his head, attempting to smother a smile. "Well, my dear, if you don't want his affection and you don't expect to live long enough to make use of the social privilege connected to his title, what is it you do want of him?"

Anne squared her shoulders, determined to face this moment with all the grace she could muster. She forced away all thought of the agony in her thigh and the feverish heat flowing through her veins.

"Your Grace, my father was a Luddite," she said softly. "He is imprisoned in Nottingham for his activities. Had his trial been conducted earlier, he would have been transported for fourteen years. Now he will surely face execution."

"A Luddite. My, my."

"The Baroness de Winter preferred my father to a small rectory, where he ministered for many years prior to his imprisonment. Now my family is near destitution, and we have no hope of hiring a barrister to speak in my father's defense. Money to speed my father's trial and release is all I would ask of your son, my lord. It is the least I can hope for as the wife of a marquess.''

"How very noble." The duke turned to his butler. "She wants to save her father."

"Apparently so, Your Grace."

"Shall we simply give her the funds and be done with her?''

"As you wish, Your Grace."

The duke leaned back in his chair and studied the young woman seated across from him. Anne tried not to stare back. She had recognized the note of sarcasm in his voice and knew where the marquess had learned it. They were a pair, father and son. Clearly each man had confidence in his own power, each acted without consideration of others' feelings, and each enjoyed manipulating people as though they were pawns in a game of chess.

Circumstances might play with Anne Webster, but people never had. She wouldn't allow it. She knew her own mind and had never felt compelled to hide her thoughts. Her father's sermons had taught her that all men were the same in the eyes of God. His participation in the Luddite movement had illustrated the importance of standing up for right and truth—no matter that one might butt one's head against authority.

"I am rather inclined not to give you the money," the duke said finally.

"I never asked a donation of you, Your Grace."

"True. You asked a more preposterous thing—the hand of my son.''

"Lord Blackthorne asked for my hand, as you well know because you were in the room when he did so. I would not reject your financial assistance, however, should you find it in your heart to help my family."

"If I hand you over the funds to pay a barrister, Miss Webster, I expect you might willingly expire rather soon.

You will have saved your father from execution, and you will see no point in struggling to overcome this grievous injury to your leg. In short, you will die, and I shall feel most melancholy at having played a part in your demise.''

Anne prickled. "If you don't want to help my family, Your Grace, simply state your intention. Your vain attempt to wash your hands of the matter by claiming to want to save my life is very low.''

"Low, am I?'' Again the duke turned to the butler. "Errand, do you take note of this girl's insolence?''

"She is most brazen, Your Grace.''

"Yes, she is.'' The duke was practically purring like a cat at a bowl of milk when he returned his focus to Anne. "Miss Webster, you are audacious, bold, and impudent. Moreover, you are arrogant.''

"I beg your pardon, sir. I intended no offense.''

"No, no, I'm quite charmed. I should very much dislike to see you die. In fact, I shall have to send the physician to tend you when he comes from London.''

"The physician has arrived,'' the butler said. "He is in the drawing room awaiting your son's return from Tiverton.''

"Is he now?''

"Your Grace, the marquess expressed the desire to have the physician examine the young lady. I thought it best to await your wishes in this matter.''

"Errand, send for the man at once.'' As the butler hurried out of the room, the duke leaned across the top of his cane and peered at Anne. "I am not going to give you any money, Miss Anne Webster,'' he said in a low voice. "Your father is a Luddite, and I despise all forms of insurrection. For all I care, the authorities can execute your father and spike his head on the town gates.''

Anne swallowed. The duke was more a devil than his son. At the thought of her father's death, she blinked back the angry tears that filled her eyes. "You are cruel," she said.

"I am rational," he retorted. "Luddites want power, and power in the hands of the masses is a deadly thing. You view the world through the tiny window of your own experience, Miss Webster. I shouldn't mind except that—like my son—you clearly have the wit to see beyond such triviality. Look, please, at life beyond the servants' hall at Slocombe House in Devon, England. Imagine the globe as a great game board spread out before you."

He plunged his cane into the rose-strewn wool carpet and forced himself to a standing position. Anne watched, almost mortified, as he walked toward her. "France, Italy, Spain," he said, stabbing the tip of his cane onto a different bouquet of roses as he called out each nation. "America. India. Africa. China. The entire earth lies at your feet. You, Miss Webster, are England. You are monarchy. Are you a great world empire? Do you rule all these little countries—enriching your coffers with their silk, wine, tea, cotton, sugar, precious gems, opium, and gold? Not yet, but you could. In the strength of the king lies the strength of England. Do you understand?"

"Yes, sir," she whispered, though she wasn't sure she did.

"Look what happened to France when the people revolted. Do you wish that a renegade like Napoleon ruled England?"

"No, Your Grace."

"Of course not! Look what happened when the American colonies revolted. Do you wish to live as those savage Americans with their barbarian manners and bizarre politics?"

Anne shook her head. She knew hardly a thing about America, but it must be a dreadful place.

"Look what happened to heaven itself when Lucifer took it upon himself to revolt. Evil was born! Hell was created!

Rebellion is a sin, Miss Webster.'' He hammered his cane on the floor. ''The people must stay in their place! Luddites are a cancer within our nation. They must be eradicated!''

Anne grabbed the arm of the settee. ''A cancer, sir?'' she said, clenching her jaw as she forced herself to her feet. ''Let me tell you what will rot away the core of your precious monarchy and bring death to your dreams of a world empire. Machines! Luddites revolted not against the aristocracy but against industrialization. Machines give power to those who own them, Your Grace. Those who own them are the middle class, the merchants. Who suffers? The common laborers, of course. But you will suffer, too.''

The duke glared at her. ''Shall I?''

''The middle class has its hands on the source of money—manufacturing,'' she said, repeating the Marquess of Blackthorne's own words. To her surprise, they made sense. ''Money is power. Power in the hands of the middle class spells doom to the aristocracy. And that aristocracy, Your Grace, is you. You would do well to listen to your elder son.''

The duke took a step closer and cocked his head, scrutinizing Anne as though she were an insect under a microscope. Then his frown softened, and one corner of his mouth tilted up.

''By heaven, Miss Anne Webster,'' he said, ''I like you.''

She clutched the settee arm to keep from wilting into it. ''Thank you, Your Grace.''

''You speak this brazenly to my son, do you not?''

''I say what is in my heart.''

''Yes, well, you have a very good heart and a very upright character, both of which attributes my elder son sorely lacks. You are also articulate, bold, and headstrong, three characteristics absent in most women of this day. Your manners are coarse, but manners can be taught. You are the daughter of a minister, and, in short, I believe we can make you do.''

''Make me do what?''

With a wink, the duke turned to his butler, who stood near the door. ''Errand, where is that damned physician?''

''In the corridor. He awaits your bidding, Your Grace.''

''Send him in, send him in.'' The duke tapped his cane on the settee. ''Sit down, Miss Webster. It will never do for you to perish on your wedding day.''

$\mathcal{S}ix$

THE TWO-THOUSAND-DEGREE HEAT OF THE FORGE RA-
diated through the door of the small smithy on the outskirts
of Tiverton. Smoke tinged with the sulfurous smell of burning coal drifted out the open windows. Carriage wheels,
horseshoes, and plowshares littered the dusty, grassless
yard. Wrought-iron pokers, cooking pots, knives, chains,
and swords hung from nails driven into the stone wall beneath the overhanging eave.

Just as he had from the time he was a little boy, Ruel
leaned against the smithy's door frame lost in rapt fascination. Inside, a tall, muscled man slammed his hammer
against a shaft of incandescent orange steel. Each ringing
blow against the anvil launched an arcing shower of sparks
that lit up the dim, sooty interior.

The blacksmith inspired the same awe he always had,
though in the passing years Ruel had grown to nearly equal
his size. A large and powerful figure at two hundred pounds
on a six-foot, two-inch frame, the smith himself seemed no
less forged in a furnace than the implements of war and
toil he produced. His straight hair, as black as midnight,
hung to the middle of his back in a tight braid. Ruel knew
that the rhythm the man hammered out sang of more than
a common laborer in a long leather apron, more than a
small stone smithy, more than a bleak existence in the south
of England.

The beat echoed of drums, battle cries, and prayers chanted in the setting sun. Did the blacksmith still remember the stories he had told the wide-eyed little English boy so long ago? Ruel had hung on his idol's every word— tales of the days when the smith had been known as Walks-in-the-Night, son of an Osage chieftain. He had lived on the banks of a river far away in America, a place he called the Middle Waters.

A warmth filled Ruel's chest as the blacksmith inspected the steel he was shaping into a carriage wheel spoke. How many times had the young boy watched the dark man scrutinize a piece of his work, eyebrows drawn together, mouth turned down? With a slight nod of satisfaction, the smith buried the metal in the firepot of his hooded forge. His young assistant leaped to pump the bellows, and the mound of coals began to glow.

"Too much heat and the metal burns, Tommy," the man reminded his striker. "Too little heat—"

"Too little, and the metal stock is hard enough to ruin your tools," Ruel finished.

The smith turned at the unexpected voice, and his taut face softened into a smile. "Blackthorne."

"I've come home."

"It was said you had died in America."

"No." Ruel swallowed at the knot that formed in his throat. "It's been a long time, Walker."

"Three years." The blacksmith gazed impassively at the nobleman for a moment longer, then he held out his arms. "Welcome home, my son."

Ruel stepped into the warm embrace of the older man and clasped him tightly. The familiar smell of the huge man's sweaty shirt, the heated dampness of his red-brown skin, the fierce strength of his powerful arms transported him to his boyhood. Ruel buried his cheek against the side of his mentor's neck and drank in the grip of solid hands on his back and the gentle rocking of the smith's body.

"Oh, my boy," Walker whispered, "you have returned."

"Did you doubt I would?"

"They said you were killed by Indians."

Ruel stepped back and took the smith's powerful shoulders. "Your people are good men, Walker, though the settlers they've raided might argue otherwise."

"You saw them? The Little Ones?"

Ruel nodded. "I lived in the home of Auguste Chouteau."

"You stayed in Sho'to To-Wo'n? Chouteau's Town?"

"The settlers call it St. Louis, and it's no longer a little town, Walker. Auguste has seen his dream grow."

"Your cousin is respected and honored among the Little People. He tries to understand us, and he accepts our religion even though he cannot approve of it. I remember many years ago he spoke on our behalf with the Spaniards."

"And later with the British and the Americans. Did you know that three years ago, after the war of 1812, he concluded a treaty of peace between the leaders of the Osage and the commissioners of the United States of America? All injuries and hostilities have been mutually forgiven, and there's been a promise of perpetual peace between the United States and the Osage."

"Perpetual peace?" Walker shook his head. "Auguste Chouteau is a good man, but he's a dreamer. So long as settlers keep moving onto our land, building houses, fencing farms, and plowing fields, there will never be peace between us, Blackthorne."

"Perhaps the Osage need a leader who can speak for them. A man like you, Walker."

"Now you dream, Blackthorne. Before you went away, I told you I can never go back. Look at me." He held out his calloused hands. His dark eyes hardened. "Remember? I'm no longer a warrior. I'm a metal-maker, like the traders and half-breeds. I haven't held a bow since I was sent to France.

Did you know I've lived in England more than a quarter of a century, Blackthorne? I have forty-five years . . . an old man.''

"Nonsense. You're still young and fit. You're the picture of health.''

"How little you understand. Why would my people want me to return? Why would they seek my advice? To tell them stories of a blacksmith in England? I can hardly remember how to speak their tongue. I have no tribal wisdom to lend the council of Little Old Men who lead the Osage. I have no wife, no daughters to pass along my bloodlines.'' His mouth grim, he turned back to his forge. "If I had a son to claim as my own, I might offer them some hope, some promise of a future. I can do nothing but bend steel.''

Ruel studied Walker as the Indian lifted the glowing rod from the furnace with his tongs. He laid the metal on his anvil and began to hammer. How many times had Ruel witnessed this man pouring his rage, his desolation, his agony into the steel? As a child, he hadn't seen the helpless impotence that bound the blacksmith as securely as the chains he forged. Now he understood it.

"I came to you because you can do more than bend steel, Walker,'' Ruel said when the pounding ceased. "I need your help.''

The blacksmith swung around, his face stony. "You're a grown man now, Blackthorne. Traveling for years at a time, living your own life. What can an old Indian do for you? I cannot make you a wheel to roll or carry you on my shoulders. I cannot tell you my stories, or take you swimming in the pond, or teach you how to catch a fish as I did in the days when you were a boy. You're a marquess now, and one day people will call you 'duke' and bow to you as though you were a god.''

He swung his hammer again, and a cascade of orange sparks lit the room. "Don't come here to tell me of your travels in America or your visits with Auguste Chouteau and the Osage. Don't make me wish for things that can never be. Go away from this place, Blackthorne.''

Ruel stood in silence as the blows rained on metal. The small room filled with the deafening sound of the ringing hammer. Walker picked up the carriage wheel spoke and shoved it into the furnace again.

''Hotter, Tommy,'' he told his assistant. ''Pump the bellows, boy.''

''A woman is dying, Walker,'' Ruel said, his voice almost too low to be heard. ''Unless you come, the surgeon will amputate her leg or let her die of gangrene.''

''A woman?''

''We are to be married.''

Walker fell silent. ''Your father will not want me in his house.''

''My father won't want a woman to die in his house.''

The Indian stared at the glowing coals. ''A woman . . . to be your wife and bear your children,'' he whispered. For a moment he stood unmoving, lost in the fire. Then he lifted his head and tossed the carriage spoke into a trough of cold water. Hot metal hissed. Steam billowed into the room.

''Tommy,'' he said, ''run to the tailor and tell him his carriage wheel will be ready tomorrow.''

''Yes, sir.''

Lifting his leather apron over his head, Walker nodded at Ruel. ''I'll get my bag.''

''Amputation might save the young lady's life.'' The physician regarded Anne through his monocle as he spoke to the Duke of Marston. ''First we must transport her to London, bleed her, dose her liberally with opiates, and then remove the limb. I trust she will have no objection.''

Anne bit her lip as she tried to reason past the pain swirling through her body. In spite of the heavy dose of laudanum she had been forced to drink, her leg felt like a flaming log jerked from a fire. She could hardly move it.

Bright red tentacles of infection crept slowly from the seeping wound toward her heart. A day or two longer and she would certainly die . . . or lose her leg.

"Vera?" She held out her hand.

"I'm here, Annie. Rest yourself now." The housemaid's gaze lifted to the physician in his fine coat and white cravat. "Don't cut off her leg, sir, I beg you. The pain would be too great to endure. Let her die in peace."

"Die she will if I don't remove the infected limb." He turned to the duke. "Your Grace, which do you prefer? Shall I perform the amputation, or shall we permit the young lady to perish?"

"Perish?" Ruel strode across the room and pushed past the physician. "Miss Webster, you do not have my permission to die."

Anne studied the face that peered down her. Gray eyes, curly black hair. Ruel. Or was it? The laudanum made her head swim. She couldn't think any longer. Nothing made sense. Permission to die? Did a person need permission to die?

"Walker, come here at once." Ruel beckoned the man waiting in the shadows near the door. "Have a look at Miss Webster's leg and see what you can do."

Waving the little blond housemaid to one side, Ruel took her place and bent over the pillow. Surprise tumbled down him like a spray of icy water. The woman had been transformed. Her long hair, artfully curled and pinned into the latest fashion, shone a deep bronze in the candlelight. The neckline of her dress, covered by no bedding, shawl, or pelisse, curved to reveal the rise of her creamy breasts. Blue eyes regarded him through a mist.

"Miss Webster," he said in a low voice, "I've brought my friend. I expect you to do exactly as he tells you and don't—"

"Blackthorne." The duke's voice was stiff. "This man is not permitted in my home."

Walker's eyes moved between the two men as the marquess straightened. "Your Grace, this is the blacksmith from Tiverton."

"I know who he is. What can you mean by bringing an Indian into my house?"

"Mr. Walker knows more about healing than any physician in the area. The townspeople visit him with their ailments. I insist—"

"I won't have him here." He turned to his butler. "Errand, remove the gentleman."

"Your Grace," Ruel cut in, taking his father's arm. "Do be reasonable. Miss Webster will do us little good without her leg, and no good at all dead. I need her whole and healthy. The physician confesses his lack of skill in this matter, and I'm convinced Mr. Walker can heal her."

"Convinced, are you? The Indian is a man of low breeding, a savage."

"He's the son of an Osage chieftain whose home I visited while staying in St. Louis. Auguste Chouteau hopes to see Mr. Walker returned to America whence he was so ruthlessly exported at the mercy of French officials who—you will recall—held him hostage and used him for the pleasure of their Society until he was able to escape to us."

"You make much of a man about whom you know little, Blackthorne."

"He fled to us here in England because of his regard for our name, yet you debase him?"

"He has no regard for the Chouteau family."

"On the contrary, he holds us in high esteem. Through the years, he has inquired after you, Your Grace, and after my mother and my sisters. Mr. Walker is the most upright gentleman I have the pleasure to know. Grateful for the haven you provided him on his escape from France, he feels he owes our family a debt, and he would be pleased to assist us in resolving this medical calamity."

The duke grunted. "You bring a wounded maid into my

household and place her in my bed. You make an engagement of marriage with a woman who is so far beneath you as to bring ridicule upon your name. Now you inflict a savage upon me. Ruel Chouteau . . . you wear my name . . . you claim privileges as my heir . . . one day you will own my titles and possess my lands. Have I erred?''

Ruel tried to read the message in the duke's eyes. He saw in them a hurt he couldn't understand. Had he been a disappointment to his father? Was it so wrong to associate with such a man as the blacksmith, even though he didn't carry the social status of a marquess?

''Your Grace,'' Ruel said in a low voice,''I give you my word I will bring nothing but respect to your name. My primary objective in this life has always been to honor you. With that aim I traveled to America and began the development of a plan to enrich the duchy. I seek nothing more from my existence than security for your properties.''

''Your associations with commoners do not please me.''

''I beg your pardon, Your Grace,'' Ruel said, his voice flinty, ''but I can consider neither this woman nor the blacksmith common.''

He let his focus drift to Anne. Her blue eyes, wide and deeply shadowed, stared out at him from her ashen face. He suppressed the panic that gripped his stomach at the thought of her death. If the duke knew the truth about his son's fascination with a servant . . . about his heir's deep affection for an Indian from the wilderness of America . . .

When Ruel looked up, he realized his father's eyes had softened. Slipping a hand around the duke's shoulder, he turned him toward the door. ''Mr. Walker will tend the woman's leg. She, in turn, will assist me in a small venture.''

''She plans to marry you, Blackthorne. I hope you know that.''

''A temporary alliance, Your Grace, I assure you.''

The duke cast a glance toward the bed. ''I actually rather

like the wench. She's a minister's daughter, did you know? Her father's a Luddite, of all things. Imprisoned in Nottingham for smashing lace machines. He has bequeathed her quite a wicked tongue. I should think she'll be good for you.''

Ruel smiled. ''I should think so.''

''If you're not going to use the physician for her, do send the man up to tend your mother. The duchess continues to enjoy the most tiresome headache.''

''Yes, Your Grace.'' Ruel watched his father work his way down the corridor, attended closely by Mr. Errand and two footmen. Once they had turned a corner, he nodded to the Indian.

''Walker, do whatever it takes,'' he said.

''You should not disappoint the duke with your behavior, Blackthorne.'' The tall Osage blacksmith removed a damp white cabbage leaf from Anne's thigh and dropped it into a bucket. ''He has been more than good to you.''

''How does her wound look?'' Ruel tried to peer around the tent of sheets Walker had erected over his patient.

''White cabbage leaves absorb pus,'' the Indian said.''They reduce swelling, too. As soon as the leaf grows hot, I take it away and place another under the bandage. I think the wound is almost clean.''

''She seems to be sleeping.''

''No, she's awake. The drug they gave her numbed her mind.'' He placed his bronzed fingers on Anne's pale brow. ''She's feeling some relief now, as the fever begins to burn away. Blackthorne, you must take great care of this woman when she's your wife. You must protect and honor her. There should be no greater love than that between marriage partners. Not even the love between parent and child should be as strong. The duke honors you as his son, but his love for his wife is enduring.''

Ruel grimaced at the thought of his self-absorbed, unaffectionate mother and lifted the bucket of cabbage leaves. "I'll take these out."

"Have I not taught you that the bonds of a family must remain unbroken? To the Osage, family ties are as strong as the sinews of the buffalo."

"Don't speak to me of family, Walker. My mother has yet to lay eyes on me since my return."

"She is not well. You should leave this woman to me and see to the duchess. If you do not stop him, that London physician will start some of his foolishness like filling her stomach with laudanum or draining her veins of her life-blood."

Ruel held out a fresh cabbage leaf. The Osage waved it away.

"Now it is time for garlic. Put down the bucket." He drew two clusters of cloves from his cloth bag. "The Little People use crushed seeds of the wild columbine to make a drink for fever. For wounds and infections, we use the wild four-o'clock or the butterfly weed. Here, I cannot find such plants, so I make this paste."

Ruel observed as Walker mashed the garlic cloves in a small bowl. The pungent aroma drifted into the room. The Indian spread the paste over the injury to Anne's thigh and covered it with a warm flannel bandage. When he had wrapped and tied the cloth around her leg, he lowered the tented sheets and tucked them under the mattress.

"She must rest," Walker said. "Her friend can tend her. You should go to the duchess."

Ruel sat in his chair at the edge of the bed for a moment and studied his laced fingers. In the passing hours, some of his fears for the housemaid had eased. Now he felt dismayed—almost embarrassed—at the lengths to which he had gone to save her life. She was nothing to him. Nothing.

"If I'm to make this worth the time I've spent on the woman," he said finally, "I've got to finish it. I've got to marry her."

"Worth the time you've spent?" Walker regarded him. "Are the lives of some humans worth less than the lives of others?"

"Of course."

"Really? But you told me you planned to marry Miss Webster. I assumed you loved her."

"No, nothing like that. The woman is a part of my plan."

"Is Miss Anne Webster only 'the woman' to you, Blackthorne? This marriage sounds like nothing but a sham."

Ruel frowned. "You can be damned annoying, Walker." He lifted his chin and dismissed his valet with a wave of the hand. "Foley, send for the vicar, and tell my father the marriage will take place within the hour."

"You intend to marry your woman today? She can hardly open her eyes. Blackthorne, your haste disturbs me."

Ruel raked a hand through his hair. "Look, Walker, I mean to make something productive of my life. I won't spend my time in the company of Society, rouging myself and lacing corsets about my waist as my brother does. I won't give myself to wasting time as my father does— having the vicar to tea in the drawing room, riding through the village and sneering at peasants, hunting foxes, for God's sake. Even you, whom I admire, have lived a futile life, haven't you, Walker? Hammering steel day after day— sweat pouring down your body, the smell of sulfur in your nostrils. You might as well be living in hell."

The Indian's eyes went as dark as ink. Ruel knew he had struck a raw place in his friend's heart. Yet he couldn't restrain his tongue. What good was a life so empty?

"My life is hell," Walker said, his tone confirming Ruel's accusations. "What will you make of yours? What is it you really want, Blackthorne?"

"Adventure. Money. Freedom."

"So you will join yourself to this maid as though she were another cog in the machine you are building to glorify and amuse yourself. In all those afternoons we spent together, did I not speak to you of tender affection, Blackthorne? Did I not tell you of the joys of family, of the blessing of a wife and children? Do you not wish for love?''

Ruel shook off the beckoning pull of the Indian's words. ''Come now, Walker, it's not like you to speak such pretty words. Family, blessing, tender affection, love? Good heavens, you'll drown me in sugar syrup.''

''Not pretty words. True words.''

''Words have no power, Walker. None. I've never lived with family joy, blessing, or tender affection. I don't believe in such drivel. Action has power. A man's own experience is his greatest teacher. I have been taught by my parents' example to desire wealth and prestige over love.''

''Oh, my son.''

''Enough of your lamenting. Just keep your eye on me, Walker. You'll see I'm right in the end.''

Ruel leaned back in his chair and stretched out his legs. He closed his eyes and gave a deep yawn. Hours of tending the ill did not suit him. He needed to be up and about, paying a visit to Mr. Heathcoat, the lacemaker, investigating the shooting incident, calling on old friends, making preparations for his trip into France.

He opened his eyes. Anne was staring at him. The bright blue of her gaze ran through him like a shower of sparks. In spite of himself, he leaned forward, elbows on his knees.

Heavens, she was a beauty. Even this close to death, the young woman shone with a strange inner light. Her skin was luminous alabaster. Her cheeks glowed a soft pink. The outer corners of her eyes tilted up, so she seemed to be smiling at him even though her full lips were still.

''Miss Webster,'' he began, not even knowing what he planned to say. ''Are you still quite content to die?''

She shut her eyes, confused. For what seemed like hours, she had listened to the Marquess of Blackthorne rant on and on. The man was full of himself, vain and obnoxious. He had not the slightest concern for others. Didn't even believe in love. Enjoyed using people. Cogs in a machine.

"Anne?" That deep voice again. So near. So gentle and warm.

She opened her eyes. Ruel. Sitting by her bed, his black hair in a tumble over his brow. How kind he was. Protecting her. Bringing that dark-eyed physician to heal her. Ruel had saved her life. Just as he'd promised.

"Ruel . . ." She reached out her hand.

"Now then, Blackthorne, can you really mean to wed the girl this afternoon?" The Duke of Marston marched into the chamber, his cane fairly piercing holes in the carpet as he hurried toward the bed. "Your mother swooned straight away at such horrifying intelligence. She cannot believe you intend to marry a housemaid. Dire, dire misfortune, she assures me. Even though I informed her the lady was a minister's daughter and not entirely unacceptable, the duchess is not to be swayed. A minister has no money, she reminded me. I certainly cannot acquaint her with the uncomfortable news that this particular lady's father is doomed to execution. The daughter of a criminal, no less! No dowry, no money, no grand wedding at St. James's in London. Your mother is quite beside herself. Quite, quite afflicted."

Ruel drew back from Anne and crossed his arms over his chest. "She's not coming down for the wedding, then?"

"Good heavens, of course not. She's predicting the stars will fall from the sky."

"May I have the pleasure of your blessing, Your Grace?"

The duke fanned himself with both hands. "Is the young lady expected to live?"

"Indeed."

"How can you actually be thinking of marrying her? I understood you hoped to spend at least a year in mourning in order to escape my constant pressure for you to marry in Society.''

"You're mistaken. I plan to make good use of my wife.''

"And then what? When she's served her purpose to you, what will you do with the wench? Cast her aside?''

"I'll see to her welfare, of course. I'm an honorable man. To my way of thinking, this action is hardly uncommon. As you well know, thirty years ago the Prince Regent himself married a commoner, that Catholic widow, Mrs. Mary Anne Fitzherbert. Ten years later, without benefit of divorce or annulment, he married Caroline Amelia Elizabeth of Brunswick. The future king of England—a bigamist. No one thinks a thing of it.''

"Nonsense! The Regent had a friend deny the first marriage in the House of Commons.''

"Would it be so difficult to deny a marriage made under these circumstances?'' Ruel gestured to Anne. "A dying woman. A deathbed wedding. A marquess and a housemaid. When I elect to terminate the situation, surely the good vicar will be able to come up with some rule or regulation we've violated here.''

"Good Lord, wouldn't it be simpler just to take Miss Webster as your mistress? If you want royal example to follow, why not emulate the Regent's brother, Prince William, Duke of Clarence? He spent twenty years with that actress what's-her-name.''

"Dorothea Bland?''

"Ah, yes. She was known professionally as Mrs. Jordan. Prince William's mistress has given birth to ten children by him, and certainly no one has condemned him. Should he accede to the throne, I suspect he will ennoble every one of his illegitimate offspring. Why not take Miss Webster as a mistress?''

"The daughter of a minister? I hardly think Miss Webster will agree to that. You've encountered the woman. She has a mind of her own and a barbed tongue to match it.''

"Ah, yes. So she does." The duke turned his attention to the young woman. He tilted forward on his cane and ran his gaze up and down her. "Going to live, are you, young lady? Well, I hope you've kept your wits through this ordeal. You will speak to the marquess as you spoke to me earlier, will you not?"

Anne managed a nod.

The duke chuckled. "Very good. Then I give your union my blessing, though one cannot deny this is dreadfully irregular. Dreadfully. Blackthorne, in spite of your common wife and ill-conceived marriage, I shall expect you to behave as a duke ought after you inherit."

"Of course, Your Grace. I shall do my utmost to honor your name and bring fortune to your property."

The duke glanced at Walker, who had warily backed into a corner and was half hidden in shadow. "That Indian's responsible for Miss Webster's health, is he?"

"Yes. We owe him our deepest gratitude."

"Gratitude?" He pointed his cane at the blacksmith, but at that moment the vicar and his entourage entered the room. Walker's exit was masked by a horde of various church and town officials, a congregation of the duke's comrades who had been summoned earlier in the day from their manors, the landowners' wives and daughters, and even a few townsfolk who seemed to have felt little trepidation on entering the duke's house to observe the momentous occasion of the marriage of a marquess.

Chaos reined until Mr. Errand and Mrs. Davies called for order. Footmen rushed to bring chairs into the bedroom for the guests. Housemaids folded away blankets and put out urns of fresh flowers they had snatched from other rooms in Slocombe House. Kitchenmaids brought in wine and silver trays laden with sweets, which Mrs. Smythe had managed to throw together upon hearing the shocking news. A lady's maid repinned Anne's hair. Another dusted scented powder on her neck. A third arranged her dress as two footmen lifted her from the bed.

"Good heavens, it smells of garlic in here!" The Duchess of Marston waved a silk handkerchief across her nose as her younger son escorted her into the room. "Someone fetch my smelling salts lest I swoon again."

"Mother!" Ruel stepped away from his valet, who was attempting to tie on a fresh cravat. He could hardly believe she had come. Like a child surprised by an unexpected pat on the head, he took the woman's arm. "May I show you to a chair, Your Grace?"

"Don't touch me, you disagreeable young man!" She swatted his hand with her fan. "Alex, darling, do tell your brother not to make such a pest of himself. He's caused enough trouble already."

Ruel's jaw tightened as Lord Alexander led their mother to a wide settee. She patted her golden hair, waved her fan beneath her chin, and fussed at the maid who was arranging her skirt. Nothing had changed. Ruel covered the familiar hurt with grim determination and turned away.

"Let's begin." He strode to the chair where Anne had been seated and took his place at her side.

Anne leaned back against the velvet cushions and tried to make sense of the unreality before her eyes. Somehow she had gotten herself into a private bedroom with the Duke and Duchess of Marston, their two sons, the vicar of Tiverton, and at least fifty other people. Viscounts and barons sipped wine. Their wives nibbled cakes. The sweet scent of perfume mingled with the overpowering smell of garlic—and both seemed to be emanating from her own body.

It was worse than a nightmare. Most confusing of all had been the snippets of conversation that now played a game of chase inside her head: *Miss Webster will do us little good without her leg, and no good at all dead. If I'm to make use of her, I'll need her whole and healthy. . . . You make an engagement of marriage with this woman who is so far beneath you as to bring ridicule upon your name. . . . I actually rather like the wench. She's a minister's daughter, did you know? He has bequeathed her quite a wicked tongue. . . . There should be no greater love than that between marriage partners. . . . I don't believe in such drivel. I have been taught by my parents' example to desire wealth and prestige, not love.*

Anne searched the room for the source of the words she remembered. The duke, there by the fire. The duchess, fanning herself on a settee. The dark-eyed healer, gone. The Marquess of Blackthorne . . .

"Dearly beloved," the vicar of Tiverton began. A wedding. Her own wedding.

A tall man with dark, curly hair knelt beside her and took her hand. She looked into his gray eyes. She thought . . . hoped . . . prayed . . . the man she was marrying was Ruel . . . but she had the terrible feeling he might be the Marquess of Blackthorne after all.

Seven

WHATEVER THE NAME OF THE MAN ANNE HAD MAR-
ried, he did not show himself again after the wedding. Instead, the dark-eyed physician came every morning to the
large, drafty bedroom to tend her. He changed the garlic
poultice—which sent Vera and all the other attendants
scampering from the room—bathed the bullet wound with
calendula lotion and sage tea, and then replaced the bandage with a clean garlic-paste poultice.

Within a week, the man—who called himself Walker and
claimed to be an Indian from America—began washing
Anne's injury with diluted calendula tincture and peach-pit
tea. He made a fresh goldenseal, plantain, and comfrey oint-
ment and packed the wound. By the end of the second
week, the wounds where the ball had entered and exited
Anne's thigh had closed. Any sign of the bits of dress fabric
the bullet had driven into her flesh finally vanished.

She began to walk about the bedroom, exercising her
muscles. Then she began to explore the corridors. In the
third week, she asked to be taken to the garden. Walker
volunteered to escort her, and Vera insisted on attending
her as well. They made their way down countless flights of
stairs, through two drawing rooms, and finally out a pair
of tall glass-paned doors onto a paved terrace. Anne took
a deep breath of the fresh spring air and looked around her.

"I'm alive, Vera," she said softly.

"Yes, you are, Lady Blackthorne." The pale-haired maid never flinched at calling her best friend by her new title, but it annoyed Anne no end. "I must tell you the truth. I never thought you would live to walk outside again."

"Nor did I." Thankful for life but dismayed at the turn it had taken, she took the arm of the tall Indian for support. "You saved me, Mr. Walker, and I'm grateful. At the same time, I can't think how I'm to go on."

"Breathe air, drink water, sleep at night, find some little work for your hands. Life cannot be so difficult for the wife of a marquess, can it?"

She sighed. "That's just the problem."

As her need for laudanum had eased during the past three weeks, Anne could no longer deny that she had, indeed, married the marquess. She was now the Marchioness of Blackthorne. Kitchenmaids dipped little curtsies when she passed them, and housemaids scurried to tend her before she even requested help. Mrs. Davies, the housekeeper, assigned Vera the position of lady's maid and increased her wages commensurate with her newly elevated stature in the House. While Anne lay in bed, Vera went to lessons given by the duchess's attendants, and now she insisted on bathing, dressing, and perfuming her mistress as she'd been taught.

Anne could hardly keep up with the changes. Not only did Vera and the other household staff wait on her hand and foot, but seamstresses traveled from London to measure her, milliners came to fit her with bonnets and hats, and shoemakers arrived to design slippers and boots. Mrs. Davies herself entered the bedroom every afternoon to instruct Anne on the manners and etiquette befitting a marchioness. Even Mr. Errand came in once or twice to give his new mistress charts of the Chouteau family's ancestry and to explain everyone's titles and how she was to address them.

Her meals could have fed the entire Webster family in Nottingham, who had learned to make do on dark bread, butter, shriveled potatoes, and strong tea. At breakfast Anne faced veal-and-ham pies, mackerel, dried haddock, mutton chops, broiled sheep's kidneys, sausages, bacon, poached eggs, toast, marmalade, butter, and fresh fruit. At luncheon she met with hashed meats, bread, cheese, biscuits, and puddings. At dinner, she encountered oxtail soup, crimped salmon, croquettes of chicken, mutton cutlets, roast filet of veal, boiled capon, lobster salad, raspberry jam tartlets, and plum pudding. No wonder the duchess's middle had expanded and the duke puffed when he climbed the stairs.

Since her wedding day, she had seen neither of her esteemed noble relations, nor had she laid eyes on the marquess or his brother. In fact, her world continued to be oddly dreamlike, as though she had stepped behind a green baize curtain in a dark corridor, had entered another existence, and couldn't remember how to get back.

"I feel lost," she said softly. "I don't know where to turn."

"You've been handed the whole world, my lady," Vera told her. "You can do anything you like. Go anywhere. See anyone. What do you want?"

"My family. I don't have any idea what's become of my father." She touched the rough white linen of her escort's shirtsleeve. "The marquess never returned my lace, did he?"

"You don't need that scrap of lace," Vera said. "As his wife, you have all the money you like. Why not send a letter to your mother on the mail coach? In the desk in your bedroom are enough pens, ink, and paper to write a hundred books if you like. Or why not dispatch a footman to inquire at the rectory in Nottingham? You could have your mother, sisters, and brother transported to Tiverton and put up in a good house."

"You say I have money, Vera. Where is it? Am I to knock on the duke's library door and ask him for a thousand pounds? Am I to go into the duchess's bedroom and rifle through her bags?''

''Inquire of Mr. Errand how you're to get at your money. Heaven knows, he's told you everything else you're meant to do.''

Anne tugged her shawl more closely around her shoulders. She might be the Marchioness of Blackthorne, but she still felt like Annie Webster. The thought of demanding anything of the formidable butler sent a knot into her stomach.

If, as Vera claimed, she could do anything she liked, she wanted to go home. In Nottingham the long hedgerows would be in full bloom—cow parsley, hawthorn, and hogweed dancing with white blossoms. Violets and yellow primroses shyly showing their faces. Ferns beginning to unfurl their green fronds. Kestrels and wood pigeons soaring on cool spring breezes as farmers turned over the rich soil.

In contrast to the wild exuberance of her beloved midlands, the Slocombe House garden was crisscrossed by narrow brick paths, twelve-foot walls covered in ivy, and hedges pruned into sharp boxes or perfect orbs. Roses had been forced over metal arches; daffodils marched in straight, even rows. They looked as miserable as she felt.

''I should like to go home,'' she said, almost to herself.

Walker stopped in the midst of the path. Turning to Anne, he took her shoulders and forced her to meet his gaze. ''You are home, Lady Blackthorne. This England, this Devon, this patch of soil near the sea, is your home. It is my home. Forces more powerful than you and I have made it so. Nothing can change that.''

''This is not a home, Walker. It's a prison.''

''No, it's just a place. Not so different from any other. If you don't learn to accept this place as your home, you will live with anger and regret. You will have no hope. Your faith in God will grow weak.''

Anne read the truth in his dark eyes. During her recovery, as she sat making lace by the window, he had told her about the land of his birth. America. He made it sound wild and beautiful and free. She had heard the longing in his voice, and she knew it echoed her own.

In silence, they walked on down the path. Stopping at a large gate, Anne peered up through the bars at the huge gray stone house with its four round turrets, its parapets, its countless chimneys, its multipaned windows and heavy iron and oak doors. Home? No wonder the marquess had been eager to escape on his adventures.

They were on the point of continuing their walk when Anne caught a glimpse of a man in the grove that edged one side of the garden. He was moving their way, and she had the sudden fear it might be the marquess. She turned around, took Vera's arm for support, and retreated down the path. But the man, near enough to see her, called out.

"It's him, Annie," Vera whispered, forgetting her subservient status. "It's the marquess. Oh, Annie!"

"Blackthorne!" The Indian lifted a hand as the nobleman strode onto the path and approached them. "Where have you been keeping yourself?"

"London, mostly. Good morning, Walker, Lady Blackthorne, miss." He took off his tall black hat and gave them a little bow. "Out for a stroll, are you? I was told I'd find you here."

Anne's legs had turned to wooden boards, and her feet might as well have been nailed to the ground. It was one thing to adjust to her new social status and come to grips with its effect on her life. It was another thing to meet the Marquess of Blackthorne face-to-face and realize he was her husband. Husband.

She could hardly force breath into her lungs. Her heartbeat hammered in her ears like an infantry drum. Husband! Husbands meant beds and babies and . . . oh, dear God.

She stared at the man. He was saying something about

the weather to Walker. His black hair curled at the tops of his ears and lay in a ruffle against his high, stiff collar. Beneath his calf-length greatcoat, his shoulders looked enormous. Under his coat were undoubtedly his waistcoat and shirt. Under them . . . his bare chest.

Mortified, Anne clutched her shawl at her throat. He had said he meant to make use of her. She had thought him odious. But it never occurred to her that he had any specific purpose in mind. She had expected herself to die and be free of him. But now . . . now!

"And your injury, my lady?" he said, turning to her suddenly. "Has Walker healed you, as I expected he would?"

She had no choice but to look straight into his gray eyes. His dark brows lifted a little in inquiry, and one corner of his mouth turned up. He leaned toward her, waiting for her reply like a cat toying with its prey.

"I'm well," she managed, horribly aware that her voice sounded like a frog's.

"Capital. Nothing could cheer me more. Then will you do me the honor of accompanying me into the arboretum for a brief tête-à-tête?" He glanced at the other two. "You don't mind, do you, Walker?"

The Indian tipped his head. "I'll return to my smithy."

"No, wait for me in the library, please. There's a charming prospect from the south windows to entertain you. I won't be long. I've a great deal to tell you."

Without waiting for his friend's answer, the marquess took Anne's hand, tucked it around the inside of his elbow, and set off toward the tree-filled park near the path. She glanced back to see Vera staring at her, white-faced with trepidation, as she was led away by Walker.

"London is abuzz with news of our wedding," the marquess began when he had walked her through the gate into the arboretum. Trees of every species in England filled the walled grove, their shadows darkening the sunlit grass.

"You and I are quite the scandal of the moment."

"I've never been a scandal," Anne spoke up.

"You'd better accustom yourself to it. A minister's daughter snaring a marquess . . . it's deliciously appalling. The predators can hardly wait to get their fangs into you. Errand assures me he and Mrs. Davies have trained you well, but I'm afraid you'll have to rely on your wit when you enter the lair of Society."

"I have no plan to go to London, Lord Blackthorne."

"Oh, and what do you plan?" He stopped walking and looked down at her. From his greater height, the woman seemed fragile and delicate, as if she might fade into the shadows or drift away in the spring breeze. He feared her fiery spirit might have been snuffed by her illness.

In the three weeks away, he had almost made himself forget the upward tilt of her eyes and the soft angle of her nose. When confronted by her memory—which happened more often than he liked—he had reminded himself she was a commoner, hardly educated, very plain, and of little consequence. In short, she was nothing.

But now she lifted her chin and turned her indigo eyes on him, and he suddenly remembered why he had been so determined to save her life. Her soft wool shawl slipped off one shoulder to reveal delicate bone and alabaster skin. Her long neck arched upward. Her pink lips curved into the smallest of smiles.

"What do I plan to do? I plan to get my lace back from you, Lord Blackthorne," she said and held out one hand. "You made me a promise."

He took her hand, turned it over, and kissed her fingers. His blue-eyed hothead had returned. "You made *me* a promise, my dear lady. To love, honor, and obey . . . until death do us part."

Anne snatched her hand away. "I was drugged, and you knew it! I believed I was going to die. Don't tell me you mean to continue this charade. Give me my lace, and let me go back to Nottingham where I belong. I've had more than my fill of roasted pheasant, bowing servants, and ivied walls.''

"Good, then you won't object to embarking on a tour of pleasure. London first, then Belgium and France. We shall stay in all the best houses, dance at the most elegant balls, and eat and drink ourselves into oblivion. You shall have new dresses every day and the latest hats—''

"I don't want new dresses and hats, sir! I was happy enough with my mobcap."

"You were not." He leaned close and took her chin. "You were trying to sell lace to my brother. You wanted more money than the laceman would give you."

Anne clamped her mouth shut. He was boorish. A rogue.

"You, my dear wife, are enterprising, visionary, and ambitious. You see curly hair where others see peeling paint. You weave silk threads better than any spider. You managed to marry yourself off to a marquess. Don't tell me you're content with a mobcap and dust cloth."

"I'm meant to be a housemaid. That's all." She knotted her hands into fists. "I won't be played with. I won't be made sport of by you. I only want . . . I want . . ."

"What is it you want, Anne Chouteau, Marchioness of Blackthorne? Tell me. What are your dreams?"

Anne turned her head away and stared into the top branches of a giant oak tree. Light green leaves rustled in the cool air. What did she want? Her old dreams had grown as tangled as the tree's budding branches. To sell her lace . . . to free her father . . . to marry . . . to start a lace school . . . to have children . . .

"I dream of things you can never give me," she said. "For all your great wealth and prestige and standing in Society, you are powerless to make me happy."

"I'll wager you're dead wrong there." He caught her elbow. Turning her against him, he molded his hand along the back of her neck. "I would wager my entire fortune on the odds I can make you happy . . . very happy. But then, you're not a gambler, are you? No cards or dice for my little saint. Tell me, wife, do you intend to read the Bible every night before we retire to our bed?''

Anne gulped down a bubble of air. His chest pressed tightly against her breasts, and she could feel every breath he took. The buttons of his greatcoat cut into her stomach. His thigh brushed against hers. His fingers against her neck were warm and firm.

For an instant, she absorbed the utter sensation of the moment—aware of the man's scent, enraptured by the contrast between his black hair and the blue sky behind him, trapped in his gray eyes, bewitched by his mouth. For an instant, she forgot her stolen lace and her imprisoned father. For an instant, she imagined she was melting into this man, enfolded in his strength and wrapped in the surprise of her own desire. For an instant . . . and then she remembered.

"Don't." The word barely escaped her trembling lips. "Don't mock me."

"Never. I always tell the truth, and I always see the truth. Don't believe you can fool me with the facade you've built around yourself—minister's daughter, housemaid, faithful Bible reader, common lace stitcher. From the moment we met, I knew you."

"You know nothing of me."

"No?" He slid his fingers down her arm and lifted her hand. Tugging away her glove, he regarded her with a confident smile. He dropped the glove into the grass and laced his fingers through hers. "I know your hands, my lady. Yours are fingers that can weave magic from silk thread. Magic and mystery. I understand how few can work such wonders. In the past three weeks I've been to the lace schools at Honiton, I've spoken with Mr. Heathcoat the lacemaker, and I've watched women bent over their lace pillows. You were quite right in your boast that day in my brother's bedroom. Few can equal the skill with which you work lace, fewer still can prick patterns in parchment with your expertise. None . . . none I saw in my journeys could design with such inspiration as you.''

''You're a devil with your bewitching words.''

''I know your hands,'' he went on, as if she hadn't spoken, ''and I know your mouth. Your words made a beggar believe she was a duchess. Your words cowed the vicar of Tiverton. Your words charmed and delighted my father. The duke simply can't stop talking about you.''

''That's not true.''

''Yes, it is.'' He drew his finger across her bottom lip. ''My lady, I know the magic of your mouth.''

She couldn't keep her eyes from his lips. Despite the hard line they often formed, at this moment his mouth was soft, his upper lip bowed at its peak, compelling.

''I know your hands. I know your mouth.'' He traced a line across her forehead with his fingertip. ''And I know your mind. You view life as you do your lace patterns— as a great weblike maze to be worked through, one which you alone understand. You hold the threads, do you not? It is you who designs the patterns.''

''No!''

''Yes, and the more you learn about the world, the more complex your design grows. You've read a few books, now you want to read more. Your father taught you to speak your mind, now you speak to dukes and duchesses. You traveled from Nottingham to Tiverton. Now I think you would like very much to see London . . . and Paris . . . even America.''

''I wouldn't,'' Anne said, even though she wasn't completely sure it was the truth.

''You would, and you will. I've ordered your trunks packed, and tomorrow we shall set off on our grand pleasure tour. Vera will wait on you, and I'll take Foley and the odd footmen. Walker will accompany us, and we shall have a capital time.''

"Stop this!" Anne pushed at his chest with both hands until he released her. "Walker said nothing to me of a pleasure tour on the Continent."

"Of course not. I haven't told him yet."

"You expect him to go with you? How little you understand the man you call a friend. Walker will never leave Devon. Only moments ago on the pathway, he told me this land has become his home. Your arrogance blinds you, Lord Blackthorne."

As she swung away, her shawl slid to the ground between them. Abandoning it, she took two steps toward the gate before whirling to face him.

"You speak as if I'm a spider, spinning webs and manipulating the threads of my own existence. It's you who are the predator, Ruel Chouteau, Marquess of Blackthorne! You chase people into corners. You mock and ridicule the innocent. You force even your friends down paths of your own choosing. What will happen after you've devoured us all? You'll be alone, won't you? As alone as you truly are right now in your empty, black soul."

He stared at her, marveling at the flush of color on her high cheekbones. Her bosom rose and fell, filling the small bodice of her green dress to more than capacity. The afternoon sunlight that filtered through the trees lit the sheer fabric of her skirt from behind, turning it all but transparent. He let his gaze wander down, absorbing the slender curve of her waist and the thrust of the rounded hip on which she had set a clenched fist. Lower, he took in her long legs and narrow ankles. Then he lifted his focus to her eyes.

"My empty, black soul does not interest me in the least," he said. "My wife, on the other hand, I find increasingly intriguing."

Anne lifted her chin. "My husband does not interest me in the least. Though I shall make it my duty to pray for his empty, black soul."

"Not at bedtime, I hope. I should dislike anything to interrupt us then."

Her cheeks hot, Anne narrowed her eyes at him. "I have no intention of performing any conjugal duties for you, sir. Though I lay drugged and injured on our wedding day, I clearly heard you assure your father that in time you mean to terminate the arrangement between us. If you think for one moment that I shall become your mistress or bear you any bastard children, you are sadly mistaken."

"Am I?" He advanced toward her, leaving her glove and shawl on the grass behind him.

"Yes, you are." She took a step forward. "I intend to speak to the vicar and ask his blessing on an annulment of this preposterous situation."

"And then what will you do?"

"I shall go back to Nottingham."

"With what money?"

"You shall give me back my lace!"

He stopped less than a foot from her. "I'm afraid I left it in London."

"You're a demon!"

"Come with me to London and Paris, Anne. Charm the ladies and disarm the men. Make them believe we adore one another, that our tour is nothing more than a grand gallivant to the Continent in celebration of our wedding."

"Make them believe?" She studied his gray eyes. They were soft, almost gentle. "*That's* what you want of me?"

"Not only that. In France, I shall use Walker's assistance in setting up my enterprise."

"Smuggled lace machines."

"Don't make them sound so evil. They're nothing but glorified stocking knitters. All the machines can do is create net. Innocent enough, and all but valueless."

"Unless they are worked over with patterns . . . by hand." A chill washed down Anne's spine. "You can't do this without me, can you?"

He smiled. "Again you hold the trump."

"You need me. You need my skill, my expertise. Without my help, you're doomed to failure, aren't you? That means I can demand of you whatever I want."

"Perhaps I shall make a gamester of you yet." He touched her cheek. "What is it you would ask of me, my dear wife?"

Knowledge of her own power sent a tingle of triumph through Anne's veins. Perhaps her prayers had been answered after all. Perhaps the marriage hadn't been such a dreadful mistake.

"My father," she said. "I want to engage a barrister to defend his case to the court."

"Already done. While in London last week, I made arrangements with the Chouteau family's private counsel. Your father should walk free by Christmas. Your mother, three sisters, and brother will be taking temporary residence in London until that time."

"London," she said with a gasp.

"Following your father's release, he will be preferred to the rectory in Ivybridge which falls within my own property. It's a rather small parish, but safely removed from Luddites and other Tory demagogues who might again tempt your father away from the straight and narrow."

Anne tried to breathe. He had done it already. Already. He had known what she wanted. He had understood her dreams. She looked into those gray eyes, suddenly afraid he did know her as well as he'd claimed.

"Anything else you would request of me, my dear lady?" The corner of his mouth tilted up in that now-familiar expression of amused confidence. "Surely hundreds of things come to mind. Jewels, perhaps? A grand house in London with liveried servants by the score? More new gowns? Hats? A country manor? A chaise and four?"

Anne shook her head. "I don't care about those things, and you certainly know it."

"Yes, I do." He ran his hand down her arm and took her bare fingers. "Remember, I know you, Lady Anne Blackthorne. You want books to read. You want a garden lush with wild roses, hawthorns, foxgloves, feverfews, and buttercups. You'd like a large, sunlit gallery furnished with a mahogany table upon which you can design lace to your heart's content. You want reams of parchment on which to prick your elaborate patterns. You want threads in silk, linen, and cotton. You want stuffed lace pillows and steel pins by the thousand. You want twenty skilled young ladies to whom you can teach your secrets. Am I close to your dreams?"

She wished his fingers laced through hers were not so large and firm. She wished he weren't looking into her eyes as if he could see straight to her soul. Most of all, she wished her heart would stop beating so fast.

"You paint a bewitching picture," she said breathlessly, "and one that tempts me. But you're wrong to believe I would ask such things of you. If so, I would only be chained more tightly to your benevolence. I won't allow that. You've taken care of my father, almost a fair trade for my assistance in your smuggling venture."

"Almost? What else would you have of me?"

"Distance." She took her hand from his. "Don't come near me again, Lord Blackthorne, or I shall tell the Regent himself of your plan. From now on I shall sleep alone and, other than performing the pretense of marriage with you in public, I shall not be forced to endure your presence."

"Endure me? Am I so odious to you?"

She swallowed the urge to confess the unsettling, tantalizing emotions he evoked in her. "Don't you know how I feel about you?" she asked, taking on the mocking tone he so often used with her. "But I thought you knew everything about me, Lord Blackthorne."

"I believed so."

"You said yourself you know my hands, my words, my

mind. Before I spoke of it, you knew my plan to save my father. You even guessed at my dreams of a lace school. Surely you know how I feel about you.''

He stared at her. She was enticing, enchanting, and he wanted her more than he'd wanted any woman. Yet even now she was garnering a promise from him that he knew he would be forced to keep. Even now she was distancing herself, backing away from him, ready to escape like a wisp of lace caught in an afternoon breeze.

''Anne—''

''You will not touch me. Swear it.''

He reached out to her.

She stepped away. ''Promise me.''

''The devil take it. All right, I won't touch you.''

She rewarded him with a smile. ''And I shall help you transform your ugly machine-made net into such sumptuous lace that every French aristocrat will shower you with ducats to possess it. But lest you become too confident in our partnership, Lord Blackthorne, do not forget there is one part of me you do not know . . . and never will know.''

He watched her as she drifted just out of reach, her dress hugging the outlines of her legs, her blue eyes shining like sapphires. ''What part of you is that, my lady?''

''My heart.'' After giving her husband a little curtsy, she turned and walked through the gate toward the house.

$\mathcal{E}$ight

"DAMNED IMPERTINENT OF YOU, WALKER." RUEL crossed his arms over his chest and leaned against the sill of the huge, multipaned window in the library. "Now is not the time to play the loyal Devonshire blacksmith."

"I don't play at my work." The tall Indian eyed the younger man. "I am a blacksmith. Devon is my home. I will not leave."

"For years, all you've spoken of is America. You've told me a hundred tales of that land. You are why I went. I had to see the place for myself, and now I have. Missouri is as beautiful as you said, as lush, as green, as populated with deer and bison and wild turkey. Your people are there, Walker."

"Your people are there. They have taken away the land."

"Not all of it. Yours are still there, too. The Osage roam the forests and streams of Missouri as they always have. How can you tell me you don't want to go back to them?"

"I have no people. I no longer remember the Osage tongue. I don't look or behave as they do. I told you, Blackthorne, with my English manners and my blacksmith's skills I'm worth nothing to the Osage."

"Then come with me as far as France."

"Never."

"Are you afraid?"

"Of course I am. I was sent to France as a hostage to ensure Osage obedience in the Louisiana Territory, but I escaped. If I were seen there again, I could be thrown into prison."

"That happened years ago. The Louisiana Territory is greatly altered. Osage land is now part of the Missouri Territory—independent of France, Spain, England, and everyone else who's tried to control it. I expect the Missouri Territory will become one of the United States before long. France certainly doesn't have time to track down an escaped hostage. Napoleon has returned from Elba, and that country is in arms. The truth is, Walker, no one even remembers your journey to France."

"How can you be so sure? You know I was not the only one. In 1725 a group of Indians—Osage, Missouria, Illini—were taken to France to meet the boy king, Louis XV. Like puppets, they were driven to the Bois de Boulogne and told to run down a deer. They were dressed in cock hats and coats trimmed in gold. They were ordered to dance at the Italian Theatre and at masked balls. They knew the bedchambers of the French aristocracy."

"You never told me this."

"Why should I? You were a little boy. You didn't need to know that mighty warriors had been sent to France as playthings for the nobility. Nor did you need to know that one of the Indian hostages was a young Missouria girl. The French named her La Belle Sauvage and lavished her with diamonds and jewels. The Duchess d'Orleans made herself the girl's godmother, had her baptized in Notre Dame de Paris, and arranged her marriage to a French sergeant."

"To what purpose?"

"Amusement. I've discovered the aristocracy sees little harm in using people to provide their pleasure if the opportunity arises." His voice dropped. "You toy with the young lacemaker, Blackthorne. She's an honest woman, and she would make a good wife for some man. She deserves a home, a hearth, children . . . a loving husband. Yet you play with her life, with her heart.''

"No more than she plays with mine.''

"Truly?''

Ruel frowned, uncomfortable at how much he had revealed. "Look, Walker, if you think I mean to make use of you for my own pleasure, you're dead wrong. Yes, your skill with metal can help me assemble my lace machine in France. I won't deny that, and I've stated my intent to pay you handsomely for your services. But I have no other purpose in taking you to America than to restore you to your people.''

The Indian gave a snort. "My people. When the Indian delegation was taken away in 1725, the Little People said they would mourn for fifteen moons. After that period, if the hostages did not return, they would be counted dead. Fifteen moons. I've been gone twenty-eight years.''

Ruel turned away in exasperation. Outside the library window, the parks, gardens, and woods that stretched for miles around Slocombe House always had been home to him. Though he couldn't imagine leaving this place for decades at a time, he felt certain he always would be welcomed no matter when he returned.

He had not expected Walker to be so difficult. He needed the man at his side for a more important purpose than assembling a lace machine, yet he didn't know how to persuade the Indian to accompany him. Should he tell the truth? Should he reveal the suspicion that had begun to gnaw on him while he was in America and now seemed all but confirmed?

"On August 16, 1787,'' Walker was saying, his voice trancelike, "Wa-Tcha-Wa-Ha and Arrow-Going-Home were called to Chouteau's Town, St. Louis. The Spanish officials of the territory demanded that some of their chieftains be delivered as hostages to New Orleans. The hostages were to guarantee Osage future good behavior. Of course, the Osage would never turn over their leaders, the Little Old Men, so they sent others . . . Padouca and Pawnee captives who had learned the Osage language and manners after living so many years with their captors . . . and Osage warriors who could defend themselves. They sent me, Walks-in-the-Night.''

Ruel had heard the story of Walker's journey to New Orleans and then to Spain as a hostage of the Spaniards. He knew all about the Treaty of San Ildefonso, signed in 1800, transferring the Louisiana Territory from Spain to France. Many times as a boy, Ruel had listened to Walker tell him how he and the other hostages had been transferred from Madrid to Paris. Walker had become certain he would never return to America, and his desperation had been intense.

Hearing words he had heard so many times before, Ruel let his focus linger on the scene outside the library window. The pathways, the knot gardens, the parks . . . the arboretum. His heart lurched. A slim figure slipped between the heavy iron gates and into the tree-filled enclosure. Her wisp of a green dress told him it was Anne . . .

Straightening, he tried to watch her progress through the trees. Just a glimpse. She appeared for a moment in a glade, then vanished again. What was she doing? Why had she returned to the place of their meeting? Did she hope to find him there? Or had she some other assignation . . . a lover?

He hadn't considered that possibility. Perhaps the woman he had married loved another man. A footman or a gardener. Maybe she loved the gamekeeper. Hadn't Ruel been told of the man's pursuit of her?

''It was in Paris that I heard again the beloved name of Chouteau,'' Walker was saying. ''Then I knew I had hope. I made arrangements to meet this man, Etienne Chouteau, uncle of Auguste, who is friend to the Little People. Etienne Chouteau is a great man, very wise and very, very old. He had me brought in a carriage from the prison to his grand house on the Champs Elysses, and there he told me that he had two brothers.''

Ruel nodded. Yes, yes, he knew the story. There were three of them—sons of Raoul and Marie Chouteau of France—Etienne, Laurent, and René. Etienne lived in Paris and was a grand patron of the aristocracy. Laurent traveled to England, where he assumed the family's duchy of Marston, married the Englishwoman Beatrice, and produced five daughters and two sons, the elder of whom was Ruel himself. René married Marie Therese and journeyed to America to seek his fortune. He became the father of Auguste Chouteau before separating from his wife and fading into anonymity.

The story was as familiar as any nursery rhyme. Ruel was much more interested in the slender woman who had vanished into a copse in the arboretum. Perhaps she was only a commoner, a housemaid, a criminal's daughter—but she was his wife. She owed her husband the pretense of faithfulness, didn't she? If she were attending a lover's tryst, couldn't she at least do it away from the grounds of Slocombe House?

The thought of Anne folded into the arms of another man sent a stab of anger through his chest. The image of her lips pressed against another man's mouth . . . of someone else placing his hands around her waist and over her breasts . . .

Don't touch me, she had said. *Promise me*. Of course she didn't want Ruel to touch her! Of course she didn't want him in her bed. She was in love with someone else. Why hadn't he seen it?

He'd been too damned busy arranging for her father's defense and sending seamstresses and milliners to clothe her in silk and feathers, that's why. He'd been too wrapped up in his own plans and too absorbed in investigating the mystery that swirled around in his head.

''It was Etienne Chouteau who helped me escape to his

brother Laurent, in England,'' Walker continued, as if he were speaking to a rapt audience. "Here in Devon, I was welcomed into Slocombe House and treated with great respect. I will honor your father always for saving me from a life in the prisons of France. That is why I shall never go back to that country. Not even for you."

Ruel scowled at the window. Where had she gone? He had a mind to walk straight down to the arboretum and publicly disgrace her and her ill-bred lover. She was his wife, for heaven's sake. She'd promised allegiance. Didn't he have the right to expect a certain degree of faithfulness?

"Did you hear me, Blackthorne?" Walker asked. "I told you I will never go to France."

"You have to come, damn it." Ruel swung around. "Someone's trying to kill me."

The Indian stared at him. "Kill you? Why?"

"Any number of reasons. Wimberly believes himself cheated of his fortune. Barkham blames me for the seduction of his wife. Droughtmoor claims I ruined his sister."

"You loved these women?"

"Of course not. They were amusements—consensual dalliances. Any man in my position can be expected to have engaged in various affairs."

"But now you're a married man. You'll be faithful to Anne, will you not?"

"Well, I . . . I . . ." Ruel glanced out the window. She was nowhere to be seen. It hadn't occurred to him that if he expected faithfulness of her, he would be held to the same exacting standard himself. Could he be loyal to only one woman for the rest of his life? Hard to imagine. Yet the thought of wanting any woman other than Anne . . . he couldn't imagine that either.

But she didn't want him. Wouldn't have him in her bed. Wouldn't allow even his hand on hers. *Don't touch me.*

"If you are settled with a wife and children," Walker said, "how can these enemies pursue you for revenge?

Surely what happened was many years ago when you were no more than a boy. Among the Osage, a peace gift is given to the one wronged. Why not present these three men with a small measure of your wealth, Blackthorne, as we do among my people?''

"Your people!" Ruel took the man's shoulder. "You admit it. The Osage *are* your people, Walker, and they always will be. Come to France and America. Help protect me."

"I cannot."

"You must. On a roadway in Missouri, I was attacked, knifed, and left for dead. At sea I was beaten senseless and expected to die. Neither time was I robbed. Both incidents were investigated, but no perpetrator was found and no motive uncovered. Three weeks ago, someone shot me through the left shoulder, six inches from my heart. When I fell, the marksman vanished. Who was it, Walker?"

"They said it was the gamekeeper, a spurned suitor of Lady Blackthorne."

"William Green was drinking ale at the Boar's Head tavern in Tiverton at the time of the shooting. Any number of reliable witnesses attested to that fact. Who wants me dead so badly he would see me tracked to the ends of the earth by his hired assassins? And if this murderer is so determined and so deceitful that he would send someone to ambush me rather than challenge me to a duel himself, how am I to defend my life? Walker, you've always been loyal to me. You've been the only man I could depend on. You were the one I came to as a boy when I was frightened or sad or angry. Help me now. I need you."

The Indian looked away, his eyes misted. "You ask much of me."

"Please, Walker."

His focus on the ground, he nodded. "All right. I'll go with you to France."

"It's not only for me." He glanced out the window.

"Anne was almost killed by that ball, Walker. She has no idea I'm a marked man, and I won't have her wounded again in my stead."

The Indian lifted his head, surprise written in his brown eyes. "You love her."

"Don't be absurd. Romance is for dandies like my brother. I merely want the woman protected . . . as a business asset as much as anything else." He put his hand on the Indian's arm and turned him toward the door. "Come now, Walker, you'd better shut down the smithy and pack your things. We're leaving for London in the morning."

"London?"

"Didn't I tell you? I've had the Grosvenor Square house opened a little early. My sister has written that she and her husband are traveling down from the highlands to meet us. Welcome the newlyweds, wish us joy, and all that fiddle-faddle."

Walker stopped. "Which sister?"

"Claire. You remember her, don't you? The eldest. She's kind and good, and really too beautiful. She has scads of children, and her husband is a jolly sort. You'll adore her."

Ruel followed his companion into the corridor. At that moment the arboretum gate swung open, and Anne slipped out of the shadows onto the path. Evening was coming on, and the breeze carried with it the chill of night. Shivering, she was thankful she had remembered to return to the arboretum before leaving Slocombe House the following morning. She pulled on the glove she had left behind and wrapped her shawl more closely about her shoulders.

Four carriages emblazoned with the crest of the Duke of Marston drew rows of spectators as they rolled into London. Ragged boys chased after them while little girls in patches waved from windows. The curious stares made Anne shrink into her seat. The city was enormous, gray, and so very crowded. Though trees had leafed out in small gardens and flowers bloomed in clay pots, dirt lay heaped in corners, soggy newspapers rotted on the sidewalks, and the smell . . . oh, the smell. She lifted her handkerchief to her nose and drank in the scent of the lavender blossoms in which the linen fabric had been stored.

"Ah, London," Ruel said. "Cesspool of England. Home to harlots, actresses, fishwives, and countless other squashed cabbage leaves of society."

Anne eyed him. For some reason Ruel was angry, and the closer they drew to town, the darker his mood grew. Now he looked a veritable volcano, smoldering inside his black traveling coat and high, starched collar. His eyes flashed a steely silver gray as he observed the city through the carriage window.

"Armpit of the Thames," he said under his breath. He had spent the journey discussing one thing and another with his brother and the Chouteau family steward, who was accompanying them to London on a financial matter. They had talked politics, world affairs, business. Though Anne was the only other person in the carriage, she might have been a tuft of horsehair protruding from the seat for all the attention the men paid her. At the coaching inns where the travelers stayed each evening, Ruel played at cards, wagering and usually winning large sums of money before he retired to a room alone.

She should have been grateful. Clearly her husband was honoring his promise to keep his distance. All the same, the situation grated.

Anne deplored gaming. She disliked bumpy roads. And she was growing to despise her aloof spouse more than ever. She supposed his ill temper toward her had to do with her insistence that he make her a vow of restraint. Too bad. The longer she'd had to think about their conversation in the arboretum, the more thankful she was that she'd had the presence of mind to extract his promise. The fact was, she didn't trust herself.

Ever since that afternoon, she'd found herself thinking about the marquess, remembering the way he'd held her so tightly beneath the trees, recalling the warmth in his eyes and the scent of his breath. She had wanted him to kiss her then. She hadn't been capable of preventing that desire, no matter how misguided it was. Worse, she still wanted his kiss, and she thanked heaven alone that she would never know it.

What would become of her if she allowed the man his husbandly rights? She would become pregnant, of course. She would bear a child, outlive her usefulness to him in the lace venture, and be cast into the streets like the poor women he termed ''squashed cabbage leaves.''

''The house on Grosvenor Square should be opened by now, but just barely.'' His low voice against her ear startled her. Lifting her head, she realized that Lord Alexander and the steward were deep in conversation, and Ruel had chosen this moment to confer privately with her.

''The servants traveled ahead of us to air out the rooms and put things right,'' he continued.

His shoulder pressed against hers, and his warm breath stirred the hair over her ear. A shiver rippled down her spine. ''How nice,'' she managed.

''For appearances' sake, you will take the suite next to mine. Your lady's maid will join the other servants, and you will not continue to allow her to sleep with you as you have on this journey.''

Anne dipped her head in acknowledgment. If she intended the marquess to keep his part of their agreement, she must keep hers and pretend to be his loving wife. If they slept in different wings, every footman and maid in the house would know. Gossip in the great houses ran rampant, as Anne well knew, and what a maid from one family whispered to a maid from another was soon common knowledge in Society.

''We shall take callers,'' Ruel went on, speaking barely

above a murmur, "give dinner parties, and attend balls. You will behave as Mrs. Davies instructed you, and your manners will be impeccable. No matter what is said of you, you will hold your head high. You will remember that you are the daughter of a minister, the heiress to a duchy, and the wife of a marquess."

"A man with whom I am deeply in love," she added.

He stared at her.

She leaned into him and whispered against his ear. "How long are we to continue our charade before Society, Lord Blackthorne?"

"Until the time is right."

"This is all about France, isn't it? You're waiting for something to happen in Paris."

"Insightful, as always."

Anne drew away and fingered the fringed curtain on her window. Then she leaned into him again to whisper her concern. "Do you expect that little emperor to do something to make your lace venture more profitable? Surely he won't permit the aristocracy their fripperies. The common people struggled far too hard to strip them away."

"The little emperor's name is Napoleon Bonaparte. You must learn to call him Boney among your new friends."

"Friends? You once called them predators ready to tear me apart with fangs and claws." She couldn't deny how much she dreaded the coming weeks in London, but she didn't want the marquess to sense any trepidation in her lest he use it to gain the upper hand. "So, this Boney . . . how can he possibly help you?"

"I'm counting on him to blunder into a major battle with England and Prussia."

"Good heavens," she said aloud. Catching a glance from Lord Alexander, she lowered her voice again. "I cannot cherish the prospect of touring France in the midst of a war."

"There are a great many things about this venture I cannot cherish.'' He studied her so intently that Anne felt her cheeks grow hot. ''I suppose you bade your farewells to everyone at Slocombe House.''

''I was sorry to leave Mrs. Davies and Mr. Errand. Even Mrs. Smythe, for all her blustering, was good to me. The kitchen staff, too, became dear friends, many of them.''

''And the gamekeeper?''

''William Green? He shot the both of us, you'll recall. Why should I be sorry to leave such a man as that?''

Ruel leaned against her, his breath hot. ''You expect me to believe you were not his lover?''

''That's preposterous!'' she exclaimed. ''Absurd!''

Aware that the other travelers were scrutinizing them, he turned to the window. ''Ah, Chouteau House at last. I see my sister is just arriving from the highlands as well. How fortunate for us all.''

Anne grabbed the edge of the leather seat as the carriage slowed. William Green? Her lover? How could Ruel possibly think such a thing of her? Where had he gotten so ridiculous a notion? But he'd said it with such confidence . . . tossed it between them like a gauntlet. She had no weapons with which to duel such a man as the marquess. How could she prove him wrong? For that matter, why did he even care?

He stepped out of the carriage and tugged the tails of his coat into place. Then he held out one gloved hand to Anne. At the sight of his cold eyes and rigid mouth, her dismay changed to anger. She set her hand in his and leaned through the door.

''I rejected the gamekeeper three times,'' she hissed in his ear as she descended. ''That is why he shot me.''

''I saw you go into the arboretum—''

''Ruel!'' The golden-haired beauty running across the front lawn stole their attention. She must have been in her early forties, but her skin was a pale, luminous pink, and her figure was small and lithe. ''Oh, my darling, you don't know how happy I am to see you! We received the most awful intelligence that you had died in America . . . been killed in a most horrifying manner . . . and then a letter arrived from Devon saying you'd come home. Oh, Ruel!''

She threw her arms around him. He caught her at the waist and swung her against him. "Claire!" His voice held muffled emotion. "Claire, I'm so glad you came.''

"How could I not? Oh, you've grown so! Let me look at you." She held him at arm's length, her blue eyes misty and her lips trembling. "Goodness me, you're enormous. Look at these shoulders! And how your face has changed. You're so lean and hard. Did they not feed you on that ship? You might very well be a pirate yourself with all this mass of black hair.'' She ruffled her fingers through his curls. "Oh, what has happened to my little boy? My darling Puggy with his gingerbread nuts and bunny rabbit . . . my precious pumpkin!''

Ruel grinned. "Claire, you do run on.''

"And who is this?" She caught Anne's hands. "Are you the new marchioness? But you're lovely! Of course, you adore her, Ruel. I can see it now. What a sweet face! And your eyes are magnificent. Oh, welcome to the family, my dear. May I call you Anne?''

Swept into Claire's arms, Anne could hardly resist the flood of warmth she felt. Enveloped in the scent of roses, she slipped her arms around the woman and held her tightly. "Please do. I'm so happy to know you, Lady Eagon.''

"You must call me Claire, and that's my husband, the Viscount Eagon, but he's Edward to you." She beckoned the portly gentleman. "Teddy, this is Puggy's bride. We're to call her Anne.''

The viscount took off his hat and gave her an elegant bow. "I wish you great joy, my lady. And you, my lord. My heartiest congratulations.''

"Oh, look!" Claire exclaimed. "There's Alex. My, isn't he the dandy these days?"

Anne stood to one side as Ruel and his sister, joined by Lord Alexander, were caught up in the swirl of coachmen unloading trunks, nannies rounding up Claire's various children, and footmen offering trays of drinks. She finally spotted Vera climbing down from a carriage and shaking out her skirts. Mr. Walker spoke a word to the young maid, pulled her shawl from the carriage, and draped it about her thin shoulders.

In spite of the marquess's more luxurious vehicle, Anne gladly would have traded places with Vera. Surely Mr. Walker would never stoop to accuse her on unfounded rumors. The blacksmith, hat pulled low on his head, took Vera's arm and was starting up the steps into the house when the marquess noticed him.

"Walker! Do come and greet the family." He caught his sister's hand. "You remember Walker, don't you, Claire? He stayed with us years ago when he'd just come from France. Mr. Walker, this is Claire, Lady Eagon, my eldest sister."

"Oh . . . Mr. Walker." Claire's hand went to her throat. "What a surprise."

Anne stepped back as Ruel's sister extended her hand. The Indian kept his eyes to the ground. "Lady Eagon. It has been many years." He took the woman's hand and pressed his lips to her gloved fingers. "I trust you are well."

"Yes . . . yes, of course. I'm married to . . . to Teddy . . . Viscount Eagon. Edward." She bit her lower lip.

"Blackthorne has told me of your family."

"Has he? Certainly he has. Of course! What am I thinking?" Her laugh held a tremble. "You live in Tiverton, I believe."

"I'm a blacksmith."

"Oh, how very nice." She swallowed and gave Anne a

smile. "Do you know Mr. Walker, Lady Blackthorne? I'm sure you do. Dear me, this is such a shock. Teddy, darling, do come and meet Mr. Walker. He's a dear friend of the family. I can't think . . . can't think how long it's been. Many years since I . . . since we saw you."

"Ten years, my lady." Walker's voice was low. "You passed through Tiverton on a journey to Slocombe House. I repaired your carriage wheel."

"Yes, you did! Has it been ten years? My goodness, how time flies."

"Claire, you're all aflutter," her husband said gently. "I fear in a moment you'll begin to weep great rivers of tears all over your brother and his friend. Do let's all go inside and retire to the drawing room. I'm nearly famished for tea, and the children are beside themselves to slide down the banister."

"Tea. What a lovely idea. You will join us, won't you, Anne? And Mr. Walker . . . if you like . . ."

"Thank you, but I am not in the custom of drinking tea. Excuse me." He gave the company a nod and continued up the stairs to where Vera stood waiting. Taking her arm, he ushered her into the house.

"The arboretum." The word was spoken so close to Anne's ear that she jumped. "I saw you there."

She looked up into a pair of eyes the color of slate. "Of course you did, Puggy," she whispered back. "You dragged me into the arboretum yourself."

"You went back there after I'd gone up to the house." He took her arm and propelled her toward the stairs. "Whom did you meet?"

She tried to think, but his hand gripped her arm so tightly and his shoulder was pressed so hard against hers it was all she could do to climb the steps without stumbling. "You should know what I did if you were so intent to spy on me."

"I was not spying. I was talking to Walker in the library

when I witnessed your secret assignation.'' He pulled her through the marble-floored hall and turned her into a small parlor hung with gold and velvet. Kicking the door shut with his foot, he pressed her up against a wall. "If you have a lover, I will know his name. Tell me."

"You say little to me for three days alone in a carriage, and now in the midst of your family you assail me!" She squared her shoulders. "What does it matter to you whom I love?"

His jaw tightened. "You are my wife."

"Don't be absurd, Blackthorne. I'm a housemaid with a gift for making lace. I'm a commoner you need for a business enterprise. I am not your wife!"

His hands on her shoulders tightened. "As long as you wear my name and my title, you will not take lovers."

"Will *you*? Or do we play our game of charades by different rules?"

"Damn it! Who was in the garden with you?"

"My glove," she snapped. "You'd tossed it away, you odious man. I went back to fetch it. And my shawl. Unlike you, I regard my material possessions with respect, and I would never think to abandon my glove in the arboretum or leave my shawl in the grass . . . or mislay a length of valuable handmade Honiton lace in London!"

As she spoke, his face lifted, and his mouth tilted into a grin. "Your glove?"

She waved her fingers in front of his face. "My glove. You might have remembered it had you not been so blind with jealousy over some imagined lover."

"Jealous, am I?"

"Are you not?" She narrowed her eyes. "Blind with it. In fact, you are the blindest man I have ever had the misfortune to know. Blind, blind, blind. Blind to the beauty of the world around you. Blind to the love of your father. Blind to the selfish greediness of your dreams. Blind to the people who surround you."

He lifted her chin with the crook of his forefinger. "I seem to see you clearly, my hotheaded beauty."

She turned her head. "Proof of your blindness. I am no beauty. Your brother declared my hair the brown of a mouse's rump."

"My brother is a fool."

"Ruel?" The female voice outside the parlor door echoed through the foyer. "Puggy, are you in there?"

"It's Claire," he whispered, pulling Anne into his arms. "Hold me quickly," he mouthed against the side of her neck.

Shivering at his touch, Anne instinctively slid her hands around his back as the door burst open. "Ruel? Oh, dear! How wicked of me to disturb you."

Ruel lifted his head. "Claire? Have we been missed?"

"Everyone's looking for you." She glanced at Anne and clapped a hand over her mouth. "Had we but considered that you might like a moment's tête-à-tête . . . do forgive us. I'm so sorry."

Struggling to breathe, Anne was certain every flame that flickered up and down her body must be visible. Her neck glowed with heat where Ruel had kissed it. Her skin felt alive and tingling. A fire burned in the pit of her stomach.

"Quite . . . quite all right," she managed.

"Yes, Claire, please try to understand." He let his warm fingers slide down Anne's arm. "We've been imprisoned in that dashed carriage for three days."

Flustered, Anne stepped away from him. "I should like to freshen up for tea. Excuse me, please."

"Darling." His voice stopped her. "I very much hope you will leave your hair hanging loose at tea as you promised. I feel quite determined to enlighten my brother's opinion of its color."

Anne suppressed a glare. How dare he ask her to wear her hair unbonneted like some wanton?

"Of course, my dear husband," she said. "At your pleasure."

He smiled. "Where you are concerned, my pleasure knows no bounds."

She dipped her head at Lady Eagon and slipped out into the hall. As she fled up the grand staircase, she could hear him chuckling behind her.

$\mathcal{N}ine$

NOTHING HAD PREPARED ANNE FOR THE ASSAULT THAT began at dinner. Mrs. Davies's instruction in manners proved useless beneath the onslaught of snide comments and digging retorts flung at the bride from "friends of the family" who gathered around the long mahogany table at Chouteau House. Mr. Errand's lengthy lists of ancestors, descriptions of coats of arms, and maps of family properties did nothing to diffuse the volley launched at the newest member of the Chouteau dynasty.

By the time the last pies and puddings had been eaten, Anne's stomach had twisted into a Gordian knot she was certain nothing could untie. Swathed in a hideous gown that Vera had pulled out from some clothier's contribution to her trousseau—a wedding cake of pink silk, pink ribbons, and rows of pink lace at the hem—she felt sure her cheeks matched her dress to perfection. Never in her life, not even when her father had been cast into prison, had she been so humiliated. The Reverend Webster's stand in support of the Luddites of his parish had held a righteous tone, and his imprisonment made him a martyr for their cause. Anne felt like nothing more glorious than a spitted pig, roasted before a fire, slowly carved apart piece by piece.

Fortunately the marquess had been seated at the opposite end of the long table, which released her from having to keep up the pretense of adoring him through dinner. Unfortunately his distant position prevented his championing his new wife. Lord Alexander, in a pair of purple bloomers and a red polka-dot cravat, drank too much wine to be anything but silly. Mr. Walker might have helped Anne, but he had declined dinner, saying he was stiff from travel and wanted to walk in the gardens. Only Lady Eagon was available to rise to her new sister's defense—which she did. But Claire, who was gentle and kindhearted, hardly had the fortitude to counter every stab.

When the ladies at last retired to the drawing room, leaving the men to smoke and drink port, Anne seized the opportunity to escape. She hurried up to her suite of rooms, dug her Bible out of her trunk, and read three chapters in I Corinthians before she felt able to go back safely into Society. Without sensible words on the qualities of Christian love—patience, kindness, forbearance—to strengthen her, she felt certain she would slap the next young lady who made mention of her "fortuitous marriage" or her "unfortunate upbringing" or her "poor, poor relations" who must be ecstatic at her "astounding and unexpected connubial state" to the "handsome and noble" Marquess of Blackthorne.

Calmed, she stepped into the drawing room and realized—to her satisfaction—that tables of cards already had been set up and filled. The pianoforte was occupied, and ladies of varying ages had gathered around the instrument to sing in high, quivering voices while their husbands discussed the latest doings of that "flagitous tyrant," Napoleon. Spotting a shelf of books, Anne made for it like a magnet to iron. She grabbed the first volume of the history of Russia, found a chair in the corner, sat down, and began to read.

"How are the tsars getting on these days?"

She knew the voice without looking up. "Famously, Lord Blackthorne."

"And you?" He knelt beside her and spoke barely above

a whisper. "Still in one piece, or have the vultures shredded you to bits?"

She set her finger on the page to hold her place and lifted her head. "Blackthorne, I—"

The look on his face stopped her. His eyes had softened to a quiet dove gray, and they searched hers as if reading them were the most important thing in the world. He took her hand and brought it to his lips. As his head bent, she gazed down at the rumple of silky black curls and felt a jolt run through her chest.

"My love, that shade of pink quite lights up your face." His expression was tender, but his mouth lifted slightly at the corners. "You're as enchanting as a new rose this evening."

And then, of course, she remembered. The game. She glanced away from him to find every eye in the room turned their way. Fixing her attention on him again, she forced her lips into a smile. "Thank you, darling Ruel. You flatter me most becomingly."

"Did you enjoy your first dinner in your new home, my sweeting?" he murmured, just loud enough for everyone present to hear.

"The leg of lamb was exquisite and the filet of veal sumptuous. My compliments to the cook. Oh, Ruel . . ." On an impulse, she reached out and stroked the side of his face with the back of her hand. At the touch of his smooth, taut skin, her heart began to hammer. Willing it to silence, she painted a coy expression on her face. "I missed you dreadfully, my dear. You seemed miles and miles away at the other end of the table."

"I was, I was." He took her hand and kissed her palm and then her wrist. Taking a deep breath, he shut his eyes. "Lavender. This was the scent you wore when we met."

"Ah, yes, we were in that enchanting arbor filled with mingled scents and succulent treats."

He suppressed a chuckle. "You are my succulent treat,

dear Anne.'' At the flush of color that spread up her neck, Ruel found he could hardly resist the charming young woman. Though she played the part of blushing bride with the skill of a London actress, he sensed there might be some genuine pleasure in her response to his flirtation. Could it be that she'd never heard such words from a man?

"You are my intoxicating cup of wine," he continued for the benefit of those guests sitting closest, "my opiate, the stuff of my dreams."

"Oh, Ruel, my love . . ." She leaned against him and whispered into his ear. "You are a blackguard."

Throwing back his head, he laughed aloud. "Little minx!"

He slipped an arm around her waist and stood, bringing Anne to her feet. Holding her closely against him, he extended a hand toward the open French doors that led onto a long walk. "A promenade, my love? The air is quite warm, and the moonlight beckons."

She tipped her head. "With pleasure."

Eyes locked in an eternal gaze, they wandered out onto the flagstone path. A ripple of sighs from the company in the drawing room was followed by the urgent return to gossip and recountings of what had just been witnessed. But the moment Anne and Ruel stepped into the shadows of an overhanging ivy, she pulled away.

"I'm going to my rooms."

"Not so fast." The marquess caught her and drew her under his arm again.

"Blackthorne! That's quite enough now."

"Enough for whom?" His grin broadened. "I find I'm enjoying our little drama immensely, my darling wife. Come stand with me here in this patch of moonlight, and let's give our guests a bit of a show."

"Whatever can you—?"

He turned her into his arms, leaned her into the pale, buttery glow of the moon, and kissed her neck for the second time that day. "I can't tell you how intoxicating I find the scent of your skin."

"Blackthorne, release me this minute!"

Her voice was a hiss of delighted desperation. He found her dismay amusing . . . amazing . . . and powerfully stimulating. "Hold me, Anne," he murmured against her ear. "We're being observed from the drawing room, and we mustn't let down our facade for a moment."

"But this is . . . this is—"

"Soft, very soft." His lips crept up her neck to her chin. "Very fragrant—"

"You promised not to touch me," she sputtered. "You made me a vow."

"You promised to prove to everyone that we're madly in love. What better way than this . . . here, in the midst of those most intimate with my family?" He lifted her chin. "Does my lovemaking disturb you, Anne?"

"Of course not. It's just that I . . . that you . . ."

"I must say I find your consternation most intriguing." He pulled her closer, relishing the curve of her hip against his hand and the slight pressure of her thigh on his. "You see, were this truly no more than a game between us, and had you nothing but contempt for me, you would merely perform your role in a perfunctory manner. Instead, you blush and sigh and avert your eyes in a very beguiling way. And every time I hold you in my arms, you seem to have the most dreadful time breathing."

"I do not!" she puffed.

"In fact, my dear Anne, I have come to the conclusion that you have never been properly wooed."

"Rubbish. William Green the gamekeeper wooed me."

"That boor?"

"As did a young man in Nottingham." She squared her shoulders. "A man I plan to marry someday."

"A weaver, no doubt."

"A farmer."

"Oh, a farmer. How charming. Tell me, Anne, did your young farmer kiss this particular place on your shoulder?" He drew a line with his fingertip down her neck to the edge of her bodice. "Or perhaps here?"

She grabbed his hand as it dipped toward the swell of her breast. "Beast!"

"Beauty." He took her hand, forced it behind her back, and pulled her hard against him. "Contrary to my original assumption, I don't believe you've ever been loved, Anne Webster Chouteau, Lady Blackthorne, and one day Duchess of Marston. I doubt you've even been kissed."

Before she could push at him again, he covered her lips with his mouth. Against him her body stiffened, and she took in a deep breath. He softened the kiss, suddenly determined to explore the fascinating shape of those lips that could speak with such vehemence and smile with such radiance. Warm . . . damp . . . hard . . . tight . . .

"Anne," he whispered against her mouth. "Kiss me."

She squeezed her eyes shut and fought the whirl inside her brain. Dear God . . . oh, yes . . . no! . . . oh, this was wrong . . . right . . . magic . . . sinful . . . His mouth was so hot, and his lips moved across hers in such a beckoning, tempting . . . yes . . .

All for the imposture, she told herself. Only for show. Prove to his friends. She softened her mouth and let him mold her body more tightly against his. Allowing herself to touch him, she placed one hand on his arm. Rock hard. She slid her fingers around the muscle, marveling. But how could she think of anything but his lips. They drank hers, endlessly pressing and sliding . . . now soft, now hard.

His hand moved up her back and onto her bare neck. His fingers slid into her hair. Tingles rippled down her skin. Moving his mouth to her ear, he stroked his lips over the sensitive shell.

"You are delicious," he murmured.

"Ohh." The moan of pleasure escaped before she could

stop it. She felt the rumble of his chuckle deep in his chest.
"Lord Blackthorne, I—"

"Ruel."

"I think we've performed quite well enough to convince
anyone."

"I'm convinced." He kissed her lips again. "Are you
convinced, Anne?"

"That you should not take such liberties again. Yes, I'm
quite sure of it. And will you please . . ."

He shook his head. "No, I will not."

The longer he kissed this woman, the more certain he
became that he had to have her. His body demanded it.
Never in his life had he felt such an explosion of need. She
was ripe and untouched, soft and more than willing. She
hungered for him whether she would admit it or not. Her
lips were red and hot, her breasts swollen against his chest.
Her breath came in little gasps, and he could hardly wait
to hear her cry out with pleasure in his arms.

"Anne, come with me." His own breath was so ragged
he could hardly force the words out. "Upstairs. We'll hardly be missed."

"No—"

"Yes!" He caught her shoulders. Staring down at her,
he could see the naked longing in her eyes. "I'll give you
anything you desire, more than you dreamed."

"Ruel, the game—"

"To hell with the game. I want you."

"Blackthorne? Are you out here?" It was his brother.
Lord Alexander stood in the doorway, squinting in the
darkness. "The guests are going, Blackthorne."

"Damn it, Alex, go and wish them off yourself."

He walked unsteadily toward them, his face pulled into
a frown. "What are you doing? Making love to the
wench?"

"She's my wife. I'll do what I like with her."

"Will you? Sire little whoresons with her, then? Jeopardize the duchy?"

Ruel clenched his jaw. "Go inside, Alex. You've had far too much to drink."

"I won't allow you to do this!"

Anne backed up against a pillar. The marquess grabbed his brother's arm. "This is not your affair, Alex."

"But it is. Do you think I'll stand by while the duchy passes from one bastard to another?"

"Get out!"

"Swear you'll not touch her!" Alex's face went red as he took a step toward Anne. "She's nothing but a housemaid. A conniving little whore."

"Stand back from her, Alex."

"Look at her." He jerked Anne into the moonlight. "She's common. She's nothing. You can bed anyone you like in this damned town. Spread your mongrel seed from Soho to Belgravia. But not her, Ruel." He shook Anne hard. "Not her."

"Take your bloody hands off my wife." He pushed his brother's chest. "You're too drunk to know what you're saying. Let her go."

"You claim to care so much for the duchy. Do you mean it? Will you keep our bloodline pure? Swear you won't sleep with her."

"He's already taken that vow," Anne said, tugging her arm from Lord Alexander's grip. She lowered her voice. "It was my understanding that you have known from the beginning about your brother's plan for the lace industry, sir. I believed you understood the purpose for this journey to London and then to France. Have you not grasped that your brother's advances toward me are merely an imposture?"

"Well, I . . ."

She looked at Ruel. "You did make me a vow of celibacy, did you not?"

His eyes narrowed as the significance of her action sank in. "I did."

Turning to Lord Alexander, she gave him a small smile. "There you have it, quite publicly presented. Your brother will not, as you say, sleep with me."

"You don't want him?"

She regarded Lord Blackthorne for a moment. Tall and dark, he awaited her answer as intently as his brother. Yes, she wanted him. She ached for him. His hands on her flesh, his mouth covering her lips, his words of passion tingling the skin of her ear . . . she craved him. *I'll give you anything you desire, more than you dreamed.* What had his avowal meant? What would it be like to be taken by this man . . . to be folded in his arms . . . to know his body? He had called her his wife, and she was. But not really. Not forever.

"What I want, Lord Alexander," she said softly, "is of little consequence. It has never mattered to you or to your brother what I think or how I feel, but only how I can be of use to you. If you learn nothing else about me in the short time I shall be your sister, know this one thing, my lord. I am not an object to be used."

"Dash it, where do you get off making a speech to me?"

"Only a warning." She took a deep breath. "The next time you encounter me, you will do it with deference. I am the future duchess. I am also the key to your brother's plans. Moreover, I am beginning to understand certain unhappy qualities of your character. Qualities that would not serve you well were they noted by those presently too blind to see them."

"What?" His head swiveled toward his brother. "What's she blathering about, Ruel?"

Anne regarded both men. Shaken by her own temerity, she could barely control the tremble in her hand as she lifted her skirt. "Furthermore," she said, taking a step toward the fair-haired man, "you will never again refer to me as a whore, nor to your brother as a bastard. You condemn your entire family with such insults.''

"Do I, now?''

"You do.'' She set her face to the door and lifted her chin. "Excuse me, gentlemen. I shall bid farewell to our guests.''

Eyes burning, she hurried back into the drawing room. It was bad enough to be called conniving and common, to have her unborn children labeled whoresons, to be regarded as impure and a fornicator . . . but to know that even now she felt aroused and breathless from the kisses of a man who toyed with her as a pawn on his chessboard . . . how awful! How hopeless and weak she was.

As she moved from one powdered face to the next, kissing cheeks and bidding empty farewells to people who despised and envied her, it was all she could do to hold back tears. The last of the gathering stepped into the hall, and she started for the corridor. To bed, to sleep, to escape.

"Anne!'' Claire caught her hand. "Oh, my darling Anne, I must tell you how well you looked tonight and how handsomely you answered every question and comment. You really are too charming.''

Anne bit her trembling lip. "Thank you, Claire. How good of you to say so.''

"Sharks, they are,'' she whispered, leaning closer. "A great school of wicked, biting, hungry sharks.''

Anne sniffled. "Y-yes. They are.''

"Oh, dear, are you gravely wounded?'' Lady Eagon slipped her arms around the younger woman and clasped her tightly. "I pray not. You were magnificent. Utterly astounding in the face of it all. I don't know how you held up.''

"Th-thank you, Claire.''

Her sister-in-law pressed a silk handkerchief into Anne's hand. "There now, you must rejoice in your victory. Dry your eyes, and hold high that lovely chin.''

Anne dabbed the corner of her eye. "Without you beside me at dinner, I should not have endured. You were more than kind to speak on my behalf. It is no wonder to me that your brother adores you so profoundly."

Claire studied the floor for a moment. "Ruel is precious to me. More precious than he knows."

"I think perhaps he does know. He told me you were more a mother to him than his own mother."

"Did he?" Her blue eyes filled with tears. "Oh, did he?"

"Was it wrong of me to tell you? I had no intent to speak ill of the duchess, only well of you."

Claire shook her head. "It's quite all right. You must understand that Ruel's birth was . . . unexpected. After five daughters, for my parents suddenly to have another baby in the family, and a boy at that, was . . . unusual. By that time, my mother was no longer young. My father had given up all hope of an heir to the duchy. As you may have seen, he dotes on Puggy."

"And your mother?"

"Anyone will tell you the duchess was not well for a very long time after the baby's birth. For more than a year she confined herself to isolation. I believe she blames him—quite wrongly, of course—for the difficulties that ensued with his birth."

Anne tried to understand, though the thought of rejecting one's own child for any reason was all but incomprehensible. "When Lord Alexander came along, I assume the duchess had accustomed herself to childbearing once again. And to the idea of sons."

Claire looked away. "Yes. Though she has never loved Puggy as she ought. And he knows it." Letting out a breath, she took Anne's hands. "That is why, my darling sister, I am delighted he found you. I feared my brother would never experience acceptance and genuine adoration. He wandered for so many years from one woman to another, from one adventure to another. He was aimless and unhappy. He drifted, making a shallow sport of life itself. But when I observe him with you, Anne, I see at last in his eyes true passion. True joy. True love.''

"Oh, Claire . . ."

"Say nothing. Merely know how greatly I esteem and admire you.'' She squeezed Anne's hands. "Love him, dear sister. Love him with all your heart.''

Anne fought the hard lump in her throat. How could she go on deceiving this generous and noble woman? What would poor Claire think when she and the marquess dissolved their union? Oh, it was too horrible.

"Good night, sweet Anne.'' Claire pressed a soft kiss on her cheek. "Until tomorrow.''

Anne stood staring after the older woman as she left the drawing room to join her husband in the foyer.

"Tell me about Mr. Walker, Vera.'' Still distraught over the evening's events, Anne stood before a tall gilt-framed mirror in her bedchamber. "I saw you bidding him good night in the corridor just now before you came to attend me.''

Vera untied the pink ribbon beneath her mistress's bodice and began to undo the row of tiny buttons at the back of her gown. "I'm sure I can't imagine what you mean to imply, Lady Blackthorne. The blacksmith accompanied me in the same carriage on the journey to London, and through our conversation we became civil acquaintances.''

"Civil acquaintances! Oh, Vera, don't patronize me. This is Anne Webster you're speaking to, not some marchioness with her nose so high in the air she can't see what's going on beneath her own chin. You fancy him, and I sense the emotion is mutual.''

"Do you prefer the rose-scented dusting powder or the lavender, my lady?''

"Vera, really!'' Turning, Anne took her friend's shoulders. "You must tell me. When he looks at you with those great brown eyes of his, you blush as pink as a carnation. Did you learn to love him as you rode to London together?"

"It's not me you should concern yourself with. I stood near you all evening at dinner and in the drawing room. The marquess could not keep his eyes from you. He worshiped you! I don't wonder why, with you dressed in this lovely gown of pink ribbons and roses, but really, Anne, you must think what you're going to do about the man. You are legally married to him, and he's besotted with you."

"I'm glad you believe so."

"Annie! Please tell me you can't mean to regard this marriage seriously. The marquess's ardor for you will never endure. He's a rake."

"You needn't concern yourself, Vera. The marquess's attentions are nothing but a ruse. Before we left Slocombe we agreed to an imposture. Everyone is to believe my husband loves me violently, though of course he doesn't. I'm to fawn over him as though he were the King of England." She tossed her evening gown on the bed. "No one in London must suspect our marriage is a sham, because the marquess wants his plans for the future of the duchy kept in utmost secrecy. No suspicions must be aroused, Vera. We must always appear to be young newlyweds madly in love."

"I could not believe it more myself."

"Good, and you mustn't betray the truth about us. For all you know, the marquess and I truly do adore one another and are intimate as husbands and wives must be."

"Will you be intimate with him?"

Anne stopped unlacing her slippers. Remembering the moment when Ruel had held and kissed her, she let her eyes drift shut. Did he truly desire her, as he'd said? Or was that part of the imposture, too? Either way, she must do nothing but continue to turn him away. Mustn't she?

"Annie?" Vera took the slipper from her hand. "Will you be intimate with the marquess?"

"Of course not." She banished her imaginings and focused on reality. "I cannot abide the man. He ridicules and mocks me. He pushes me about and questions my virtue. He is stubborn, demanding, and disputatious. I have warned him not to touch me, or I shall reveal his schemes to the authorities."

"Anne! How very bold of you."

"Careful is a better word." She tugged the ribbon from her hair. "Are you being careful, Vera?"

The slender maid picked up a comb and began working through her mistress's long hair. "Mr. Walker is . . . wonderful," she said softly. "He's very kind and gentle."

"People do not treat him well."

"That is their loss."

"The Duke of Marston abhors him—"

"While Mr. Walker has nothing but kind words for the duke. He regards the duke as his savior. In fact, I have never heard him speak an ill word of anyone."

"Then you do love him, Vera?"

"Yes." She clasped the comb to her breast and shut her eyes. "I love him, Annie, I love him . . . and nothing will come of it."

"Why do you say that?"

"He's more than twice my age."

"Does it matter?"

"I think it does." She shook her head. "Mr. Walker has been badly wounded in his life. There is a great emptiness in him, a sorrow so deep I can never touch it."

Anne sank onto her bed. "It's the loss of his homeland. He loved America, and he was taken from it."

"Perhaps. But as you said yourself, people have used him ill. I cannot believe the root of his pain is caused by anything other than human cruelty. What can one scrawny young serving girl like me do to overcome that?''

''First of all, you're lady's maid to a marchioness now, a position that gives you esteem, power, and value in everyone's eyes—including his. Second, it is your abiding love for Mr. Walker that will overcome his pain. My father always preached that love has the power to destroy or the power to heal.''

''Did he now?'' The voice from the doorway drew the attention of both women. ''Most ministers I know hold forth on hellfire and damnation.''

Vera let out a squawk, grabbed a combing gown from the bed, and tossed it to her mistress. Anne yanked the filmy garment up to her throat and made a vain attempt to cover her corset and petticoats with the swath of silk and lace.

Lord Blackthorne's face softened into a wicked grin as he strode into the room. ''Hellfire and damnation, indeed,'' he said.

*T*en

"HOW ENCHANTING YOU LOOK THIS EVENING, MY DEAR wife."

Ruel studied Anne's face as he walked toward her. Her almond eyes, tilted up at the corners, glittered like sapphires in a pool of clear water. Enchanting? Wickedly delectable was more like it. He could just make out the lacy upper edge of her corset and the swell of her breasts rising above it. Pale and velvety, her fair skin begged for his touch. Her hair, loose from its pins, tumbled around her shoulders like a cascade of dark whiskey. Her full lips beckoned.

"You have no need to act your little drama here, Black-thorne," she retorted, pursing that damask mouth in the most naively seductive manner. "This is no drawing room, and Vera is privy to our secrets."

He glanced at the slender maid, vaguely recalling she had been Anne's friend when both women worked at Slo-combe. Vera had been the one to run to Tiverton for help when they'd been shot on the road, had she not? Flushing bright pink, the young lady had backed so far into a corner it was a wonder she didn't vanish into the wall altogether.

Nothing to worry about from that one, he decided. She didn't have the temerity to use the secrets of the highborn to her advantage. It was his wife he needed to keep his eye on.

As he had climbed the stairs to his rooms that evening

after the gathering, it occurred to him that he might use Anne's innocence to his advantage. Were she truly a trollop, as his brother had implied, she would never succumb to a severe case of infatuation. Were she accustomed to the easy dalliances of his society, she would not likely believe herself—or him—to be in love.

But his wife was a minister's daughter. Shy. Untouched. Pure. If she became convinced she had fallen deeply in love with her husband, she would be nothing more than a lump of clay in his hands. He could mold her as he wished. He could take her wherever he liked and coerce her into laboring at his lace venture for as long as he wanted. And he would never have to fear her betrayal. Women in the throes of romantic passion, he had been given to understand, would do anything for their beloved.

As he approached her, a stain of color spread from her neck into her cheeks. It would be more than a little enjoyable to make this woman his. Despite her heartfelt avowals to the contrary, she did want him. And he wanted her.

"You may go," he said, dismissing the little maid.

"Stay, Vera," Anne countered, holding out a hand to stop her. "I have not concluded my toilet."

The young woman's eyes grew round and frightened as she glanced from her mistress to her master. Ruel squared his shoulders. "You may go," he repeated. Then he lowered his voice. "Should you wish to retain your position in my house, miss, I suggest you obey."

"Yes, my lord. Of course." Eyes darting to Anne one last time, Vera grabbed her skirts and fled. As she shut the bedroom door behind her, Ruel tugged the knot from his cravat.

"Obedient," he said. "I like that in a woman."

"Have you something important to say to me, Blackthorne?" Anne gripped her combing gown tightly and hiked it an inch higher until the knot of fabric was jammed against her throat. "It's late, and I'm scheduled to go calling at seven houses in the morning. I should very much appreciate my privacy.''

''What happy manners you have, my lady. Mrs. Davies certainly taught you well.''

''And you poorly. You failed to knock. You did not announce yourself. You drove away my lady's maid. And you have continued to stay when you are not wanted.''

''Am I not wanted?''

She glanced away, but only for an instant. ''As I told you, I'm fatigued. If you have something to tell me, say it quickly and be gone.''

Determined to stay until he had begun his successful seduction of the young lady, Ruel walked across the room to a window, drew back the heavy drapes, and peered outside. He had resolved to know what her true feelings were toward him—and to see that she acknowledged aloud her growing passion. Equally important, he wanted to discover what it was about this glorified housemaid that so intrigued him. Was it those blue eyes and that tiny waist of hers? Was it her saucy conversation that amused and challenged him so? Or was it the bright spark of her obvious intelligence that drew him?

''You have a charming prospect of Grosvenor Square from this room,'' he said, setting one knee on the window seat. ''Did you know I used to sleep in this room when I was a little boy? These quarters were the nursery in those days. I would sit in this window for hours watching carriages come and go, studying ladies and gentlemen out for their promenade, spying on housemaids as they flirted with policemen and vegetable boys. What do you think of town, Anne?''

When he looked at her again, he saw to his dismay that she had managed to slip her arms into the white combing gown and tie its pale blue ribbon at her throat. Gone was his wicked temptress. She looked chaste. Ethereal. Angelic.

Damn.

He had come into the room intending to make her his conquest. Now she looked like a creature from heaven, not some silken vixen awaiting his touch. A minister's daughter. How could he seduce that?

She glided slowly across the carpeted floor and joined him at the window. Peeking between the drapes, she studied the lamplit city.

"I prefer the wilds of the Midlands," she said in a soft voice. "Through my curtains in our little rectory in Nottingham I watched butterflies dance above yellow primroses and saw hedgehogs scurry through the fern. I memorized the songs of the blue tit, the wood pigeon, and the wren. Bumblebees in the knapweed and ladybirds on the dandelions fascinated and charmed me."

"Bumblebees and ladybirds?"

"Do you know," she said, turning her blue eyes on him, "that I see lace in the commonest things? In the spiral of a cobweb . . . in the white blossom of a hawthorn shrub . . . in the curls of a small green moss on a gray stone. Sometimes I think I'm quite mad."

He couldn't hold back a smile. "You have a gift."

"Not a very useful one . . . unless you're a marquess with grandiose dreams."

"Which I am." He pulled his cravat from his neck and unbuttoned the top button of his shirt. "Do you believe I want only to make use of you, Anne? You implied as much tonight with my brother."

"Have you any other purpose?"

He focused on the window again, remembering his plan to make a conquest of her. More and more often, he was finding it easy to scheme while alone in his chamber—and impossible to carry out his plans in the presence of this woman. She was too good. Too gentle. Too damnably moral.

"No," he said, standing suddenly. "I have no purpose other than the plan we made. Perhaps I am using you in my commercial venture, but no more than you have used me to accomplish the release of your father.''

"My father! Have you had any report of him?"

"A note from the barrister I engaged. Nothing new."

"I see." She sank down onto the window seat.

Annoyed with himself and with her, he started for the door. "Look, I must apologize for my brother's behavior tonight in the garden. Alex can be quite revolting when he drinks."

She had tucked her knees beneath her chin and was staring out the window. Her gown draped in a puddle of white silk on the floor. "It must be very hard for you to be so unloved."

"Unloved? My dear lady, I have been loved a great deal more ardently than you, I should think. I believe my reputation with women preceded my own person into the kitchen on that very first day we met."

Her focus never left the window. "I do not speak of physical passion. I believe true love has little to do with the body and far more to do with the spirit. The soul is the repository of love, and without love the soul withers and dies."

Religious gibberish. Romantic nonsense. Frowning, Ruel had the sudden urge to take his little zealot straight to bed and teach her how very much the body did have to do with it. She sat there so smugly virtuous. What did she know about the world?

"I never think about anyone's affections or disaffections toward me," he said, taking another step toward the door.

"Do you not?" She laid her cheek on her arm and observed him. "Then I fear you are more empty inside than Mr. Walker."

"Empty? Good Lord, what gives you that idea?"

"Claire."

He rolled his eyes. What had his doting elder sister gone and done now? "Claire tended me when I was a baby. She married the Viscount Eagon the year after I was born, and I saw her rarely after that. My sister hardly knows me. And what gives you to think Walker's life is empty?''

"Vera. She spoke with him at length on the journey to London. They rode in the same carriage." She narrowed her eyes at him. "Tell me, Blackthorne, do you observe nothing?"

"I see the important things."

"Yes, your great financial schemes and capital adventures. What about the people around you?"

"I avoid people when I can. Unfortunately I've been surrounded by them all my life. I endure their mincing and gossiping and preening until I'm nearly ill from it. Only in America was I ever able to escape such posturing—and then but briefly. In general, people annoy me, Lady Blackthorne. Especially those who labor on and on in conversation of little consequence."

As though she hadn't heard him, she continued in her soft, magnetic voice. "There are those people around you whose characters run deep. Some of them love you. Others despise you. You would do well to find out which are which."

"Your character runs rather deep, I should think. Tell me, do you love me or despise me?" When she didn't answer, he smiled. "Well, Lady Blackthorne, which is it?"

"If by this time you do not know my feelings for you, then you are far more blind than I thought." She stood and faced him, her soft gown swirling at her stockinged feet. Lifting that delicate chin, she narrowed her eyes at him. "I pity you. You are friendless and loveless, and your soul is blacker than the night outside this window. I find you self-centered, disputatious, and immoral. I dislike you very much."

He leaned against the door frame and studied her. Damn it, why couldn't she be like the other women he knew—

moldable and silly, eager for baubles and about as visionary as clams.

"Then you despise me," he said.

"I dislike you . . . but I cannot despise you."

"If you cannot despise me, then you must love me. In your grand speech moments ago, you left no other option." As he spoke, Ruel walked toward her. The blue light in her eyes changed from defiance to uncertainty to dismay. All her bold words to the contrary, she was afraid of him. Afraid of the emotion he evoked in her. And her fear gave him power.

"In fact, I believe you do love me, Anne," he said, advancing on her. "You find me intriguing and intelligent. In spite of yourself, you are curious about me. You admire my brashness and my disrespect for Society. You are attracted to my bold tongue, my sense of foresight, and my enterprising nature. It is you who would wish to save me from myself. It is your love that you would have fill my empty, black soul."

He stopped a breath away from her and stared down at her upturned face. "Am I right?"

"No."

But her eyes said yes. He searched them, awed by the intensity of need that he saw in their depths. This was not a woman he could toy with and then cast aside. Her love really might fill his soul . . . fill it up . . . and overflow it . . . and possess him.

"Dear God in heaven," he whispered. "You frighten me, Anne Webster. You frighten me as much as I frighten you."

"Go away, Ruel. Please." Her voice held a husky note that transfixed him. "Go now, and leave me in peace."

She took his shoulders and pushed him through the door. When she had shut it, he stared at the blank wood until he heard her singing softly in the next room. It was a hymn.

* * *

After reading her Bible and saying her prayers, Anne lay in her bed for nearly an hour watching the moon rise through the open curtains. London. Grosvenor Square. A marchioness. What had become of her?

She hadn't worked on lace in weeks. She hadn't seen the inside of a kitchen or scrubbed a floor or brushed crumbs from a tablecloth in ever so long. She had traded the happy chatter of the servants' quarters for the sniping and back-stabbing of the upper class. She had exchanged bowls of hot oatmeal and hearty roast beef for hare soup and ragout of duck. She had given up the silly flirtations of vegetable boys and fishmongers for a man whose desire simmered openly in his eyes.

And what of Vera? If only Anne could relinquish this enormous, overstuffed bed for her narrow cot in the upstairs room with her best friend. How cozy that had been, all the young women chatting after dark and giggling over this and that. Happy hours of making lace by the window . . . lighting candles in the corridors . . . arranging bouquets of fresh flowers in the drawing rooms.

Anne sat up in bed and threw her combing gown over her shoulders. Vera would understand. She just had to. Vera had always given such clever advice. Maybe she would know what to do about the marquess and his magical kisses.

Aware that the full moon would cast enough light in the corridors for her to see her way to the servants' quarters, Anne elected not to light a candle. She stepped into a pair of soft slippers, pushed her loose hair over her shoulders, and peeked through the doorway. The corridor was deserted. Shutting the heavy door behind her, she crept down the hall past the marquess's chambers, edged around a corner, and finally tiptoed up a short flight of stairs and through a green baize curtain.

"I came when I found your note in my room."

The male voice was only paces away, and Anne froze in

surprise. A chill washed down her skin. The hour was much too late for anyone to be about.

"Thank you for coming. I felt I had to speak with you."

A woman! Anne backed through the curtain and stood breathless on the other side, certain her heartbeat could be heard a mile away. Was this a tryst? A lovers' assignation? But who were the speakers?

"It is not wise to meet in secret," the man said. "You are a married woman now, and I—"

"I couldn't help myself. I had to see you alone."

Anne leaned against the wall and shut her eyes. She knew those voices. But who? Could the man be Blackthorne? His voice was similar—deep and resonant.

"Are you well?" The woman's words were soft and fearful.

"Well enough. You?"

"I'm all right. Everything has become common now . . . the routines of life."

"Yes."

"I would never do anything to hurt anyone. I hope you understand that. I simply . . . I wanted to talk to you."

"I do understand."

"Do you . . . do you ever think of me?"

Knowing she should go, Anne found she could do nothing but stay, her back pressed against the wall and her breath shallow. It was wrong, she knew, for these two to meet in such a way. It was secret and shameful and probably a terrible sin. What if the man were her own husband—caught up in an affair of the heart?

Yet she could hear the torment in the voices of these two lovers, and for some unexplainable reason she responded to their pain. The agony of their separation drifted over the surface of every word they spoke.

"I think of you every day," the man said in his graveled voice.

The woman sniffled. "Not a morning passes that I don't

wonder about you, pray for you . . . long for you.''

"Don't say that! Please.''

"But it's true. I've done what I had to do, and I'll go on doing as I must. But my heart . . . my heart . . .''

"My own heart is dead.''

"Dear God!''

The woman was openly weeping now, and it was all Anne could do to hold back her own tears. Who were they, these forlorn, lost, and hopeless lovers? She carefully drew back the edge of the curtain.

"Will you take me in your arms again?'' the woman sobbed. "Only for a moment?''

"If I touch you, I will die.''

"I can't bear it! I can't bear another minute. To live the rest of my life and never know . . . never touch you again . . . never have your love.''

"You have my love.''

The two figures stood in deep shadow. Anne could see only that one was tall, the other much smaller, with long, shimmery hair. They were separated by mere inches, yet neither touched the other.

"I shall love you until the day I die,'' the woman whispered through her tears. "You must never, never forget that. You must promise me you will always know of my love for you.''

The man let out a low groan of smothered anguish as he swept the woman into his arms. When their lips met, Anne dropped the curtain and collapsed against the wall. How terrible. How wonderful. How hopeless.

Anne knew she would never know love like that, such depth of passion. To think that these two had experienced it—and lost it . . .

Was the man Ruel? Whom did he love? She must be some woman from his past . . . some great beauty who had married another. Perhaps her marriage had taken place when he was in America . . . or when he was believed dead.

Now everything made sense. Ruel had felt no serious qualms about relinquishing an untainted future in order to marry—and later divorce—an impoverished little housemaid with no family ranking and no dowry. *I never think about anyone's affections or disaffections toward me*, he had told Anne.

Of course he didn't. *My own heart is dead*, he had said to the woman in the corridor. The marquess's true love was married to someone else, and to her his heart would always belong. And now Anne understood the facade he wore at all times. Every flirtation was a sham, every sweet word a lie.

Yet how could she hate him? His love for this woman was so pure . . . and so impossible.

"Never again." The man pushed back the curtain and stepped into the corridor as Anne pressed into the shadows. "We cannot."

He ran through the hall to the stairs. Never looking back, he vanished down the narrow passageway. In a moment, she heard a door shut in a corridor somewhere below. No doubt it was the door to the chambers of the marquess.

Eyes closed, Anne rested her head on her arms. The abandoned woman had sobbed softly behind the curtain for a long time. Anne had listened to the mournful sound as the sleeve of her own gown grew damp. And then the woman had sighed, sniffled one last time, and slipped away.

Anne's legs felt stiff and cold when she finally moved. Her wild impulse to fling herself into Vera's arms and pour out her heart to her best friend had faded. Her dismal lot in life was nothing compared with the utterly hopeless future of her husband. *I have been loved a great deal more ardently than you*, he had said. To live forever in love with a woman he could never have . . . what worse fate could there be?

Perhaps only one. To be married to such a man.

Anne brushed her fingertips over her cheek as she crept down the stairs. What a great muddle she had made of her life. What an equally great fool she was. How could she have thought Ruel's kiss in the garden held any real ardor? Worse, how idiotic to have responded to that false passion with feeling of her own.

She had melted into his arms and shivered at his touch. For longer than an eternity she had drifted in rapture. She had actually been deceived by her own charade! How stupid!

Not only had Lord Alexander believed his brother was making love to Anne . . . not only had all the company gathered in the drawing room believed it . . . not only had Vera believed it . . . but Anne had believed it, too! What a buffoon she was.

She stepped into her room and shut the door behind her. The air felt stuffy and humid, so cloying she thought she might be sick. Stepping out of her slippers, she walked to the window and opened it. As she gazed down into the square, she thought of Ruel's words to her not long before—the way he had portrayed himself as looking down on the grand comings and goings of this great city. He had seemed gentle then, almost like the little boy he had described. But all the while he had been thinking about the note he had discovered in his room . . . about the tryst he would have later in the dark corridor . . . about another woman.

"Sleepless?"

Anne sucked in a breath and whirled around. He lay on her bed, his great gray eyes luminous in the moonlight. "Ruel! But you . . . I thought you were—"

"Awaiting your return? I was." He cocked his arms behind his head on her high white pillow. "Perhaps you might share with me your whereabouts for the past half hour."

"I was in the corridor . . . on my way to see Vera."

"Vera?"

"I . . . I wanted someone to talk to." She met his even stare. He wasn't behaving the least bit lovelorn. In fact, the man seemed his usual cocksure self. "And you, my lord? Where were you this past half hour?"

"Here, of course, wondering what my wife was up to."

"Ah, yes. Of course you were." She sat down on the window seat. He would say nothing about the woman and their forbidden love. She might use such knowledge against him.

"I remembered something I'd forgotten to tell you," he said, his voice light. "As you know, in less than a fortnight, the Season will be under way. Everyone will be in town, and we'll have hardly a moment for private conversation. Anyone of significance in the military, most of the peerage, and usually the Regent himself spend the evenings attending one or more balls. The most influential gentlemen in England go to these dashed things, and our own presence is crucial. So is our performance."

"Performance."

"It will be our labor to convince Society of our undying love," he said, coming to his feet. "We must be as one. Husband and wife."

Anne held her breath as he walked toward her. Still dressed in his half-buttoned white shirt, sleeves rolled to the elbow and collar loose, he loomed huge and dark in the moonlit room. His curly black hair spilled over his brow and onto his neck. His eyes never left her face.

"There are things you should know about me," he said.

She nodded. "Yes, my lord." Please let him tell her about the woman tonight . . . now. She could bear the ruse much easier this way. "I understand. Tell me everything."

"Tongue. I loathe it."

"What?"

"Pickled, boiled, garnished with Brussels sprouts—no matter how it's prepared, I won't eat tongue. Can't bear the stuff. You should know that about me. Turnips. I never touch them. Head cheese. I find it revolting.''

"Head cheese? But . . . but the corridor . . .''

"I like rum and port.'' He began to pace. "Wine and whiskey are suitable. I never touch champagne. I'm partial to gingerbread nuts with my tea—''

"What are you talking about?''

"Me, of course. If we're to convince everyone of our love, we must know about one another. Turkish delight and treacle are particular favorites, and I'm fond of trifle. I like my coffee black, my tea the color of caramel, and my toast piping hot. You?''

Anne swallowed. This wasn't at all what she'd expected. What about the woman in the corridor? The tears . . . the anguish . . . the unrequited love? And now he was speaking of tongue and Brussels sprouts!

Worse, he had stopped his pacing and begun walking toward her. His black hair was silvered by the light. His gray eyes drank hers. "Anne,'' he said, his voice husky. "What do you like?''

"Everything,'' she said quickly.

"Everything? How fascinating.''

She gulped down a bubble of air. "Except eels. I despise eels.''

"Do you sugar your tea?''

"Two lumps.''

"Coffee?''

"I don't drink it.''

"Your favorite color is . . . pink.''

Remembering the dress she'd worn that night, she had to smile. "Hardly. blue.''

"Green for me. The color of the Atlantic Ocean off the coast of Florida. My favorite book is Chaucer's *Canterbury Tales*. Yours is—''

"The Bible.'' Their words overlapped, and he chuckled.

"Of course it is. Tell me, Anne, have you ever read Solomon's song?''

"I heard a sermon on it once. My father says that book is a dramatic interpretation of Christ's love for the church. Christ is the bridegroom, and the church is the bride."

" 'Let him kiss me with the kisses of his mouth,' " Ruel murmured in a low voice. " 'His left hand is under my head, and his right hand doth embrace me.' "

"It's meant to be symbolic."

"Symbolic? I should like to hear your father interpret this: 'Behold, thou art fair my love; behold, thou art fair; thou hast doves' eyes within thy locks . . . Thy lips are like a thread of scarlet, and thy speech is comely . . . Thy two breasts are like two young roes that are twins, which feed among the lilies. . . . thou hast ravished my heart—' "

"Stop!" She put out her hand and pushed at his chest. "It's sacrilegious."

"I'm only reciting what I read as I waited for you. It quite mesmerized me to think of you alone in your bed, wearing nothing but this little slip of a gown, and reading such intriguing poetry. 'The joints of thy thighs are like jewels,' " he began quoting again, only this time he reached out and ran his palm over her waist and down the curve of her hip. " 'Thy navel is like a round goblet . . . thy neck is like a tower of ivory; thine eyes like the fishpools in Heshbon . . . ' "

He stroked the side of his thumb up her neck. She shivered, paralyzed with confusion. How could he? How could a man so in love with one woman be able to woo another with such ease? He was a rogue. A devil. With his warm breath, magic fingers, and silken words, he wove his evil spells, and she was as susceptible to them as any drunken sailor to a siren's song.

" 'How fair and how pleasant art thou, O love, for delights,' " he whispered, drawing her against him. " 'This thy stature is like to a palm tree, and thy breasts to clusters of grapes. . . . thy breasts shall be as clusters of the vine, and the smell of thy nose like apples, and the roof of thy mouth like the best wine.' ''

His lips covered hers, and what could she do? She had thought of nothing but his mouth all evening . . . nothing but the brush of his rough cheek against hers . . . nothing but his hands rubbing her shoulders . . . and kneading her back . . . and tracing lines down her bodice.

''Wicked man!'' She shoved him away and sank down onto the window seat. Burying her face in her hands, she conjured up the image of that forlorn woman in the corridor—so convinced she had his eternal, undying love.

''You wicked, wicked creature,'' she cried. ''You're a demon. You vowed never to touch me, but you came into my bedroom and attempted the most boldfaced seduction. You misspoke the very Scriptures in your unholy lust! Have you no conscience? You use and abuse every poor, poor woman who falls prey to your charms. You are horrible! Horrible! Go away from me.''

''Anne—''

''No! Don't talk to me. I can't bear the sound of your voice.''

''Anne, I spoke the Scriptures as they were written. I cannot believe those words are some high symbolic portrayal of a holy bond between the church and God, no matter what your father preached. Those words are words of love from a man to his bride. Words of desire.'' He knelt beside her and took her hands away from her eyes. ''Wanting the man you married is not wrong. It's no sin to desire your own husband, Anne. Passion and ardor—if you can believe Solomon's song—are sacred.''

''Passion and ardor! Bedding every creature in skirts, as Lord Alexander said? That's not sacred! That's . . . that's sinful!''

''I cannot deny my past. But I never took what wasn't offered.''

''You are disgraceful.''

"Anne, look at me."

"I can't. You repulse me."

"I entice you."

"You're repugnant."

"Tempting."

"Lies!" She grabbed the shirt fabric on his shoulders and squeezed it into fists. "Lies!"

"Truth." He leaned forward, taking her mouth again, pushing her against the window. "Love me, Anne. Love me."

His fingers slid into her hair as his lips roved over hers. Tears squeezed from the outer corners of her eyes as she thought of the forlorn woman . . . the hopelessness of loving such a man as this. And yet even as she thought such things and wept over them, her fingers slipped apart, and she took his shoulders in her hands. She let him kiss her neck with feather-light brushes of his mouth, let his lips nudge at her ear, let him lay her across the window seat.

"Anne, I have wanted you from the moment I heard your voice," he murmured. "The way you wove that magic tale for the little girl in the kitchen. A duchess, you called that child. I wanted to make you my own duchess. I wanted to know the touch of fingers that could make lace as you make it. Touch me, Anne."

When she wouldn't, he took her hand and stroked her fingertips down his own neck. As they ran between the edges of his shirt, she felt the smooth, firm muscle of his chest. She shuddered from the unexpectedness of it and pulled her hand away.

"Please," she whispered.

But his hand had found the side of her breast, lifted it, cupped it. He buried his face in the gathers of her combing gown, and nuzzled the sensitive skin between her breasts. Anne held her breath, unable to push him away as his hand tugged apart the tiny silk ribbons and slipped onto her bare skin.

"Anne, don't be frightened of me," he murmured against her cheek. His mouth covered hers again, drawing every shred of resistance out of her body. When she felt his tongue stroke across her bottom lip, she arched upward from the sheer pleasure of it.

"Tell me you want me." His hand molded over the fullness of her breast, gently squeezing. The tip of her nipple hardened as he nudged it between his fingers. "Tell me, Anne. Say the words."

"Ruel, I . . ."

His kisses drifted from her mouth to her cheek to her temple. "Say it, Anne. I won't take you unwilling. You must want me as much as I—" He stopped and kissed her temple again. "Your hair is damp. You're crying."

Lost in the rapture of his touch, she could do nothing but push her breast upward into his hand. "Oh, Ruel."

He pulled away abruptly and looked down at her. "I've made you cry."

She looked at him. "And more."

*E*leven

"WHY ARE YOU CRYING?" RUEL STUDIED ANNE'S FACE in the moonlight. Beautiful, and good, and far too pure, she was beyond him. He assumed he might seduce her if he wanted. She had responded . . . and would respond to his touch until he had won her into his bed. But suddenly he didn't want it. Not that way.

"The woman," she whispered, brushing her temple where the tear had fallen. "In the corridor . . . I thought about you and . . . all those poor women who have loved you . . ."

"You weep for me because of my past—my black soul, as you put it? Yes, I've known other women, but . . ." Damn it all. How could he explain that those encounters had been nothing? Youthful gallivants, that's all. And nothing to feel particularly proud of, especially when he looked into Anne's blue eyes.

"To make a woman believe you care for her," she was saying, "to convince her she's the only creature you desire . . . that your heart belongs only to her . . . and then to . . . to . . ."

"But you *are* the only woman—"

"No!"

"No." Ruel jumped to his feet, sweat breaking out across his brow. "No, you're quite right about that. I don't know why I said it. Good Lord, what's come over me?"

He wiped a hand behind his collar. Had he lost his mind? Telling her she was the only woman in his life. Insane. He'd gone insane. Three years without a woman in his bed would do that to a man. Three years was a hell of a long time. Too long. But his travels hadn't left time for liaisons, and on the journey he had met no woman he cared to bed. No wonder he was acting the fool over this creature in her white gown and blue eyes. He needed a good romp.

"Please, Ruel," she whispered. "You mustn't play with women's hearts. If she loves you truly, a woman will be loyal to you no matter what happens. She will hold the candle of her passion for you through separation and obstacle and the passage of countless years. Nothing will snuff it out. Nothing."

"I don't want that." He turned away, unable to face her. His words were a lie. For the first time in his life, he did want that. He craved a woman's passion, her commitment, her faith in him through the years. He wanted someone to weep over him and laugh with him. He wanted it all. And he wanted it with Anne.

"Damn it, woman." He swung on her, finger outstretched. "You will make lace, and you will pose as my wife, and that is all. Do you understand?"

"Yes."

"You will not talk to me about watching hedgehogs from your bedroom window or dreaming of moss on gray stones. You will not gaze at me with those great blue eyes and lecture me about passion and love. And if I am called upon to woo you in public, you will not respond with anything but sham emotion. Do you understand that?"

"I understand perfectly." She stood and set her hands on her hips. "And should I discover you slipping into my private quarters, or lying in my own bed, or laying me across my window seat and kissing and caressing me, how am I to respond then, Lord Blackthorne?"

"I assure you, those things will not happen again."

"I am greatly relieved to hear it. Then will you do me the honor of leaving my presence so that I may restore my dishabille?"

"Gladly."

He walked to the door that joined their suites. She watched him go, his broad back so familiar to her now. She had touched that back, stroked those shoulders, known the pressure of that body against hers. The ache spreading through her chest hurt so deeply that she clutched her arms tight around herself.

Go away, Ruel. Go away and don't make me want things that can never be between us. Even if you were not a rake and a libertine, a liar and a tormentor . . . even if there were no other women . . . I am only a temporary bride. I am only a housemaid, and one day you will be a duke. Even if all the other things that separated us were to vanish, that will hold us apart forever.

"Good night, Lady Blackthorne," he said, turning in the open doorway.

She lifted her head. "I'm only Anne."

He leaned a shoulder against the frame. "Good night, then, Anne. My lady."

Their eyes held until the door shut between them.

"You slept with him, Annie!"

Vera's squawk dragged Anne out of the depths of sleep. She squinted at the sunlight pouring through the open curtain. What time was it? And what on earth was Vera screeching about?

"You slept with the marquess!" she repeated, staring in horror at Anne. "Here are his cravat and his shoes and his coat! Right on the floor by your bed. And his own bed was still made this morning. Unrumpled and perfectly flat! Everyone's gushing about it, of course, wondering when the first little heir will make his appearance. Oh, Annie, how could you? Really, how could you?"

"What are you going on about, Vera?" Anne edged up on her elbows and stared down at the clothing on the floor.

"I hope you know you'll be cast out into the streets. You'll become nothing more than a trollop! What future will you have? Don't think he'll keep you just because you've borne him a son. They don't. They cast their mistresses aside like so much dirty laundry. Oh, Annie!"

"Vera, stop it at once." She swung her legs over the side of the bed and slid to the carpet. Crouching, she picked up the dark gray coat and the pale cravat Ruel had worn the night before. "This is not at all what you think. The marquess was lying on my bed waiting for me when I—"

"Lying on your bed! Oh, then it's true. We must get you away from London at once. We'll run down to the vegetable market this morning and beg you a ride on one of the carts going back to Nottingham. You can hurry home and pray you've not conceived a child by him. And if by some miracle—"

"Will you be quiet, Vera, and stop your blabbering." Anne tucked the coat and cravat under her arm. "The marquess wanted to speak with me last night, and he waited for me here."

"In your bed?"

"Yes. He was reading the Bible."

"Oh, Annie, you're a dreadful liar."

"It's the truth," she retorted, aware of Vera's disrespect for her mistress but thankful they finally could speak as friends. "Nothing happened between us, Vera, believe me. You've let your imagination run away with you. All the same, you must encourage people to go on thinking the marquess and I sleep together, and you must urge them to speculate about an heir. It can only be good for his enterprise. In the meantime, have no trepidation on my behalf. I would never give myself to such an untrustworthy man as the marquess, and I should hope you have more faith in me than that.''

"But he sent me out of the room to be alone with you . . . and I saw the way he was looking at you all night . . . the way he follows you with his eyes and how he was kissing you in the garden—"

"It was a ruse. I told you that already. Really, Vera, when will you start believing me?"

"I'm so frightened you'll accidentally be seduced by him."

"Oh, please. The marquess is a cad. Of that I have incontestable proof. Late last night after the house fell silent, I heard someone in the corridor. A man."

"It was Mr. Walker."

"Walker?"

"I heard him go out of his room and come back only much later. Hours perhaps. And then he was so distraught he paced all night."

"Walker?" Anne repeated dully.

"I confronted him about it this morning. He was startled at first to know I had heard him, but I reminded him his room is just below the servants' quarters. When I assured him I had not followed him but had only thought of him and been concerned as to his temperament, he was much relieved. He told me how unhappy he is in this house, and how very much he wishes he had never left Tiverton. He said he had walked out his restlessness in the corridors, but even so, he is thinking of leaving London."

"Walker was in the corridor?" Anne sat down on the bed. "I thought the man was Ruel."

"The marquess was about last night, as well. I had just crept downstairs to look in on Mr. Walker when I saw him. The marquess appeared most unhappy. Most distraught. I think perhaps you had just rejected him, Anne."

"It wasn't my rejection that disturbed him," she said.

"He was leaving another woman. A mistress. I inadvertently overheard their conversation in the corridor. My husband loves someone else—or at least she loves him. Their parting was most pathetic."

"Are you quite sure it was the marquess you overheard? Perhaps it was Mr. Walker."

"How could it have been Walker? Those in the corridor were two people most violently in love. The only woman Walker loves is you, Vera."

"Me? Do you think so?" She flushed a bright pink. "Oh, I don't know. He's so very remote."

"He's deep."

"I won't deny that." She thought for a moment. "The man you heard—could it have been Lord Alexander? He was in the corridors last night."

"Good heavens, was no one asleep?"

"I hardly think so. You know how these houses are in the Season. People creeping up and down the stairs, passing love notes in the pudding, meeting in the gardens for a roll in the grass—"

"Vera!"

"It's quite true. Once everyone arrives for the Season, you'll have any number of men after you, Anne. You mustn't be so naive. All summer long, these lords and ladies play the most wicked games of adultery. They are hardly better in their country houses in winter. I should think what you overheard last night was nothing at all. A mere episode in someone's repertoire. Give it no more credence than you should—it was a warning to you. Men will pursue you. The marquess will pursue you. And if you don't want to end up selling your body on the corner of Tottenham Court Road, you'd do well to keep your mouth shut and your bedroom door locked."

Vera lifted the lid of the teapot and peered inside. Her soft, open demeanor faded, and her face went stiff as she reassumed her role. "If you will excuse me, Lady Blackthorne, I shall return to the kitchen to fetch a fresh pot of hot water for your morning tea.''

''Thank you, Vera.''

''Yes, my lady.'' Sweeping the tray of cold breakfast into her arms, Vera hurried to the door. ''When you have eaten and dressed, madam, your carriage is waiting to take you on your morning calls.''

Anne watched the door shut behind the little maid. She studied the rumple of clothing in her arms. Had Ruel been in the corridor with another woman? Or had he been lying on her bed waiting for her all that time? Were his kisses merely the common dalliance of a man accustomed to ''wicked games of adultery''? Or were they born of genuine feeling for her?

It was all too confusing. As she stood to begin her toilet, Anne lifted the bundle of his clothes. The faint whiff of spiced rum and cedar drifted under her nose. Burying her face in the folds of rough, tweedy fabric, she drank in the scent.

How much better is thy love than wine! And the smell of thine ointments than all spices! The words of Solomon's Song of Songs—words she had read for so many hours last night alone in her room—came back to her. *Thy lips, O my spouse, drop as the honeycomb; honey and milk are under thy tongue; and the smell of thy garments is like the smell of Lebanon. . . . Make haste, my beloved, and be thou like to a roe or to a young hart upon the mountains of spices.*

''Two lumps as always, my dearest?'' Ruel held the silver sugar tongs over Anne's teacup.

''Thank you, darling.'' She tried to keep her hand from shaking as she stirred her tea. It was the first time they had been together among so few people since that night she had heard him in the corridor. Or thought she had. Two weeks had passed—two miserable weeks of paying calls and re-

ceiving calls, of going to parties and giving parties, of curtsies and gossip and innuendo and slander.

Now Anne's beloved mother had come to call on her
daughter and new son at Chouteau House on Grosvenor
Square. In the past week, Mrs. Webster, the children, and
all their belongings had been transported from the rectory
in Nottingham to a large, quiet house in London. The
house, of course, was owned by the Chouteau family, and
the Websters were provided for by mysterious funds delivered by a footman each Monday morning promptly at nine.
The baroness Lady de Winter had not abandoned the Webster family; she insisted on spending the first week in town
helping the parson's wife settle into her new quarters.

The four of them were seated beside a large window in
the drawing room, a prospect of sunlit summer gardens
stretching out beyond them. The round table had been laden
with scones, clotted cream, strawberry jam, and all manner
of tiny sandwiches and tarts. The baroness, adrift in the
scent of rose water, rustled with purple silk and countless
rows of Nottingham lace. Mrs. Webster, small and timid in
such grand surroundings, perched like a little brown wren
on the edge of her chair.

"Thank you, Annie," she whispered when her daughter
offered her a petit four. "Lady Blackthorne, I meant to
say."

Anne smiled, wishing to heaven she could throw herself
into her mother's arms and tell her everything. "You're
quite welcome," was all she could manage. "Lady de Winter? A petit four?"

"Thank you, my dear. Ah, delicious!" The baroness
continued to speak between bites of the small iced cake. "I
must tell you, when I first received intelligence of the love
match between darling little Annie Webster and the Marquess of Blackthorne, I could hardly believe such happy
tidings. To see you risen from such dire, dire circumstances
to this grand a height of opulence is most rewarding to me,

my dear. How pleased I am to have played but a small part in your happiness.''

"Lady de Winter," Anne said quickly, "your role has been anything but small. I shall never forget that you preferred my father to the parish before anyone ever dreamed the ensuing events might lead me to such a station in life as this.''

"Quite true." The elderly lady's face folded into lines of pleasure. "Such happy, happy events.''

Anne glanced at her mother and then at Ruel. He had warned her long ago that the baroness was a formidable force in the lace industry of the Midlands. Her employees' smuggling ventures had been undertaken with great derring-do. She had been known to export her contraband wares to France in coffins, their lifeless contents luxuriantly swathed like lacy Egyptian mummies. She had even sent dogs wrapped in lace across the forested borders from Belgium into France, where the smuggled wares were unwrapped and sold to the aristocracy. Lady de Winter's coffers boasted the rich results of her success.

The night before this tea, Anne had received a cryptic letter from the marquess warning her not to mention his own plans for smuggling lace-making machinery into France. Further, he had cautioned her that the impression she made on the baroness—more than on any other person in Society—would count toward his success or failure. No matter that her own mother would be in the room, Anne was not to drop for a second her facade of true love for the marquess.

"You may recall," Anne went on, determined to make the most of the situation, "it was you, Lady de Winter, who sent a letter of recommendation to Slocombe House on my behalf. Without your backing, I should never have met the Duke of Marston or have come to be introduced to his charming . . . gallant . . . generous son.''

"Indeed, we are eternally grateful to you, Lady de Winter." Ruel took one of Anne's hands in his and rubbed his fingers back and forth, heating the skin beneath her glove. "My marriage to this beautiful woman has made me the happiest of men."

"And you, Anne . . . Lady Blackthorne," Mrs. Webster asked softly. "Are you happy?"

"My goodness . . . well, of course." She tried to smile. Vera had told her she was a terrible liar, and never had Anne felt it more than now. Gazing into her mother's blue eyes, a mirror of her own, she felt sure her every emotion was written plainly on her face.

"Your daughter and I have a great deal in common, Mrs. Webster," Ruel said, slipping his arm around Anne's shoulders. "Though it is quite true we come from very different backgrounds, we immediately discovered wonderful threads of similarity in our interests and avocations. Did we not, my sweetness?"

Anne glanced at him. He was too close, too warm. He smelled of cedar and spice, and she felt dizzy and faint from it all. "Yes," she fumbled. "Of course."

"Really?" Mrs. Webster was staring at her daughter. "I cannot imagine that. What sorts of things do you have in common?"

When Anne couldn't respond, the marquess filled in. "We're both avidly fond of the out-of-doors. Anne has told me all about the quaint prospect from her bedroom window in Nottingham. Hedgehogs scurrying through the knapweed. Wood pigeons and blue tits in the hawthorn tree. Curly moss on that . . . that . . ."

"On that gray stone. You know the one I mean, Mother?"

"Near the oak tree?"

"That's it," Ruel said with a triumphant grin. "The gray stone near the oak tree."

Mrs. Webster laughed in relief. "I almost feel as if you've been there, Lord Blackthorne."

"So do I. Your daughter has such a way with words."

"And what else?" Anne's mother asked. "Do tell us the other things you enjoy in common."

Ruel glanced at Anne. She had paled to an ashy white. "Food," he said quickly. "We have similar culinary likes and dislikes. Neither of us can bear eels."

"Eels?"

"And . . . and two lumps of sugar in our tea. We both like that, though Anne won't drink coffee, and I won't go without it in the morning. She prefers blue, and I like green, but what of that? They're only colors, aren't they?"

Mrs. Webster stared at her daughter. "You both like the out-of-doors and despise eels. Anne, have you made a marriage on nothing more substantial than this?"

"Not only those things, Mother." She squeezed Ruel's hand, trying to think of something. "My darling husband and I both adore . . ."

"The Bible," he said.

"The Bible!" The baroness dropped her spoon. "Lord Blackthorne?"

"I've become an avid reader."

"He can quote entire passages," Anne put in.

Ruel couldn't hold back a chuckle. "Yes, I'm quite the scholar."

"I'm happy to know that." Mrs. Webster stirred her tea. "Anne's father will be more than pleased when I write to him. My husband has been most . . . most distressed at the turn of events."

"Distressed? Mrs. Webster, my wife is a marchioness, a ranking of no little power, wealth, prestige. What better fate could you and your husband wish upon your daughter?"

"We're grateful, of course, for your backing in all our affairs. But you must understand that our daughter's happiness is of great importance as well. Our Annie is . . . well, Annie is special." Mrs. Webster lifted her chin in exactly the manner of her daughter. "Lord Blackthorne, if I may be so bold as to ask . . . do you know anything of my daughter's talents in the design and making of lace?''

''Anne is a genius. I am deeply in awe of her skill and artistry.''

''Is that so?''

''Indeed. You might like to know that I carry a bit of her work with me at all times.'' He slipped his hand into his pocket and drew out the panel of lace Anne had hoped to sell to his brother. ''Can you see the family crest in the center? My wife designed this as a gift for our wedding.''

Anne sucked in a breath as he turned the lace this way and that. He carried it with him, the scoundrel! The delicate scrap shivered as she reached for it.

''Ruel, darling, may I see that?''

He gave her a quick kiss on the cheek and stuffed the lace back into his pocket. ''Anne is always thinking how she might rework it. I consider this lace a masterpiece, and I'm not about to let her touch it.''

''How lovely,'' the baroness said, beaming. ''How very sentimental and charming of you, Lord Blackthorne.''

''I hope you won't try to keep Annie from her dreams,'' Mrs. Webster said softly, ''as you keep her from that lace. You do share Annie's dreams, do you not?''

''Some of my dreams have changed, Mamá.'' Anne removed her hand from Ruel's and leaned toward her mother. ''Things are very different for me now. You must try to understand.''

''But you always had so many dreams—a head filled with them! You dreamed of a lace school of your own. You always wanted to teach others your patterns and your techniques. You talked often of marrying a man you could love forever, as I love your father. You wanted to live with him in a small stone house with a fireplace where you could sit and make your lace. Dear Annie, have you given up those dreams for grand palaces and golden furniture?''

''Oh, Mamá—''

"And what of children? Has that hope changed, too? Do you no longer ache for handfuls of little ones dancing across the hillsides, playing in the primroses and picking pails of blackberries? You wanted them to run in bare feet . . . swim in the farm pond . . . stand under the thatched roof in the rain . . ."

She wiped her eyes. Her voice was a throaty whisper when she spoke again. "Oh, Annie, did you give it all up . . . did you make this marriage . . . for the sake of your father?"

"Nonsense!" the baroness bellowed. "Lady Blackthorne can have anything she likes. As her husband said, she's a marchioness now and one day she'll be a duchess. What woman would want barefoot children and lace schools when she can have silk slippers and private tutors?"

"Annie did."

"Mamá, please try to understand." Anne fought the lump in her own throat. She couldn't cry. Couldn't. "I'm very, very happy with Lord Blackthorne. I adore my husband. Our future is . . . is . . ."

"Bright and wonderful." Ruel took her arm and pulled her back until he had her safely tucked against him. "We shall have handfuls of children, and they can all run as barefoot as they like. Dear Mrs. Webster, please be assured of my undying devotion to your daughter and all her dreams."

"Yes," the woman said uncertainly.

"My wife's happiness is the focus of my entire being." Concerned that the tea party would end up with both Webster women dissolved in tears and all his plans exposed before the baroness, Ruel rose. He kept Anne firmly ensconced under his arm as he gestured at the table. "Would you like another cup of tea, Mrs. Webster, or must you be going?"

Sniffling, Anne's mother gathered up her bag, stood, and shook out her skirts. "Thank you so much, my lord, but I must be getting home."

"Indeed," the baroness added, rising. "Mrs. Webster's furnishings arrived yesterday morning, and things are all at sixes and sevens."

"We do appreciate the loan of the house, Lord Blackthorne," Anne's mother said, "and all your efforts on behalf of our dear daughter."

After interminable farewell speeches, the baroness and Mrs. Webster were seen out of the drawing room by a waiting footman. The moment the door shut behind them, Anne flung herself at Ruel. "Give me my lace this instant, you beast!"

$\mathcal{T}$welve

ANNE REACHED FOR RUEL'S POCKET. "I WANT MY lace, and you have no right to it. Give it to me!"

He grabbed her wrists and braced his feet to hold her back. "And have you racing back to Nottingham so you can buy a little stone house and marry some weaver who will give you lots of barefoot children? Not a chance."

"What do you care how I live?" She lunged at him, barely missing his face with her nails. "Your little ruse is never going to work! The baroness saw through you instantly. The Bible!"

"Eels!" he scoffed, pushing her down onto the settee.

"Hedgehogs in the knapweed."

"Stop fighting me!"

"Give me my lace!"

"Never. What else do I have to hold you?"

"You have me. I'm your prisoner, aren't I? Bound to do as you tell me, or you'll throw my family to the dogs and let my father be executed or sent away on a convict ship."

"Bound to do as I tell you? But you're failing miserably at that! You can't bring yourself even to pretend to admire me." He pressed her down into the cushions, his face a breath away and his gray eyes crackling. "Look how your mother wept at your piteous declaration. 'I'm very, very happy with Lord Blackthorne.' You might as well have told her I'm torturing you on the rack."

"You are!"

"How? Any other woman would be ecstatic to be married to a marquess—to have countless properties, the prospect of Seasons in London and winters in the country, the finest gowns from the best seamstresses, shoes and jewels and scores of hats. What do you want?"

She searched his eyes, unable to trust herself to speak.

"Do you want stone houses? I've stone houses enough for ten wives. This is a stone house, damn it! Slocombe is a stone house. You can have them both. They're yours. You want to make lace? I'll import two thousand bales of silk thread to keep you and fifty lace schools busy for a hundred years. Why can't you be happy?" He gripped her shoulders. "What do you want?"

"What do you care if I'm happy or not?"

"I care. I need you, Anne." He caught himself, aware he'd said far more than he meant . . . more than he should. "Look, if you're miserable, you're likely to go racing back to Nottingham or blurting my plans to Lady de Winter. You're important to the success of this entire venture. You're . . . you're an ingredient in the recipe. A cog in the wheel, so to speak. Why is it so damned difficult to pretend to like me?"

"Because I don't know you."

"This again? What do you want—a recitation? I loathe tongue, I like the color green—"

"Those things are not you. Any number of men might recite the very same litany." She searched his face. "How am I to go on pretending to adore you when it's clear to everyone we share nothing of the heart? The things that matter in a marriage are not a taste for the same foods or an affinity for the same colors. What counts is a common purpose in life, shared dreams and hopes, a united faith in a mutual creed."

"That is romantic nonsense, my dear lady. My parents have been married for forty-two years, and they share few interests beyond entertaining acquaintances and playing whist. They have no common purpose other than getting through life in the most comfortable fashion possible. As to shared dreams and hopes . . . I can't think they've spoken together long enough at one time to approach the subject.''

"Do they love each other?"

He paused for a moment, pondering. "What difference does it make? Love has nothing to do with the reality of marriage.''

"Does it not?" She studied the hardened, cynical line of his mouth. "My parents taught me by example that when two people are anchored in the same God, and when they place their love for each other above all worldly concerns, they do far more than get through life in the most comfortable fashion possible. They have a deep-burning love, an unquenchable passion, a bond that nothing can sever.''

Ruel looked into Anne's blue eyes as she spoke, and he knew she believed completely in what she said. She had witnessed such true love. She possessed utter faith in the reality of such love. And she had committed herself to sharing such love someday with a man.

He felt suddenly at a loss. He had no idea how to achieve such a pinnacle in life—nor even how to pretend he had. Worse, a curl of envy gripped his chest as he thought of the man who one day would capture this woman's heart and share her faith, her passion . . . her love.

"You told me you want everyone to believe I adore you," Anne said softly. "Then you must wish us to feign a marriage of love, as my parents truly have. I cannot go on pretending—not in the face of my own mother—unless I know something of the depths of your heart. You heard my dreams. What are yours?"

"I've told you already. My dreams are neither romantic nor ethereal. I have only practical goals, those I can achieve through physical effort and the application of my own intellect. I want to save the Chouteau dynasty from financial ruin. I want to establish a mercantile trade with America and France.''

''Then you want to make something from nothing. As do I.'' Unable to stop herself, she reached up and touched a curl that had fallen onto his forehead. Dark and shiny between her fingertips, it entranced her. ''Commerce from bankruptcy. Lace from silk thread. Something from nothing.''

At her touch, a sprinkle of sparks shimmered across his flesh. He looked down at her, sapphire eyes soft and alluring. He could almost swear she was asking him to kiss her. A smile tugged at the corners of his mouth. ''Something from nothing. There, my Lady Blackthorne, we have discovered what we have in common.''

''But I abhor your lace machines.''

''Only because you see life in too narrow a manner. You must open your eyes wide and look ahead. The world is on the threshold of great things. There is power in steam, power we've barely begun to harness. I believe that one day London will grow into an enormous city with factories and commerce at its hub. England perches on the verge of world dominance. Our nation has the potential to become a mighty empire.''

''England? I trust you are jesting with me now. England is nothing more than a tiny, foggy island populated by shepherds and fishmongers.''

''Anne, the world waits at our doorstep. America . . . you should see the untouched treasures there. France . . . and India . . . and China. Even Africa! They'll all be woven together one day by the threads of commerce. I want to be a part of that.''

''You want to make a lace out of the whole world.'' She shut her eyes and leaned back into the settee cushion, envisioning his words woven into a length of the finest Honiton. ''Here is England with her roses and misty moors. Here's China with little footbridges and peonies. Here's

India with mysterious temples and twining cobras. Here's Africa with coconut palms and jewels. And here's America—''

"Wildflowers and oak trees and mighty rivers."

She opened her eyes. "Threads twine and swirl from each continent all meeting at one central motif. The crest of the Chouteau family."

He grinned. "A bit grandiose, is it?"

"Grand, not grandiose. I hope your dream comes true for you." She touched his arm. "Lord Blackthorne—"

"Ruel."

"Ruel . . . when you've harnessed the world with your threads of commerce and woven your empire with machines of steam, I pray you will not forget all the common people who can dream of nothing but the next loaf of black bread they hope to eat."

"People who live in small stone houses and teach at lace schools?"

"All who survive by the labor of their hands. Those who will be ruined by your machines."

As though he hadn't heard her, he stroked his thumb down the side of her cheek. "I will never forget you, Annie Webster. I can't think how you came to haunt me in the first place."

"You stole my lace."

No, he wanted to tell her. *You stole my heart.*

But it wasn't true, was it? He'd never thought he had enough heart to matter one way or other. He hadn't received much love in his life, and he knew he had precious little to give away. So why did this common creature with her almond-shaped blue eyes and her saucy mouth fill his thoughts night and day? Why did it tie his stomach in knots to contemplate the reality of someday sending her into the arms of a Nottingham weaver with a stone house?

"I must go, now, Lord Blackthorne," she said softly,

sitting up and folding her hands in her lap. "Our tea is completed, and I cannot speak with you in peace. You stole my lace, and you made my poor mother weep. You dream of the whole world, whilst I dream only of a home and a family of my own. What you want, I cannot give you. And what I want, you cannot give me."

"Is that true?"

"It is true. And what is worse, the longer you stare into my eyes and hold my hand, the more I begin to forget how very impossible you are and how very much I dislike you." She stood stiffly. "The more I forget how truly abominable you are, the more I want you to kiss me again as you did in the garden. And the more I want you to kiss me again, the more hopeless my future becomes."

"Anne!" He rose and caught her around the waist.

"Good afternoon, Lord Blackthorne," she whispered, pulling away and running toward the door.

It was given out about London that the Marquess and Marchioness of Blackthorne would depart Society for a pleasure tour of the Continent at the height of the Season. For three months, they would enjoy boating along the Rhine, climbing through the Alps, basking on the seacoasts of southern Spain.

Their holiday would begin with a short stay in Brussels. It was common knowledge that every fashionable English aristocrat was making plans to visit Flanders, and of course the marquess and his wife would want to be there, too. In fact, the London Season quickly disintegrated as more and more members of important Society booked passage for the exciting arena of Europe. After all, in the past two months Napoleon had been declared an outlaw, and all the sovereigns of the Continent had agreed to unite forces against him. No one wanted to miss out on the possibility of such an exciting campaign.

Assuming that all political upheaval was settled in France

by early September, Lord Alexander would then wed Gabrielle Duchesne, daughter of the Comte de la Roche. The Duke and Duchess of Marston would journey from Devon to Paris for the happy nuptials, and then all the family would return to England together for the start of winter and the foxhunt season.

Anne counted the days until she could depart London. She made a list of every ball and party she had to attend, and she crossed them off one by one. With utmost effort, she slowly reduced the barbs of Society's dowagers to brief snide remarks, and she managed to make civil acquaintances of more than one of the young wives who hadn't yet skipped away to the Continent. It was impossible to say she had friends. Vera remained Anne's only confidante, and she dreaded the thought of ever separating from her.

Shortly before the marquess and his party were to depart for Brussels, Anne returned from a round of paying calls to discover a note on her dressing table. Picking up the letter, she recognized the dark, bold script at once. It was dated that morning.

"My darling Anne, I shall be visiting several properties in the country the next two days, as I told you last night. How dreadfully I shall miss you!"

Anne frowned. Properties in the country? The marquess had not mentioned anything of the sort the night before. In fact, they had dined at opposite ends of a huge table in a long, mirrored hall at the home of Lord and Lady Something-or-other. Later, she had been compelled to dance with so many different men she'd hardly laid eyes on her husband. This letter was clearly not intended to be private. The marquess expected its contents to have been read and spread about by the household staff. She scanned the page again.

"In preparation for our journey to the Continent," he wrote, "I have had your trunks sent out to various clothiers in Town. I hope you don't mind, darling. I took the liberty of ordering a substantial number of items for your wardrobe. I'm sure you'll be pleased.''

Pleased? She didn't need new clothes. She already had more gowns than she could wear. What on earth could this mean?

''Your trunks will be returned to you locked, but please don't fret, my sweetness. I do so want you to be surprised when you see what I've selected for you, and I am determined to be on hand to observe the happy alteration in your countenance. The thought of the light in your blue eyes will keep my heart in eager anticipation of the moment when I shall hold you in my arms once again. Until then, my pet, do think of me often and remember how very much I adore you. Your loving husband—B''

Anne stared at the letter in confusion. Properties in the country. Clothiers in Town. Locked trunks. It must have something to do with their planned journey. But what?

Determined to discover at once the meaning of the letter, she debated whom to approach. Lord Alexander, of course, would know everything his brother had planned. But the thought of meeting privately with the foppish young nobleman held no satisfaction whatsoever. Anne knew she could expect insult from him at the very least. He might even attempt to seduce and humiliate her, as he had in his rooms at Slocombe House. Lord Alexander considered his brother's wife nothing better than a whore, and she knew she could never trust him.

Mr. Walker would know Ruel's plans, as well. She would find him and bluntly ask the meaning of the message. If anyone could be depended upon to speak the truth, it was Walker. Anne pulled a white muslin pelisse over her soft blue-and-white-striped dress and hurried out into the corridor. After the housekeeper and the butler said they hadn't seen Walker for hours, Anne went down two flights of stairs to the library.

From that room she knew it was possible to see all the back garden, the kitchen garden, and part of the drive. If Walker were anywhere about the property, she probably could spot him through the library windows.

Anne pushed open the door and stepped into the room. Instantly she realized the curtains had been drawn apart no more than half a foot, and a slender, silhouetted figure stood peering between them.

"Excuse me?" she said softly.

"Oh!" Claire, the Viscountess Eagon, whirled around and dropped the curtains. She flushed bright red, as though she were a child caught with a finger in the pudding. "Who's there?"

"It's Anne. Lady Blackthorne. Forgive me for startling you. I was looking for someone."

Claire exhaled. "Puggy's away touring properties. I spoke with him at breakfast this morning just before he went off. He said he had left a note in your room explaining the circumstances of his absence."

"Yes, he did." Anne walked toward the window. "It's not my husband I'm seeking. Have you seen Mr. Walker today?"

"The blacksmith? Perhaps he went with Puggy."

"I don't think so. The housekeeper told me she'd seen him here in the library reading several hours ago."

"Here?"

Just as Anne stepped around the viscountess and took hold of the curtain, it occurred to her she might find someone hiding behind it. Someone Claire very much did not want her to see. Someone tall and dark. Someone who had spoken of love in a corridor and had held a small, weeping woman in his arms . . . this woman, perhaps.

It was too late.

She grasped the curtain and pushed it aside before she could stop herself. There was nobody behind it.

Anne let out a breath of relief. What if a man had been

there? What if it had been some illicit lover? How dreadful to have discovered such a thing. She must learn to be more prudent.

"It's bright outside, isn't it?" she commented, dropping the curtain quickly. "Perhaps Mr. Walker went for a stroll. Vera tells me he is partial to daily meanderings along the Serpentine River. She believes the summer verdure of Hyde Park and the beauty of the river must put him in mind of America."

"Vera?"

"My lady's maid. I believe some measure of affection is growing between her and the blacksmith. She tells me Mr. Walker speaks more and more often of his homeland these days. Vera thinks—"

A sniffle stopped Anne's words, and she realized Claire had begun dabbing her eyes. A wisp of golden hair had escaped her cap and lay on her shoulder in disarray. Her shawl, a lovely scrap of lace with long fringes, dropped to the floor at her feet.

"Have I distressed you with my chatter, Claire?" Anne asked, taking her hands. "I know I'm running on about nothing. The amours of a lady's maid and a blacksmith are of no consequence to a woman such as yourself. Having come alone to the library, you certainly wanted privacy. Please believe I never meant to cause you a moment's unhappiness."

"You mustn't mind me." Attempting a smile, the older woman tucked her handkerchief inside her cuff. "I believe I'm becoming quite the sentimental fool. I find things . . . difficult these days. So very difficult."

"Is your husband not well?"

"The viscount could not be in better health. No, it's . . . it's . . ." Her face crumpled again. "It's Puggy, I suppose. I feel I've only just gotten him back, and he's off again. I do dread these long absences."

Anne nodded. "You had such a fright the last time he

was away. Rumors of his death must have dismayed you terribly.''

''Yes, and now . . . now he'll go off again with you and Alex and . . .'' She pulled out her handkerchief and blotted her cheeks. ''. . . and Mr. Walker and everybody. It's a great deal for me to bear.''

''You must come with us, Claire. Bring all your children and your husband, too.'' Anne squeezed the poor woman's hands, all the while wondering what on earth she was saying. Claire couldn't possibly accompany the party to Europe. They were smuggling lace machinery—

Lace machinery! That's what was in her trunks. Of course. How could she not have known at once? But how appalling to carry the unassembled loom in her own trunks! What if the parts were discovered there by authorities? Anne herself would be accused, of course. She would take all the blame.

But that must be the very reason she was to carry the equipment. The marquess would never allow himself or his brother to be discovered smuggling. Were his common, ill-bred wife to be caught, she could fall to her doom with little discomfort to anyone. After all, her father was already in prison. Such intelligence could be put about Society as a perfect excuse for Anne's illicit activity. ''Her father is a Luddite, you know,'' she could hear them whispering. The marquess could cast her off as easily as a snake sheds its skin.

''You've gone quite pale, Anne,'' Claire said, touching her arm. ''Do sit down and let me ring for tea. I'm afraid I've upset you with my tears.''

''No, it's something I've just thought of. Something . . . dreadful.''

''Really? Has it to do with my accompanying you on your tour?'' Claire seated Anne in the leather sofa near the window and sat beside her. ''I cannot go with you, you know. The viscount and I could never be away from our home for so long. Teddy has properties to oversee, tenants to look in on. The children would not do well on such an extended journey. And I ... well, I have to manage the household, of course. No, I won't come. I'll ... I'll let him go." She bit her lower lip and dabbed at her eyes. "I shall let him go once again, as I always must."

Anne watched in a daze as the sobbing woman did her best to dam the river of tears pouring down her cheeks. Claire was miserable, but Anne knew no one could possibly feel as terrible as she did at this moment. What was the temporary absence of a brother? Nothing compared to the reality of that very man's willingness to betray his own wife.

"I must go," Claire whispered.

Anne put out her hand. "Are you well?"

"I'm all right. I should be quite accustomed to his absence. Everything has become common now ... the routines of life." She tucked her handkerchief away once again. "Thank you, Anne."

As Claire walked across the carpeted floor, Anne lifted her eyes to the curtains. *Everything has become common now ... the routines of life.* She had heard those words before. In a darkened corridor. Spoken by a woman in a man's arms. A woman in tears.

Anne drew apart the curtains as the slender figure slipped out of the library and shut the tall door behind her. It hardly mattered if Claire had been the woman in the corridor. As Vera herself had said, these aristocrats were forever creeping in and out of bedrooms. Society evenings during the Season often disintegrated into little more than amorous circuses. Anne wanted nothing to do with such immorality, and she was always thankful the marquess chose to depart every gathering at an early hour.

The marquess. Anne studied the long rows of clipped hedges in the garden outside the library window. Ruel really was the scoundrel Vera insisted he was, and Anne must never forget it. Never mind his hypnotic kisses and sensual words. Never mind his warm hands and hungry looks. He was a rogue with no more scruples than a common criminal—a man who would use his own wife to smuggle goods and let her take the consequences if discovered.

Vera would smile in satisfaction to know how correct she had been all along. Anne shook her head, then straightened in surprise when she saw that very young woman stroll from behind a hedge onto a patch of green lawn in the garden. The next instant she was joined by none other than Mr. Walker.

"Vera!" Anne gasped.

Bonnet cast aside, Vera threw back her head and laughed. Her hair of pale gold shimmered in the bright sunshine. She stretched out her arms to the blacksmith, beckoning, welcoming. After only a moment's hesitation, he took both her hands. She swung backward, lifting her face up to the sky.

Anne had never seen anyone so beautiful. Certainly not Vera, with her sallow skin and limp hair. This young woman glowed. Radiated. Her cheeks had blossomed into pink roses, and for the first time her pert nose looked perfectly at home on her bright, lively face.

Anne leaned forward on the windowsill, entranced. The blacksmith said something to Vera. She laughed and whirled away from him, lifting her skirts in her hands and spinning in giddy circles like a nymph at a bacchanalian revelry. His own face transfixed, Mr. Walker set his hands on his hips and watched the young woman, a smile softening his dark, craggy features.

"Vera!" Anne whispered. "Vera, is that really you?"

Golden hair flying, the little maid skipped across the grass toward the blacksmith and flung her arms around him. With a look that somehow mingled both sadness and joy, he caught her up against his full length, swung her around, and kissed her gently on the mouth.

"Oh, Vera, you are in love," Anne murmured. "And Mr. Walker is in love with you."

As she let the curtains fall together, she discovered she was crying. She drew her handkerchief from her sleeve and buried her face in it, understanding at last why Claire had wept. It was self-pity, of course, but she could not think how to rise above it.

What could be more hopeless than the certainty that *everything had become common . . . the routines of life*? What could be more numbing than to exist, as Ruel had said of his parents, in a marriage with *no common purpose other than getting through life in the most comfortable fashion possible*?

Anne pressed her handkerchief into the corner of her eye and stared down at her lap. Existence as the wife of the Marquess of Blackthorne, too, offered at its best nothing better than routine and getting through life. At its worst, it might bring her a prison sentence.

There was only one thing to be done. Put all romantic nonsense of her husband into the rubbish heap where it belonged, do her best to maneuver through the coming few weeks without becoming trapped like a spider in the marquess's web of intrigue, and then hope . . . wish . . . pray that somewhere, somehow she might find a true love who would lift her up, swing her around in his arms, and kiss her gently on the lips.

Though fear nearly paralyzed her breath at dockside on the Thames, Anne watched her baggage loaded into the ship's cargo hold without incident. Of course, it hardly mattered if she arrived in Flanders with a lace machine in her trunks. It was not there but in France that both the lace and the looms had been prohibited.

Barely in time to board the same ship transporting his party to the Continent, the marquess arrived from his purported inspection of his properties. By that time, everyone in the group had settled into their rooms. Too angry to confront him about her trunks, Anne avoided her husband at every turn.

The group sailed the short distance across the North Sea from England to Flanders. They then traveled by carriage to Brussels, where they put up in the Gothic fifteenth-century Hotel de Ville near the center of the city. Anne took a large suite next to her husband's rooms, but she could not bring herself even to dine with the man. Though she would have no choice but to accompany him to balls and parties each evening, she refused to consider spending time with him alone. Instead, she ordered all her meals sent up to her, and she watched the city through her long, open windows.

Brussels. Anne could not have been more filled with wonder had she been escorted into heaven itself. Flanders was the birthplace of lace. Each city's artisans had developed their own special techniques and decorative styles. Antwerp lace, known for its vase-and-lilies motif, was called pot lace. It symbolized the Annunciation, for lilies in a pot were shown often in early illustrations of the visit of the Angel Gabriel to the Virgin Mary. At Bruges, the very best lace cravats were made, and no English gentleman of an aristocratic bent would be without one. The marquess himself owned five, though Anne felt humbly certain that her own length of Honiton far surpassed them. Beautiful lace also was made at Ghent, Mechlin, and Ypres. Anne had heard of a parasol cover once made in Ypres using eight thousand bobbins.

But Brussels . . . ah, Brussels! The best of all Flanders lace always had been made in Brussels. Lacemakers in that city used exceptionally fine thread to work the most delicate creations Anne had ever seen—she had been privileged to witness such lace only twice in her lifetime. The webbing was so fine, in fact, that it was too easily discolored by the workers' hands. To overcome this, each airy bit of handwork was powdered with either white lead or lime.

Anne treasured the hope of visiting lace schools in Flanders, or at the very least speaking with some of the designers and pattern prickers. She mentioned her desire on their second evening as she and the marquess were returning to the hotel after a particularly late ball. He informed her that what little lace still was being made in Flanders was created by nuns in closed religious communities.

"Abandon your interest in lace for the time being," he whispered to her, leaning against her shoulder as they entered the foyer. "The less you are associated with the subject in people's minds, the better."

"Shall I deny the essential quality of my character for your enterprise?" she snapped in return, annoyed that he must always look so handsome and smell so intriguing when she wanted nothing more than to despise him. "You jeopardize my person with your illicit activities. Will you also jeopardize my very soul?"

Turning on her heel, she started up the stairs. He caught up with her and took her elbow. "Anne, what are you talking about?"

"I'm speaking of the lace machine, of course."

"Shh!"

"I assumed we would depart as all proper smugglers do from Devon—that we would leave from Mount Pleasant Inn in the Warren or from Sladnor House near Torquay. I imagined we would slip away from England into France with our cargo secreted on some small boat. Instead we sailed gallantly away from London as though we had no other purpose than a pleasure tour. We're smugglers, aren't we, Blackthorne? And if so, where have you hidden the lace machine?"

"*Will* you be quiet?" He opened her door and pushed her roughly into the room. "Do you want the whole of Brussels to know our plan?"

"*Your* plan."

"Your own life is at stake in this, Anne."

"Thanks to you." She tore off her gloves and flung them on a side table. "Where is the loom?"

"It's better that you not know the exact location."

"And why is that? So I may be properly shocked when the authorities in France open my trunks and discover your machine neatly packed away in my possessions?"

"Lower your voice, please." Suddenly hot, he stripped off his coat and tugged his cravat loose. "What leads you to believe the loom is in your trunks?"

"Is it not?" She walked over to the stacked metal and wood boxes and gave the bottom one a swift kick. "Locked, are they? Filled with a brand-new wardrobe for your darling wife, are they?"

"Did you not believe my letter to you?"

"Not a word of it."

"Of course not." He drew a set of keys from his pocket, pulled one from the chain, and tossed it atop the nearest trunk. "Open it, then."

Anne stared at him. Could she have been wrong? He wouldn't have bought her all new gowns, would he? Of course not. Or would he?

"Open it," he repeated. "Go on, Anne. Open the trunk."

Thirteen

"HAVE A LOOK AT THE GLORIOUS MACHINE I HID IN your trunks," Ruel said, gesturing at the locked chests.

Suddenly unsure, Anne eyed them warily. Pandora's boxes? Would she open them to find beauty and delight in the form of a hundred new gowns—or all the evils of the modern world in the shape of hard, cold machinery? All at once she wasn't certain she wanted to see what was inside at all.

"If the loom is not in my baggage," she asked the man who stood so cocksure before her, "where is it?"

"As I told you, it's better for you not to know." He took a step toward her and slipped his hand behind her neck. Warm fingers pressed against her skin. "Are you frightened, Anne?"

She clenched her jaw against an unbidden shortness of breath. "I prefer to know what is to befall me."

"What is to befall you is nothing more than the Duchess of Richmond's ball. It takes place tomorrow night, the fifteenth day of June, 1815, and it will be attended by some two hundred persons. I feel certain you will look magnificent in one of your many new gowns."

"And after the ball?"

"Another ball. And then, perhaps another."

"I can't bear this game of endless waiting!" She jerked off her headdress of ostrich plumes and diamonds. "I'm suffocating in feathers and silk. When will we go to France?''

"When the time is right. As the daughter of a minister, Anne, you should know better than anyone how little control we have over our lives. No one can really determine his own fate.'' He tilted her jaw upward with his thumb, forcing her to meet his eyes. "We'll go to France when the situation there warrants.''

"Are you the only judge of that?''

"I'm doing what I believe to be right. Please trust me.''

"Have I any choice? You claim we have no control over our lives, yet you control everything about me. You say where I may go and when. You predetermine how I must behave and what I must say. You regulate everything about my existence from what I do each day to how I dress. You even lock my trunks to keep my own clothing from me! I feel as if I'm hemmed in by walls of your construction— a prisoner to your every whim.''

"Far from it.'' His mouth fell into a grim line. "Far from it. Though you may feel confined by our present situation, I am no more able to capture you than a man can capture a hummingbird.''

"You speak in riddles.''

"Hummingbirds are found in America. They're small, very bright, totally entrancing. Their wings move so quickly they cannot even be seen as the little birds hover to sip nectar from red and orange flowers. A man is free to observe them and to be both enchanted and mystified. But to make a hummingbird a prisoner? Impossible.''

Disturbed by his words, Anne found she could no longer meet his eyes. She turned away and went to the window. Was it possible her husband was as tormented as she by this impossible marriage they had made?

Opening the curtains, she looked down on the tree-shaded boulevards and imposing monuments that characterized the city. She had hardly admitted to herself the torture of endless hours in his presence—unable to touch him as she desired, hardly able even to look at him. She felt as though she were burning up inside, like a volcano that had simmered far too long.

How could she endure another ball? He would take her in his arms and hold her tightly, her breasts cresting against the rough fabric of his coat. She would smell that maddening scent of cedar and spice that clung to his skin and clothing. She would hear the rumble of his deep voice inside his chest, feel the warmth of his breath against her ear, and look into eyes whose messages of intense desire belied every glib and careless word from his mouth.

Everything about the man was familiar now—as common to her as her own reflection in a mirror. She knew the exact breadth of his shoulders, knew the solid ripple of the muscle in his arm, knew the curl of his hair at the back of his neck. She knew what made him laugh and what made him angry. She had memorized the shape of his hands with their long fingers, large, strong, and far too brown to be fashionable. She was intimate with the ridge of toughened skin on the inside of his palm where he had labored at some task in America of which he would not speak. The veins that coursed down his arms like narrow blue ropes had held her spellbound. Even the crop of short black whiskers that he daily shaved away were as familiar to her as old friends.

"You asked if I were frightened," she said softly. "Well, I am. I'm terrified."

"Why?"

Could she tell him? Could she admit that her own feelings for him frightened her beyond words? Could she let him know how deeply it had hurt to believe he might have meant to betray her to the authorities with his damnable machine? Could she tell him how she ached at the things that separated them—their conflicting beliefs, their values, their backgrounds? Of course not. She could reveal nothing. She must go on playing their game of charades until he finished what he had to do and could cast her aside.

"Anne?" he asked, touching the bare skin of her arm. "What frightens you? You must tell me."

She swung around, replacing her anguish with anger. "You and your friends continue to play at silly balls and parties as though the arena of war were nothing more than a picnic ground. Everyone in your elegant Society has come to Brussels as they would flock to a cricket match or a game of croquet. Are they so completely ignorant of the potential for violence here?"

Ruel walked toward her, aware he was breaking his own rule for keeping his distance, yet perturbed by her spirit. When confronted by his brother about Anne's nerve and stamina, Ruel had defended her with utmost confidence. The closer they came to the moment of adventure, he had predicted, the more alive and fiery she would become. Anne would plunge into her differing roles with relish and would be a key to the success of their efforts.

Instead, she had grown almost fragile. With moonlight silvering her face, Anne had transformed again into his angel. Her brown hair, caught up in rosebuds and ringlets, tumbled down her back. Her blue eyes searched the stars. Her gown, a wisp of pale violet crepe over a satin slip, clung to her hips before draping softly to her ankles.

If not for the twin scraps of gathered fabric that barely covered her bosom, Ruel might have thought himself impervious to regarding this woman with anything but courtesy and respect. But as he approached, he took note of the shadow that had mesmerized him all evening at the ball. Soft and blue, it slid between the creamy mounds of her breasts and vanished beneath a central lace rosette. The image of sliding a finger down that shadow, of knowing the velvet whisper of her skin, tormented him.

If he came too near, he would hear her words, smell the scent of lavender on her skin, and want to touch her. Want it too much. Did she want him?

Her eyes were luminous as she observed him. Large and blue, they shone with an inner light that held him transfixed. "I do not believe you have known violence, Lord Blackthorne," she said in a low voice. "But I have."

He frowned, unable to imagine it. "Where?"

"You must not forget my father is a Luddite. I observed the secret meetings of his fellows, heard their plans, witnessed the fire of righteous indignation burning in their eyes. I saw those men take their hammers and their axes and rush to the factories. And I saw them when they returned—bloodied, injured, ultimately defeated."

She held her folded hands to her lips, lost in memory. He laid a hand on her shoulder, aware of every small bone, spellbound by the silken warmth of her bare skin. "Anne, I will protect you throughout whatever befalls us."

"So you say. But you must understand that the passion to right wrongs stirs deeply within my own blood. I know what sort of ardor leads to war. I myself feel convictions so strong I would fight to the death to defend them." She lifted her head. "I cannot believe that the forces of Napoleon in France and the companies of English and Prussian troops stationed here in Flanders are willing to lay down their lives for a cause so unworthy as to be made a spectacle of by the aristocracy. For those soldiers and for the people they defend, the issues at stake have nothing to do with balls and parties. These are men who would kill and die for what they believe. We are wrong to treat their cause so lightly."

"Do you understand their cause, Anne?"

"I do not, nor do I care to. I only know that to dance blindly into the midst of their war as though waltzing through a ballroom is a mistake. To believe we can transport ourselves and our great load of lace machinery across a battleground is foolish. If we mince out into the open country—me garbed in a silk pelisse and satin gown, Lord Alexander in his cossack bloomers and corseted waist, you in your tall hat and polished boots, we shall be cut to pieces, and we shall deserve it.''

She was right, of course. Why hadn't he expected her to see through everything? Again, he had failed to give Anne's wisdom and insight the credit they deserved. This woman was no giddy debutante. Like the hummingbird, she was aggressive and fearless in the face of attack. She had witnessed violence, she understood it. She would never passively allow herself—or anyone else—to be injured senselessly.

''I made you a vow on our wedding day,'' he said, taking her shoulders. ''I swore to protect you, Anne, and I will.''

''You have made me far too many vows—few of which you have kept.''

''What promises have I broken?''

''You swore if I married you, you would return my lace. You have not done so.''

Letting out a breath, he turned away and stalked to the trunk. ''If you won't unlock it, I shall.'' He inserted the iron key, gave it a turn, and stepped back. ''Open the trunk, Anne.''

She drifted to his side, curiosity conquering her uncertainties for the moment. Bending, she grasped the heavy lid and lifted. The moment she saw what was inside, she gasped. A gown of fragile blue satin lay draped across a length of white silk. Like nothing she had ever seen, the garment shimmered in the lamplit room. Its low neckline had been edged with delicate white lace, and the puffed sleeves were trimmed in a pale gold fringe. From the short gathered waist, a divided overskirt of blue crepe cascaded down in luxurious folds. And carefully stitched to the very center of the satin slip, in prominent view, lay . . .

''My lace!'' She caught up the dress and hugged it to her bosom, her dark mood suddenly vanished. ''Oh, it's the most beautiful gown I've ever seen!''

"It's blue."

"So it is!" She laughed in spellbound disbelief. "You had my lace worked into the gown! I can hardly believe it!"

"I couldn't very well go traipsing into France with a panel of elegant Honiton in my pocket, now could I?" He grinned. "Besides, it is your lace, and I promised to return it to you."

Beside herself with delight, Anne danced across the room to the tall gilt-framed mirror in the corner. "It's splendid. It's magnificent." She laughed again, turning this way and that with the gown held in front of her. "And . . . yes, it is a soft sky blue! My favorite shade. Oh, my lord—"

"Ruel." He shoved his hands into the pockets of his breeches to keep himself from taking her in his arms. "You must call me Ruel."

"Just look how the fabric sets off the lace. It's perfect. I might have created it for this very gown."

"I'm pleased you like it."

Her cheeks glowing, she smiled at him. "Thank you. Thank you for the gown, and thank you for keeping your vow to me. I felt sure you would never return this lace. I thought you meant to keep it forever. After all, it does bear your crest."

"And yours."

"Yes," she whispered.

He watched her drape the gown across the trunk again. "Still feeling like a prisoner in a dungeon?"

"I was certain that you had put the loom into my trunks. I believed that if the trunks were opened and the machinery discovered, I would take the blame. I believed you would betray me into the hands of the authorities with little compunction. Now I feel as if I've betrayed you."

Without thinking, he drew two fingers down the length of her arm. "Anne, I must ask you to trust me without question in the days to come." He took her hand and wove his fingers through hers. ''When the moment comes for us to leave Brussels, things may happen very swiftly, and not at all as you expect. I cannot predict each event and its consequence. If I tell you everything I plan, you may fall into danger yourself. There are those who . . .'' The words drifted off as his voice fell.

''What?'' she asked softly.

''You are no fool, Anne. You are aware I have enemies who would rejoice in my downfall and would think nothing of using you to bring it about. It is for your own protection that I must keep you innocent. And protect you I shall, no matter the cost. But I must have your trust.''

Her heart thudding heavily, Anne looked into his gray eyes. He had said she was no fool. Was she foolish to believe his words now? Or did he speak the truth?

''You have kept your vows,'' she replied. ''That is certainly a start.''

''I have not kept them all, and you well know it.'' He fingered a ringlet that curled down her shoulder. ''Resisting the temptation to touch you is quite impossible. I find your eyes alluring and your lips far too sweet. Can you release me from that promise, Anne?''

She held her breath as he trailed the tips of his fingers up the side of her neck. ''To what end?''

''I should like to kiss you again. This time away from the eyes of family and friends.'' He took another step, bringing her lightly against him. ''Anne, may I?''

Yes, she thought. *Oh, please.* But if he kissed her, then what? Then she would want to know the brush of his mouth on her neck. The pressure of his hands on her waist. And the delicious magic of his fingers tormenting her flesh . . .

''Yes,'' she said quickly. She had meant to say no, she was sure of it. But his arms went around her and pulled her into the hardness of his body. His hands tilted back her head, his eyes drifted shut, and he kissed her. Lips warm, sensitive, hungry. Hands molding the length of her back, pressing her close and hard. Bodies touching, curves and hollows melded into one silhouette.

Anne drifted. As always, this man smelled of the woods and the exotic lands to which he had traveled. He tasted of wine. His breath came labored in his chest, and she heard her own shallow gasps echo his. She slipped her hands over the rigid muscles in his arms. Yes. Yes, she was glad she had said it. Yes, yes, yes!

And then she felt his tongue moisten the seam between her lips. Oh, heaven. Something burst apart inside her, something damp and hot. Clutching his broad shoulders, she parted her lips and touched his tongue with hers. He let out a low groan and pulled her hard against him. She melted, drowning in sensation as his mouth moved over hers, his tongue probing and tasting her. Invaded, her body willed complete surrender as she met his explorations with searching of her own.

Oh, and his mouth was magnificent! Alternating hard and soft, his lips drew her into a magical realm of rainbows. Her eyelids blocked the moonlight, but still she drifted in colors . . . blue and pale green and damask pink. The fortifications in their war—the ritual, the formal talk, the polite nothings—had been breached. He was inside her. She was in him.

"Anne . . ." He spoke against her open mouth. "Anne, this pretense between us is maddening to me. Touching you, holding you . . . wanting you every day and night. I'm the one who has lived imprisoned."

"No more than I."

"You're my wife . . . my desire . . . and damn the consequences of it."

As he kissed the length of her neck, his lips sending flickers of lightning up and down her arms, she tried her best to remember what the consequences were. She could see the angry face of Lord Alexander . . . the terrified eyes of Vera . . . she knew it must be a mistake to want this man so much.

But the only effects of his kiss that seemed real to her were the shivers that skittered down her spine like marbles. His nose touched the side of hers, his chin grazed her skin. Opening her hands on his back, she reveled in the bunched muscle. She could feel his fingers slipping slowly around her torso, molding her ribs beneath her sheer gown, splaying over the curves of her hips. Wonderful consequences. Magical consequences.

Her knees warm and liquid, she allowed him to form his large hands around the swell of her bottom. As he drank her mouth, he lifted and settled her firmly against him. Minister's daughter she might be, but Anne knew the significance of the hard ridge that pressed so deliciously into her pelvis. Oh, the consequences of that!

Ripples of heat swept through her chest. Her heart slammed against her ribs as she felt her breasts blossom and her nipples tighten. Would he stroke them as he had before? She hardly dared to hope. It had been all she could think of as she lay alone in her bed. That touch, that incredible sweet torture.

"Anne," Ruel groaned, "I have never . . . never in my life . . . desired a woman as I desire you."

He could hardly believe he had said such words, and yet they were true. The way she melted into him, her mouth puffed and pink from his kisses and her slender legs so innocently pressed against his, had lifted him to the peak of arousal. Her firm, shapely breasts pushed against his chest as though demanding his attention. Reluctantly he drew his mouth from Anne's and traced the horizon of her shoulder with his lips. Her skin felt like pure silk as he grazed the low edge of her bodice.

"Ruel." She gasped, clutching his head. "I can't bear it."

"My beauty." He stroked the velvet shadow with his lips. "My succulent treat."

"I can hardly breathe."

"Don't try." Palming the weight of one breast, he nudged it upward until the bud of her nipple peeked out from her bodice. Heaven, she was magnificent. She threaded trembling fingers through his hair as he kissed her bare breast, suckled it lightly, nicked it with his teeth.

"Oh, Ruel!" She knotted her fingers around his hair, lost in the display of lights that sparked on and off behind her eyes. He thumbed her bodice off its tenuous perch on her shoulders, and the fabric sighed like a fallen flower around her waist. With a tug, he stripped it away and cast it to the floor.

"Stay with me, Anne. Don't be shy." He lifted her chin and forced her to meet his eyes as his hands worshiped her body. "You are my wife. That I desire you cannot be wrong. That I touch your flesh can only be right . . ."

"I'm a maiden," she whispered.

He looked into her blue eyes and understood for the first time what those words meant to such a woman as she. A maiden. Untouched. Sealed. She had never cast herself lightly into any man's bed. That she even considered giving that gift to him tore at his heart.

"Anne," he ground out, "I will never take what you cannot freely give."

As he spoke, his thumbs roved in errant circles around the pink buds of her breasts. She could hardly think beyond it. Hot velvet ribbons ran deep in the pit of her stomach, pulling and tightening until she could hardly breathe. Her back ached, and all she could think about was the unbearable, unbidden dance of her hips against his. Flooded with fire, she felt as though she had melted inside, like a dripping, waxy candle that would never burn out.

"I cannot reason," she managed. "My mind has completely ceased to function."

He smiled as he kissed her. Her tongue slid recklessly into his mouth, and she gripped his shoulders. Driven by the unexpected force of her passion, he cupped her buttocks and rocked against her. He nudged her legs apart and inserted his thigh between hers, cocking it firmly into her warm nest.

Again, she gasped. "Yes!" As her head fell backward and her body began to sway, he realized she had given him her answer. Yes, she wanted him, would have him at any cost.

Sweeping her into his arms, he let out a moan of disbelief. "Anne, my Anne."

Her arms entwined his neck, and her mouth drank his as he carried her to the bed. She covered her breasts with her hands, whether in shyness or out of a desire to know the majesty of her own arousal he did not know. It hardly mattered. In moments, he had stripped away his own clothing and the remainder of hers.

"Anne, look at me," he murmured as he stretched out against the length of her naked body. "Look into my eyes. Know what you offer and who I am that you give it to."

"I know." She smoothed her hands over his body, marveling in the hard muscle beneath the satin smoothness of his skin. "I know you, Ruel Chouteau, and I cannot think beyond the heaven of your kisses and the silver in your eyes. I want you . . . please."

It was enough. He drenched her mouth with his kisses, demonstrating with his tongue what he would do with his body—caressing, dipping, plundering, tormenting, ultimately pleasing. Her hands flowered on his skin as though she were weaving a lace, moving here and there, setting his flesh on fire with her quick, light touch. A sheen broke out across his forehead as he struggled to wait . . . wait . . . wait until she was ready.

He teased her nipples with his fingertips, tugging and circling them until she was writhing with need. And then he smoothed his hand down her flat stomach, molded the powder puff of tiny dark curls, and tested the sweetness of his untouched bride. As his fingers stroked and feathered her, she began a hypnotic dance across the bed, her hips swaying to an ancient music.

"Ruel," she panted, "Ruel, Ruel, Ruel," as though his name had become a part of her breath. "I don't know what is . . . I'm afraid I shall . . . I can't bear to . . ."

"Let us enjoy one another, my lady." Cradling her head, he looked deeply into her eyes as his knee spread apart her thighs. "This is the touch only my wife shall know."

He allowed his body to take the place of his fingers, stroking and lifting her upward into the stars that danced over her head. She arched back in pleasure. As her arousal poised on the brink like a butterfly at the lip of a flower, he came into her. She held her breath as he breached the fragile barrier of her maidenhood.

"Wife," he whispered again. "My wife."

He stroked her deeply then, eager to know her completely, to possess her wholly with himself. The moon cast silver beams across them as she brought her legs up to grasp him tightly. They swayed . . . swam . . . danced across the galaxy. When she was certain her body would fragment into a thousand silken shreds, he grew still and rigid, staring entranced and heavy-lidded into her eyes. And then he shuddered. As his seed spilled into her, she tumbled over the falls in a crashing, exploding arc of lights.

The cry that was torn from her throat echoed through the deep growl in his chest. Damp and sinuous in release, their bodies rocked together, limbs twisted and fingers twined. Their skin seared together, melting them into one flesh. When the undulations eased, they lay panting, gasping for breath through parched throats and swollen lips.

"Dear God," Ruel muttered, and the phrase held more reverence than any words Anne had heard fall from his lips.

She licked a fine line along his shoulder, and he drew a

matching pathway down her back. For long moments, neither could speak. Anne drank in the scent of male satisfaction on his skin, her nostrils flaring with the utter sensuality of it. She brushed her nose against the ruffle of his hair and tasted the salty tang of his skin. He was magnificent. A wonder. She had never known such majesty in all her life.

"You please me," she whispered.

With a groan, he reared up on his elbows and captured her face in both his hands. "Anne, you cannot understand! You have no idea the significance of such pleasure. What passed between us was . . . it went far beyond . . ." He pulled away from her and rolled up into a sitting position. "Dear God," he repeated, staring blindly at the moonlit sky.

"What is it?" Alarmed, she leaned forward, touching his arm. "What's wrong?"

He looked at her, his gray eyes red-rimmed. Glimpsing again the ethereal beauty of her perfect breasts, tipped with bright, hard buds, he shook his head in disbelief. By heaven, the woman was a miracle. A damned miracle.

He had meant to seduce her, use her, bend her to his own will. Instead he felt certain he would do anything this creature asked. Weakened by her, aching inside for her, he longed for nothing more than the silken pressure of her arms around him and her sweet mouth moving against his. He craved her blue eyes gazing into his the first thing each morning and her magic fingers weaving lace on his flesh each evening.

Damn the lace machine! Damn Alex and his accusations! Damn the entire fornicating, adulterous aristocracy! He wanted this poverty-stricken little minister's daughter in his bed every night for the rest of his life.

"Ruel?" She slipped her fingers around his arm. "Have I upset you?"

"Upset me?" He leaned over her, gathering her hair in his hands and crushing it. "You've destroyed me."

"I'm sorry!" She bit her lower lip. It was all too clear what he meant. It was possible she might even now carry the seed of his child. If the child were a son, his hopes for the future of his beloved duchy would be tainted . . . if not completely ruined. Were his own wife to bear him an heir, he could never cast her off. He might put her away somewhere, but everyone would know the child was his—and must be acknowledged as his heir. His heir . . . with nothing better than a common housemaid for a mother.

Fighting the growing lump in her throat, Anne stared into Ruel's eyes. She had wanted him, craved him, coveted him. Now with her passion she had toppled him. Yet how could she regard the possibility of a baby as anything but miraculous? Their child! Bone of their bones and flesh of their flesh. Could such a creation be anything but precious?

"I intended nothing but your happiness," she told Ruel finally, her voice low. "And my own, of course. I shall never lose faith no matter what this union may bring. My father taught me that all things work together for the good of those who love the Lord and are called according to His purpose. How can I believe that anything less than good will come of our union? We are married in God's eyes, and as husband and wife we both desired what came to pass. Now we shall make the best of any consequences."

He shook his head as he gazed into her blue eyes. The woman was paralyzing. One moment she took him to a higher sexual peak than he could ever have imagined . . . in the next breath she was quoting Scripture. One moment she danced like a nymph in his arms . . . the next she spent clearly reasoning out every action she had just undertaken. She was light and wonder and miracle. She had the mind of an intellect, the body of a sylph, the spirit of an angel.

"Dear God," he said for the third time. He stroked his hand down the side of her face as if he were examining a rare porcelain statue. With the tip of one finger he gently turned her head one way and then the other.

Perfect. To think that such a creature had come into his life . . . at just such a time . . . in just such a way. Perhaps she was right. Perhaps there was a God after all. And perhaps He had planned something good even for such a man as himself.

"We should sleep," Anne said softly, gesturing toward the door that divided their rooms.

"Come, then." He took her in his arms and laid her across the bed again. Nesting her head against the curve of his neck, he pressed her warm body close to his. She was beautiful and good, and she was his wife.

His own wife. Dear God.

Fourteen

ANNE WOKE TO FIND HER BED EMPTY AND THE DAY
half gone. Perhaps what had happened the preceding night
had been but a dream. She hardly knew whether to hope it
had or to fear it had not.

When she moved from the bed, there could be no doubt.
A telling pain tingled between her thighs as she stood and
looked down on the damp bedding. A bright stain had
seeped through the linen. Blood. Her own maidenhood.

She gathered up the sheets, fighting the knot in her
throat. She had been broken . . . entered . . . by him. And
she had wanted it. How she had wanted it. Worse, she
wanted it still.

Anne folded the bedding in her arms and breathed in the
scent of the man she had lain with. It had been wonderful.
Too wonderful. Too perfect . . . until she had seen the look
of dismay in his eyes.

You've destroyed me.

Hearing the echoed refrain of his words in her mind, she
rinsed the sheets and proceeded to move numbly through
her day. She bathed. Dressed. Ate. Paid three calls. Took
tea. Changed clothes again. Received five calls. And then
it was time to dress for the Duchess of Richmond's ball.

Anne put on the blue lace-trimmed gown and sat while
Vera arranged her hair in curls and ringlets. During the day
she had turned over in her mind what she might say to Ruel

when she saw him that evening. "Let's pretend it never happened." "Don't worry. Should a baby be born of our union, I shall take care of it myself." "I'm sorry. I never meant to destroy you." "You beast, you've destroyed me." Nothing sounded right. Nothing *was* right.

And then word came that the carriages had arrived, and she was expected downstairs. As she carried her skirts down the long staircase to the foyer below, she could see Ruel engaged in conversation with his brother. His face intense, almost angry, the marquess hammered his palm with a fist. Anne's stomach twisted in unhappy anticipation of the moment she must face him again.

In the midst of Lord Alexander's equally agitated response, Ruel suddenly lifted his head, and his eyes focused on Anne. His grim mouth went slack, the gray in his eyes deepening to charcoal. He pushed past his brother and strode to the bottom of the staircase as he regarded the descending woman.

Palms damp inside her gloves, Anne managed the last few steps without tottering. "Good evening, Lord Blackthorne," was all she could say in spite of her hours of rehearsal. He looked unbearably handsome. Single-breasted black coat with gold buttons, white waistcoat, starched white cravat, black breeches, black stockings, and black gold-buckled shoes—he might have been a king, for all Anne knew. With his black hair and searching gray eyes, he could have swept her away as Sir Lancelot had entranced fair Guinevere.

But Blackthorne was no knight in shining armor. He was an angry marquess who disdained the lowborn wife who might be bearing his child. She must not forget it.

"My lady," he said, removing his tall hat and taking her hand. Before she could descend the final step, he bent and kissed her fingers. "I have never seen you more radiant." He lowered his voice and spoke against her ear as he escorted her across the hotel foyer. "Only once have I seen you more beautiful. Last night."

"Ruel, I—"

"Where's that damned redskin?" Lord Alexander cut in. "The ball began more than an hour ago. Ruel, have you seen the blackguard?"

"Lady Blackthorne," Ruel said in a low voice, handing Anne to his brother, "Alex will escort you to the carriage. I must see what's keeping our reluctant Mr. Walker."

Before Anne could respond, Lord Alexander was escorting her out into the cool evening where a line of carriages stood to receive partygoers. It would be a night like all the others, she knew, yet somehow everything felt different. Ruel had been much too polite. The normally bustling streets were silent, as if everyone had paused in anticipation of something. Hotel guests hurried in purposeful solemnity out to their carriages. The air seemed to crackle around Anne's ears. And Alex . . .

"You've been sleeping with him," he spat as he hustled her down the walk. "Don't lie, wench. Everyone says it's true. My brother has bedded you, has he not?"

Flushing, Anne tried to pull her arm free. "If your brother wishes you to know his business, sir, he will tell you himself."

"You cannot deny it, can you? Then it's true! Damn! Damn you to hell!" He shoved her up the carriage step and through the door. Hurling her against the seat, he uttered a string of vile curses. "You seduced him, you little whore!"

Anne recoiled. "I've never seduced anyone."

"Rubbish! That is utter rubbish!" he hissed into her face as he sat down beside her, crushing the blue gown. "You intend for your bastard brat to inherit the duchy. Are you with child? Tell me!"

He grabbed her shoulder and wrenched it until she cried aloud. "I shall thank you to ask your brother what it is you wish to know! I am nothing in this but a pawn, and I won't—''

''Lady Blackthorne?'' The blacksmith stepped up into the carriage. Seeing her face, he paused. ''Are you well?''

''Mr. Walker.'' Anne flicked open her fan. Stirring the air around her face, she tried to catch her breath. ''Do sit down. How fine you look this evening.''

Regarding her curiously as he folded his tall body into the carriage, the older man ran a finger around the inside of his stiff cravat. ''I prefer my collarless shirt and leather breeches.'' He leaned toward her. ''Are you feeling all right?''

''Yes . . . of course.''

''Walker, a fine evening for a ride, don't you think?'' Ruel entered the carriage. ''Anne and Alex, you must be especially good to our American friend tonight. He has come only at my sternest insistence, and I'm afraid he's feeling rather more foreign among us than usual.''

Lord Alexander moved to the seat opposite Anne, but his eyes never left her face. As the horses drew the visiting aristocracy down the streets of Brussels, Ruel took Anne's hand. She stared at their twined fingers, well aware that such action meant her husband was returning them to their charade. He would feign adoration all evening. She must smile and laugh and swoon against his shoulder. All the while, she would know how deeply he must regret the turn his life had taken.

The house rented by the Duke and Duchess of Richmond was a grand structure, large and somber on the outside but a gilded masterpiece of marble columns, crystal chandeliers, and statues inside. Nearly every member of London's upper class and half the British military gathered in the large ballroom with its rose-and-trellis-patterned wallpaper.

Uniformed gentlemen mingled with feather-bedecked and diamond-studded ladies around long tables on which silver platters held enough food to fill everyone twice over.

Rising above the comestibles, huge gold statues of Grecian women lifted trays laden with grapes, quinces, figs, cherries, and strawberries. Swags of roses and ivy draped from the elbow of one statue to the elbow of another. Fountains gurgled with rich red wine or white champagne. Above all, saturating the very air, swam the strains of waltzes played by a large, liveried orchestra.

When Ruel began to greet acquaintances, he slipped an arm around Anne's waist. "This is my wife," he introduced her. Then again, "My wife, the Marchioness of Blackthorne." And again, "My wife."

Cringing inside, Anne pasted on the best smile she could muster. How many times had he uttered those words the night before? Were they merely a rote recitation from this same drama he had played with her so many times before? Of course they were. She had been such a fool to believe his avowals held any essence of truth.

They strolled through the ballroom, meeting colleagues they had recently seen in London and enduring introductions to countless members of the Brussels elite. Royalty fairly infested the place. The Duke and Duchess of Richmond chatted with the Duke of Brunswick, who bounced the little Prince de Ligne on his knee all the while. Talk of Napoleon mingled with inquiries about health and holiday plans.

The arrival of the Duke of Wellington, commander of the allied armies, produced an excited stir. With his patrician nose and strong jaw, the duke cut an imposing figure as he strode into the ballroom a good two hours late. Anne noticed that Mr. Walker took advantage of the hubbub to fill a plate with bread and fruit and escape through a pair of long glassed doors. She would have traded her title to have done the same.

Ruel came to Anne's side as people gathered around the Duke of Wellington to admire and greet the handsome military leader. His uniform adorned with jeweled medals, bright sashes, and loops of gold cording, he seemed to carry all of England's majesty with him. Having battled to victories in India, Hannover, Portugal, and Denmark, he was considered a masterful soldier. His success in the recent Peninsular War against Napoleon had led him to be honored with large estates, cash awards, and the title of Duke of Wellington. Now that Napoleon had escaped Elba and returned to France, Wellington's powerful presence in Brussels captivated everyone.

When the dancing began anew, Ruel guided Anne across the crowded floor. "I must speak with you alone for a moment," he murmured. "Walker told me he witnessed my brother assaulting you in the carriage tonight. Can that be true?"

"Lord Alexander . . . he questioned me." She glanced up, but the look in Ruel's eyes made her turn away quickly.

How dare he gaze at her with such feigned adoration? She could never take lightly what had happened between them, and he knew it. Their lovemaking had been nothing more than another fleshly escapade to him, but she had surrendered herself completely, irreparably. Did that mean so little to him? His easy ability to slip into the role of doting lover infuriated her.

"Alex questioned you about what?" He took her elbow and turned her toward an alcove near the long windows. "Anne, you have no obligation to speak to my brother about anything. What occurs between you and me is none of his affair."

"Ruel, people are beginning to stare at us."

"Let them." He slipped his hands behind her head and tipped her chin up, forcing her to meet his eyes. "I don't care what anyone thinks. Nothing matters but—"

"Someone is coming." She looked over his shoulder at the three men approaching the alcove. "Ruel, please. Talking can only make things worse between us. I acknowledge my own responsibility in what occurred last night, and you may rest assured it will never happen again."

"Never hap—?"

"Blackthorne." One of the three men tapped him on the shoulder.

His dark brow furrowed, Ruel swung around. "What?" Seeing who stood there, he let out a breath. "Droughtmoor, Wimberly, Barkham. Good evening, gentlemen."

"We've come to speak with you."

"At this moment I am busy, as you can see."

"This is a matter of utmost urgency. We can wait no longer."

"No longer? I returned from America three full months ago, yet you choose to address me only now?" He lifted one eyebrow. "Ah, yes, I forget myself. You've been missing from Society in London these past months. How we all have regretted the absence of your delightful and charming company."

"Enough of your nonsense, Blackthorne," Droughtmoor said. "We have an item of business to attend."

"In such a place as this? Sirs, you will forgive my bluntness, but this is a pleasure ball. I have only lately arrived with my new bride, and I intend to spend the evening dancing with her, tending to her every desire, and at every turn demonstrating to her my undying ardor. Matters of business are not on my agenda."

He made as if to lead Anne away, but Droughtmoor grabbed his arm. "You know damned well why we've come, Blackthorne, and if you think you will escape our mission this time, you are sorely mistaken. You have besmirched each of us in a method most unforgivable, and we require recompense."

"Besmirched you, have I?" Ruel squared his shoulders. "Droughtmoor, your inability to resist the bottle has blackened your name far more effectively than I ever could. Barkham, your dalliances with ladies dwelling in the West End of London are far more damning than any premarital indiscretions your wife may have committed with me.''

"Upon my word!" Barkham exploded.

"And Wimberly," Ruel continued. "Dear old Wimberly. Your fondness for gaming surpasses my own. Unfortunately you are famous only for your outstanding losses. Equally unfortunate, you failed to abandon your fondness for cards when it became clear they were ruining you, while I have had the good sense to relinquish gambling to the faded recesses of my past.''

"Now then, Blackthorne—" Wimberly began.

"Gentlemen, far be it from me to lay claim to besmirching your honorable names. You have succeeded admirably without my assistance.''

Ruel took Anne's hand, but before he could lead her out of the alcove, Droughtmoor stepped in front of him again.

"Bastard," the man spat. "Don't think your fine words will release you from your debt. This time you cannot flee to America to escape us. I'm calling you out.''

Ruel turned, a slow-burning anger suffusing his face. "Anne, perhaps you would like to go and speak with the Duchess of Richmond's daughter for a moment. I understand Lady Georgianna has been eager to make your acquaintance.''

Handed the opportunity for escape, Anne suddenly knew she couldn't take it. Ruel had been called out. A duel. She studied the hard angle of his jaw and understood at once the gravity of the matter. If he were to retain his honor, he could not decline.

"Excuse me," she said in a low voice. Leaving the alcove, she headed straight for the long French doors.

Were Ruel to face this Droughtmoor in a duel, he might be killed. The thought of it ripped through her stomach like a knife. No! She couldn't let it happen. Spotting the blacksmith alone at the far end of the walkway, she lifted her skirts and ran to him.

"Mr. Walker, you must come inside at once!"

"Lady Blackthorne?"

"Three men are confronting Ruel in the ballroom. They've called him out and mean to kill him! You must stop them!"

"I'll do what I can."

In moments, Anne had directed Walker to the knot of men gathered in the alcove. She knew she should stand aside. But how could she? Ruel was her husband. No matter how little he cared for her, she cared for him. More than that. She had given herself to him. She loved him. Against all reason, she loved him.

"Dear Lord, help!" she whispered, starting toward the men. She had to do something. Had to stop this madness.

"Tomorrow morning, then." Droughtmoor nodded at Ruel. "Pistols."

"At first daylight."

"No!" Anne cried. "No, Ruel, you mustn't—"

Her words were drowned by a shout. "War! Napoleon has crossed the Sambre. He has taken Charleroi by storm and is now marching toward Brussels!"

"War!" A cacophony of shrieks and screams erupted. Music faltered. The dancing stopped. Disorder broke out at the long tables. A lady swooned. Another collapsed into the arms of her partner.

As the room erupted into chaos, Anne clutched her fan and stood on tiptoe, searching for Ruel among the swarm of men. The Duke of Brunswick leapt to his feet, dropping the little Prince de Ligne to the floor. The Duchess of Richmond clutched her throat. Soldiers dashed to gather around the Duke of Wellington, who stood in earnest conversation with the messenger who had brought the news. Through the open windows, the roll of drums began to thunder through the night air. Trumpets called out from every part of the city.

"Anne!" Ruel caught her around the waist. "Stay near me."

"Dear heaven, will Napoleon really come to Brussels?"

"Brussels and then Vienna, if he has his way. Wellington will oppose him."

"But I read in *The Times* that Napoleon has amassed two hundred thousand French troops. Wellington has far fewer men—and less than a third of them are British."

"The Russians are on their way through Poland to assist him. Austrian troops will join Wellington, as well."

"The Austrians are needed against him in Italy!"

"Never underestimate the Prussians. Field Marshal Blücher is a canny man."

As he spoke, a second courier arrived. The crowd parted to allow the caped soldier to approach Wellington. The man presented the duke with a leather packet, and the Englishman opened it. He scanned the documents enclosed, then lifted his head.

"Napoleon has attacked Field Marshal Blücher," he announced. "Due to the considerable force of the enemy, the battle has become serious. As reported earlier, the French have captured Charleroi. Now I am told they have gained some advantage over the Prussians." He paused, looking around at his men. "The English will march in support of our allies. Gentlemen, prepare to depart the city at once."

Amid gasps and cries, Wellington strode out of the ballroom. Most of the uniformed men went with him. A few stayed behind to take a hasty leave of their wives. Women hurried to help their husbands, fathers, or brothers pack up. In the confusion, half the band remained and began to play some frantic little tune. The other half rushed to join the departing troops.

"Droughtmoor!" Ruel spotted his accuser as he and Anne joined the throng pouring through the doors. "What of your challenge?"

"Tomorrow at dawn!"

"Impossible. We're leaving the city tonight."

"I shall have my revenge on you, Blackthorne!"

Droughtmoor vanished into the corridor and was lost to them in the flood of pushing, shoving people.

Ruel wrapped his arm around Anne's shoulders and pulled her close. "We'll return to the hotel at once," he murmured, speaking against her ear so she could hear above the cries of the people. "Our plan begins immediately. A plain blue dress, black shawl, and bonnet lie in a paper-wrapped box in your trunk. Put them on, pull the shawl over your head, and go downstairs. Take your lady's maid with you, but explain nothing to her. No one must recognize either of you. Walker, Alex, and I will carry down the baggage. A vegetable cart will arrive at the back door of the hotel. Get in and pay the driver with this money. Do you understand?"

"Yes." She nodded as she took the wallet he handed her.

"Send the driver away, and wait with your maid until we come. Have you seen Walker?"

"He's over there." Anne lifted her hand to point out the tall man in the throng, but the blacksmith was already lunging toward them, his eyes wide and his mouth open in a cry of desperation.

"No!" he shouted. "No!"

Anne smelled the scent of black powder just as Ruel crumpled onto her. She heard nothing but the roar of the crowd, saw nothing but the spurt of crimson blood that burst before her eyes, felt nothing but the weight of the man dragging her down to the hard marble floor.

"Ruel!" Walker screamed the name as he threw himself across his fallen friend. "Ruel!"

Anne lay pinned beneath the marquess, unable to move. A foot stepped into her hair. Another tangled in her dress, tore the fabric, hurried on. Someone leapt over the two fallen people. She tried to breathe, tried to speak, and found she couldn't.

"Lady Blackthorne?" The weight lifted off her, and a

hand slid under her neck. "Are you injured?"

"No," she said with a gasp. "Ruel?"

"He's been shot in the face," Walker cried. "Ruel, lie down. You are bleeding everywhere."

"Anne! Where is she? I can't see. Can't see her."

"I'm here." She pushed out from under the man, wiping at the blood that dampened her own face. "Ruel . . . dear heaven!"

"Are you hurt, Anne?" He grabbed her shoulders hard and shook her. "Did the ball strike you?"

She stared into his face. His right cheek had been slashed open, ripped downward into a gaping flap of torn skin. Blood poured from the wound, covering his white cravat and waistcoat.

"Walker!" she screamed. "Walker, you must help him!"

As she cried out, the blacksmith was tearing the white cloth from around his own neck. "We must find a physician," he said, pressing it against the wound in Ruel's face. "The wound must be stitched."

"Ruel? Good God, what happened?" Lord Alexander skidded to a stop and crouched at his brother's side. "A saber?"

"A coat pistol," Walker barked. "Fetch a physic."

"They'll all be leaving with Wellington. Damn it, Walker, who did this? Was it Droughtmoor? Did you see?"

"I saw only the pistol." The Indian scooped Ruel into his arms. "We must return to the hotel."

"I shall sew him myself," Anne said. "I've never worked in flesh and blood, but the Lord has given me skill with a needle."

Dabbing tears and blood from her cheeks, she followed the men down the steps to the waiting carriage. All around them the city continued to erupt. Bugles sounded. Drums thundered. Horses clattered through the streets. Men loaded baggage wagons, and soldiers harnessed artillery trains. Officers rode toward the Place Royale while their men marched along with knapsacks on their backs and rifles on their shoulders. Flags went up, and children cried.

"Bleed him," Lord Alexander commanded. "If you don't bleed him, he'll die."

Walker settled Ruel in the back of the open cart and wrapped a blanket around the semiconscious man. "He can lose no more blood, or he surely will die."

Seated beside Vera, Anne tucked the frayed and blood-spattered blue silk gown around her legs and lifted Ruel's head into her lap. She hadn't had time to put on anything except the black shawl, and she hardly cared. Vera had spent the last hour dosing Ruel with laudanum and trying to stanch the flow of blood while Anne had carefully stitched the terrible wound in his face.

She had worked in spite of her horror. The ball had entered from the front just to the side of Ruel's nose and had torn its path of destruction all the way to his ear. Though the cheekbone had just been nicked, the flesh had been raggedly sliced all the way to the teeth. Had the pistol been aimed an inch to the left, Ruel would be dead.

"Mr. Walker speaks the truth, Lord Alexander," she said firmly. "You must trust your brother's treatment to the blacksmith now. He knows how to keep the wound clean and prevent infection. Ruel has lost far too much blood already. A bleeding would kill him."

"You think this damned redskin can save his life?"

"He saved mine."

"And aren't we grateful for that." With a snort, Lord Alexander slapped the side of the wagon. "Go on, then, all three of you. Take my brother to France. I'll meet you in Valenciennes, as we planned. Two days."

"Give us three." Walker climbed onto the bench and took the reins. "We may have some trouble."

"Does Ruel know any mode of existence other than

causing trouble? Gaming, smuggling, whoring, being shot at by angry assassins bent on revenge?'' He shook his head. ''Be at the fountain in Valenciennes in three days, or I'll ride for Paris.''

''Paris?'' Anne stared at him. ''You would not come searching for us? But you know we're traveling directly toward the French border just behind Wellington's troops. Anything can happen.''

''How do you suppose I shall get to Valenciennes myself? Fly?''

''You're armed and on horseback. We have nothing to protect us but this old cart filled with half-rotted vegetables.''

''At least you'll have something to eat.'' Still wearing his ball costume, Lord Alexander slipped his foot into the stirrup and swung onto his horse.

''Why will you abandon us, my lord?'' Vera cried out suddenly. ''Your brother needs you.''

''I'm merely following Ruel's own command to me. In fact, Mr. Walker and I were originally scheduled to journey together. My brother wished to travel separately from me in order to arouse the least amount of suspicion toward your trunks there.''

Anne stared at the baggage in the cart. ''Is the lace machine in my trunks?''

''Of course. Where did you suppose it was?'' With a flick of the reins, Lord Alexander spurred his horse. ''Three days, Walker, or I'm off to Paris and the arms of my affianced. Gabrielle Duchesne has been kept waiting far too long.''

Anne stared at the man's back as he vanished down the alley. Then she turned to the trunks lying amid piles of cabbages and baskets of green peas, strawberries, and early potatoes. ''Mr. Walker,'' she whispered, ''is the loom truly in my trunks?''

The Indian jostled the reins and set the two horses to

pulling the cart toward the sunrise. "Yes, Lady Black-thorne. Not many days before we left London, Ruel returned to Tiverton and packed Mr. Heathcoat's unassembled lace-making machine inside the trunks. It has been with us all along."

"With me, you mean." She let her focus drift down to the man who lay on her lap. Sleeping from the laudanum he had been given to drink, Ruel looked nothing like the devil she knew him to be. A tangle of dark curls fell over his pale brow. Thick black lashes lay like twin fans on his cheeks. The lips that tilted so easily into a cynical curl had softened. Only the wound that slashed across his cheek reminded her that this man was scarred both outwardly on his flesh and in the depths of his black heart.

He had lied to her. Dared her to open the trunks. Counted on her to trust him. Counted on her to believe his every word and not to use the iron key he had tossed so casually onto the trunk lid. She had trusted him, of course. Trusted him, fallen into his arms, loved him.

The cart rolled out onto the main road, and Walker headed the horses toward a little town called Waterloo.

Fifteen

THE CART HAD TRAVELED FEWER THAN FIVE MILES
when English soldiers put a halt to the journey. Camped
along the high ground near the main road into Brussels, the
troops wanted no interference from wandering vegetable
sellers. Seeing the wounded man in the cart, they sent the
four travelers to wait out the expected confrontation with
the French in one of the stone barns of a landowner named
Hougoumont, whose château had been converted to an English stronghold.

While Walker tended Ruel, Anne and Vera climbed to a
window in the top of the barn and studied the French troops
camped fourteen hundred yards away on the opposite ridge,
a place they called La Belle Alliance. Her heart hammering
and her palms clammy with helplessness, Anne witnessed
two battles that day. Both times, Napoleon's men forced
their enemies to retreat. Even though the French were unable to defeat them, the allied troops suffered countless injuries. Gradually the barn filled with wounded men, and
both young women went down to help Walker and the military physicians who arrived to treat the victims.

All the following day, the seventeenth of June, rain
poured, turning the hard ground to deep, sucking mud.
Lightning slashed across roiling gray skies, while thunder
made the barn's thick rock walls shake. Wellington's men
assured Anne that this was a wonderful omen. Every one

of the duke's peninsular victories, they told her, had been preceded by violent storms. This hardly encouraged a woman who put her faith in God and not in atmospheric portents.

Inside the barn, soldiers sat in clusters, smoking, playing at cards, singing. Others helped tend the wounded. Any plans for engaging the enemy in battle were abandoned. The rain made fusils, cannons, and most of the other weapons useless.

When night fell, Anne sank onto a pile of dank hay beside the vegetable cart. Mr. Walker and Vera sat in the hay together, the little maid lying half asleep on the older man's shoulder.

"So . . . how is he?" Anne asked.

"Who?" the blacksmith returned.

"The marquess, of course."

"I am surprised you ask. You have not visited your husband's side a single time today."

Anne closed her eyes and let out a breath. "As you and Vera both know very well, Ruel is my husband in name only."

"He would not agree."

"How little you understand him, then."

"I know him better than I know any man. In you, Lady Blackthorne, he believes he has found the healing of his heart."

"Not three days ago, he told me I had destroyed him."

"You have destroyed the former man, perhaps. But you have created someone new."

Anne let out a bitter laugh. "Was it the new man or the old who elected to store contraband in his wife's baggage? Is it the new man or the old who would see this woman who has supposedly healed his heart turned over to the authorities and imprisoned should her trunks be opened and the lace machine discovered?"

Walker sat up, his dark eyes piercing. "Is that what you believe?"

"How can I think otherwise?"

"Have you looked at the trunks since we began our journey from Brussels, madam?"

"No." Anne glanced at Vera, whose pale face shone in the darkness of the barn. "I've been tending the wounded."

"Your name was painted over, Annie," Vera whispered. "I thought you knew. A new name and direction were inscribed on the trunks."

Her pulse racing, Anne scrambled to her feet and took hold of the iron spokes of one of the cart's wheels. Pulling herself on tiptoe, she peered into the wagon bed. Lying on a pallet of rough blankets, the Marquess of Blackthorne turned his head to gaze at her.

"Mr. Hezekiah Cutts," he said in a low voice. "Tailor."

Anne's focus darted to the trunk. As he said, the name had been newly inscribed. "Tailor?"

"Tailor." His mouth twisted into a pained grin.

When he spoke, she could see how difficult it was for him to form the words, yet she felt no compassion. She intended to hear how he would explain himself. "Who is this Mr. Cutts? Where is he?"

"Lying in a vegetable cart with his face half peeled away by an assassin's ball. I'm the tailor, Anne, although I won't deny you are much handier with a needle. Before Droughtmoor shot me, I didn't have time to tell you about the disguises we were to take on. I'm Cutts, a poor tailor traveling from village to village, and these trunks contain my wares—gowns of every size and hue."

"Gowns." Her voice held disgust.

"Gowns." He repeated. Then he dropped his voice. "False-bottomed trunks are the smuggler's stock-in-trade, you know."

Anne frowned. "And Mr. Walker?"

"Walker is our friendly village vegetable seller. Vera's his wife. And you, I trust, are still mine."

Anne tightened her fingers on the wheel spoke. "Why did you lie to me?"

"I have never lied to you. You asked me that night in Brussels if the machine was in the trunks. I gave you the key to open them and discover the truth for yourself. You chose not to." He shifted on the hard plank wagon bed, a grimace contorting his face as pain shot through him. Touching the bloodied bandage on the side of his face, he lay still for a moment, breathing hard.

Then he turned his gray eyes on her. "I wanted you that night, Anne. I knew if I told you about the loom you would be angry with me on too many counts. I am well aware you despise my intended industry, and you disdain my machine and all it stands for. I also understand you feared I would betray you. But far more important to me, I knew your safety depended on your ignorance. It still does. I cannot forgive my brother for telling you about the trunks' contents. It was not his place to do so. The machine is my responsibility, and I alone intend to bear the consequences of my deeds."

Confused, unwilling to believe he told the truth now when she had been so certain he was a lying devil, Anne studied the livid laceration across Ruel's cheek. "You already suffer the consequences of your deeds, my lord."

"What do you mean?" He bolted up, stared at her for a moment, then suddenly grabbed her hand. "Are you with child? Anne, you must tell me the truth!"

"I speak of your wounded face. It's far too soon to know what will become of our ill-spent night." She pulled away. "Lie down. Your exertions may cause you to bleed again."

He slumped back onto the pallet. "Send Walker to me, will you please? I must have more laudanum."

Anne stayed at his side for a moment, watching the pain write shadows and lines across his face. What had his reaction to the possibility of a baby meant? Did he hope for such an event—or dread it? She never knew what to make of this man.

How dare her heart ache for him? How dare her heart beckon her crawl into the cart and curl against him and lend him her warmth? This was a man who relied on no one but himself—his own wisdom and his own strength. This was a man other men tried to kill, a man who thought nothing of breaking laws for his personal gain, a man who might betray those who loved him most.

Loved him? Yes, it was true. Terribly true, and Anne loathed herself for it. Mr. Walker said she had made Ruel a new man. He insisted she had brought him a healing of the heart. Her father had always preached that men's lives could be changed, sinful creatures born again, black hearts washed as white as snow. His eldest daughter, faithfully seated in the front pew, had believed every word from her father's mouth.

God's love, she had no doubt, could change a person. But could one lowborn woman—admittedly stubborn, impatient, and far too selfish—actually heal a man's heart? Was there hope for such a transformation in a man like Ruel Chouteau, the Marquess of Blackthorne?

"Hezekiah," she said softly. "Do you know the meaning of the name you have chosen?"

Ruel's eyes fluttered open. "No."

"Jehovah strengthens." She reached out and gently laid her hand over the wound on his face. "Be strong in the Lord."

Dawn of June eighteenth brought new trepidation to the band of travelers as the sun emerged over the horizon and the rain stopped. On the opposite ridge, the highly trained French troops began to assemble and prepare their artillery. Far outnumbering the seventy thousand English soldiers, Napoleon's two hundred thousand troops were openly contemptuous of their rivals. They shouted insults, taunting the English that any battle between them would be nothing more than eating breakfast.

Just when Vera whispered to Anne that she almost believed the French taunts herself, the enemy attacked. Napoleon's brother, Jerome, led the assault down from La Belle Alliance, across the valley, and up toward the château of Hougoumont. Four full regiments—highly trained and brilliant in their tactical skills—battled Wellington's fusiliers, storming the stone houses and steadily fighting all the way up to the courtyard of the farm.

Screaming in terror as the French burst through the old iron gates, Vera ran into the blacksmith's arms. While the enemy poured into the courtyard, Walker beckoned Anne, and the three of them climbed into the old vegetable cart with Ruel. If the barn itself were taken, they all knew they stood little chance of living through the assault.

Around them soldiers fell, and cannonballs exploded. Clods of dirt flew into the air, men cried out in pain, bullets rang against the barn's walls and shattered the stone into bursts of razor-sharp shards. The four travelers huddled together, clutching each other. Vera wept. Anne prayed. Ruel fought to work his way out of a drugged haze. Walker alternated between hovering over the injured man and the women and darting to the window to check on the status of the battle.

By noon it was clear that a miracle had occurred. The defending English somehow had managed to repel the better-armed French. But the victory was short-lived. Wellington's men hardly had taken time to catch their breath when a thunderous cannonade announced the second advance of the French infantry. The ground shook, and the air around Anne's ears vibrated. Covering her head, she could no longer hold back the trembling that overtook her.

"Dear God, we shall all die," Vera sobbed. "We can never hold them back again!"

Anne squeezed her friend's hand. "Take courage, Vera. Death is hardly the worst thing that can happen."

"Oh, Annie! How can you be so calm?"

"My wife is quite prepared to die," Ruel uttered from his pallet. "She spoke those words to me once, and I've never forgotten them." He inched up onto his elbows and attempted a wink. "Mrs. Cutts, would you care to accompany me upstairs to the loft? I believe our party shall find greater refuge there than here."

With effort, he rolled to a sitting position, took out his chain of keys, and unlocked one of the trunks. He lifted out a small firearm and pulled it to half cock. Then he handed it to Anne. "This is a coat pistol. It's loaded, so look where you're pointing it before you pull the trigger."

He removed three more weapons and a powder flask from the trunk before locking it again. "Another coat pistol for Miss Vera, also ready to shoot, a blunderbuss for Mr. Walker, and a German Jaeger rifle for me. Shall we go up?"

"Ruel, the laudanum dulls your thinking," Walker said gruffly. "You should stay here and rest."

"Walker, you know as well as I what the coming hours may bring. The night Droughtmoor shot me, I vowed it was the last time I would meet any foe unprepared." He forced a lighter note to his voice. "Come along, ladies. Let's secure our own little fortress against the storm."

Walker grudgingly helped Ruel climb down from the cart, and with the ground shaking beneath them, they all made their way up the stone steps to the barn's loft. In an alcove near the window, Walker and Ruel built a rough barricade of hay bales and feed sacks. Gripping her weapon, Anne helped Vera nestle into the protected corner. Walker knelt beside her, his eyes trained on the stairway for any sign of invasion.

Ruel had no intention of hiding. He had led these people into the midst of hell itself, and he would not sit by and allow them all to be killed—no matter how prepared Anne was to meet her Maker. He propped one shoulder against the window frame and looked out on the battle.

"You must not overexert yourself." The soft voice at his side was unexpected. "You lost more blood the night of your shooting than I knew flowed through any man's veins."

"Did you believe I would die?" he asked, turning. When he looked into Anne's face, he saw that the pink had washed from her cheeks in fear, but the light of determination burned brightly in her blue eyes.

"Yes," she said.

"Did you care?"

"Yes," she said again, then looked away for a moment. "As I recall, you were unwilling that I should perish of my leg injury. You brought Mr. Walker to take care of my wound. As the recipient of your benevolence, how could I wish for you to die?"

"Tit for tat, then."

"If you wish to believe I would press your flesh together with my bare hands, stanch your blood, and pierce your living skin with a needle merely from a sense of obligation, I can offer nothing to counter your opinion." She lifted her chin. "By the same token, if you wish to believe I would willingly ride into the thick of battle simply because I bear your title, or covet your inheritance, or long for more gowns and jewels, I can say little to sway you. And if you think I would give away my maidenhood for nothing more than hedonistic pleasure, how can I convince you otherwise? If I have learned one thing about you, Lord Blackthorne, it is that you will believe as you please, think as you wish, and do exactly as you see fit."

"Is that so?" He reached out and fingered the tattered gold fringe on her sleeve. "Then you believe yourself powerless where I am concerned? How very wrong you are."

As she looked into his eyes, Ruel realized for the first

time that his desire for this woman went beyond compre-
hension. And dear heaven, what had he brought her to? Her
lustrous hair hung limp and tangled against the rough black
shawl around her shoulders. The blue gown bore splatters
of blood. His own blood. While suspecting betrayal at her
own husband's hands, Anne nevertheless had not hesitated
to sew up his wounds and to follow him into the unknown.

"What manner of creature are you?" he asked in a low
voice.

"You know exactly who I am." Her eyes narrowed, and
she set her hands on her hips. "Ruel, you must come behind the barricade. You are not well, and I'm afraid you
will—"

"Dear heaven, listen to you!" Overwhelmed that she
would continue to place his welfare above her own, he took
her into his arms. "Anne, if you should die . . . if I have
led you to this . . ."

"Shh," she whispered, laying her cheek on the rough
fabric of his coat. "Please don't distress yourself."

He knew he should release her. In spite of all she had
done for him, clearly she felt little in her heart for him
beyond animosity and responsibility. Her words to him in
all the past weeks of their marriage had held little but re-
pugnance. She had instructed him not to touch her, told
him she disliked him, accused him of betrayal, and repeat-
edly referred to his black heart.

Why then did he want nothing more in life than to hold
this woman? Hold her forever . . . smell the scent of her hair
against his nose, stroke the smooth skin of her arms, hang
on to the musical sound of her voice, taste the sweetness
of her lips . . .

"Anne, I beg you to forgive me for bringing you to
this," he choked out. "Were it within my power, I would
see you taken far away from here. Back to Nottingham, if
you like. I would grant you that stone house you dream of.

That lace school. Those hedgehogs in the brush and that gray stone with its curling moss.''

He stroked his hands over her thin shoulders, memorizing the feel of her body. He could not bring himself to wish her a farmer or a weaver for a husband. No matter how deep her distaste for him, he wanted her as his wife. He loved her. He loved her, and he would tell her, no matter the consequences to his battered ego.

"Anne—"

"Oh, God! Oh, heaven!" She pulled from his arms and dropped onto the stone sill. "Look, Ruel! They're coming!"

"Get back!" He pressed her away from the window and grabbed his rifle. "Walker, take her! Guard the women."

Leaning against the window, Ruel looked out onto the sight that had terrified Anne. Sixteen thousand infantrymen, rifles shouldered and sabers flashing in the sunlight, swept down from La Belle Alliance and rushed across the valley toward Wellington's fusiliers. Despite Wellington's brave defense, the French surrounded the second of the two farms occupied by the English.

"Napoleon has stormed La Haye Sainte," he called to Walker. "Wellington has sent his own infantry to meet them."

He watched as the two armies clashed and men fell. The acrid scent of gunpowder drifted through the air as shouts and screams of pain mingled with the report of rifles. Minutes ticked by, and neither side made headway.

"What now, Ruel?" Walker called.

"Wellington is sending out the cavalry."

"Who rides?"

"I can just make out the Scots Greys and Life Guards ... and there are the Inniskillings and the King's Dragoons." He paused, observing the incredible sight of the huge English war horses slashing and biting as they galloped against the enemy. "Wellington is forcing back the

French! . . . Yes, Napoleon's men are retreating . . . racing back across the valley! Wellington is pursuing. He's captured two of their standards and several guns!''

"Thank God!" Anne cried. "Ruel, we must take the cart and flee this place at once!"

"Impossible. There are far too many soldiers in the fields. Wellington's cavalry is still chasing after the French.'' He paused, his breath hanging in his chest while the horses thundered up the hill toward La Belle Alliance. "Dash it! Can't they see they must turn back now? Sound the retreat, damn it! Napoleon will call in his reserves!"

Ruel stared in helpless frustration as the giant horses churned the mud across the cornfields, their riders crying out "For England!" and "Scotland Forever!" The trumpeters called the retreat again and again, but the dragoons rode on. Ruel watched in horror as his fears were realized— Napoleon's reserve troops turned on the English.

"It's too late!" he cried out. "Too late to turn back. Napoleon's men and horses are fresh. The French lances are far longer than our short swords. Our whole bloody cavalry is doomed!"

The minutes slipped into hours as Ruel called the agonizing news of the battle to the others in the alcove. "Their cannons are slaughtering us . . . blowing our men to pieces. The Lancers are mowing us down, unhorsing and mutilating us! . . . They're killing the men as they try to crawl away."

"How many are dead?" Anne asked.

"Three hundred Greys at least. I count only a few dozen riding to safety."

"Where is Wellington in all this?"

"He rides among them, here and there, rallying the Brunswickers, leading the cavalry back into position. He's magnificent! But the devastation is too great."

"Are we defeated?"

"The English center holds, but only just."

"And the Prussians? Where is Blücher?"

Though it had seemed impossible that Wellington's allies could reach the battleground in time to join the fray, Ruel spotted the Prussians advancing down the road from a great distance.

"Blücher is coming!" He glanced at the others. "He's on his way."

"He's too far," Walker said. "To hope for victory would be preposterous."

"I'm afraid so. It's clear the French are better trained, and their guns are superior. Now . . . now, Napoleon comes at us again. Dear heaven, it's Marshal Ney! His cavalry is charging La Haye Sainte again. Look, he's riding straight into our guns! What a fool! I don't believe it!"

Unable to stay in hiding any longer, Anne joined Ruel at the window. It was six o'clock in the evening and drawing toward dusk, but the orange light revealed the full horror of Ney's light cavalry riding directly into the wall of English musket fire. As the Frenchmen were mowed down by their still hopelessly underarmed foes, Ruel made his decision.

"The fields are blanketed with smoke and fog," he told Walker quietly. "Mud covers everything. We must use the chaos to make our escape."

With Vera protesting and Anne half numbed with the horror of what she was witnessing, the men urged the women down the stairs and into the wagon. "You and I shall guard either side of the cart," Ruel instructed Walker. "Shoot any man who comes at us. Anne, you and Vera must lie down in the midst of the wall of trunks. They will barricade you from the bullets."

"Who will lead the horses?" Anne could see that the men would never be able to shield the women and direct the cart through the sticky muck at the same time. "I shall take the reins. No, don't even attempt to argue with me, Ruel. There's no choice in this matter. You know as well as I the horses will never go willingly into such conditions.''

She pulled her shawl around her head and clutched the leather reins. ''Shall we go?''

Ruel breathed the first prayer he had prayed in twenty years. ''Lead out,'' he said as he opened the barn door. Lifting his rifle against one shoulder, he fought the pain in his cheek. He must protect her. Must guard her life. Must save her.

The horses pulled the cart out of the stone barn, across the courtyard littered with bodies, and into the battlefield. Choking against the smoke, Anne jerked on the reins, attempting to guide the cart toward shelter in the forest nearby. The two horses tossed their heads in fear. Walking wounded staggered toward safety. Riderless horses, crazed with terror, galloped aimlessly, colliding with the onrushing cavalry. Scattered corpses blocked the path, and Anne fought to keep the cart moving.

''Walker!'' Ruel shouted as a steaming horse bolted from nowhere across their path. His voice was lost in the explosion of a cannonball not ten yards away. Clods of wet dirt splattered over him. Vera lifted her head in an agonized scream, but Ruel heard nothing, deafened by the cannonade.

He looked up at Anne. Chin set, she flicked the reins against the horses' backs. Her loose hair streamed behind her. Mud peppered her face and gown. Glancing down at him, she nodded encouragement. ''It's all right,'' her mouth seemed to say, forming words he could not hear.

''Anne!'' He wanted to tell her, had to tell her of his love for her. As he spoke, another missile exploded directly in front of the cart. The horses shied, threw back their heads, bolted. ''Anne!''

He struggled to hold the harness, but the horses tore it from his hands, pulled away, and cantered straight toward the battle lines. Sprinting through the fog, Ruel could just make out the cart lurching toward the line of Wellington's fusiliers, who somehow still held the French forces fewer than two hundred yards at bay.

"Anne!" he bellowed. A bullet shattered the corner of one of his trunks. Wood chips flew. He plunged through a cloud of smoke, chasing the runaway horses, leaping over corpses, sloshing through bloody mud. Walker ran at Ruel's side two paces away, his face stoic.

"Anne!" Ruel shouted her name until he was hoarse. She never turned. In the distance he could discern Vera clambering onto the seat beside Anne, grabbing at the reins, attempting to control the horses.

A cannonball exploded in front of the two men. They both fell, lay stunned for a moment by the impact, then scrambled to their feet again and continued to run. Bouncing, jolting over ruts, the cart again vanished behind a wall of smoke. Another ball exploded, and another.

Ruel looked to his side. Walker had vanished. He ran on toward the front line. Anne. Had to get to her. Had to save her. A bullet zinged past his ear. Another knocked his hat from his head. A soldier tumbled from his horse and fell writhing to the ground at Ruel's feet. Ruel leaped over him and ran on.

"Anne!" He spotted the cart through a clearing in the smoke. It had stopped, tilted crazily to one side. Dear God! No! Coughing, he jumped across a ditch and fell to his knees at the side of the cartwheel. The horses lay dead, mangled by a cannonball's explosion. Ruel pulled himself to his feet and reached over the side onto the seat. His hand closed on soft blue fabric.

"Come, Ruel!" Walker's words were shouted into his ear. The Indian appeared as if by magic at his side. "Nothing can be done here."

As Walker tugged his hands from the cart, Ruel looked into the wagon. Both women lay sprawled across the seat, their faces, hair, gowns drenched in blood. Breathless, lifeless, they hung like limp mannequins, arms dangling and mouths opened in wordless screams.

"Anne!" Ruel howled her name again and again as Walker dragged him away from the cart, across the muddied fields, and finally into the safe haven of the forest.

Crumpling, Ruel sobbed against the ground as he clutched handfuls of damp earth. He had killed her. He had led her to her death. Killed the woman he loved, the only woman he would ever love.

"We must get out of here!" Walker spoke against his ear. "The French are coming!"

"I won't leave her."

"She's gone, Ruel. They both are. You saw them."

"I want to bury her."

"Impossible. It will be done with dignity. Nothing you can do will bring her back, Ruel. We must save ourselves now. Come!"

"No!" He grabbed the Indian's shirt and twisted it in his fist. "I love her! I love her!"

Speaking into Ruel's face, Walker enunciated each word. "Anne . . . is . . . dead. Dead!"

"God!"

"Yes, God. He will watch your woman now . . . and mine. We have been spared. We have work to do. We must go to Valenciennes and meet your brother. Lord Alexander may still be waiting."

"No. I won't go to France." He gritted his teeth. "Napoleon—"

"England, then. We'll return to England. The duke will rejoice to see your safe return."

Ruel shook his head. "I cannot go back there. Slocombe, where she worked . . . the arboretum . . . the road to London . . . Chouteau House . . . the room where I loved her . . ."

Walker laid a hand on his friend's arm. In the distance, he could see the Prussian troops arriving to bolster Wellington's forces. Would they be enough? It hardly seemed possible. The French pressed on, driving the English lines back closer and closer to the forest.

"We must go, my son. We must find a place of refuge."

"Refuge?" Ruel lifted his head. "I can think of only one place where my heart may find peace."

"Where?"

Rising unsteadily to his feet, the younger man set his face toward the west. "America."

Sixteen

SPILLED SUGAR. THERE IT LAY, SCATTERED ACROSS the tablecloth, a grand mess to be cleaned up before Mrs. Smythe would notice. The sugar sparkled and glittered in the firelight from the cooking hearth. The tea cloth, a smooth expanse of lustrous black velvet, stretched on and on along the huge table. Sugar . . . endless, endless sugar . . . like stars in a deep, ebony night . . .

Stars! Anne sat up. A breath of fog whispered past her face. She shivered. Where was Mrs. Smythe? And the sugar . . .

"Vera?" she called, but her voice made no sound. The kitchenmaid would be about, watching for mistakes. "Sally Pimm?"

But this wasn't Slocombe House after all, was it? Anne looked around her, searching for signs of the familiar fireplace, the long work tables, the black-and-white-tiled floor. Instead of the massive stone hearth and blazing logs, she saw lights in the distance, the flash of swords glinting in the starlight. Rather than basking in the smell of baking cinnamon and roasting duck, she choked on smoke. Black, cloying smoke with the tangy scent of gunpowder. In the place of the laughter and fuss of the kitchenmaids, she heard . . . nothing. She heard nothing!

"Vera!" Her own voice made no sound. She had gone deaf! Panic gripped her heart. This was not the kitchen at

Slocombe. This was the battlefield. Waterloo!

"Ruel?" Again, she heard nothing, not even the word she had shouted at the top of her lungs.

Frantic, she felt around her, groping, touching. Her fingers fell on something soft and sticky. A hand gripped hers, and she screamed. Again, nothing. No sound.

Vera's moonlit face formed in front of hers, a ghoulish mask of caked blood and terror. Vera's lips moved, forming words but saying nothing. Panic widening her eyes, she covered her ears and shook her head violently at her inability to hear. She clutched Anne's arms, tears running down her cheeks.

Oh, Vera! Anne threw her arms around her friend. They must be deaf, both of them. Deafened by the cannonade. The men . . . where was Ruel? And Walker? Dear Lord, look at the poor horses! Dead!

They had to get away from this place. In the distance, the battle continued. It hardly seemed possible.

No matter what the outcome of the war, Anne knew she and Vera had to find Ruel and Walker. Oh, she couldn't reason clearly. If the men were alive, they would have gone on to Valenciennes, wouldn't they? Were they alive? Or dead? No! Anne could hardly think beyond her unbearable thirst and the ringing in her ears. Not dead. Ruel was not dead. He couldn't be.

She set Vera away from her and pointed toward the forest and safety. Vera nodded, seeming to understand. Hoisting her skirts around her knees, Anne climbed down from the cart and began to unharness the mangled horses. It was hard, unpleasant work, but determination to escape drove her. Too many times in the past days, she had witnessed near victory only to see it followed by another onslaught of Napoleon's forces. Though it looked as though the French were retreating and the Prussians and English were racing behind, slaughtering their enemies without mercy, Anne feared to trust her eyes.

Gesturing and mouthing silent words, she indicated to Vera that they each must capture another horse from those wandering loose on the grisly battlefield. They must take the cart with them, or they would never make it to France.

Coming out of her shock, Vera slipped down to the ground. Together the women stepped over and skirted clusters of dead soldiers until they found two horses milling aimlessly but calm enough to approach. They led them to the cart, harnessed them, and climbed back onto the wooden seat.

Anne pointed toward the west. "France?" she queried.

Vera's lower lip trembled as she nodded. Both knew it might be easier to drive back to Brussels and find refuge there. Even if Napoleon took the city, there would be food to eat, water to drink, and hope for passage back to England. But Anne had no doubt where her friend's heart belonged. They must find the men.

The horses slowly pulled the cart across the gruesome battlefield. Anne shut her eyes, allowing the creatures to take the lead until she could bear to look again. Her thoughts drifted as she tried to make sense of her situation.

What had happened to her and Vera in the passing hours? The last thing she recalled, a cannonball had exploded in front of the cart, and the horses had bolted in fear. She remembered Ruel clinging to the harness, trying to stop the escape until he could hold on no longer. Though she had fought for control, the cart had bounced and jolted directly toward the front line. Men had been screaming, mud flying, hooves thundering. And then . . .

Oh, yes. Then the soldier . . . the poor, poor soldier. Speared by a French Lancer, already dead, he had flopped against his frantic horse as it galloped toward the women on a direct course for collision. Frenzied, the animal had crashed full force into the cart, and the soldier's limp body had tumbled onto Vera and Anne. Soaked by the man's blood, they had barely pushed him away when a second cannonball came whistling toward them. Falling. Falling.

Anne could remember nothing after that. Not the ball hitting the earth. Not the explosion. Not the death of the horses or the cart slamming into the pit created by the blast. Nothing. Where was Ruel during all that time? Had he been killed? No. Surely not.

Yes. Anne squeezed her eyes more tightly shut against the reality. If he had been alive, Ruel would have come for her and Vera. Anne had doubted much about her husband, but this one thing she knew for certain. Alive, he would never have abandoned her on that battlefield.

Glancing at Vera, Anne saw that her friend had come to the same conclusion. She sobbed into her skirt, shoulders shaking in sorrow. The men were dead. Ruel, her husband. Walker, Vera's lover. Dead.

The moonlit night brought little comfort. The two horses pulled the cart down lanes and byways, westward away from the battle and toward France. Anne took turns with Vera driving the wagon and sleeping in the back amid the trunks. Neither woman could hear the other, but it hardly mattered. Lost in their grief, they had nothing to say.

Two full days and nights passed before Anne and Vera crossed the border into France and drove their little cart into the city of Valenciennes. After leaving the battlefield safely behind, they had stopped along a river, slaked their thirst, and washed the blood from their bodies. Though Ruel had taken the keys to the trunks, Anne used her coat pistol to shoot off the lock on one.

The women dressed in two of the simple gowns they found inside—pale cotton garments and soft woven shawls. Their hearing slowly returned as they drove their little cart through one village after another, but they had no way of understanding the news of the battle. Was Napoleon defeated or victorious? And how would either result affect them—two young Englishwomen in France?

"The fountain," Anne said, tugging on a rein to turn the horses down a street in Valenciennes. "That's where Ruel agreed to meet his brother."

"We had but three days to travel from Brussels, and many more than that have gone by, Annie. You know Lord Alexander will have gone to Paris to stay with his fiancée."

"Then we shall write him a letter."

"You will. I can barely scratch out my own name." Vera studied her workworn fingers. "Oh, what's to become of us, Annie? I cannot have such faith as you that Lord Alexander or . . . or the other men . . . or anyone is here waiting for us."

"I have little faith in it myself. I only know it was Ruel's plan for everyone to meet in Valenciennes. If we have any hope of finding help, we must find that fountain."

"What then? Do you really mean for us to stay here? What shall we do with ourselves in France? We know no one here, and we cannot speak a word of the language."

Anne surveyed the town with its bustling market, narrow streets, and crowded half-timbered houses. "Ruel must have planned to meet someone other than his brother in France. He surely knew someone here who would work with him to set up the machine."

"In this town? This is hardly a commercial center. I presumed he would be going to Paris himself eventually." Vera fingered her shawl as she scanned the streets, her eyes brimming with hope. "Annie . . . do you think it's at all possible Lord Blackthorne and Walker are here already? Could they really be waiting for us?"

Even as Vera spoke the words, Anne knew they were impossible. Not only would the men not be here, but she and Vera already were in jeopardy. The two women had driven a cart full of contraband lace machinery into a country where the people spoke no English and where most everyone was loyal to Napoleon Bonaparte.

"I only know we must find the fountain," Anne said

softly. "Perhaps someone will help us there."

As she guided the horses toward the center of the little town, she thought about what she and Vera must do after the reality of their situation became inescapable. It was all but foolish to believe Ruel and Walker would be there. Lord Alexander would not be there either. No one would help them.

Perhaps they might sell the horses and cart, sell the gowns in the trunks . . . even sell the lace loom. With the money, they would have some hope of returning to England. But what waited for them there? Anne thought of her father languishing in prison. His case depended on the goodwill of the Marquess of Blackthorne.

Without him . . . without Ruel . . .

"There it is!" Vera cried, pointing. "The fountain."

Anne flicked the reins and sent the tired horses the last few yards to the stone fountain. Surrounding it, small booths with colorful canopies offered cheeses, fresh strawberries, wooden clogs, and iron pots for sale. Ladies filled their shopping baskets with goods while their children played in their skirts. It was a scene that brought Nottingham market to Anne's mind, and for the first time in weeks she felt the tension begin to slide out of her body.

"It's almost like home," she said softly as she pulled the horses to a stop. "The little houses. The gardens. The vendors."

"But there's no one here. No one is waiting for us."

"No. There's no one."

Anne drew her shawl from her shoulders and folded it into her lap. In the silence of the morning, she could hear birds twittering in the trees overhead. Someone laughed. A puppy yawned.

"Ruel wished this for me, Vera," Anne whispered, suddenly unable to keep back the tears. "We stood in the barn window at Waterloo watching the horrors, and his words took me far away from those fields of slaughter. He told

me he wanted me to have a stone house and a lace school
and . . . and hedgehogs. Oh, Vera, I would trade a hundred
stone houses to see Ruel again!''

"Anne." Vera folded her friend into her arms. "He
loved you, Annie. He loved you so."

"No, Vera," she muttered, "he didn't love me at all. I
was mulish and impertinent. I could hardly bear the society
of his acquaintances, and he knew it. I learned the proper
manners and the decorous speech, but I never belonged in
his world. Worse than my own incompetence was my harsh
tongue. I accused Ruel of having a black heart, and I told
him I found him stubborn, disputatious, and difficult. I was
never anything but trouble to him.''

"But he loved you all the same."

"No, Vera."

"Walker swore he did. He told me of the events of one
night at Chouteau House in London. Do you recall the first
evening of our stay there? After dinner, the marquess held
you in his arms in the garden outside the drawing room.
You said the embrace had meant nothing. You swore Lord
Blackthorne was merely acting out a drama for the benefit
of visitors to the house. But much later that night, after
Walker had spoken with someone in the corridor—''

"In the corridor? Who?''

"An old friend. I don't know the name, and it doesn't
matter, Annie. This friend and Walker discussed the past,
and their words reminded him of the unhappy days when
he first had come to England from America. Distressed, he
went down the stairs to Lord Blackthorne's bedroom. The
marquess, too, was distraught.''

"That was Walker?" Anne could not think beyond the
realization that one of the two parties in the tryst she had
overheard in the corridor had been the blacksmith. But who
was his lover?

"Anne, have you forgotten that night already? Lord
Blackthorne told Walker he was ready to abandon all his

dreams for the future if only he could make you truly his wife. Yet he was convinced you loathed him and he would never win you over.''

"Loathed him? But I didn't!''

"Walker felt certain it was at that moment in the garden the marquess began to love you. Already Lord Blackthorne was an altered man, you see. Altered by his acquaintance with you. But not until the garden did he truly love you. From that time onward, though the marquess himself could not acknowledge it, his heart belonged to you and you alone.''

"Vera, I never had faith in Ruel's constancy. I believed he toyed with me for his personal gain.''

"You were wrong, Annie. Walker knew Lord Blackthorne better than anyone did. He had loved the marquess himself since Blackthorne was but a little boy loitering outside the blacksmith forge in Tiverton.''

"Madame? *Bonjour.*''

At the heavily accented voice, Anne looked down from the cart to discover a small, wiry man smiling up at her. With a pair of gleaming spectacles perched on his large hooked nose, he looked to Anne like one of the fairy-tale shoemaker's elves.

"I'm sorry,'' she said, "I can't speak French.''

"No, no. I have a little English. I see the . . . how you say? . . . the boxes here in your cart. The name is Cutts, and I am waiting for you many days. Hezekiah Cutts? He is not with you?''

"No, he is . . . he was . . .'' She gestured toward the distance. "We were separated at Waterloo.''

"Waterloo?'' The man frowned. "*Ma foi!* He is killed?''

Anne bit her lower lip. "I believe so.''

The man lowered his head and slowly took off the small leather beret that covered his bald pate. "*C'est la guerre.* Very sad news. Very sad. His brother will grieve.''

"Is his brother here?''

"In Paris. He waits for Monsieur Cutts there."

"He waits in vain." Anne studied the little man for a moment. "May I ask your name, sir?"

"I am Monsieur Pierre Robidoux. And you?"

"Mrs. Cutts. Anne."

"Your lovely *compagnon de voyage*?"

"I'm Vera Walker." The slender young woman held out her hand. "Pleased to meet you, Mr. Robidoux. Can you tell us, sir, how you know of Mr. Cutts and Mr. Walker? Were you their friend?"

"*Oui*. Friend and business acquaintance. Perhaps you come to my house? We talk? Eat?"

Anne glanced at Vera. Wholly taken with the little man, Vera would have leapt at the chance for a glass of wine and a loaf of fresh bread. Anne had no such confidence in him. All she could think of were the trunks in the back of the cart and the dangers they represented.

"Thank you, but we must find lodging here in Valenciennes," she said before Vera could protest. "We shall wait here for a few days in the hope that my husband may arrive."

The man nodded slowly, then he spoke in a low voice. "Douai is a better place to wait, Madame Cutts. Your husband sent a letter instructing me to prepare a small house and also a place for your . . . for the boxes in the cart." He regarded her for a moment. "It was his plan."

"How shall I trust your words are true, Monsieur Robidoux? We have only just met."

"Monsieur Cutts told me you were *la belle dame d'esprit*. The beautiful lady of wit." Robidoux favored her with another warm smile. "I tell you this. The name of your new house is the Black Thorn. *Oui?*"

She shrugged. "A good name."

"You are not convinced. Then I tell you this of which I know. I am the finest weaver of stockings in the whole of Nord-Pas-de-Calais. My looms are in the town of Douai

near Valenciennes. Mr. Walker, I believe, was the finest
blacksmith in all of southern England. And you, Mrs. Cutts,
I am told are the finest lacemaker in all of Nottingham.''

Anne clapped her hand over his to stop him from saying
more. "Enough. Take us to Douai.''

"I shall drive the cart,'' he said as he climbed onto the
seat beside the women. "You must think what it is your
husband would want to happen to his plans now.''

"What do you mean?''

The cart turned into a narrow alley. "I mean this, Lady
Blackthorne,'' Robidoux whispered. "Napoleon was defeated by Wellington at Waterloo. The general was expected to arrive in Paris this morning. There will be an
uproar in that city.''

"Civil war? But Lord Alexander is there!''

"Not war. The Chamber will argue about what to do,
and perhaps Napoleon will abdicate to his son, Napoleon
II. But Fouché, who was Napoleon's servant, also wishes
to seize power. Of course, England and her allies want to
put King Louis XVIII onto the throne of France. The strug-
gle for power will be vicious, but it will not last for many
days. A week or two at the most.''

"What does all of this have to do with us?''

"We have only this short time to make our decisions and
act on our plans. I believe King Louis will be returned to
France by the English within a month or two. By that time
our machine must be assembled and prepared to operate.
We must be the first to weave lace with the new English
machine. We must obtain French patents for the looms.
Everything must be done in order, or others will take our
place at the forefront of this new industry.''

"But how can we do all that ourselves? Lord Blackthorne is . . . I think he must be dead.''

"Even so, you are his wife. Lord Alexander supports us,
and he will inherit the duchy. Things do not change so
greatly, do they?''

"Everything is changed! I have no husband. I have nothing."

"You have everything, Madame. You have the name, the title, the inheritance, and most important, the skill. If you are able to design patterns as beautiful as Blackthorne swore to me you could, you and I can develop the most important lace center in all of France here in the region of Calais. Perhaps we will rival Nottingham itself one day. We have the machines. We have the buildings. We even have the funds your husband established here to begin the work."

"But we don't have him. Lord Blackthorne was the vision behind this plan. It was his dream, not mine."

"Then do this for him. Make his dream come true." He looked into her eyes and gave a solemn nod. "Do this for the man you love."

For a long time Anne rode without speaking. Fear urged her to leave the cursed machines with the little Frenchman and hurry back to England and her mother's arms. If nothing else, she could take another position as a housemaid or a kitchenmaid.

She had not been brought up to smuggle contraband or apply for a patent or manage a business or establish a lace industry. She didn't want to rival Nottingham's lace dynasty, and she didn't want to live in a country teetering on the brink of revolution. She certainly hadn't been raised to promote the very machines her father was imprisoned for destroying. Reason told her to leave. Common sense insisted that she abandon the machine and return to safety.

But her heart . . . She shut her eyes and allowed the jostling cart to rock her body with its rhythm. In her mind's eye she pictured him then. Ruel. His gray eyes beckoned her. The curls of his black hair seemed nearly within reach. She could almost see that familiar grin on his face, one corner of his mouth turned up and his lips twitching with suppressed laughter. Was he truly dead? The thought of him lying on that grisly battlefield was too much. If he had died, he had lost his life trying to save hers. If that was not a sign of love, what was?

Perhaps . . . perhaps in spite of everything she had said to him and everything lowborn she had brought to their marriage . . . perhaps Vera was right. Perhaps in his own way he had loved her.

If so, what right had she to abandon his dreams? Monsieur Robidoux was right. Ruel had given her his name, his titles, his wealth. He had trusted her to be his partner. And he had given his life for her.

"I shall stay," she said softly. "Until my husband's goals are achieved, I shall stay in France and help you."

Monsieur Robidoux patted her on the hand. "*La belle dame d'esprit.* Your husband knew you well."

Ruel leaned over the ship's rail and looked down into the gray-green water swirling below. Beside him, Walker reclined with his back against the rail, his eyes searching the vivid blue sky.

"My life runs in a circle, like the flight of those weary seagulls who follow our ship," the Indian said. "My existence is one of endless repetition. Everything I have loved has been taken from me. My family. My home. The woman I loved."

"I didn't realize you cared so much for the little housemaid," Ruel said.

"I speak of days long ago."

"You were once in love?"

"More than once. I lost everything then. Now I have lost my world again. When Vera entered my life, I began to believe something good might come to me after all. The woman had such faith in the goodness of the Creator."

"Like my Anne."

Walker nodded. "Vera was young and full of hope. So pale and beautiful. You know, she did not care about the color of my skin. She told me I was handsome.''

Ruel glanced at his friend. A wry smile was written on the older man's face. Ruel smiled in return.

"You are handsome, Walker. You're tall and strong. I suppose in a way you're rather striking."

"I have the face of a buzzard." He gave a rueful laugh and then let out a shuddering sigh. "She was my wife, Ruel. Did you know that? I married Vera in London."

"I had no idea. I'm so sorry." Ruel shut his eyes against the recurrent sight of the two bloodied women sprawled on the wagon bench. "At least Vera knew of your love for her. I never told Anne. Couldn't bring myself to admit it, let alone say the words. I didn't know I was even capable of such an emotion. I imagined love was a pastime for dandies and women. Romantic nonsense, I always maintained. To me, marriage was an arrangement for social benefit and the procreation of children. Secret liaisons took care of the rest. That was it. All I thought life had to offer. Love? I didn't think I had it in me."

"The day you came to see me at the smithy in Tiverton I recognized you loved that woman. The look in your eyes was one of terror. She might die, you said. 'You have to save her, Walker'. So I did."

"A lot of good it did her. I led Anne from one catastrophe to the next. If she wasn't being shot through the leg, she was being coerced into transporting contraband across land and sea. If she wasn't being forced to carry contemptible lace machines in her baggage, she was forced to drive a cart through a bloody battlefield. She spent her days as my wife either fending off verbal barbs from those in my Society or ducking lead balls being fired by someone trying to assassinate me. Oh, I did well as a husband, Walker. Damned well."

The Indian rested silently against the rail for a long time. His eyes combed the clouds as though he might read answers in them. "All the same," he said finally, "your grief has led you to flee from your responsibility. The duke will believe you dead. You would have been wise to send a letter to him before we embarked.''

''I'll write from New Orleans.''

''In the meantime, your brother may inherit your title.''

''Let him have Marston. Alex is more comfortable in that world than I have ever been.''

''You know Lord Alexander will squander his position. The family wealth will run through his fingers as flour through a hair sieve.''

Ruel studied the waves slapping against the side of the ship. Overhead the masts creaked and the sails snapped. The scent of salt water stung his nostrils, easing in his chest the agony that had weighed on him like a millstone.

''I'll write to Alex,'' he said in a low voice. ''I'll see that he knows I shall never relinquish my title. I'll send instructions to my father for the management of our properties. My brother's fingers will be kept out of the finances. When I return to England, I'll again see to my responsibilities there.''

''This would be wise.''

''I'm a damned fool. I had everything, and I couldn't see it. Now I have nothing. Nothing.''

''You're young. Intelligent. Not without means. You have enough.''

Ruel slammed his fist on the rail and turned away. Striding down the deck toward the ship's stern, he fought the black mist of hopelessness. What good was youth if he had no one with whom to enjoy the long years to come? What use was intelligence if there was no one to match his wit? Of what benefit was wealth in an empty bed in the middle of a cold night?

Yes, he would go to America and build his factory. He might even save the duchy from financial ruin. He came to a standstill on the slick wooden planks and lifted his head to the billowing white sails. But what good was it? What good was anything without her?

Seventeen

ANNE SETTLED INTO A SMALL HOUSE IN THE TOWN OF Douai on the western border of France. Like many other homes in the region of Calais, Anne's had been built of stone, its walls plastered white and its steep roof heavily thatched. Vera slept downstairs near the kitchen, and she insisted on continuing to serve Anne as a lady's maid. Her mistress took an upstairs bedroom with a view of the River Somme.

Using funds previously deposited by the Marquess of Blackthorne and managed by Monsieur Robidoux, Anne purchased pots and pans for the cozy kitchen. She furnished the small living area and bought a table and four chairs for the dining room. She hired a cook, planted a vegetable garden, and employed a tutor to teach her to speak French.

As the days passed, Anne again learned that though some might have thought her husband a wastrel, he had not earned that label. Ruel had been no fool. His plan to enrich the duchy of Marston had been a good one, and his trust in Monsieur Robidoux was well founded. The little Frenchman was a master stockinger with a profitable weaving business, a leader in the town. He told Anne he had met Ruel many years before, but their partnership in the lace business had been undertaken solely through letters. Anne felt certain that had he lived, Ruel would have seen his enterprise successful.

After settling the women into their house, Monsieur Robidoux had driven the cart into one of his large warehouses on the outskirts of town, opened the trunks, and removed the machinery. It took him and his employees two weeks to assemble the equipment. Though the English-made machine had been adapted from a common stocking loom, it required another month for Robidoux to decipher its intricacies, learn how to thread it, and begin to operate it. When the first inch of lace net rolled off the loom, even Anne felt a measure of pride.

Thanks to English intervention, France began to settle back into the once-familiar rhythms of monarchy. The change had not come easily. Following his defeat at Waterloo, Napoleon had indeed abdicated in favor of his son, Napoleon II, just as Robidoux had predicted. But the Chambers denied the young man recognition, and Fouché took the president's chair. As Wellington and Blücher advanced on Paris, the Chambers drew up a new agenda and scrambled to proclaim Napoleon II emperor. His defeated father left the country by sea on July 8, the same day the English escorted King Louis XVIII into Paris in a coach.

Though Wellington wanted Napoleon handed over to the King of France, the little man managed to board the ship *Bellerophon* and sail for England, where he hoped to solicit mercy from the Regent. On July 20, buckling to allied pressure, eight hundred French generals and senior officers surrendered in Paris. Everyone from Napoleon's former regime—his son, brothers, members of the Chambers, and even his foe, Fouché—was expelled from the country. Napoleon's defeat was complete. Four days later, the *Bellerophon* arrived in England near Torbay.

Anne could not have been more disgusted at the news accounts Monsieur Robidoux translated for her from the French newspapers. Rather than living in shame, Napoleon was treated by English Society as the celebrated emperor he once had been. Sightseers in boats surrounded the *Bel-*

lerophon and called to the diminutive figure every time he paraded on deck. When he was moved to Plymouth, nearly ten thousand gawkers crowded around his ship in boats to gaze at him and exclaim on his fine features and excellent manners. Newspapers in France reported that Napoleon had charmed everyone in England and had become popular beyond belief.

If not for the French people's fawning admiration of all English citizens, Anne would have been mortified to let her nationality be known. Everywhere in France, Napoleon was vilified, while Parisians cheered as English troops marched in parade down the Champs Elysées. Following the expulsion of Napoleon's loyal entourage, the former emperor was formally outlawed in Paris by treaty. It was mid-August when the news finally arrived that Napoleon had boarded the ship *Northumberland* bound for the island of St. Helena, where he was to spend the rest of his life in exile.

With the monarchy restored, Hezekiah Cutts's smuggled machine went to work. The sudden voracious demand for lace by everyone from the wealthy aristocracy to the humblest peasants took even Monsieur Robidoux by surprise. As the summer months flew by, Anne hardly had time to breathe. The spectacled little weaver became positively frenetic.

French fashion again rose to the forefront of interest across the Continent, and echoes of the war filtered into even the simplest designs. Soon after Waterloo, men began wearing full-skirted frock coats modeled after military wear. The single-breasted coats featured distinctive Prussian collars without lapels. Wellington's name was given to every type of clothing from coats to pantaloons to boots. A method of tying the cravat was even dubbed after the disgraced Napoleon, and it was as popular as any other of the fourteen most favored neckwear styles.

The end of the war reintroduced a spring tide of French

fashions for women. Ornamental epaulets covered the shoulder seams of pelisses. Hats grew to astronomical heights. Straight-edged lace went completely out of fashion, while scalloped edges began to creep in. Whitework embroidered on muslin came into vogue. Blonde lace began appearing on everything from dresses to aprons.

In a headlong rush to escape her memories, Anne flung herself into making Ruel's dream a success. Aware that many of the elderly former lace workers in Calais had abandoned their techniques, and no young women knew the methods, she started a lace school in a little house down the lane from the one she shared with Vera.

At first she had to be satisfied with teaching her students how to embroider the muslin and net that rolled off the machine in Monsieur Robidoux's warehouse. But as the weeks passed, she urged her experienced and her more talented young employees to begin enriching parts of the white embroideries with sumptuous fancy fillings in needlepoint stitches.

In early September Anne wrote a letter to the Viscountess Eagon, telling Claire of the events that had taken place on that horrible June day at Waterloo. Though she felt she must send the letter as a matter of record, she expected to hear nothing in return. After all, there was no doubt the Chouteau family preferred to pretend that a brown-haired housemaid named Anne Webster never had existed.

Alexander, who was now titled Marquess of Blackthorne and heir apparent to the Duke of Marston, had answered none of her missives to him in Paris. The duke himself was said to be deep in mourning over the death of his elder son at Waterloo. He had failed to respond to the letter Anne had sent him shortly after she arrived in Douai. If not for letters from her mother in London assuring her that their financial assistance continued, Anne would have believed the Chouteau family had dismissed her entirely.

One glowing pink evening just at sunset, Monsieur Robidoux arrived at Anne's house bearing a letter. Anne left Vera at the fireside and went to the door to greet him.

"If the Duke of Marston has disavowed you, Lady Blackthorne," the Frenchman said as he presented the letter with a deep bow, "have no fear. Our industry here in Calais grows beyond our dreams. You may be assured of financial comfort for many years to come, and it is not beyond imagining that you and I together may grow wealthy. I beg of you to consider my words with much seriousness."

"*Merci*, Monsieur Robidoux." Anne dipped a curtsy and tried to return the man's gracious smile.

How could she explain to him that she had never wanted wealth or security? Her father's health and safety had been uppermost in her heart for so many years she had hardly been able to think beyond it. Now, the latest letter from her mother had assured Anne her father was to be released from prison within the month. In fact, the barrister Ruel had employed had managed to prevent the case being brought to trial.

With her family safe and her own financial security assured, Anne knew she should be content. She never would. She had tasted the cordial of Ruel's passion, and nothing could quench her thirst for it.

"*En ami*, I tell you I am an honorable man, madame," Robidoux continued, tugging at his lapels. "I will see to your care. Here in France we say. *Il faut cultiver notre jardin*. We must cultivate our garden. It means we must tend to our own affairs. No matter the contents of this letter, you have no need for concern."

"*Bien entendu. Merci beaucoup, monsieur,*" she said softly as she broke the seal on the letter. It had not been written by the duke, but by his daughter, the viscountess. "*Bonsoir, et Dieu vous garde.*"

"*J'y suis, j'y reste. Bonsoir, madame.*"

As the Frenchman walked down the lane to his carriage, Anne read Claire's letter. Her words mirrored their composer—light, chatty, sparkling with half-finished sentences and exclamation points. Claire had written to tell Anne that her brother would marry Gabrielle Duchesne, daughter of the Comte de la Roche, in Paris at the end of the month. Would Anne be so good as to come to Alexander's wedding?

"Claire has asked me to travel to Paris," Anne told Vera as she shut the door behind her. "She wants me to see the Marquess of Blackthorne married."

"Really?" Vera looked up from her knitting. "That's wonderful!"

"I can't go."

"Whyever not?"

"Alexander Chouteau won't want me at his wedding, and seeing Claire will only remind me of Ruel. I'll have to answer a thousand questions and try to explain what he and I were doing at Waterloo. I'll be forced to relive everything. I can't bear it."

"You must go, Anne. You have no choice. You're the Dowager Marchioness of Blackthorne, and you must represent your husband at his brother's marriage. If you don't attend the wedding, everyone will believe you have something to be ashamed of, hiding away from Society as you have all these months."

"I'm not hiding!"

"Are you not? You go nowhere but to the warehouse and the lace school. You wear those horrid black dresses day after day. You never attend balls or teas, though you've been invited plenty of times. You won't pay calls, and you're reluctant to receive visitors. You might as well be invisible, for all the joy you display."

"I won't deny my lack of liveliness, Vera. These past months have been very difficult for me. But I'm not hiding."

"Then go to Paris and sit in the chapel with the Duke of Marston and his wife. Take your place in the family, or they will cut you out of everything you're owed."

"I'm owed nothing, Vera, and you know it. Ruel and I were hardly married under normal circumstances. Everyone hoped I would die soon after the wedding, and when I didn't I was little more than an embarrassment to the family."

"The Viscountess Eagon would not have invited you to her brother's wedding had you been nothing but an embarrassment. She wants you there. You must go, Anne."

Dropping into her chair, Anne stared at the fire. "Do you want to know something strange, Vera? At this very moment, I have everything I believed I might have wanted in life. I possess my faith in God, the well-being of my parents, even this house. A little stone house. Do you know . . ." She stopped, struggling against tears. "Do you know, I always wanted a lace school . . . and now I have one. I even . . . I believe Monsieur Robidoux wishes to marry me." She gave a laugh that was half a sob. "He informed me yesterday at the warehouse that he has been thinking we should wed. Oh, Vera, I shall have my stone house and my lace school and even . . . even my weaver."

"You make it sound like a death sentence. It's not so bad, is it? Monsieur Robidoux is a good man, after all. He treats you fairly, and he respects your skills. Why not marry him?"

"I don't love him!"

"Nor does he love you. But look what love got us. You're the widow of a man who died leaving you nothing but aching memories. And I'm . . . I have nothing at all. Nothing but the emptiness." Her voice bitter, Vera stood and tossed her knitting into her chair. The ball of yarn tumbled to the floor and rolled toward the hearth.

"Better to marry for security and comfort than for passion," she went on. "Marry Monsieur Robidoux, Anne. At least you'll have a home of your own and a husband who won't go plunging across bloody battlefields and getting himself killed. That should be happiness enough.''

Humiliated at her own selfishness, Anne brushed a tear to keep it from rolling down her cheek. ''I'm sorry, Vera.''

''No, I'm sorry! Would that I had a man like Monsieur Robidoux asking for my hand. But I had to love Walker, had to fall into his arms, had to melt at the sound of his voice. I thought him magical, and he was. He was so magical he vanished. *Pfft!* Look at me, Anne. Can't you see what's happened?''

Anne lifted her head, puzzled at the near-hysterical tone of her levelheaded friend. ''Vera?''

''I'm pregnant, Annie! I'm going to have Walker's baby.''

''Oh, Vera!'' Anne leapt up from her chair and clasped her friend to her breast. ''Vera, why didn't you tell me? How long have you known? When will the baby be born?''

''I'm not sure. March, I think.'' Tears trickled down Vera's pale cheeks. ''I loved him, Annie. I loved him so much, and I'll never see him again. I love him still—and I hate him, too, for dying and leaving me alone. He swore he'd watch over me. The day we were married—''

''Married? Vera, when?''

''In London. I believed my life had just begun. I'd never known such happiness. Such peace. And then . . . oh, Anne, how can I go on without him? What shall I do?''

Anne lifted her head and stared at the blank white ceiling. Hearing her own despair echoed in Vera's cries, she suddenly knew what must be done. As clearly as she could picture the proper placement for every one of a thousand pins on a parchment pattern of bobbin lace, she saw a solution to their problems.

''We shall travel to Paris together, Vera.'' She drew in a deep breath. ''Before the wedding, I shall request a tête-à-tête with the Duke of Marston. I shall put my affairs in order with the Chouteau family and ask that I be given some recompense for my title. I believe the duke may settle as much as four or five thousand pounds on me.''

"Four or five thousand pounds? But that's nothing! How can you live the rest of your life on such a small fortune?''

"Quite easily. As the wife of Monsieur Robidoux, I shall want for nothing. When we return from Paris, I shall marry my weaver.''

"Annie, you can't marry Monsieur Robidoux! Truly, I didn't mean what I said before about him. I was ranting.'' Vera's eyes filled with tears again. "He's far too old for you, and he's hardly as tall as your shoulder. You can't possibly learn to love him, no matter how decent and respectable he is. Be his partner, but not his wife.''

"Don't be ridiculous, Vera. Men form partnerships with other men. Monsieur Robidoux respects my talents, but he will never make me an equal with him in the lace business. I am little more than a highly valued employee. If I don't marry him, once my skills have reached the end of their usefulness, I shall be cut off.''

"You'll never be useless here in France.''

"How little you know. The women of Calais have lace-making talents as brilliant as the most skilled in Nottingham. One of my elderly ladies once worked a magnificent *point d'Alençon*. She showed me the length of the rich, heavy lace she had helped to make, and I was truly astonished at its complexity. The blonde laces from Chantilly are superb, and even the Lille and Arras laces evidence great skill.''

"Perhaps so, but it was you who smuggled in the loom, you who set up the school, and you who manage the women turning Robidoux's plain and boring machine-made net into wonderful lace. You're invaluable not only to him but to the entire lace industry in France.''

"Vera, your loyalty touches my heart, but you must face reality. It will not be many months before other Englishmen arrive in France with lace machines of their own. Others will found lace schools, and the competition for skilled labor will be fierce. Calais promises one day to be the center of French lace manufacture."

"And Monsieur Robidoux its emperor."

"Shall I not be his empress?"

"Oh, Annie, don't be silly. You've never wanted fame or fortune."

"No, but I mean to ensure security for your child. As Madame Robidoux, I can continue to pay you a livelihood, and we shall make certain your little one never faces the ignominy of poverty."

"You would do that for me?"

Anne thought of her own past as she looked into Vera's large, sad eyes. Once she had walked away from her desire for security in order to save her father's future. Again, she had walked away from safety in order to marry Ruel and give his dreams a future. How could she do less for Vera?

"Of course I would," she said softly. "Now, stop your worries and pick up your ball of knitting wool before it rolls into the fire."

Setting her friend aside, Anne walked to the window. The last fingers of sunset threaded through the trees on the hillside. The baby was Vera's, and for Vera alone Anne would do almost anything. But the baby was also Walker's child. Ruel had loved Walker. How could Anne do less than to provide this son or daughter a heritage?

"Vera?" she asked, her focus still on the horizon. "Light a candle for me, will you please? I must write a letter to Monsieur Robidoux telling him I accept his offer and shall marry him on my return from Paris. Then we must begin packing our trunks."

As Vera moved across the room toward the candle box, Anne studied the sky. A wisp of black smoke drifted across the evening, and once again she knew the ache of memory. Perhaps it was only her gift for seeing patterns where others saw the common objects of life. Perhaps it was her tendency to envision lace where others saw nothing.

All the same, she was certain she saw in that breath of smoke the curl of a man's black hair. In the rustle of evening breeze against the windowpane, she heard the whisper of his voice. In the dark pearl of the sky, she saw the gray of his eyes. And she was quite sure, at that moment, he was looking into her soul.

The wedding of the Marquess of Blackthorne to the daughter of the Comte de la Roche promised to be everything his elder brother's should have been. Anne had never witnessed such pomp and pageantry as that taking place in Paris in the days leading up to the wedding.

It seemed as though France's aristocracy viewed the marriage as a symbol of their happy alliance with the country that had so magnificently restored their beloved monarchy. To the French nobility, the wedding presented a grand opportunity to uncork every bottle of champagne stashed away during the years of war, to unfurl every yard of lace that had been hidden, to display every diamond and emerald in the realm.

In sharp contrast to the glitter, Anne dressed in her wardrobe of crepe mourning gowns decorated with nothing more than black bugle beads, black roses, black velvet Vandykes, or black chenille. She wore no jewelry but a jet brooch at her neck, and she carried a black silk handkerchief in her reticule. It was the least she could do in Ruel's memory. Only the Duke of Marston and his eldest daughter seemed to remember there had ever been another Marquess of Blackthorne.

Alexander strutted from tea party to ballroom arrayed in the very finest of dandy fashion. With his corseted waist, rouged cheeks, and billowing cossack trousers, he outshone even his buxom fiancée. He tinged his palms with vermilion and whitened the backs of his hands with enamel. An aura of sweetly scented perfume drifted always about his noble person. Anne learned she could find her brother-in-law simply by sniffing him out in a crowd.

Claire's four younger sisters, too, reveled in the celebration. Lucy, Elizabeth, Charlotte, and Rebecca, a bevy of lovely blondes, each had brought their husbands and children to France, making a grand Continental holiday of the event. Their mother paraded about as though she were the Queen of Sheba. Her ample figure swathed in lace and satin, the duchess fairly billowed like a ship asail as she floated from one event to another.

"I should think Her Grace the Duchess of Marston would recognize what bad form she displays," Vera fretted one afternoon as she dressed Anne for tea. "At least the duke wears a black armband and seems still to truly mourn his son's death. And I've not seen the Viscountess Eagon in anything but the darkest of colors. She wore a midnight blue at breakfast today. Did you see? It wasn't even a morning dress, and I thought it so grand of her to wear it."

Anne nodded. "Claire is very good."

She could hardly think beyond counting the days until the wedding was over. Her first obstacle had been surmounted two days before. In a private meeting with the Duke of Marston, she had informed him of her desire to remarry. Expressing sympathy at the loss of her first husband and great satisfaction at her intelligent decision to rewed and remove herself from the Chouteau family, the duke bestowed on her a fortune of ten thousand pounds. Far more than she had expected—or deserved, considering the humiliation and grief she had brought on the family— the money would go a long way toward securing the future of Vera's child.

"In my opinion," Vera said, draping a black shawl around Anne's shoulders, "all the duchess's daughters save the Viscountess Eagon are as vain and shallow as their mother. They haven't one drop of the character your husband displayed and nothing of their eldest sister's wit and charm.''

"Vera, please don't say such—''

"Lady Blackthorne, forgive my interruption.'' The duke's own valet executed a crisp bow in the open doorway of her bedroom. "Your presence is required in the drawing room immediately.''

"Required?'' Anne glanced at Vera as she stood up from her dressing table. "Not requested?''

"The Duke of Marston requires your presence, my lady. At once.''

"Of course.'' Anne grabbed her gloves from the table and tugged them on as she followed the valet into the corridor. "Vera, stay here and wait for me. You can take your tea a little late today.''

"Yes, my lady.''

Anne picked up her skirts and hurried after the valet. "What has happened that the duke wishes to see me?''

"I know only that the family has been requested to gather.''

"Has someone fallen ill? Is the wedding in jeopardy?''

The valet lifted his chin. "I know nothing, Lady Blackthorne.''

"Of course not.'' Her heart hammering, Anne had to be content to race along one corridor after another, down three flights of stairs, and through two receiving rooms before she reached the drawing room where the Chouteau family was assembling.

Slipping into the room behind two of Ruel's sisters, she could see at once that something profound had taken place. Claire sobbed into her handkerchief, the portly viscount kneeling solicitously at his wife's side. The Duchess of Marston reclined in a deathly swoon as her youngest daughter fanned her ashen face. Alexander was nowhere to be seen.

When everyone was seated, the duke stood, balanced

himself on his cane, and fitted his monocle to his eye. "An event of great import has occurred," he said. "I have had a letter from Ruel."

"Ruel!" A collective gasp went up. Anne gulped down a cry of shock. The duchess closed her eyes and emitted a loud groan. Claire dabbed her eyes.

Trembling, hardly able to breathe, Anne watched as the duke shook out the folds of a sheet of white paper and began to read. "August 13, 1815. My dear father, as I pen this letter, I am fast at sea on a ship bound for America. I shall entrust the letter's delivery to you via the next vessel we encounter. My traveling companion and friend, Mr. Walker, previously employed as a blacksmith in Tiverton, has convinced me of my error in failing to write to you sooner. I trust you will understand the circumstances of this omission once I have explained them.

"On leaving Brussels, Anne, the Marchioness of Blackthorne, and I inadvertently were caught in a battle at Waterloo between the forces of Wellington and Napoleon. Father, I have never witnessed such a display of carnage, nor do I have intelligence as to its outcome. During this battle, we attempted to escape. My wife was killed."

"Killed?" Anne jumped to her feet. "But I wasn't killed! There was a cannonball, you see." She sucked in a sob. "Oh, sir, is Ruel truly alive?"

"Sit down, Lady Blackthorne, if you please," the duke said. "I have endured histrionics enough for one day. I shall continue the epistle."

Shaking with disbelief, Anne sank into her chair.

"My wife was killed," the duke repeated. "Of that event, I am able to write nothing further, nor can I bring myself to speak of it even to Mr. Walker. On our escaping to safety, I made the immediate decision to travel to America without delay. I trust you will respect my desire to spend the time of mourning in a place other than England. While I am away, please entrust all financial and legal mat-

ters regarding my properties to my brother Theodore, the
Viscount Eagon, husband to my eldest sister, Claire. I trust
his judgment implicitly and have not the slightest reluctance
to place my affairs under his excellent care.''

"Teddy?'' Claire exclaimed to her husband.

"Indeed,'' the viscount said with a nod. "I have been
given a letter from Blackthorne as well. Your Grace, do
carry on.''

"Thank you, Teddy,'' the duke said, returning to Ruel's
letter. "Please place into the hands of the proper authorities
the matter of an attempt on my life following the Duchess
of Richmond's ball in Brussels.''

"Father—'' Claire cried.

"Alexander will supply you with the particulars of Lord
Droughtmoor's part in this unhappy event,'' the duke read
on. "Until I return, you may write to me at the home of
your nephew, Auguste Chouteau, in Saint Louis. My
warmest regards, etc. Ruel Chouteau, Marquess of Blackthorne, etc., etc.''

The duke allowed his monocle to drop from his eye. He
turned to Anne. "My elder son is alive. What do you know
about that?''

Eighteen

"I KNOW NOTHING, YOUR GRACE," ANNE SAID TO THE duke. "As I have told you both in letter and in private conversation, I was rendered unconscious on the battlefield at Waterloo. When I awakened, night had fallen, and I discovered myself to be alone with my lady's maid. I could see little in the moonlight save the countless thousands of dead around me. I had no doubt my husband was among them."

"You failed to search for my son's body?" the duke asked.

"Your Grace, the battle continued not many yards from where I had been stricken. For all I knew, the French would sweep down on us again, as they had so many times before. My lady's maid and I unharnessed the dead horses, captured two others we found wandering loose on the field, and fled into the forest. We assumed that had my husband and Mr. Walker been alive, they would have taken us to safety themselves."

"The last you saw my son he was alive?"

"Yes, Your Grace. Lord Blackthorne was attempting to capture the runaway horses. We were separated, and I never saw him again. I was certain he had died. I had no doubt of it. Even though I've heard you read his letter, I cannot believe that if Ruel were alive and uninjured he would have left me alone and unconscious on that battlefield."

"Why not? He believed you dead."

"But I wasn't!"

"You were dead enough for him," the duchess said suddenly, rising from her couch like a gray ghost. "Clearly he saw little point in rescuing you, dead or alive. He left you there to die, young lady, and he counted on you to do so. But you didn't, did you? Assuring all of us that *he* was dead, you made your merry way to France, where you spent the marquess's money investing in the manufacture of lace. Then you, the Marchioness of Blackthorne and bearer of our family's proud name, proceeded to find yourself a Frenchman to wed. And a merchant at that!"

"I believed my husband dead, Your Grace."

"You wished him dead and yourself the richer for it," she said bitterly. "But now he's alive, and Alexander has gone off to fetch him back."

"But the wedding . . ."

"Postponed." The duchess shook her handkerchief at Anne. "Ruel is alive, Alex is gone, the wedding is off, and it's all your fault! Your fault, you shameless creature! You've spoiled everything."

"Spoiled everything?" Anne slowly rose. "Ruel is alive. Alive!" Turning to the viscountess, she gave a laugh of disbelief. "Ruel's alive, Claire! We thought him dead, and now he's alive! And Mr. Walker's alive! Oh, I must tell Vera. I must go upstairs at once. I can't see why anyone could be anything but happy."

"Can you not?" the duchess barked. "Tell her then, Laurent. Tell Ruel's faithless wife why he is better off dead."

"That's enough, Beatrice!" the duke shouted. "This is a family matter."

"But the little housemaid is as much family as her bastard husband. Tell her, Laurent."

"Beatrice!" The duke hammered his cane into the floor. "Lady Blackthorne, you came to me not two days ago informing me of your desire to leave this family and marry again. I settled on you a sum of money with the agreement that you wed this Frenchman of yours and never trouble us again. I consider your relationship with our family at an end.''

Anne stared at the wizened man. ''Then you err, Your Grace.''

''Of course!'' the duchess burst out. ''Now that she sees she can sink her claws into us again, humiliating us before everyone, she leaps at the opportunity.''

Anne turned on the duchess. ''I shall say again as I have said before. Every action I undertook from my journey to France to my association with the man who has asked for my hand stemmed from the belief that I was a widow. No, madam, I shall not walk out of this family, despite the fact that I am despised and rejected by you. There is one factor you forget. I loved your son. I love him still.''

''Love, love, love,'' the duchess spat. ''Every ruinous event in my life has resulted from that hideous emotion. Run to your beloved husband, then. See how happy he is to take you back after Alexander informs him you promised your hand to another man within three months of his supposed death.''

''No!'' Anne gasped. ''Lord Alexander has gone to tell Ruel that?''

''And to bring him back,'' the duke cut in. ''Now, we shall settle this matter once and for all. Before my son returns, Lady Blackthorne, I propose you carry out your plan to wed the Frenchman. I intend to see it accomplished within the week. You will remarry under the public misconception that Ruel is dead, before the news leaks out that he is alive. This will leave everything cleanly resolved.''

''Resolved?'' the duchess shrieked. ''It will only be resolved on Ruel's grave.''

''How can you wish your son dead?'' Anne shouted back. ''You are the wickedest mother I have ever known!''

"I am not Ruel's mother!"

Silence dropped like a damp blanket over the drawing room. Everyone turned to stare at the hysterically weeping woman.

"You aren't?" Anne breathed the words. "Then who is?"

"Of course she's his mother," the duke roared, his voice bouncing off the high ceiling. "Ruel is my son. My first-born. My heir. I took him in, gave him my name, made him mine. I love him, by God, and he'll wear my title no matter who sired him! Do you hear me, Beatrice? Ruel is my son. Your son!"

"He's not! He's not, you demon!"

"Shut up, Beatrice. Shut up and sit down!"

"I wish him dead," the duchess shrieked. "He destroyed my life!"

"And you destroyed his." Anne glared at the woman. "Ruel believes you his mother whether you are or not. He has sensed your rejection, your hatred. You planted every seed of bitterness in his life. You nurtured every root of unhappiness. You revile him for his inability to build a family dynasty, my lord duke, yet you never taught him the treasure of home and hearth. What he has been for too many years is thanks to both of you. What he can become lies only in the hands of God."

Unable to face them any longer, Anne turned and ran out of the drawing room. Ruel was alive. It was all she knew. Ruel was alive, and Alex was going to him to tell him she didn't love him.

As she lifted her skirts and took the stairs two at a time, she made the most difficult—and the easiest—decision of her life. She would go to America.

"You were at the marquess's side the night of the Duchess of Richmond's ball," the Viscount Eagon said to Anne as they stood on the pier at the edge of the port city of Le

Havre, France. "Did you see Droughtmoor fire the pistol?"

Anne tried to sort through her memories of that night. So much had whirled past her in the two weeks following the arrival of Ruel's letter. On hearing that both Ruel and Walker were alive, Vera immediately had decided that she, too, would travel to America. Walker needed to know his wife was alive and bearing his child—even if he had left her on that battlefield. Neither Vera nor Anne could believe the men had simply abandoned them to die.

Anne dreaded traveling such a distance with Vera. The rough journey might cause her to lose the baby. Though the birth was not expected until March, Atlantic crossings had been known to take as long as five months, especially at this time of year. Equally distressing was Anne's fear of how Ruel might react when Lord Alexander told him she was alive, yet engaged to marry someone else. What if he turned to another woman in St. Louis? What if he already had? Anne could hardly bear the thought of Ruel's arms around anyone but herself, his hands touching any woman's skin but her own. Unable to rest, she had written to Monsieur Robidoux to inform him of the situation. Then she had made immediate plans to leave the country.

Finding passage on a ship was another matter. Winter was at hand, and few vessels risked venturing into the stormy seas. Anne knew it was possible that Lord Alexander would arrive weeks ahead of her and Vera, no matter how quickly their ship crossed the Atlantic.

Claire's kindhearted husband had taken Anne in hand from the moment she told him of her plan to go to America. Viscount Eagon had located a merchant vessel, booked passage, and arranged to take the two women to Le Havre. Again, she was impressed by Ruel's selection of the person who would manage his affairs.

"I can hardly piece together how my husband was shot," she told the viscount. "At the news of Napoleon taking Charleroi, everyone began rushing through the corridors of

Richmond's house, out the doors, and into the streets. I recall Mr. Walker shouting something—a warning, I suppose. I smelled black powder. And then Ruel fell on me.''

"Did you actually see Droughtmoor?"

"Not in the crowd, but I have no doubt he was the assassin. Earlier I heard him challenge Ruel to a duel. When news of the war broke out, Ruel told him their assignation the following morning would be impossible, and Droughtmoor vowed to have his revenge. The next thing I knew, Ruel lay bleeding in my arms.''

"The assassin was not Droughtmoor."

"How can you be certain?"

"More than one witness can testify to his presence moments after the news of Napoleon arrived. Barkham, Wimberly—''

"Droughtmoor accomplices. Of course they defend him!"

"The Duke of Richmond is also a witness on behalf of Lord Droughtmoor. The duke was given intelligence of the hostile exchange between the men. He followed Droughtmoor outside to have a word with him, meaning to put a stop to any duel of honor on foreign land. The duke was speaking with Droughtmoor in the roadway when word of Blackthorne's shooting came.''

"Then it must have been Barkham or Wimberly."

"Both were with the duke." The viscount shook his head as he stared out at the large ship being loaded with cargo. "Someone else shot your husband, Lady Blackthorne. He has been shot at more than once, as you well know. Have you any idea who might want him dead?"

A sickening chill surged over Anne as she remembered the earlier incident involving Ruel. Everyone had assumed the spurned gamekeeper wanted to kill Anne. But he, too, had an alibi. Then she thought of the family meeting when the Duchess of Marston had reviled Ruel and wished him dead.

"The duchess?" she whispered. "Could Her Grace have hired an assassin?"

The viscount lifted his eyebrows. "Possibly. She minces no words concerning her dislike for him."

"No," Anne said suddenly. "It wasn't the duchess. She despises Ruel, but she has allowed him to live as heir apparent for far too many years. If she'd wanted him dead, she would have seen to it long ago. The stalker is someone else. Someone who stands to gain the most by my husband's death."

Viscount Eagon stared at her. "Can you be thinking—"

"Lord Alexander."

"Surely not! I watched them grow up together. They were bosom friends and the closest of brothers all their childhood. I've seen Alex express nothing but the deepest love for the marquess. He rushed to America the moment he heard Ruel was alive. I cannot believe—"

"Lord Alexander is a more accomplished actor than even his mother. When Ruel was in America and rumored to be dead the first time, she surely told her son of his brother's heritage. On Ruel's return, she must have been devastated at Alex losing the title and fortune."

"Enough to urge Alex to murder Ruel?"

"I think Lord Alexander was capable of such evil on his own volition. You witnessed only his public facade. I saw him too many times in private rages to believe him incapable of such action. He had the motive and the opportunity."

"Lady Blackthorne," the viscount said in a low voice. "Lord Alexander will arrive in America long before you or any letter of warning we might send. If Ruel believes Alex loves him . . ."

"Alex will kill him." She swallowed. "For all his impenetrable exterior, Ruel is vulnerable. Lacking his mother's love, he has become both hardened and vulnerable at the same time. No one knows the chinks in Ruel's armor better than his brother." Her fingers tightened on her shawl as she thought about what might happen. "Even if I arrive in time to caution him, he may not believe what I tell him about Alex."

The viscount regarded her for a moment without speaking. Then he took her hand. "Lady Blackthorne, do you love your husband as you vowed you did?"

"At first the marriage was little more than an arrangement between us. I thought of it as another of his games." She looked away. "I learned to love Ruel. These past months . . . thinking him dead . . . have been unbearable. The truth is . . . I don't care where we live or what his properties or who his family. I love him, Teddy. I love Ruel, and if . . . if I lose him again . . ."

"You must make him believe in your love. Nothing else may convince him of his brother's evil wishes." He kissed the back of her hand. "It's time you boarded the ship, Lady Blackthorne. I shall see to your properties until you return to assume them. It will be my prayer you return with your husband at your side."

Anne gave the viscount the bravest smile she could muster. "God bless you, Teddy," she whispered.

"And you, Anne."

By the time the sailing vessel arrived in New Orleans in January of 1816, Anne had completely restored the panel of lace she had removed from her bloodied blue gown. Vera had doubled in size around the middle, but her face was more sunken and her eyes deeper and larger than Anne had ever seen them. She had not lost her baby, but it seemed almost impossible that the child—or its mother—could survive the rigors of the continuing journey.

Vera was determined to go on. Knowing that Walker lived, she became obsessed with seeing his face again. She plagued Anne with questions that had no answers. Would Walker have reverted to his Indian ways? Might he have taken another wife? Would he want to make a life with her and their baby? Could she possibly live in this backward wilderness so far from the beaches of Devonshire?

Anne knew little beyond her own drive to keep going. In New Orleans, she had inquired about previous passengers on various merchant ships recently docked from the Continent. Alexander Chouteau, she discovered, had arrived in the city just before Christmas, barely a month ahead of her and Vera. She traced him to a hotel and learned he had stayed there a fortnight and had wagered prodigious sums at the gaming tables before engaging a coach to take him on the frozen roads north to Missouri.

Two weeks. Alex was only two weeks ahead. Might she catch up to him? Might she stop him? She brushed aside Vera's objections and booked them passage on one of the few steamships plying the Mississippi. Once Ruel had insisted these mechanical monsters were the hope of the future, and there was no doubt that a steamship could outdistance any horse-drawn coach.

Terrified of the belching smokestack and flipping paddle wheel, Vera huddled in their berth all the way up the river from New Orleans to the mouth of the Ohio. When the steamboat could go no farther, the two women disembarked and joined other passengers in a small, worn coach drawn by four ill-tempered horses.

Never had Anne known such bitter cold, such dark nights, such uncertain days. Food was scarce and all but inedible. There were no inns or hostels. Few towns. Nowhere to wash or change clothing or rest. As the days turned to weeks, Vera visibly withered. She clung to Anne's hand, fretting constantly over the impending birth of her baby in this frozen wasteland. But never once did she mention turning back.

On the twentieth day of March, when the snows had melted, the dirt tracks had turned to sucking mud, and the flowers on the white dogwoods had begun to bud out, the

coach rolled into St. Louis, Missouri. It was hardly the grand
city Anne had imagined from Ruel's descriptions of its wonders.

On the drive to the home of Auguste Chouteau, she
counted seven live pigs, three dead ones, and eight cows.
Mangy dogs yapped in front of the market house, while a
duck paddled across one of the countless mud holes in the
street. Soldiers, boatmen, Indians, and slaves mingled easily
with other residents. Some of the women she saw were
outfitted in outrageous French fashion, while others wore
rags.

Anne estimated that there were hardly more than two
hundred homes in the area, nearly all liberally coated with
whitewash. Some had been built of stone and some of
brick, but most of the houses were little more than rough-
hewn log cabins. Signs identifying shop and office locations
had been printed in both French and English. In addition
to a few mercantiles, several fur-trading posts, and a news-
paper office, she spotted a small school and two volunteer
fire companies.

"Do you think they'll be here, Annie?" Vera asked for
the hundredth time. "Are you certain it was Auguste Chouteau they were visiting and not some other person?"

Anne nestled Vera's head against her shoulder. "We'll
know everything soon," she said softly.

The coach drew up to the front of an imposing white-
washed stone house with a wraparound porch on the second
floor, dormers in the roof, and two enormous chimneys.
When the coach pulled to a stop, Anne helped Vera down
the steps while the footman threw their trunks to the
ground. In moments, the coach pulled away, leaving the
two bedraggled women standing at the door.

"*Oui*, madame?" The servant who answered their knock
stared in disdain at Anne's dusty skirt and unwashed face.

"The Marquess of Blackthorne?" she asked. "Is he
here?"

"And Mr. Walker?" Vera put in. "Where are they?"

"Have you a calling card, madam?" His language changed from French to English, but his demeanor never altered.

"Tell the marquess that his wife, the Marchioness of Blackthorne, has just arrived."

The footman glanced behind her, as if looking for someone else. Anne let out a sigh. "It's me, sir. I'm Lady Blackthorne."

"I beg your pardon. Will you not come in?" He stepped aside and ushered the women into a cool, stone-floored hall before hurrying up the long staircase.

Anne's heart leapt for the first time since she had heard the duke read from Ruel's letter. He was here! Would he recognize her? Would he want her? Oh, she looked terrible.

"Vera, my hair. Is it—"

"Anne?"

She looked to the top of the stairs. He stood outlined in the morning sun, tall, raven-haired, magnificent. White shirt. Black trousers. Leather boots. A quill dropped from his fingers to the carpeted landing.

"Anne?" he repeated.

All these months, and she hadn't planned what to say. Hadn't imagined how it would be to actually see him again.

"I'm here, Ruel," she said. "I've come from France."

Nostrils flaring, he gripped the bannister as he started down the stairs. He gray eyes burned silver. "Anne, is it really you?"

She left Vera's side. "I thought you had died at Waterloo—"

"But it was you—"

"No, I was alive. I . . . we went to France and—"

"You're not dead?"

"No, but I thought you were until the letter came. The duke—"

"Dear God!" He leapt down the last five steps, tore

across the hall, caught her up in his arms, and swung her around and around. "It's a miracle! Anne! Dear Lord, you're alive!"

Laughing, crying, she clung to him. "I can't believe it's really you!"

"It's a miracle!"

"Ruel, I was certain I'd never see you again. So many months—"

"Almost a year." He let her slide down him until her feet touched the floor. Searching her eyes, he shook his head. "You're beautiful."

She thought of all the miles she'd come, all the days without a wash, all the wrinkles in her dress and tangles in her hair, and none of it mattered. To him she was beautiful. Beautiful!

"I believed I would never hold you in my arms again," he murmured. "I saw you dead on that battlefield. Your blue dress was drenched in blood. You lay lifeless, as did Vera. The horses were mangled and the cart half blown to bits. Dear heaven, how many times have I recalled that vision in my mind. Your mouth hung open . . . your eyes were rolled back . . . your head lolled to one side. You were dead, Anne."

She shook her head. "Vera and I lay unconscious for hours. It was night when we awoke, and the battle still raged on all around us. Our ears had been deafened by the blast of the cannonball, but we could see the fallen men lying in great tortured heaps. At first we thought you must have gone to France. Later, we had no doubt you and Walker were among the dead at Waterloo."

"You were mistaken. After finding you on the front line, we knew we had no choice but to flee the battleground. Walker insisted we run. He said we'd be killed, too." He gripped her shoulders. "Anne, I've grieved you all these months."

"Have you? Vera and I thought perhaps . . . after we had

your letter, we believed you and Walker . . . well, Vera said
. . . Vera?'' She turned, seeking her friend.

Vera had collapsed beside the door. Doubled over, she
clutched her stomach as a trickle of water dampened her
stockings and formed a puddle on the floor between her
feet.

''Vera!'' Anne tore away from Ruel and ran across the
hall to her friend. ''Vera, what's the matter? Are you ill?''

She lifted her head, her great eyes bright with fear. ''I
don't know, Annie,'' she whispered. ''It's a terrible pain.
I think I'm dying.''

''Ruel, send for an apothecary at once!'' Anne shook his
arm. ''Vera mustn't die, do you understand?''

''Where's Walker?'' Vera groaned.

''He's been living with his people in the Great Osage village near Fort Carondelet,'' Ruel said, crouching at Vera's
side. ''He's in St. Genevieve right now negotiating—''

''He's left me. Ohhh, Annie!''

Anne gathered her friend to her breast. ''Ruel, you must
send for Walker immediately. Vera's bearing his child.
Go!''

Racing to the door, Ruel ran out into the sunshine. Still
reeling with disbelief, he summoned a carriage and sent it
down the hill to fetch one of St. Louis's thirteen physicians.
For a moment, he considered riding after Walker himself.
He knew St. Genevieve well, and he had no doubt he could
find his friend more quickly than anyone. But Anne was
here, and he was not about to leave her again.

He sent a rider to the town where Walker was negotiating
on behalf of the Osage. Ruel's message urged Walker to
hurry to the home of Auguste Chouteau at once. As he
watched the horse's hooves send up a line of dust along
the road, he paused on the porch. His mind still struggled
with the realization. Anne! Anne had come back from the
dead. She was inside the house. How could that be?

He had been haunted by her memory. Though certain

that he loved her, he had failed to tell her at Waterloo. Then she had been killed on the field. Killed. He had been so sure of it. Every mile of ocean he had crossed had been etched with his agony. Regret. Anger. Disbelief. Sorrow. Self-hatred. Fury. Rage. Tears.

How many tears had he wept over her? When he thought back on his life, he could not recall shedding a single tear about anything. Ever. Grieving Anne had torn the edges of his heart.

Once in America, he had gone on living. Existing. In partnership with his elderly cousin, Auguste, he had spent the months working toward the dream that once had possessed him. He had negotiated contracts with cotton farmers in the southern states. He had invested in a steamship company that planned to dock merchant vessels in St. Louis within two years. He had sent cotton cloth, silks, hardware, and cutlery to New Mexico on a trail that could be negotiated in fifty days or less and had turned a profit of two thousand percent. Everything had gone well.

Still, he had felt dead inside.

In the past weeks, despairing of hope, he had found his only comfort in God. There were no cathedrals or abbeys like the ones he had known in England, so he sought strength in the congregation that met in the little log Baptist church on Fee Fee Creek. But Ruel could hardly accept that God's grace, His free gift of love, could reach down and touch his own life so profoundly. The most undeserving of men, he had been remiss in too many ways.

But now God had brought Anne all this way to him. Feeling like a young colt set free in a spring pasture, he bounded back across the front porch and burst through the door.

"Oh, Ruel, I think Vera's dying!" Anne cried. "She's in terrible agony."

A cluster of household servants had gathered around the writhing woman who lay on the floor, pillow beneath her head. Anne held her friend's hand, stroking it helplessly. At the commotion, Ruel's cousin hurried in from the garden behind the house, his much younger wife on his arm.

"Blackthorne?" he asked. "I am told your wife has come from England? I thought she was . . . What happens here?"

Realizing there was no time for introductions, Ruel took his cousin to one side to explain. Thérèse Chouteau parted the servants and knelt at Vera's side. Matron of the house, she took the young woman's hand away from Anne, felt Vera's brow, asked her several questions, then began to issue commands to the servants in rapid French.

"What are you telling them?" Anne asked, unable to translate. "Madame, she's my best friend—"

"And she will have her first baby very soon." Thérèse patted Anne's hand as the servants lifted Vera and carried her up the stairs. "Why do you worry, Lady Blackthorne? The baby is due, *n'est-ce pas*? And now it comes."

"Now?"

"*Oui*. There, there. I have given birth to many children myself, and in St. Louis we have three fine midwives. Your friend will be well."

"Anne?" Ruel appeared at her side. "She's to deliver the baby?"

Anne nodded. "I'm frightened for her. Vera's been so ill. All that has held her together is the hope of seeing Mr. Walker again. Has he truly gone back to the Indians?"

"Lady Blackthorne," Auguste Chouteau put in, "the Osage and I have a long and profitable history in this territory. I have traded furs with them, built forts and trading posts, and helped them to negotiate with the French and Spanish. You will not find a better people than the Osage. Even if he chooses to remain with his people, Walks-in-the-Night will deal fairly with this woman."

"Walks-in-the-Night?"

"Walker," Ruel said. "It's his Osage name."

He took the time to make a the brief but necessary introductions. At sixty-six, Auguste was the most powerful man in St. Louis, leader of the landed elite, and wealthy from the fur trade. His children and grandchildren had married within the controlling Creole families, and his ability to influence and manipulate events was unsurpassed. At one time, Ruel would have been concerned that Anne make a good impression on Auguste and Thérèse. Now he didn't give a fig that her dress was dirty and tears had streaked through the dust on her cheeks.

"My wife," he said proudly.

"So pleased to meet you." Auguste awarded her a deep bow. "Blackthorne, I was given to believe this young lady had perished . . ."

Anne hardly listened to the discussion drifting back and forth in front of her. Only three things mattered. Ruel was alive and well. Vera was to have her baby in the protection of this house. And Lord Alexander had failed to convince Ruel that she had abandoned him for another man. He also had been unable to kill Ruel . . . if that had been his plan at all.

"Come, *mon chéri*," Thérèse said gently to Anne. "You will be shown to your husband's suite of rooms, and I will order a basin of hot water sent up to you. Your trunks will be taken upstairs, but should you lack anything, I can supply you with gowns, shawls, bonnets, anything. Tea will be taken at four o'clock in the garden."

Reluctant to move away from Ruel's side, Anne squeezed his hand. "I shall look forward to tea," she said softly. "I should enjoy the flowers and the opportunity to rest after my arduous journey. But first I'll look in on Vera, and I must request a tête-à-tête with Lord Alexander."

"Alex?" Ruel said. "Alex isn't here."

"But he was ahead of us."

"Alex is coming to America?"

"Yes. Once he heard you were alive, he abandoned his

wedding plans to come at once. He arrived in New Orleans at Christmas. He traveled north by coach, leaving two weeks before we arrived there.''

''And how did you make the journey?''

''Steamboat.''

''Of course you outpaced him! You raced ahead aboard the transportation of the future.'' Ruel's grin broadened. ''Auguste, you hear that? My brother's on his way. Alex is coming!''

Nineteen

ANNE WASHED HERSELF THOROUGHLY WITH FRAGRANT, steaming water, then slipped her arms into the silky sleeves of a white combing gown. As she worked her comb through her hair again and again, unknotting every tangle, she reflected on the impending arrival of Lord Alexander.

In France, she had been certain he meant harm to Ruel. The duchess's admission that she was not Ruel's mother put her husband in a precarious position. Alex would want the Duchy of Marston for himself. There could be no doubt about that.

But would he kill his own brother? Common sense argued against it. Alex—with his rouge, perfume, and bloomers— was too much the fop. Anne had never seen him carry so much as a coat pistol. He had always been loving toward Ruel, and his dislike of her could hardly be termed irrational. In the eyes of most, she was the lowly housemaid who had entrapped the grand marquess. Her child might become a duke. It was enough to infuriate any true blueblood. No, Alex might be annoying, but he didn't seem evil.

Perhaps the duchess herself had been behind the attempted assassinations. She certainly was wicked enough. It stood to reason she would prefer her own son to inherit the duchy, and her rage at Ruel had been appalling to witness.

Or perhaps the villain was some other enemy. Certainly

Droughtmoor, Barkham, and Wimberly longed for revenge.
Their hearts had been bent on murder that night at the ball,
even though the viscount had been quick to defend them.
The Viscount Eagon. Perhaps he had something to gain by
Ruel's death. Would he be in line after Alex for the duchy?
Or would Claire's eldest son stand to inherit?

Anne laid the comb on the dressing table. She realized
she could destroy her sanity in the attempt to pinpoint
Ruel's enemy. The most important thing was not to fear
death but to be thankful for life. Before Alex arrived with
the news of her engagement to Monsieur Robidoux, she
must convince Ruel of her love for him. She must win his
heart. Nothing mattered more than their future.

She splashed the scent of lavender on her wrists and
elbows and pondered what to wear to tea. She had brought
very few gowns, and most of them had been worn in the
dust and rain. But there was one . . .

Lifting the lid of her trunk, Anne pushed aside her dirty
dresses until she came to a soft, tissue-wrapped packet tied
with a silk ribbon. Would Ruel understand what she intended by wearing the blue gown she had so lovingly re-
created after the fashion of the one he had given her?
Would he know the significance of the Honiton lace panel
she had rescued, bleached of its bloodstains, mended, and
stitched onto the gown's underskirt? She could only hope
so. She drew it out of the trunk and turned toward the bed.

Ruel stood in the room near the closed door. His gray
eyes burning, he walked toward her. "I've looked in on
Vera," he said. "A midwife is attending her. She's said to
be doing well, though the baby is not expected for some
time."

Anne's heart stumbled and began to thud. He was taller
than she remembered, broader of shoulder, his hair much
blacker. Had he grown it longer? She thought so. It gave
him a wild appearance, like that rugged man she had met
in the kitchen so long ago. A faded scar trailed in a curve

across his cheek, and she remembered the night a lead ball had nearly taken his life.

"Walker should arrive early tomorrow," he said. "St. Genevieve is not far."

She clutched the bedpost. "His people have accepted him?"

"As a hero. He's been made one of the Little Old Men— the name they give their leading elders. They respect his wisdom, his experience, his knowledge of the outside world, his ability to speak English. He's seen as a valuable asset to the tribe."

"I'm so glad. But Vera will be . . ." She stumbled as his hand reached out and his fingers trailed up her neck. "Vera is so very . . ."

"Anne, I'm not the least bit interested in Vera at the moment." He slipped his fingers through her hair, cupping the back of her head. She trembled slightly as she drifted toward him. "I still can hardly believe you're here. Sitting in the library moments ago, I began to doubt my own senses. Perhaps you hadn't really come. Perhaps I'd dreamed it. I had to see you."

She smiled and rubbed her cheek against his hand. "I felt the same bewilderment the moment your father read your letter. Until this moment, I've existed in a sort of trance, able to do nothing but move forward until I could prove to myself you really were alive."

"Anne, at Waterloo something happened . . . no, it occurred long before that. The moment I first laid eyes on you, I think I knew. The moment I heard your voice. The moment I listened to you weave a spell around that little urchin in the kitchen." He folded her into his embrace. "Anne, you're the magic in my life. You've brought me such joy, such fulfillment, such . . . such laughter."

Holding him close, she heard a chuckle deep in his chest and had to respond. "We're quite a pair. We've played at charades, danced, argued—"

"I stole your lace just to annoy you."

"Did you?"

"You're the only woman who ever verbally fenced with me. And you parried my every move." He traced his finger over the outline of her lips, anticipating the moment he would claim them. "You have a wicked tongue, little Annie Webster."

"I'm wicked?" A glowing heat began to pulse at the base of her spine. "You're the man who turned Solomon's song into a lyric of seduction."

"Isn't it?" He rubbed the pad of his thumb down her cheek.

"Perhaps."

"Seducing you was once my uppermost priority. I had little beyond it in my thoughts, and I was willing to try anything to win you." The corner of his mouth bent up. "King Solomon and I succeeded, didn't we?"

She could have told him it took far less to seduce her. The rough fabric of his coat beneath her fingers aroused her. The scent of his skin was an aphrodisiac. The touch of his hands on her bare flesh inflamed her. She sank against him, molding her body to his.

"Oh, Ruel, I can hardly believe you're real," she murmured. "After that night together in Brussels, I wanted nothing but you. And then I lost you for so long."

"Never again."

She looked up into his eyes, marveling at the depth of passion in their gray pools. His hands wrapped around her hips, settling her against the evidence of his own arousal. His breath came hard, ragged, but she knew he wanted to speak. There were things he had to say, but she could hardly listen beyond the beckoning of her own body.

"Anne," he whispered, "as a man, I . . . I find it difficult to suppress my desire. I see you . . . your body . . . your eyes . . . your mouth, and I want you beyond all reason. When I touch your skin, I become consumed with need.

Should I kiss you, Anne, I . . . I would not be able to . . ."

"Kiss me, Ruel," she begged. "I've ached for this moment."

"No." He swallowed and gritted his teeth. Taking her shoulders, he set her a little away from him. "I will not speak these words in the heat of passion. I will not say what I have to say to you in any way that it could be misconstrued. Nor will I wait another moment until I have spoken my heart."

He gripped her arms, forcing her to meet his eyes. "Anne, I love you."

"Ruel . . ."

"I love you, Anne. You must hear it, and hear it again. This is not a charade, not a game, not a ruse. I say it not for the benefit of witnesses and not to manipulate you in any way. I love you, Anne."

She bit her lip to hold back the tears and nodded.

"I felt it from the moment we met," he went on, "but I didn't understand it until Waterloo. I knew it. I meant to say it. And then I lost you. I've lived with that pain until it has nearly broken me."

"Oh, Ruel!" She threw her arms around him and buried her face in his neck. "I felt your love, or I wouldn't have come all this distance in the hope of finding it again. Ruel, I love you. I love you."

He cradled her head and pressed his lips to hers. Unsure whether he tasted his own tears or hers, he drank of her mouth. Her lips were soft, warm, pliant with response, and he captured them again and again. Her hands worked the muscles of his back, her fingers sliding under his shirt and stroking his heated skin.

Wanting to know her as he had before, he moved his hands around the back of her neck, over her shoulders, down her arms. Her breasts pressed against his chest, and he savored the sweet pressure of those two swollen mounds. Again he fitted her to him, nesting himself in the crevice of her thighs. She sighed, parted her lips, and invited him in.

Half a pace took them onto the bed, where he tugged apart the edges of her combing gown. He looked into her blue eyes as he pushed the fabric aside and cupped her breast. "Are you still mine?" he murmured.

"Yours alone." She sucked in a breath as his fingers closed around her rosy nipple, teasing and plucking it erect. Damp heat spread from her spine to the nest between her thighs. She could hear her own breath barely coming in little gasps. When he bent over her and wet her breasts with his tongue, she clutched at his shirt.

"Ruel, I'm in torment!" Her fingers massaged the hard muscle of his buttocks. "I must know you."

His own need reflected in her words, he quickly stripped away his clothing to lie naked beside her. As she slipped out of her gown, his hands covered her flesh, setting it ablaze. She threaded her fingers through the thick hair on his chest, suckled his hard brown nipples, danced against his thigh. He played her body to a tune that left her breathless and writhing. His fingertips worked magic, now stroking, dipping, twirling, now holding back and teasing with featherlight caresses that made her want to scream out in need.

"My wife," he groaned again and again as he played with her body like a man drunk on a heavenly cordial. She was magnificent, her breasts full and ripe. Her narrow waist and rounded hips entranced him. Her legs twined with his, and her sweet fingers stroked him to the apex of carnal pleasure.

"Ruel, take me," she pleaded. "I've been without you so long, and my body can bear this no longer. Please, I must have you."

"I love you, Anne," he said again and again.

As he rose over her, she spread herself to receive him. Eager, hungry, she took him deep inside herself. He stroked the core of her being, once, twice, and then she plummeted.

Crying out, she writhed beneath him while he absorbed the utter miracle of her release.

"Oh, Anne," he said, shuddering with pleasure. His body hovered, drifted, sang with hers, and then he too plunged into a freedom only love could bring. Holding her tightly, he touched her tongue with his as they floated together. Their bodies burned and pulsed and thrummed.

And finally, they lay glowing like the last embers of a bonfire.

Teatime came and went. Anne lay in the bliss of Ruel's arms. The sun drifted down toward the horizon casting lacy shadows from the oak trees outside her window. She tried to remember important things. Vera. America. The duchess. Lord Alexander.

All she knew was this man whose embrace folded her in security and love. He was just as she had remembered him. And different, too. The scar on his face made a fitting emblem for the new man. His pain was more open now, more easily revealed. But so was his love. He had been scarred, wounded by loss. But he had healed into a more compassionate human being.

He traced a fingertip over her bare breast. "I'm building a stone house," he said. "It's just at the edge of the city—half in forest but facing the road to the docks. You could have a lace school, Anne, if that is still your dream."

She winced at the memory of France. "Ruel, I must tell you what has become of your machine."

"Never mind the loom. I'm making my way here in America, and I'm doing well enough to begin sending money to Marston. Is Viscount Eagon managing my properties?"

"Yes, and so is Monsieur Robidoux."

Ruel lifted his head. "Robidoux? You know him?"

"I drove your machine into France, and we set it up at Douai. Hezekiah Cutts has been a great success. You are the owner of a thriving lace industry with a lace school and a clever manager. Monsieur Robidoux is a fine man.''

Throwing his head back on the pillow, Ruel laughed aloud. ''*You* took my machine to France? You set it up? My little Luddite?''

''How could I not?'' she said softly. ''It was your dream.''

Sobering, he rolled over onto his side. ''Thank you, Anne. I know it was a sacrifice. Have you news of your father?''

''He was released without trial, and for that I thank you. But now we must speak of other matters. Drought-moor—''

''Droughtmoor is far away and forgotten. I shall deal with the man when I return to England. My life is here now. St. Louis is my destiny. I feel it somehow deep within me, Anne. It's as though my spirit comes to life here. The Mississippi River, the great fields of wheat, the steamboats, the bustling town, even the politics. I embrace it all. And Walker—''

''But it's about Lord Alexander,'' she cut in. ''Ruel, I'm afraid he may have had something to do with the attempt on your life in Brussels.''

He scowled. ''My brother?''

''Ruel, you stand between him and the duchy.'' She sucked in a breath, trying to force herself to tell him what had occurred that day the duke had read his letter. ''It's all very complicated. Your father read Lord Alexander your news, and he departed for America at once, leaving his bride in the lurch. The duchess was . . . distraught.''

''In a snit, no doubt. I'd ruined her plans once again. Anne, you must understand how my mother looks at life and pay her no mind. If I have my say, she will trouble us little.'' He paused, seeking her focus. ''My mother, Droughtmoor, Society and its fopperies—they have no consequence here. But you do. Will you stay with me, my love? Can you live in this place, become a part of its future, make a home with me here?''

Forgetting all about Lord Alexander, Anne turned against him and slipped her arms around his neck. ''I have not set foot in the town of St. Louis, nor do I have the acquaintance of a soul here. Yet, I'm at home already.''

He trailed his fingers down to her breasts and molded his hands around them both. ''My home is in your love,'' he whispered.

''And mine is in your heart.''

When he began to kiss her neck, the world slipped away. Dinnertime came and went. No one knocked. No one rang. Or if they did, neither of the lovers heard a thing.

In the purple-pink light of dawn, Anne crept down the corridor to sit beside Vera. The midwife told her the baby was expected at any moment, though its mother appeared too weak to push the little creature into the world. Vera was losing ground quickly.

Anne dipped a towel into a basin of cool water and wiped it over her friend's brow. ''You are quite the rock of strength, Mrs. Walker,'' she admonished softly. ''I hope you know how marvelous a mother you'll be.''

Smiling weakly, Vera took Anne's hand. ''You . . . you must be my baby's mother,'' she whispered. ''You, Annie.''

Anne sat up straight. ''Don't speak such nonsense, Vera. I'll do nothing of the sort. This is your baby. Yours and Walker's. He's on his way here from St. Genevieve and should arrive this morning. One look at you and that baby—''

''Ohhh!'' Vera gripped Anne's hand as a contraction twisted through her.

''Push, *chéri*!'' the midwife cried. ''Push now! For the love of God!''

Vera writhed, moaning and white-faced as Anne stared

in dismay. "Push, Vera!" she urged. "You can do it. You must do it!"

The moment passed, and Vera lay gasping, drenched in sweat, as white as the wall beside her bed. Anne glanced at the midwife who shook her head.

"I cannot take the child out myself," she said with a shrug. "It is her labor. She is so tired after such a journey. But if she does not find the strength to push . . . You understand what I am saying, *n'est-ce pas*?"

Nodding, Anne knelt on the floor beside her friend. "Oh, Vera, what can I say to make you go on?" She lifted a prayer, tried to remember anything that could inspire Vera, wished for Walker.

"Ohhh!" The shriek echoed into the marrow of Anne's bones as Vera clung to the bed, a new contraction beginning to wrack her.

"Push, Vera!" Anne urged again. "This is Annie, and you know I mean what I say. Now push it out!"

Vera gripped the edges of the mattress and pushed until her white face turned red. Less than half a minute passed before she sagged back onto the pillow.

"I can't, Annie," she puffed. "I'm going to die."

"You're not. I won't have it. Now, Vera, the next time I want you to think about Walker. Think about . . . oh, heaven . . . think about that day in London at Chouteau House, in the garden outside the library window."

"Ohhh, Annie! It's coming again. I need to rest . . . need to . . . ohhh!"

"You danced out into the garden with your hands outstretched. You twirled around and around and your hair drifted in the sunshine. Remember?"

Sobbing, Vera nodded as she strained to free her child. "Annie, I can't do it!"

"And then Walker came out from behind a hedge. He followed you onto the grass."

"Oh, Annie, help me!"

"He took you into his arms—"

"And I held you tightly." A dark figure slipped into the room, knelt at the bedside, and took Vera's hand. "I swung you up and turned you around so many times we both were dizzy."

"Walker!" Vera gasped and tried to sit up. "Oh, Walker!"

"I asked you to be my wife, and you told me you would."

"Yes, oh, yes." Crying, she allowed him to enfold her and tenderly kiss her forehead.

"Now you must bring our child into this world, my love," he whispered. "And you must not lose your own life in the birthing of another's. Can you agree to that?"

Anne watched Vera nod and squeeze her husband's hand as another wave seized her. Walker hardly looked like the man Anne remembered. His black locks had all been shaved from the sides of his scalp. Only a thin strip of hair remained along the top, and it had been interwoven with long beaver fur to create a spiked crest. A hatchet decorated with feathers was tucked into his belt. A large round mussel shell hung from a leather thong about his neck, and he wore leather buckskins, a breechcloth, and a colorful robe tossed over his shoulders. Yet Vera lay puffing and panting, aware of nothing but that her husband had come for her. Wishing them solitude, Anne slipped out into the corridor.

"Thank you, God!" she murmured. Perhaps her prayers had been answered in time. Perhaps . . . perhaps Vera could do this thing.

Ruel. She must find him. Must tell him Walker had come. He must hear about Vera and the baby. Oh, would she ever give birth herself? Could she possibly bear such an ordeal?

Hurrying down steps filtered with early morning light, she heard voices in the foyer. It would be Auguste and Thérèse Chouteau. Maybe Madame Chouteau would be so

kind as to visit and encourage Vera. Surely Auguste
thought well of Walker and would—

Anne stopped.

"She did *what*?" Ruel demanded.

Lord Alexander lifted his head, spotted her, and straightened. Garbed as always in the height of fashion, he took
off his hat. "Ah, here she is now, our little minx. So, you
used the steamboat to outpace me."

Her heart hammering, Anne gripped the bannister as she
made her way down the final steps. "Alex, what have you
been telling Ruel?"

"Alex, is it? The last intelligence I had, I was to wear
the title of lord."

"Anne?" Ruel stepped around his brother. "Is it true?
Did you betroth yourself to a wealthy French merchant
within three months of our parting at Waterloo?"

"Monsieur Robidoux can hardly be considered
wealthy."

"Robidoux?" Ruel's anger softened. The short Frenchman with his large nose and spectacles was something less
than a romantic rival. Ruel knew that, and so did Anne.
But Alex clearly did not. Why had he come all this distance
only to burst out with this as his primary news of the family?

"Believing you dead," Anne was saying to him, "Monsieur Robidoux asked for my hand. He considered me an
asset to the lace industry in Calais. On learning of Vera's
plight, I knew I must do something to provide for her child.
I was aware I could not rely on the charity of the Chouteau
family forever. Not one of them had responded to my many
letters—"

"Lies!" Lord Alexander cut in. "She will freely admit
she was invited by letter to my wedding. Her mother and siblings were provided for. Her own Luddite father was freed
from prison. How can she claim our family ignored her?"

"Until Claire's invitation arrived, I had heard nothing from any of you. Alex, you know how many times I wrote to you in Paris, yet you didn't trouble yourself to respond."

"Never mind that, Anne." Ruel took her hand. "Did you hold any affection for Robidoux?"

"Nothing more than a business arrangement passed between us. Vera can attest to that, as will Monsieur Robidoux himself. Ruel, please, you must believe me."

Taking Anne protectively against him, Ruel made no answer. "Alex, why have you come to America?"

He flushed, pale eyes widening. "To prove to myself you were alive, of course," he blustered. Pointing at Anne, he added, "Why do you suppose *she* came?"

"Anne is my wife. We made a vow to spend our lives together." Uneasy for the first time in the presence of his brother, Ruel searched his mind for answers to nagging questions. "Alex, you knew damned well I was alive. My letter proved it. Why have you come?"

"I've been traveling for months, Ruel. Is this the sort of greeting I deserve?" Alex gave his brother his old disarming grin. "Now, then, where's this famous cousin of ours? Auguste Chouteau. How many stories did we grow up on with him as hero?"

Ruel's shoulders relaxed. "Auguste is every bit as colorful as the tales. Come on, I'll show you and Anne the gardens, and then we'll sit down to breakfast. He can tell you more adventures than would fill ten volumes."

Clapping his brother on the back, Ruel started across the foyer with Alex. Anne stood for a moment. Her mind told her all was well. Her heart turned in terror.

"Alex, you never answered Ruel's question," she said.

The men stopped and looked back at her.

"You came at your mother's bidding, didn't you?" She squared her shoulders. Could she get Alex to admit the truth without hurting Ruel with the facts of his birth? Could she frighten the man enough to leave them in peace without betraying Ruel's love for him?

"I know what the duchess told you, Alex," she said carefully.

His face hardened. "What do you know?"

"Everything. She related the whole story at the reading of Ruel's letter."

"What have you said to him about it?"

"Nothing, of course. The duke means to keep everything as it has always been. Do you intend to alter your father's plans?"

"Anne, what are you talking about?" Ruel asked. "Alex?"

"You haven't told him?" Alex demanded to know.

"No, but the moment I feel it necessary, I am prepared to reveal everything." Trying to breathe normally, Anne faced down her brother-in-law. "You must go back to England, Alex. Go back to Gabrielle and make a good husband of yourself. Go back to Slocombe and tend to your affairs."

"What affairs? Claire's husband has been put in charge of everything. I have nothing! Nothing, do you hear me?" His face reddening, Alex took a step toward Anne. "You little whore, you took it all. You got your claws into the bastard heir to the Duchy of Marston, and you'll bear us yet another bastard heir."

"Alex!" Ruel cut in.

"You've slept with him since you came, haven't you? Couldn't wait to get him into bed and try again for a little by-blow!"

"Damn it, Alex!"

"You know nothing, Ruel. She's onto the secret now, aren't you, little Annie the housemaid? She thinks she can weasel her way back into your bed and back into my money. Well, it's my money, do you hear? Mine!"

"Alex, the title is mine by birthright." Confusion and

gathering anger darkened Ruel's features. "You know I'm heir apparent."

"*I'm* the rightful heir," his brother exploded. "You've boasted of nothing all your life—whoring, gaming, spending my money on your damned little schemes. Lace! Lace, for God's sake!"

"Alex, you're raving."

Ruel reached to try to calm his brother, but Alex leapt backward. Drawing a small pistol from his pocket, he pointed it at his brother. Anne saw at once he carried it on the half cock.

"Alex, stop!" she screamed.

"You're not the heir. I am!" He leveled the weapon at Ruel's heart. His voice dropped. "That's right, dear brother. Neither the duke nor the duchess will rightly claim you. They merely took in a little bastard pup, brought him up, gave him their name. My father agreed to such a despicable arrangement out of fear he would never have a son of his own. But my mother bore me within two years' time. I'm the child of their union—not you!"

"Alex, what are you saying?" Ruel looked from his brother to his wife. He could hardly believe the words he was hearing, yet he saw confirmation in his wife's eyes. "Anne?"

"The duke willingly made Ruel his heir," she spat at Alex. "He never wanted that changed. Never. He loves Ruel as his son and always will. Ruel was brought up for the duchy, and he's meant to have it. Alex, put down the pistol and—"

"Never! I've spent years of my life trying to see this whoreson dead. I sent assassins after him to America. They failed to kill him. I shot at him myself from the roadway near Tiverton. Don't look so shocked, Ruel. I wore my hunting greens into the forest and followed you from the churchyard out onto the road. Had you seen the weapon aimed your way, you would have noted it was a fine German Jaeger rifle.''

''Damnation, Alex.''

''I tried again in Brussels. Thought I had you that time. All the confusion. The crowds. I knew you'd been sleeping with your little wench by that time, knew you'd try to produce an heir to work me completely out of the picture. Hell of a clever thing.''

''Alex, don't—''

''I missed again. Deuced. But not this time. Not this time. This is America. Let the savages try to lock me up for murder.'' He pulled back on the metal hammer, setting it at full cock. ''Think I won't do it? Too much of a dandy? Pity, Ruel.''

As he pulled the trigger, Ruel jerked a pistol from his own coat, cocked it, and fired. Anne screamed. Alex's ball tore past his brother's left shoulder and splintered into the wooden front door. Ruel's ball ripped into flesh, shattered bone, shredded organs. Alex stiffened, his eyes wide with disbelief.

As he fell forward, Anne saw a feathered hatchet buried in his back, its blade severing his spine. In shock, she looked to the top of the stairs. On the landing stood Walker, one hand still outstretched toward his victim, the other cradling a newborn baby.

''Anne!'' Ruel gathered her to his chest. ''Dear God!''

''Oh, Ruel!'' She clung to him, shaking with tears of horror and relief. ''It was Alex all along. I didn't want to believe it.''

Wracked by grief and disbelief, he crouched beside his fallen brother. ''Damn you, Alex . . .'' he murmured, stroking the golden hair of the dead man. ''It wasn't worth this.''

Anne knelt near him. ''Ruel, he would have killed you.''

''Yes, this time he would have. His aim was too close, too sure.'' Struggling against the knot of anguish in his throat, he looked up at the man descending the staircase. "Walker, you threw him off. You saved my life."

"As you saved mine more than once." The Indian struggled to hold back tears. "All those years in England, I lived for only one thing, Ruel. I lived for you . . . for my son."

"What?" He stood, his word barely a breath.

Walker set the newborn in his arms. "Meet your little sister. Vera and I have named her Hope."

A chill ran through him as Ruel looked down at the tiny, puffy face. Dark skin, easily tanned like his own. Black hair . . . just like his. He lifted his focus to Walker. The same copper skin. The same black hair.

"You're my father," he whispered.

Unsmiling, Walker nodded. "You were born into the household of my patron the Duke of Marston, much as this little one was born in the home of the great Chouteau, friend to the Osage. The duke had no son, but he chose to take you as his own, to love you, to place his name on you. He wanted you to hold his lands and titles, Ruel, and he never diverted from that course."

"Walker speaks the truth," Anne said, joining them. "I was in the drawing room when the duchess revealed everything. Never once did the duke back away from his vow to you. He called you his son. He loves you as his own child."

Unable to look at them, Ruel stared into the face of the little girl in his arms. Walker was his father. And the duke was his father. Both men had played their part. Walker had given Ruel the heritage of blood and bone. Laurent Chouteau had given him the heritage of land and title and honor. Both had endowed him with their example, their values, their love.

"Who is my mother?" he asked in a low voice.

"A woman I loved." Walker's words shook with emotion. "Until I knew Vera, she was the only woman I ever loved."

"Her name?"

Walker paused, unable to speak.

Anne slipped her arms around her husband. "Your mother is Claire," she said softly.

Epilogue

THE BABY GIRL SMILED UP AT THE LACE BOBBIN DANgling over her cradle. "Touch it!" Anne cooed. "Come on, little one. Reach up and touch it. You can do it."

"You'll have her making lace before she's a year old," Vera said with a laugh.

"I certainly hope so."

"Anne?" Ruel burst through the front door of the stone house. "Anne, you must come at once. It's here!"

In the bedroom, Anne glanced at Vera, a smile lighting her eyes. "It's the *Zebulon M. Pike*. Will you come down to Market Street with us?"

"You'd take the babies into all that bustle?"

"I mean to take my little Claire. If she's to grow up sharing all her father's dreams, she must witness the first steamship to pass the mouth of the Ohio."

"And learn to make Honiton lace. And read every book in Auguste Chouteau's huge library. And go to church twice a Sunday—"

"Why not?" Anne scooped up her daughter and popped a tiny mobcap over her dark curls. "Lady Claire, don't you want to see the steamship?"

The baby gurgled. Ruel flung open the bedroom door. His gray eyes bright with the fever of happiness, he threw his arm around Anne. "Come on, you'll miss the docking!"

"Will Walker come for you before I return?" Anne asked Vera.

"I should think so. We'd like to set out for the village before nightfall." Vera flipped her long golden braid behind her back and stood up on moccasined feet. She called to little Hope, now seventeen months old, who had been digging through the ropes of pearls in Anne's jewelry box. As Vera walked her friends to the door, Hope ran to hide in her mother's skirts. "I'll come to visit you again in a month or two, Annie."

"You recall, we've had word the duke may be in his final days. If we leave for England before you return, I shall send you a letter. It may be some time after that until we can get back."

"You *will* come home to St. Louis again?"

Anne gave her friend a quick hug. "Without a doubt."

As Ruel pulled Anne down the steps and into the street, they spotted Walker arriving in his wagon. He lifted a hand in greeting, but waved them on. After leaving his wife with her friend for two weeks, he would be more eager to welcome her and Hope back into his arms.

"You should see the steamship," Ruel said. "Unbelievable. The paddle wheel is enormous. The smokestacks are huge. The decks. The engines. Everything. Such promise!"

Anne snuggled her baby against her breast as she followed her husband down the streets of St. Louis, away from their large, stone house, toward the busy docks.

"Such promise," she repeated softly. "Such hope. Such a future."

Ruel stopped suddenly. Turning, he slipped his arms around her and their baby. He held her tightly, savoring the scent of lavender on her skin, delighting in the tilt of her almond-shaped sapphire eyes, warming to the call of her sweet lips.

He covered her mouth with his for a moment. "Such love, Anne. Such love."

Author's Note

I ENJOY HEARING FROM MY READERS. YOUR LETTERS inspire and enlighten me—and I always respond. To round out the historical picture of the world of *Sometimes Forever*, let me add these few words.

In the years to come, St. Louis continued to flourish. With the advent of the steamship, the town became the major terminal and shipping point for the produce of Missouri and upper Mississippi River settlements. The Indian fur trade dominated commerce for many years. As the Gateway to the West, St. Louis saw the building of churches, banks, schools, and countless mercantiles. Rene Auguste Chouteau lived to witness Missouri's admission to the United States in 1821. By the time he died in 1829, Jefferson City had been established as the state capital, and St. Louis was thriving. Though most of the streets were still mud, and ships had to unload in the sand because there were no wharves, St. Louis was on its way to becoming the grand city of Chouteau's dreams.

Freed from the restrictions imposed by Napoleon, the lace industry in France blossomed. Calais quickly became the most important lace center in the country. Most Alençon workers abandoned handmade lace and began to embroider machine-made muslin and net. Napoleon died in exile on St. Helena in 1821, and ten years later more than a thousand lace machines were at work in France.

The English lace industry also flourished. On Oxford Street alone, five lacemen set up shop. By the time King George died in 1820, steam power was being used to drive lace machines. Though members of the royal family wore Honiton lace wedding gowns to encourage home industry, handmade lace manufacture continued to decline. Refinements in lace-making machinery led to the employment of 150,000 English workers producing net lace and working patterns on the net by needlerun. In 1837, the first year of Queen Victoria's reign, the jacquard system of incorporating patterns into machine-made lace was developed.

Though the Industrial Revolution eventually made handmade lace too expensive to be produced in quantity, I feel there is no substitute for its exquisite beauty. Thanks to talented women like Anne, techniques for making bobbin lace by hand have not been lost. In Bruges, Belgium, in Calais, and in Nottingham, handmade lace can still be purchased.

In America, women still pin intricate parchment patterns to lap pillows. As they twist the fine threads of a thousand bobbins around countless tiny silver pins, they echo those who went before them. In these patterns, genius lives on.

Thomas Wright wrote of women like Anne Webster Chouteau in *The Romance of the Lace Pillow*. "The patterns," he said, "are their most jeweled thoughts stereotyped in parchment, just as the work of an inspired author is the expression of his inmost soul imparted . . . to the printed page. They did great things, for their thoughts were hitched to the stars. In moments of ecstasy, say the old philosophers, the soul divests itself of the body. In the finest of lace, as in a precious book, we seem to come into contact with the detached soul of a great personality."